JoAnn Ross

Legacy of Lies

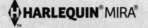

HARLEQUIN® MIRA®

Recycling programs
for this product may
not exist in your area.

ISBN-13: 978-0-7783-1526-1

LEGACY OF LIES

Printed in U.S.A.   www.Harlequin.com

To Jay,
who gives my life meaning

Dear Reader,

During a time when Jackie Collins was dishing about Hollywood wives, and readers worldwide had fallen in love with Princess Daisy, I was writing hardcover glitz novels featuring spunky heroines with glamorous careers who traveled in the world of the ultra-rich, where they'd fall in love with scrumptious, complex men, battle evil and decadence, and in the end, finally receive the happy ending they so deserved.

I was thrilled when *Legacy of Lies* was chosen to be one of the launch novels for Harlequin MIRA and am delighted that they've chosen to reprint Alexandra Lyon's story. I hope you'll enjoy traveling with Alex first to Paris, then Hollywood, as she encounters passion, obsession and betrayal on her personal journey to discover the truth behind a legacy of lies.

Happy reading!

JoAnn Ross

Prologue

Santa Barbara, California
April 1958

It rained the day Eleanor Lord buried her only son. A cold wind, bringing with it memories of a winter just past, blew in from the whitecapped gray sea. Not that the inclement weather kept anyone away; it appeared that the entire town of Santa Barbara had turned out. Rows of black umbrellas arced over the grassy knoll like mushrooms.

Nothing like a scandal to draw a crowd, Eleanor thought. After all, it wasn't every day that the scion of America's largest department store family and his wife were murdered.

If a double homicide wasn't enough to set tongues wagging, the fact that the victims were two of the town's leading citizens added grist to the gossip mill. Then there was Anna....

Eleanor's heart clenched at the thought of her missing two-year-old granddaughter. A sob escaped her tightly set lips.

"Are you all right?" Dr. Averill Brandford asked with concern. He was holding an umbrella over her head; his free arm tightened around her shoulders.

"Of course I'm not all right!" she snapped, displaying a spark of her usual fire. "My son and his wife are about to be put in the ground and my granddaughter has vanished from the face of the earth. How would you feel under similar circumstances?"

"Like hell," he answered gruffly. "Don't forget, Robert was my best friend. And Anna's my goddaughter."

Averill Brandford and Robert Lord had grown up together. Clad in rainwear and shiny black boots and armed with shovels, rakes and buckets, they'd dug for clams in the coastal tidelands. Robert had been the pitcher of the Montecito High School baseball team; Averill had been the catcher. Together they'd led the team to three district championships in four years. Inseparable, they'd gone on to USC, pledged the same fraternity and only parted four years later when Robert went east to Harvard Law School and Averill to medical school, making his father, the Lords' head gardener, extremely proud.

Eventually they were reunited in the Southern California coastal town where they'd grown up. These past horrendous days, Averill had been a pillar of support. He'd arrived at the house within minutes of Eleanor's frantic phone call, rarely leaving her side as she waited for the kidnapper's call.

Tears stung her eyes. Resolutely Eleanor blinked them away, vowing not to permit herself to break down until her granddaughter was home safe and sound.

She thanked the minister for his inspiring eulogy, not admitting she hadn't heard a word. Then she turned and began making her way across the mossy turf.

In the distance the Santa Ynez Mountains towered majestically in emerald shades over the red-roofed city; a few hardy souls were playing golf on the velvet greens of the Montecito Country Club.

Out at sea, draped in a shimmering pewter mist, a tall masted fishing boat chugged its way up the Santa Barbara Channel. Watching the slicker-clad men on the deck, Eleanor felt pained to realize that people continued to go about their daily lives, that the earth had not stopped spinning simply because her own world was crumbling down around her.

As she neared her limousine, Santa Barbara's police chief climbed out of his black-and-white squad car, parked behind it, and approached them. The look on his face was not encouraging.

"Good afternoon, Chief Tyrell." Though there were shadows smudged beneath Eleanor's eyes, her gaze was steady and direct.

The police chief lifted his fingers to his hat. "Afternoon, Mrs. Lord." He doffed the hat and began turning it around and around between his fingers. "The FBI located your granddaughter's nanny in Tijuana, ma'am. Rosa Martinez checked into a hotel under an assumed name."

"Thank God, they've found her," Eleanor breathed. "And Anna? Is she well?"

"I'm afraid we don't know."

"What do you mean, you don't know?"

"She didn't have a child with her when she checked in."

"But surely Rosa will tell you where Anna is. Even if

she refuses to cooperate, don't you people have ways of encouraging people to talk?" Thoughts of bright lights and rubber hoses flashed through her mind.

"I'm afraid that's impossible." His voice was heavy with discouragement. "The nanny's dead, Mrs. Lord."

"Dead?"

"She hung herself."

"But Anna…" Eleanor felt Averill's fingers tighten on her arm.

"We don't know," Chief Tyrell admitted. "With the nanny gone, no witnesses and no word from the kidnappers, we've run into a dead end."

"But you'll keep looking," Averill insisted.

"Of course. But I'm obliged to tell you, Mrs. Lord," the police chief said, "that the little girl's nanny left a suicide note asking for God's—and your—forgiveness. The FBI's taking the note as a sign that your granddaughter's, uh—" he paused, looking like a man on his way to the gallows "—dead."

No! For the first time in her life, Eleanor felt faint. She took a deep breath, inhaling the mild aroma of petroleum wafting in from the offshore oil derricks; the light-headed sensation passed.

She heard herself thank the police chief for his continued efforts, but her voice sounded strange to her own ears, as if it were coming from the bottom of the sea.

Back at her Montecito estate, she forced herself to remain calm as she accepted condolences from mourners. Finally, mercifully, everyone was gone, leaving her alone with Averill.

"Are you sure you want to stay here tonight?" His handsome face was stamped with professional and personal concern.

"Where would I go? This is my home."

Needing something to do with her hands, Eleanor absently began rearranging a Waterford vase filled with white lilies. The house was overflowing with flowers; the rich profusion of sweet and spicy scents was giving her a blinding headache.

"Would you like some company?" Averill asked solicitously. "I'd be glad to stay."

"No." She shook her head. "I appreciate your concern, Averill, but if you don't mind, it's been a very long day and I'd like to be alone." When he looked inclined to argue, she said, "I'll be fine. Honestly."

He frowned. "If you can't sleep—"

"I'll take one of those tablets you prescribed," she assured him, having no intention of doing any such thing.

She'd succumbed to his medical prompting that first night, only to discover that the pills made her feel as if her head were wrapped in cotton batting. It was important she be alert when the police called to tell her they'd located Anna.

Although he appeared unconvinced, the young doctor finally left. Eleanor sat alone for a long silent time. After being in the public eye all day, she was grateful for the opportunity to allow herself to droop—face, shoulders, spirits.

Finally, when she thought she could manage the act without collapsing, she got to her feet and climbed the elaborate Caroline staircase to the nursery, where she kept her vigil far into the night.

Chapter One

Paris
December 1981

Oblivious to any danger, Alexandra Lyons ran full tilt across the icy street, deftly weaving her way between two taxis, a gunmetal-gray Mercedes and a jet-black Ferrari. Her hooded, red wool cape was like the brilliant flash of a cardinal's wing against the wintry gray Paris sky and the falling white snow.

Her long legs, clad in opaque black tights and pointy-toed red cowboy boots, earned a quick toot of the horn and an admiring second look from the driver of the Ferrari.

It was Christmas in Paris. Glittering semicircles of Christmas trees had replaced Rond Point's formal gardens, and garlands of lights had been strung up in the city's leafless trees, turning the Avenue Montaigne and the Champs-élysées into great white ways, reminding one and all that Paris was, after all, the City of Light.

But Alex's mind was not on the lights, or the joyful season. Her concerns were more personal. And far more urgent.

She was on her way to the *atelier* of Yves Debord to try again to win a coveted position with the French designer. And though she knew her chances of winning a position at the famed house of couture were on a par with catching moondust in her hand, even worse than failing would be to grow old and never have tried.

Emerging ten years ago as haute couture's *enfant terrible,* the designer had been immediately clutched to the *décolleté* bosom of the *nouveaux riches.* Fashion celebrity oozed from the perfumed corners of his *atelier,* glinted off the windshield of his Lamborghini, glowed from the crystal chandeliers in his many homes.

Hostesses in Los Angeles, Dallas and New York fawned over him. He skied in the Alps with movie stars and was welcome at presidential dinner tables in Rome and Washington and Paris.

During Alex's student days in Los Angeles, the Fashion Institute had shown a documentary about the designer directed by Martin Scorsese entitled *Pure Pow: The World of Debord.* Enthralled, Alex had sat through all three showings.

She now paused outside the showroom to catch her breath. Adrenaline coursed through her veins at the sight of her idol's name written in gleaming silver script on the black glass.

"You can do it," she said, giving herself a brisk little pep talk. "The answer to all your dreams is just on the other side of this door. All you have to do is to reach out and grasp it."

She refused to dwell on the fact that after months of

daily visits to the *bureau de change* to cash her dwindling supply of traveler's checks, she was almost out of funds.

Her night job, serving beer and wine at a Montparnasse nightclub, barely paid her rent. The hours, however, allowed her to search for work in the fashion houses during the day, and if sleep had become a rare, unknown thing, Alex considered that a small price to pay for a chance to fulfill a dream.

Throwing back her shoulders, Alex lifted herself up to her full height of five feet seven inches and then, with her usual bravado, entered the showroom. Behind her, the door clicked shut with the quiet authority of a Mercedes.

The front room, used to greet customers, was a vast sea of cool gray. Modern furniture wrapped in pewter fabric sat atop silvery gray carpet that melded into the gray silk-covered walls. Marie Hélène, Yves Debord's sister and house of couture directress, was seated behind a jet lacquer table.

She was dressed in black wool jersey, her platinum hair parted in the center and pulled into a severe chignon at the nape of her swanlike neck.

When she recognized Alex, she frowned.

"I know," Alex said, holding up a gloved hand to forestall the director's complaint. She pushed back her hood, releasing a thick riot of red-gold hair.

"You've told me innumerable times in the past six months that there aren't any openings. And even if there were, you don't take Americans. But I thought, if you could only take a look at my work—" she held out her portfolio "—you might consider showing my designs to Monsieur Debord."

Alex's chin jutted out as she steeled herself for yet another cool rejection. *Nothing ventured, nothing gained.*

To Alex's amazement, Marie Hélène didn't immediately turn her away as she had all the other times. "Where did you say you studied?" she inquired in a voice as chilly as her looks.

"The Fashion Institute. In L.A."

"Los Angeles," the directress said with a sniff of disdain, as if Alex had just admitted to being an ax murderer. "You're very young," she observed, making Alex's youth sound like a fatal flaw. "When did you graduate?"

"Actually, I didn't. I felt the curriculum put too much emphasis on merchandising and too little on technique." It was the truth, so far as it went. "Besides, I was impatient, so I quit to go to work in New York."

She felt no need to volunteer that a more urgent reason for leaving school had been her mother's diagnosis of ovarian cancer.

As soon as Irene Lyons had called her with the dark news, Alex had gone to the registrar, dropped out of school and, with a recommendation from one of her professors, landed a job with a Seventh Avenue firm that made dresses for discount stores.

"New York?" Marie Hélène's brow climbed her smooth forehead. "Which designer? Beene? Blass? Surely not Klein?"

"Actually, I worked for a company that made clothing for department stores."

She lifted her chin, as if daring Marie Hélène to say a single derogatory word. While not couture, she'd worked damned hard. And although her suggestions to bring a little pizzazz to the discount clothing were more often than not rejected, she was proud of whatever contribution she'd been allowed to make. After her mother's death, no longer having any reason to remain in New York, she'd followed her lifelong dream, making this pilgrimage to the birthplace—and high altar—of couture.

"But I continued to design on my own," she said, holding out the portfolio again.

When the directress continued to ignore the proffered sketches, Alex steeled herself to be rejected once more.

Instead, Marie Hélène rose from her chair with a lithe grace any runway model would have envied and said, "Come with me."

Unwilling to question what had changed the director's mind, Alex rushed after her through the labyrinth of gray walls and silver carpeting. They entered a small Spartan room that could have doubled as an interrogation room in a police station. Or an operating room.

Though the steel shelves on the walls were filled with bolts of fabric, there was not a speck of lint or dust to be seen. Open-heart surgery could have been done on the gray Formica laminated plastic table in the center of the room.

Beside the table was a faceless mannequin. Marie Hélène took a bolt of white toile from one of the shelves, plucked a sketch from a black binder, lay both on the table along with a pair of shears and said, "Let us see if you can drape."

"Drape? But I came here to—"

"I had to dismiss one of our drapers today," the

directress said, cutting Alex off with a curt wave of her hand.

Her fingernails were lacquered a frosty white that echoed her glacial attitude. A diamond sparkled on her right hand, catching the light from the fixture above and splitting it into rainbows on the white walls. Those dancing bits of light, were, along with Alex's crimson cape, the only color in the room.

"I discovered she was sleeping with a press attaché for Saint Laurent." Marie Hélène's mouth tightened. "Which of course we cannot allow."

Uncomfortable with the idea of an employer interfering in the personal life of an employee, Alex nevertheless understood the paranoia that was part and parcel of a business where the new season's skirt lengths were guarded with the same ferocity military commanders employed when planning an invasion.

"With the couture shows next month, we must hire a replacement right away," the directress continued. "If you are able to drape properly, I might consider you for the position."

Draping was definitely a long way from designing. But Alex wasn't exactly in a position to be choosy.

She glanced down at the black-and-white pencil sketch, surprised by its rigid shape. Debord had always favored geometric lines, but this evening gown was more severe than most.

"Is there a problem?" Marie Hélène asked frostily.

"Not at all." Alex flashed her a self-assured smile, took off her cape, tossed it casually onto the table, pulled off her red kid gloves and began to work. Less than five minutes later, she stood back and folded her arms over her plaid tunic.

"Done," she announced as calmly as she could.

Marie Hélène's response was to pull a pair of silver-rimmed glasses from the pocket of her black skirt, put them on and begin going over the draped mannequin inch by inch.

Time slowed. The silence was deafening. Alex could hear the steady tick-tick-tick of the clock on the wall.

"Well?" she asked when she couldn't stand the suspense any longer. "Do I get the job?"

The directress didn't answer. Instead, she turned and submitted Alex to a long judicious study that was even more nerve-racking than her examination of Alex's draping skills.

"Where did you get that *outré* outfit?" Marie Hélène's nose was pinched, as if she'd gotten a whiff of Brie that had turned.

Imbued with a steely self-assurance that was partly inborn and partly a legacy from her mother and twin brother, who'd thought the sun rose and set on her, Alex refused to flinch under the unwavering stare. "I designed it myself."

"I thought that might be the case." The woman's tone was not at all flattering. "My brother prefers his employees to wear black. He finds bright colors distracting to the muse."

"I've read Armani feels the same way about maintaining a sensory-still environment," Alex said cheerfully.

The directress visibly recoiled. "Are you comparing the genius of Debord to that Italian son of a transport manager?"

Realizing that insulting the designer—even unintentionally—was no way to gain employment, Alex quickly backtracked.

"Never," she insisted with fervor. "The genius of Debord has no equal."

Marie Hélène studied her over the silver rim of her glasses for another long silent time. Finally the directress made her decision. "I will expect you here at nine o'clock tomorrow morning. If you do not have appropriate attire, you may purchase one of the dresses we keep for just such an occasion. As for your salary…"

The figure was less than what she'd been making at the nightclub. "That's very generous, madame," she murmured, lying through her teeth.

"You will earn every franc."

Undeterred by the veiled threat, Alex thanked the directress for the opportunity, promised to be on time, picked up her portfolio and wound her way back through the maze of hallways.

As she retraced her steps down the Avenue Montaigne, Alex's cowboy boots barely touched the snowy pavement. Having finally breached the directress's seemingly insurmountable parapets, Alexandra Lyons was walking on air.

"If you can make it here, you can make it anywhere," she sang as she clattered down the steps to the metro station. Her robust contralto drew smiles from passing commuters. "I love Paris in the winter, when it drizzles…. Or snows," she improvised. "Boy, oh boy, do I love Paris!"

She was still smiling thirty minutes later as she climbed the stairs to her apartment.

The first thing she did when she walked in the door was to go over to a table draped in a ruffled, red satin skirt that could have belonged to a cancan dancer at the Folies Bergère, and pick up a photo in an antique silver frame.

"Well, guys," she murmured, running her finger over the smiling features of her mother and brother, whose life had been tragically cut short when his car hit a patch of ice and spun out of control on the New Jersey turnpike six years ago. "I got the job. I hope you're proud."

Alex missed them terribly. She decided she probably always would. They'd both had such unwavering confidence in her talent. Such high hopes. Alex had every intention of living up to those lofty expectations.

When she'd left New York, two days after her mother's funeral, she'd been excited. And nervous. But mostly, she'd been devastated.

As the plane had reached cruising level thirty thousand feet over the Atlantic, she'd collapsed and to the distress of the flight attendants, who'd tried their utmost to uphold the Air France tradition of *esprit de service*—even bringing her a glass of the cognac strictly reserved for first-class passengers—she'd wept like a baby.

For the first time in her life, she'd been truly alone. And though she'd been raised to be independent, deep down inside, Alex had been terrified.

Now, against all odds, she'd achieved the first part of her goal. She'd gotten her boot in Debord's black glass door. Next, all she had to do was prove to the designer she was worthy of the opportunity. Once Debord recognized her talent, she'd be bound to win a promotion.

Could she do it?

Her full lips curved into a wide grin. Her amber

eyes, touched with golden facets that radiated outward, lighted with Alex's irrepressible lust for life.

"You bet," she decided with a renewed burst of her characteristic optimism.

Chapter Two

Paris
February 1982

Alex's knees were aching. She'd been kneeling in the close confines of the *cabine* for hours, laboring under the watchful arctic eye of Marie Hélène.

Alex was grateful to still have a job. Last week, at the season's *défilé de mode* held in the gilded splendor of the Salon Impérial of the Hôtel Intercontinental, Debord had experienced the fashion media's ugly habit of chewing up designers and spitting them out.

"Fashion for nuns," American *Vogue* had called his totally black-and-white collection. "A *tour de force* of hideous taste," Suzy Menkes of the *International Herald Tribune* declared, attacking the designer's androgynous black jersey for its dismal, breast-flattening style. "A cross between Grace Jones and Dracula," *Women's Wear Daily* said scornfully. Its sister publication, *W,* gave the collection a grade of *S*—for scary—

and said Debord's depressing black shrouds looked as if they came right out of the comic strip *Tales from the Crypt.*

After the disastrous showing, the *femmes du monde,* accustomed to making twice-yearly pilgrimages to this revered salon, deserted the French designer, rushing instead to Milan and Debord's long-detested rival, Gianni Sardella.

Surprisingly, Sophie Friedman, daytime television producer and wife of Hollywood mogul Howard Friedman, paid no heed to the fashion mavens. On the contrary, she amazed even the unflappable Marie Hélène by ordering six evening dresses and twice that number of daytime suits.

Considering that each garment was literally built onto the client, Mrs. Friedman and Alex had spent most of the past week locked in the cramped fitting room together.

"I think it makes me look fat," Sophie said, raising her voice over the classical music played throughout the building.

"It is only the white toile that makes it appear so, Mrs. Friedman," Marie Hélène assured her smoothly. "Once it is worked up in the satin, you will discover that black is very slimming."

"Do you think so?" Sophie ran her beringed hands over her substantial hips, tugging at the material. Alex bit back a curse as the pins she'd just inserted pulled loose. The zaftig woman looked unconvinced. "What do you think?" she asked Alex.

Alex was unaccustomed to being addressed by a customer. A mere draper, she was in the lower echelons of the profession.

But Sophie Friedman had already proved herself to be one of Debord's more eccentric clients. Unwilling to accept the idea that man was meant to fly, Sophie eschewed airline travel. The first day in the fitting room, she'd explained how she'd taken a private Pullman from Los Angeles to Grand Central Station, then the *QEII* to Cherbourg, thence to the Avenue Montaigne by Rolls-Royce.

The woman might be eccentric, Alex thought. But she was no fool. "Madame is correct about black being slimming," she hedged.

"So I won't look fat?"

Alex didn't want to alienate Marie Hélène. Those who dared question the directress were summarily dismissed. Without references.

A tendril of unruly hair escaped the chignon at the back of Alex's neck. Buying time, she unhurriedly tucked it back into place. "You're certainly not fat, Madame Friedman."

Actually, that was the truth. So far as it went. If she was to be totally honest, Alex would suggest that Debord was not the right designer for this middle-aged woman. The designer believed women came in two categories: polo ponies—those who were short and round—and Thoroughbreds—tall and slender. He prided himself on designing for the Thoroughbreds.

Using Debord's criteria, Alex decided he would probably consider the tall, robust Mrs. Friedman to be a Clydesdale.

"I've always had big bones," Sophie agreed. "But I still think this dress makes me look fat."

Alex's innate sense of honesty warred with her common sense. As she'd feared, honesty won out.

"Perhaps," she suggested, ignoring Marie Hélène's sharp look, "if we were to use a softer material than satin, perhaps a matte jersey. And draped it, like this." With a few quick changes she concealed the woman's short waist and broad hips and emphasized her firm, uplifted bustline.

Sophie Friedman's eyes lit with approval. "That's just what it needed." She turned to the directress. "Would Monsieur Debord be willing to make the changes?"

"Of course." Marie Hélène's words were tinged with ice, but her tone remained properly subservient. "It is *Madame's* prerogative to alter anything she wishes."

"Then *Madame* wishes." That settled, Sophie looked down at her diamond-studded watch. "*Madame* is also starving."

"We will take a break," Marie Hélène murmured on cue. "It will be my pleasure to bring you lunch, Madame Friedman."

"No offense, Marie Hélène," Sophie said, "but I could use something more substantial than the rabbit food you serve around this place." She looked down at Alex. "How about you?"

"Me?"

Startled, Alex dropped the box of pins, scattering them over the plush gray carpeting. Marie Hélène immediately knelt and threw three handfuls of pins over her shoulder. Alex had grown accustomed to the superstitions accompanying the business. Baste with green thread and you kill a season. Neglect to toss spilled pins over your shoulder and you've guaranteed a dispute. Lily Dache, legendary hat designer, would show on the thirteenth or not at all. Coco Chanel would wait for Antonia Castillo's numerologist to schedule Mr. Castillo's shows, then schedule her own at the same time. The irate designer was rumored to have used a Coco doll and pins for retaliation. Debord himself was famous for not shaving before a show.

"I could use some company, Alexandra," Sophie announced. "It is Alexandra, isn't it?"

"Yes, Madame Friedman," Alex answered from her place on the floor as she gathered up the scattered pins.

"Well, then," Sophie said with the no-nonsense air of a woman accustomed to getting her way, "since I hate to eat alone and you need to eat, why don't you let me buy you lunch?"

Alex could feel the irritation radiating from Marie Hélène's erect body. "Thank you, Mrs. Friedman, but I'm afraid—"

"If you're worried about your boss, I'm sure Monsieur Debord wouldn't mind." Sophie gave Marie Hélène a significant look. "Considering the dough I've dropped in his coffers this week."

Marie Hélène got the message. Loud and clear. "Alexandra," she suggested, as if the idea had been her own, "why don't you accompany Madame to *déjeuner.* Monsieur Debord has an account at the Caviar Kaspia, if Russian food meets with Madame's approval," she said to Sophie.

"Caviar Kaspia it is," Sophie agreed robustly.

Ten minutes later Alex found herself sitting in a banquette at the legendary Caviar Kaspia. The Franco-Russian restaurant, located above a caviar shop, had long been a favorite of couture customers with time to kill between fittings.

Across the room, Paloma Picasso, wearing a scarlet

suit that matched her lipstick, was engrossed in conversation with Yves Saint Laurent. Nearby, Givenchy's *attaché de presse* was doing his best to charm a buyer from Saks Fifth Avenue. Renowned for her no-nonsense, hard-as-nails approach to the business, the buyer had walked out midway through Debord's showing.

"You're an American, aren't you?" Sophie asked as she piled her warm blini with beluga caviar.

"Yes, ma'am."

"So what the hell are you doing here in Paris, pinning overpriced dresses on women with more money than sense?"

Not knowing how to address the last part of that question, Alex opted to focus on her purpose for coming to Paris. "I've wanted to be a designer for as long as I can remember.

"My mother had her own dressmaking business for a time, but she was a single mother—my father left before my twin brother and I were born—and since taking care of two children took up too much time to allow her to continue designing, she ended up doing alterations for department stores and dry cleaners."

Alex frowned as she fiddled with her cutlery. "I've always felt guilty about that."

"Oh, I'm sure your mother never considered it a sacrifice," Sophie said quickly, waving away Alex's concerns with a plump hand laden down with very good diamonds.

"That's what she always insisted whenever I brought it up," Alex agreed. "Anyway, she taught me everything I know about sewing. When I was little, I designed clothes for my dolls. Eventually I worked my way up to creating clothes for her."

"Lucky lady," Sophie said. "What does she think of you working for Debord?"

"She died before I came to Paris."

"I'm sorry."

"She was ill for a long time. In a way, her death was a blessing. After leaving school, I worked on Seventh Avenue for a few years." Alex continued her story, briefly describing her work at the design firm.

"I'll bet you didn't come clear to France to be a draper," Sophie said as she topped the glistening black caviar with a dollop of sour cream.

Alex shrugged, unwilling to admit to her own impatience. Her mother had always cautioned her that destiny wasn't immediate. But Alex couldn't help being in a hurry.

"All my life I've wanted to work in couture. Paris *is* couture." In Paris, entering a house of couture was taken as seriously as entering a convent; indeed, in French, the expression to enter *une maison* was applied to both cases. "And Debord is the best."

When she was in high school, Alex had pinned pictures of Debord cut out of fashion magazines on her bedroom wall, idolizing him in the way other girls had swooned over rock stars.

Although the photographs had come down years ago, she still harbored a secret crush on the designer.

"He *was* the best," Sophie corrected. "This season his stuff stinks to high heaven. In fact, I'd rather suck mud from the La Brea tar pits than wear one of that man's dresses in public."

Secretly appalled by the direction her idol had taken, Alex found herself unable to defend his current collection. "If you feel that way, why are you buying so many pieces?"

"My soon-to-be ex-husband is buying those clothes," Sophie corrected. "And since your boss is the most expensive designer in the business, he was the obvious choice. Even before last week's disastrous show."

Alex realized that Sophie Friedman had come to Paris to buy "fuck-you clothes." Although haute couture's clientele traditionally consisted of wealthy clients linked together in a solid-gold chain that stretched across continents, mistresses and angry discarded wives made up a remarkable percentage of Debord's customers.

American women were infamous for borrowing couture. The always thrifty French purchased *modèles*—samples. Only the Japanese, along with shadowy South American drug baronesses and Arab brides paid full price. In fact, a recent Saudi wedding was all that was keeping the house from going bankrupt.

"Of course, I'm giving the stuff to charity as soon as I get back to L.A. It does my heart good to think about that two-timing louse buying couture for some Hollywood bag lady." Sophie grinned with wicked spite. "Although, you know, the changes you made on that evening dress made a helluva difference," she allowed. "I think I'll keep that one."

She chewed thoughtfully. "What would you think of having it made up in red?"

Alex, who adored bright primary colors, grinned. "Red would be marvelous. Coco Chanel always said that red—not blue—was the color for blue eyes."

Sophie nodded, clearly satisfied. "Red it is."

The woman appeared in no hurry to leave the restaurant. Finally, after a third cup of espresso that left her nerves jangling, Alex reminded the client of her afternoon fitting.

"First, I want to see your designs," Sophie declared.

"My designs?"

"You do have some examples of your own work, don't you?"

"Well, yes, but…"

Ambition warred with caution in Alex's head. Part of her knew that Marie Hélène was waiting for them to return. Another part of her was anxious to receive someone's—anyone's—opinion on her work.

She had given Marie Hélène her sketches, hoping they might find their way to Debord. For weeks she'd been waiting for a single word of encouragement from the master. Undaunted, she'd begun a new series of designs.

Giving in to her new friend's request, Alex took Sophie to her apartment. It was located two floors above a bakery in a building that boasted the ubiquitous but charming Parisian iron grillwork, dormer windows, a mansard roof and red clay chimneys. She'd sublet the apartment from an assistant to an assistant editor of *Les Temps Modernes,* who'd taken a year's sabbatical and gone to Greece to write a novel.

The first time Alex had stood at the bedroom window and stared, enchanted, at the Jardin du Luxembourg across the street, she'd decided that the view more than made up for the building's temperamental old-fashioned cage elevator that more often than not required occupants to rely on the stairs.

Alex could have cursed a blue streak when the unpredictable elevator chose this day not to run. But Sophie proved to be a remarkable sport, though she was huffing and puffing by the time they reached Alex's floor.

"Oh!" she exclaimed, looking around the apartment. "This is absolutely delightful."

"I was lucky to find it." Viewing the apartment through the older woman's eyes, Alex saw not its shabbiness, but its charm.

Near the window overlooking the gardens, a chintz chair was surrounded by scraps of bright fabric samples; atop the table beside it was a box of rainbow-bright Caran D'Ache colored pencils and a portfolio. The Swiss pencils, the very same type Picasso had favored, had been an extravagant birthday gift from her mother. Two days later Irene Lyons had died.

But her memory lived on, just as she'd intended; Alex never sat down to sketch without thinking of her.

Drawn as if by radar, Sophie picked up the portfolio and began leafing through the sketches.

"These are wonderful." The fluid lines were draped to emphasize the waist or hips, the asymmetrical hemlines designed to flatter every woman's legs.

Alex glowed. It had been a long time since anything she'd done received recognition.

Sophie paused at the sketch of a long, slip-style evening gown of ebony silk mousseline with midnight lace and a low, plunging back. "This would be perfect for Angeline."

"Angeline?"

"She's a character on *The Edge of Tomorrow*," Sophie revealed absently, her attention captured by a clinging silver gown reminiscent of films of the thirties and forties. "A former hooker turned movie star turned romance writer."

"Oh, I remember her. I watched that show all the time when I was going to fashion school."

"You must watch a lot of old films, too," Sophie guessed.

"I love old movies."

"I figured that. Your artistic vision definitely has a cinematic scope. So, although television admittedly isn't the big screen, how would you like to come to work for me?"

"For you?"

"I've currently got three soaps in production. Since my shows are famous for their glamour, we keep three costumers shopping overtime to supply outfits for each one-hour drama. The after-six wear and lingerie is the toughest to find, so I've been considering hiring someone to design specifically for us. From what I see here, you'd be perfect."

The idea was tempting. Especially after all the months trying to land a job, then these past weeks laboring away in obscurity. But Alex was not yet prepared to let go of her dream.

"It's not that I'm not flattered," she began slowly, choosing her words with extreme caution. "Because I am...."

"But you're hoping that one of these days, that idiot Debord will open his eyes and realize what a talented designer is toiling right beneath his nose."

Alex felt herself blush. "That's pretty much it."

Sophie shrugged her padded shoulders. "Well, if that scenario doesn't happen, just remember, you've always got a job with me." She opened her bag, pulled out a business card and a pen and scribbled a number on the back.

"Here're the phone numbers for my office at the studio, my car, my home and my pager. Give me a call sometime, even if it's just to talk, okay?"

Alex took the card and stuck it away in a desk drawer. "I'd like that. Thank you."

When Alex cast another significant glance at her watch, Sophie sighed with ill-concealed resignation. "All right, I suppose we'd better get back before Marie Hélène sends the fashion police looking for us."

When Alex and Sophie returned to the salon, they found Debord waiting in the *cabine*. Clad in his smock, his sable hair pulled back into a ponytail to display his Gallic cheekbones to advantage, he looked every inch the temperamental artist.

Dior and Balenciaga had started the tradition of the white smock; Yves Saint Laurent and Givenchy continued it. Debord, always pushing against the boundaries of tradition, had altered it to an anthracite gray. Brightening the breast of the gray smock was the red ribbon of the *Chevalier de la Légion d'honneur*. Although he was not tall, beneath the smock, Debord possessed the broad chest and shoulders of a Picasso etching of a bull.

"Ah, Madame Friedman," he said, greeting her Continental style with an air kiss beside each cheek, "it is a pleasure to meet such a discerning woman."

"I like your stuff," Sophie lied adroitly, "although I have to admit, it was a toss-up between you and Gianni Sardella."

The room went suddenly, deathly still. The only sound was the soft strains of Vivaldi playing in the back-ground. Marie Hélène, normally a paragon of composure, blanched.

Alex's dark eyes widened. Surely Mrs. Friedman knew of the antipathy between the two designers! Stories of their mutual loathing were legion. Not only did Debord not permit his rival's name to be spoken in his presence, last spring he allegedly pushed a client down the grand staircase of the Paris Opera for wearing one of Sardella's beaded evening gowns.

All eyes were on Debord. The back-and-forth motion of his jaw suggested that he was grinding his teeth. His eyes had narrowed to hard, dark stones; a vein pulsed dangerously at his temple. Just when Alex thought he was going to explode, he forced a flat smile.

"I am honored you chose me," he said between clenched teeth.

That, more than anything, displayed to Alex how far her employer had fallen. Before this season's showing, he would have shouted something about philistines and demanded Mrs. Friedman leave these hallowed halls and never darken his doorway again.

Sophie appeared undaunted by the tension surrounding them. Indeed, Alex considered, from the twinkle in her eyes, she appeared to be having the time of her life.

"Your reputation is equaled only by your prices, *monsieur*," she said. "I hope you realize how lucky you are to have Alexandra working for you."

He looked at Alex, as if seeing her for the first time.

"What I can't understand is why she isn't a designer," Sophie declared. "With her talent, along with her Seventh Avenue experience, I would have thought you'd have wanted her creative input on this season's collection."

"A designer?" Yves looked at his sister. "You did not tell me that Mademoiselle Lyons was a designer."

Marie Hélène looked as if she could have eaten an entire box of Alex's straight pins and spit out staples. "She designed day wear. Little polyester American dresses," she tacked on dismissively, her tongue as sharp as a seamstress's needle.

"They may have been polyester, but if they were like any of the designs I saw this afternoon, they must have sold like hotcakes," Sophie shot back.

Debord turned to Alex. "You have sketches?"

"Yves…" Marie Hélène protested.

The designer ignored his sister. "Do you?" he asked Alex again.

Alex finally understood why her sketches had been rejected without comment. Debord had never seen them. Alex shot a quick, blistering glare Marie Hélène's way. The directress responded with a cool, challenging look of her own.

Knowing that to accuse his sister of treachery would definitely not endear herself to the designer, Alex bit her tongue practically in two. "My portfolio is at my apartment." Anger and anticipation had her heart pounding so fast and so hard she wondered if the others could hear it.

"You will bring your sketches to my office first thing tomorrow morning. I will examine them then."

Ignoring his sister's silent disapproval, Debord turned again to Sophie. "I hope you enjoy your gowns, *madame*. As well as the remainder of your time in Paris."

"If the rest of my trip is half as much fun as today

has been," Sophie professed, "I'm going have one helluva time." She winked conspiratorially at Alex.

For the first time in her life, Alex understood exactly how Cinderella had felt when her fairy godmother had shown up with that gilded pumpkin coach.

Her idol was finally going to see her sketches!

And when he did, he was bound to realize she was just what he needed to instill new excitement into his fall collection.

Alex indulged in a brief tantalizing fantasy of Debord and herself working together, side by side, spending their days and nights working feverishly to the sounds of Vivaldi, united in a single, brilliant creative effort.

As she returned Sophie Friedman's smile with a dazzling grin of her own, Alex decided that life didn't get much better than this.

Chapter Three

Alex didn't sleep all night. As she dressed for work, running one pair of black panty hose and pulling a button off the front of her dress in her fumbling nervousness, all she could think about was the upcoming moment of truth. When Debord would view her designs.

When she entered the salon, Alex was met with the cold, unwelcoming stare of Marie Hélène.

"Bonjour, Madame," Alex said with far more aplomb than she was feeling.

Marie Hélène did not return her greeting. "Debord is waiting in his office."

Taking a deep breath that should have calmed her, but didn't, Alex headed up the stairs to the designer's penthouse office.

As she paused before the ebony door, with its *Défense d'Entrer* sign, Alex had a very good idea how Marie Antoinette must have felt on her way to the guillotine. Sternly reminding herself that a faint heart never achieved anything, that this was what she'd always wanted, she knocked.

Silence. Then, Debord's deep voice calling out, *"Entrez!"*

Squaring her shoulders, clad in an uplifting, confidence-building scarlet hunting jacket she'd defiantly worn over her black dress, she entered the designer's sanctum sanctorum.

Debord was talking in English on the phone. After gesturing her toward a chair on the visitor's side of his desk, he spun his high-backed chair around and continued his conversation. From his tight, rigidly controlled tone, Alex sensed that the telephone call was not delivering good news.

She took advantage of the delay to study the office. Like the workrooms, everything was pristine. The desk had such a sheen Debord was reflected in its gleaming jet surface. On the stark white wall behind the desk, Debord appeared in triplicate in Warhol portraits.

"Of course, Madame Lord," Debord was saying. "I understand your reluctance to commit funds just now."

Alex watched his fingers twist the telephone cord and had an idea that the designer would love to put those artistic fingers around Madame Lord's neck.

She'd heard about the possibility of Debord designing a line of ready-to-wear for Lord's, the prestigious department store chain. After last week's debacle, the gossip around the *atelier* was that the designer was desperate for such a deal in order to salvage a disastrous season.

Now, unfortunately, it appeared that Eleanor Lord, like everyone else, had deserted Debord.

"Certainly. I will look forward to seeing you at the

fall *défilé* in July. We shall, of course, reserve your usual seat. *Certainement,* in the first row."

That statement revealed how important he considered the American executive. Seating was significant at couture showings; indeed, many fashion editors behaved as if their seat assignments were more important than the clothes being shown.

"*Au revoir,* Madame Lord."

The designer muttered a pungent curse, but when he turned toward Alex, his expression was bland. He did, however, lift an inquiring brow at her jacket. When he failed to offer a word of criticism, Alex let out a breath she'd been unaware of holding.

"Americans," he said dismissively. "They cannot understand that risk-taking is the entire point of couture."

"Mrs. Friedman bought your entire collection."

"True. However, I cannot understand why she chose my designs when they are so obviously inappropriate for her figure."

"She told me she likes your work." Alex was not about to reveal Sophie's actual reasons for buying Debord's collection. "And Lady Smythe seemed pleased with that black cocktail dress."

That particular purchase had been viewed as a positive sign, since Miranda Smythe not only happened to be Eleanor Lord's niece and style consultant for the Lord's London store, but was rumored to be the person who'd brought Debord to the department store executive's attention in the first place.

Unfortunately it appeared that when it came to business Lady Smythe had scant influence with her powerful aunt.

"I would feel a great deal better about the sale if

Miranda Smythe had actually paid for the dress," he countered. "I cannot understand Marie Hélène. The discounts she allows that woman are tantamount to giving my work away."

Alex was not about to criticize Debord's formidable sister. "I suppose it doesn't hurt to have the wife of a British peer wearing your designs," she said carefully.

"Such things never hurt. But the British are so damnably tightfisted, they seldom buy couture. The average Englishwoman would rather spend her money on commissioning a bronze of her nasty little dogs, or a new horse trailer. Besides, Lady Miranda is about to get a divorce."

Alex had heard Marie Hélène and Françoise, Miranda Lord Baptista Smythe's personal vendeuse, discussing the socialite's marital record just yesterday.

"Let us keep our fingers crossed," Debord decided. "Perhaps, with luck, this time the fickle lady will wed a Kuwaiti prince. They never ask for discounts."

Alex laughed, as she was supposed to.

At last she couldn't stand the suspense a minute longer. "I know you're very busy, Monsieur. Would you like to see my portfolio now?"

"In a moment. First, I would like to know why such a beautiful woman would choose to labor behind the scenes when she could easily be a successful model."

"I'm not thin enough to be a model. Or tall enough. Besides, I've wanted to be a designer forever."

"Forever?" he asked with a faintly mocking smile.

"Well, ever since I watched Susan Hayward in *Back Street*. That's an old American movie," Alex explained at his questioning glance. "She plays a designer. The first time I saw it I fell head over heels in love."

"With Susan Hayward?" He frowned.

"Oh, no." Alex laughed as she followed his train of thought. "Not the actress. I fell in love with the glamour of the business. It became an all-encompassing passion." Her grin was quick and appealing. "Some of my friends would tell you that designing is all I think about."

"Really?" Debord's eyes, so like his sister's, but much warmer, moved slowly over her face. "I find that difficult to believe. A beautiful young woman such as yourself must have some other interests—parties, dances...men. Perhaps one particular man?"

He was watching her carefully now, the blue of his eyes almost obscured by the ebony pupils. Alex swallowed.

"Let me show you my designs." The portfolio was lying across her knees. She began to untie the brown string with fingers that had turned to stone. "I should probably tell you right off that most of the teachers at the institute didn't really like my style," she admitted. "But since I believe this is my best work, I'd really appreciate a master's opinion." Her words tumbled out, as if she were eager to get them behind her.

"I do not understand why Marie Hélène did not tell me about your talent," Debord said as Alex continued to struggle with the thin brown fastener.

Personally, Alex had her own ideas about that, but knowing how close Debord was to his sister, she kept them to herself.

"She's very busy." *Finally!* Cool relief flooded through Alex when the maddening knot gave way.

Yves Debord took her sketches and placed them facedown on the desk. Before looking at them, he pulled a gold cigarette case from his jacket pocket. After lighting a Gauloises, he turned his attention toward the colorful presentations.

Alex was more anxious than she'd ever been in her life. She kept waiting for him to say something—anything!—but he continued to flip through the sketches, front to back, back to front, over and over again.

Did he like them? Hate them? Were her designs as exciting and modern as she perceived them to be? Or were they, as one of her instructors had scathingly proclaimed, clothes for tarts?

Time slowed to a snail's pace. Perspiration began to slip down her sides.

"You are extraordinarily talented," Debord said finally.

"Do you really like them?"

He stubbed out his cigarette. "They are the most innovative designs I've seen in years."

Alex beamed.

"They are also entirely unmarketable."

The words hit like a blow from behind, striking her momentarily mute. "You have flown in the face of tradition," he said in a brusque no-nonsense tone that didn't spare her feelings. "This is costuming for the theater. Not the real world."

She'd heard that accusation before. But never had it stung so badly. "I was trying to be innovative. Like Chanel in the twenties with her tweed suits. And Dior's postwar New Look. The sixties' revolution, when Yves Saint Laurent introduced the pantsuit. And of course, Courreges's minidress."

She took a deep breath. "You just said that couture was about risk. All the great designers—Norell, Beene, you yourself—have gained fame by insisting on having a spirit of their own."

"You have talent, but you do not understand couture," he countered. "A designer must see women as they *want* to be seen."

"That's true," Alex conceded, even as it crossed her mind that, instead of *telling* women what they want, designers should *ask* them what they want.

Patience, she could hear her mother warning her.

"This design, for example." He held up a sketch that happened to be one of her favorites. An evening gown of tiered gold lace over black chiffon, cut like a Flamenco dancer's dress. "This gown would make a woman look as if she were dressing for an American Halloween party."

That hurt. "I can't see what's wrong with thinking of life as a party." *Patience.* "Besides, I thought it was sexy."

"The first thing you must learn, Alexandra, is that husbands want their women to look like ladies. Especially American husbands, who have a habit of marrying younger and younger brides without really knowing their pedigree."

He ignored Alex's sharp intake of breath. "Since the husbands are the ones paying the bills, a wise couturier designs with them in mind."

"That's incredibly chauvinistic."

"Perhaps. It is also true. The British have a saying," Debord continued. "Mutton dressed as lamb. Never forget, Mademoiselle Lyons, that is precisely what we are paid to do."

"But what about celebrating the female form—" Alex couldn't help argue "—instead of focusing on androgynous, sexless women?" When he physically bristled, Alex realized she'd hit uncomfortably close to home with that one. After all, Debord's disastrous new line had carried androgyny to new extremes.

His stony expression would have encouraged a prudent woman to back away. Unfortunately caution had never been Alex's forte.

"You say we must design for the husbands," she said, leaning forward. "I can't believe any man really wants his woman looking like a malnourished twelve-year-old boy."

"Not all men do," Debord acknowledged, his steady gaze taking in the softly feminine curves her stark black dress and scarlet jacket could not entirely conceal. "But the fact remains, Alexandra, wives should look like ladies. Not sirens."

In Alex's mind, there was absolutely nothing wrong with looking like a lady in the daytime and a siren at night. After all, this was a new age. Having proven they could do men's work, Alex believed it was time women started looking like women again.

"May I ask a question?" she said quietly.

"Certainement."

"How can you consider me talented when you hate everything about my designs?"

"On the contrary, I don't hate everything about them. I love the energy, the verve. I think your use of color, while overdone, is *magnifique*."

"Well," Alex decided on a rippling little sigh, "I suppose that's something."

"It's important." He stood and smiled down at her. "It is time we found a proper outlet for your talents."

"Do you mean—"

"I'm promoting you to assistant designer," Debord confirmed. "I shall inform Marie Hélène that you will be moving upstairs. Immediately."

Joy bubbled up in Alex. It was all she could do to keep from jumping up and flinging her arms around Debord's neck. She knew the broad grin splitting her face must look horrendously gauche, but couldn't keep herself from smiling.

"I don't know how to thank you, *monsieur*."

"Just do your best. That is all I expect." Debord walked her to the door.

Feigning indifference to Marie Hélène's cold stare, Alex moved her colored pencils and sketch pads into the design office located above the showroom floor.

She was hard at work at her slanted drawing table later that afternoon when Debord entered the office. He made his way slowly around the room, offering a comment on each designer's work. Some were less than flattering, but all were encouraging. Until he got to Alex.

"A zipper is inappropriate," he declared loud enough for everyone in the room to hear. His finger jabbed at the back of her evening gown design. "This gown lacks spirit."

He plucked the slate pencil from her suddenly damp hand and with a few deft flourishes, sketched in a row of satin-covered buttons. "There. Now we have passion."

The buttons running from neckline to hem were admittedly lovely. They were also highly impractical. Alex wondered how a woman would be able to wear such a dress without a maid to fasten her up. And then there was the little matter of getting out of the gown at the end of the evening.

"It would seem to me," she countered mildly, "that trying to deal with fifty tiny, slippery satin buttons running down the back of a dress would tend to stifle passion."

There was a gasp from neighboring tables as the others in the room realized that this newcomer had dared argue with the master. Debord shot her a warning look.

"The way couture differs from ready-to-wear is in the decorating," he said shortly. "Specialness comes from the shape, the cut, the workmanship.

"Embellishing. Some fringe here." He ran his hand over her shoulder. Down the notched black velvet lapel of her scarlet hunting blazer. "A bit of beading here.

"We all must eat, Alexandra. Yet who among us wouldn't prefer a steak tartare to one of your American hot dogs? A glass of wine to water? A *crème brûlée* to some diet gelatin mold?"

"Are you comparing the designs of Debord to fine French cuisine?" Alex dared ask with a smile.

"Bien sûr." He rewarded her with an approving smile of his own. Alex could have spent the remainder of the day basking in its warmth. "I knew you would be an adept pupil, Alexandra."

As he leaned forward, his arm casually brushed against her breast. "Now, let us review your interpretation of a Debord dinner suit."

Chapter Four

The house, perched dramatically atop a hill, was draped in fog. Inside, candles flickered in Wedgwood holders. A fire blazed in the high, stone library fireplace.

Beside the fireplace, two women sat at opposite sides of a small mahogany table. Eleanor Lord wore an ivory silk blouse and linen slacks from Lord's Galleria department.

Across the table, theatrically clad in a lavender turban and a billowy caftan of rainbow chiffon, Clara Kowalski reached into a flowered tapestry bag and pulled out a small amethyst globe.

"The crystal is radiating amazing amounts of positive energy today," Clara said.

"Do you really believe Jarlath can locate Anna?"

Clara clucked her tongue. "Jarlath is merely a guide, Eleanor. Aiding you to evolve to a higher dimension."

"I'd rather he skip the evolution stuff and find my granddaughter," Eleanor muttered.

Eleanor considered herself a logical woman. She had always scoffed at those tales of farmers being kidnapped by aliens. Nor did she believe in the Bermuda Triangle, Bigfoot or the Loch Ness Monster. From the beginning of her marriage, Eleanor had been an equal partner in The Lord's Group, the department store chain established by her husband. When James Lord had died of a heart attack nearly thirty years ago, she took over the business without missing a step.

Despite her advanced years, despite the fact she now preferred doing business from her Santa Barbara home rather than trek down the coast to the chain's Los Angeles headquarters, Eleanor remained vigorous and continued her quest to keep Lord's the most successful department store in the world.

That same single-mindedness that had made Lord's a leader in fashion merchandising contributed to another, even more unrelenting obsession.

Eleanor had vowed to find her granddaughter, whatever it took. And although twenty-four years had passed, she had not stopped trying.

Each year, on the anniversary of Anna's disappearance, she'd place an advertisement offering a generous reward for information regarding her granddaughter's abduction in numerous metropolitan and small-town newspapers.

Thus far, once again, the advertisement had yielded nothing.

A less stubborn woman would have given up what everyone kept telling her was a futile search. But tenacity ran deep in Eleanor's veins. Besides, some inner sense told her she'd know if her granddaughter had been killed. Anna was alive. Of that, Eleanor had absolutely no doubt.

"As a businesswoman, you utilize your left brain, your logical side," Clara was saying. Eleanor returned her thoughts to the séance. "Jarlath will help you get in touch with your intuitive side. Once that doorway is open, you will have your answer."

Eleanor admitted to herself that the medium sounded uncomfortably like one of those frauds Mike Wallace was always unmasking on "60 Minutes." But, not wanting to leave any stone unturned, she was willing to try anything. Even this dabbling in the occult, which undoubtedly had all her Presbyterian ancestors spinning in their graves.

"Well," she said briskly, "let's get started."

Clara placed an Ouija board between them, took a chunk of quartz from her bag and placed it in the center of the board.

"Rock quartz is allied to the energies of the moon," she said. "I've found it makes a more sensitive channel than the usual pointer. The amethyst shade is exceptionally powerful."

Eleanor nodded and wondered, not for the first time, what had made her agree to this farfetched idea.

"Now," Clara said as she lit a stick of incense, "you must clear your mind. Banish all doubts. All cynicism."

Just get on with it, an impatient voice in Eleanor's cynical mind insisted. She shifted restlessly in her seat.

"I'm sensing negative energy," Clara chided. She began to sway. "Jarlath will not come if he is not welcome. Write your negative thoughts on a mental blackboard. Then erase them."

Immensely grateful that no one she knew was witnessing this outlandish scene, Eleanor took a deep breath and tried again.

"Ahhh." Clara nodded. "That's better. Relax your body, Eleanor. Feel yourself growing serene. Open your mind. Allow your physical and spiritual states to become harmonized and aligned," she intoned. She placed her fingers on the chunk of quartz. "Jarlath. Are you there?"

Eleanor watched as the violet stone slowly slid across the board, stopping on *Yes*.

"Welcome, Jarlath. This is my dear friend, Eleanor Lord. She needs your help, Jarlath. Desperately. She is trying to locate her granddaughter, Anna."

Although she knew it to be impossible, with the fire blazing nearby, Eleanor thought the air in the room suddenly felt cooler.

She leaned forward. "Ask him if he's seen Anna."

"Patience," Clara counseled. "Jarlath reveals in his own time." Nevertheless, her next words were, "Is Anna with you?"

No. "I knew it!" Eleanor crowed triumphantly. Clara's guide was saying what she'd always known herself. Anna was alive!

There was a long pause. Then the gleaming rock moved to *A*. Then *N*. Then *O*. It moved slowly at first, then faster and faster until it had spelled out *Another wishes to speak*. The flames of the candles suddenly shifted dramatically to the right, as if a wind had caught them. Caught up in the drama of the moment, Eleanor forgot to disbelieve.

"Who is with you?" Clara questioned. "Who wishes to speak with Eleanor Lord?"

This time the amethyst stone raced across the board. Candlelight reflected off its crystalline surface. *Dead.*

"Dear Lord, perhaps it's James. Or Robbie." Eleanor's voice trembled at the thought of her son. "Or Melanie." Her son's beautiful, tragically unhappy wife. Anna's mother.

No.

Clara frowned across the table as if to remind Eleanor just who was in charge of this séance. "Who, then?"

Silence.

"Place your fingers on the stone with mine," Clara advised. "It will increase the energy flow."

Eleanor did as instructed. Haltingly, the quartz began to move. *R. O.* Heat seemed to emanate from the amethyst. Eleanor's fingertips grew warm. *S.*

"Rosa," Eleanor gasped. Anna's nanny.

Confirming her thoughts, the crystal stopped on *A.* Eleanor felt light-headed. Spots danced in front of her eyes. The fire flared. Though there was no wind outdoors, the glass panes in the windows began to rattle. Then everything went dark.

"You're overreacting," Eleanor insisted an hour later. She was still in the library. And she was a very long way from being in a good mood. "It was merely a little heart flutter. Nothing more."

Dr. Averill Brandford frowned as he took the seventy-one-year-old woman's pulse. "That's your opinion. I hadn't realized you'd gotten your medical degree."

Having been called here from the yacht harbor where he moored his ketch, Averill was casually clad in a blue polo shirt, white duck slacks and navy Top-

Siders. His face was tanned and his hair was sun-streaked from sailing excursions off the coast.

"You always did have a smart mouth, Averill," Eleanor returned. "I remember the summer you boys turned seven and you taught Robbie to curse. Although I'll admit to finding the episode moderately amusing, James did not share my feelings. It was a week before Robbie could sit down."

"It was winter. And we were nine." A tape recorder on a nearby table was playing Indian flute music. He turned it off. "And for the record, it was Robbie who taught me." He went over to the desk. "I'm checking you into the hospital for tests."

"That's ridiculous. I'm fine."

"Let's just make certain, shall we?"

"Do they teach all you doctors to be such sons-of-bitches in medical school?"

"The very first semester. Along with how to pad our medicare bills."

"Smart mouth." Eleanor shook her head in disgust. Her hair, like her attitude, had steadfastly refused to give in to age. It was as richly auburn as it had been when she was a girl, save for a streak of silver at her temple, which had occurred overnight, after the tragic double murder and kidnapping.

"I think you should listen to Averill, Eleanor," the other man in the room, Zachary Deveraux, counseled with quiet authority.

"This isn't fair. You're ganging up on me."

"Whatever it takes," the tall, dark-haired man returned easily, appearing unfazed by her blistering glare.

Zachary was leaning against a leather wall, arms crossed over his chest, his legs crossed at the ankles.

Unlike the doctor's recreational attire, Zach was wearing a conservative dark suit, white shirt and navy tie. His shoes, remarkably staid for even this Republican stronghold, were wing tips.

"As president of The Lord's Group, it's my responsibility to do everything I can to keep the company strong. You're more than a vital asset, Eleanor," he said with a slight French-patois accent that hinted at his Louisiana Cajun roots. "You're the lifeblood of the chain. We need you."

His dark eyes, more black than brown, warmed. His harshly cut masculine lips curved in a coaxing smile. "*I* need you."

Although she might be in her eighth decade, Eleanor was a long way from dead. Was there a woman with blood still stirring in her veins who could resist that blatantly seductive smile?

Before she could accuse him of pulling out all the stops to win his way, the library door opened and Clara burst into the room. An overpowering scent of orrisroot and clove emanated from the silver *pomme d'ambre* she wore around her neck.

"Eleanor, dear." Moving with the force of a bulldozer, she practically knocked both men over as she rushed to the side of the sofa. "I've been absolutely frantic ever since your two bodyguards banished me from the room."

She shot a blistering glare first at Averill, then another directly at Zach, who merely stared back. The only sign of his annoyance were his lips, which tightened into a grim line.

Eleanor's slender hand disappeared between the woman's two pink pudgy ones. "I'm fine, Clara. Really," she insisted. "It was merely a flutter. Nothing to be concerned about."

"Of course not," Clara Kowalski agreed heartily. "Don't you worry, dear. I have just the tonic you need in the greenhouse."

She smiled reassuringly. "A little extract of hawthorn, followed by some pipsissewa tea. That will definitely do the trick."

"I believe you've done enough tricks for today, Mrs. Kowalski," Averill said.

Crimson flooded the elderly woman's face, clashing with her lavender turban. "I am not a magician, Doctor. I do not do tricks."

"Oh, no?" Zach countered, scowling at the Ouija board. "Looks like just another fun evening at home with Hecate."

"Zachary," Eleanor murmured her disapproval. "You mustn't talk that way. Clara's my friend. And she's been very helpful. We almost had a breakthrough."

"A breakthrough?" He didn't conceal his scorn concerning Clara Kowalski's alleged psychic powers.

"We nearly made contact with Rosa, Anna's departed nanny." Clara's eyes, nearly hidden by folds of pink fat, dared him to challenge her claim.

"Clara's guide said Rosa was willing to talk to us," Eleanor said.

"Ah, yes, the infamous guide," Zach agreed. "What was the guy's name again? Jaws?"

"Jarlath!" Clara snapped.

"That's right." Zach nodded. "Summer sales could be stronger this season. How about asking old Jarlath to see what he can do about bringing more shoppers into the stores?"

"Jarlath does not control things," Clara replied waspishly. "He is a spiritual guide, not a fortune-teller."

"Sounds a helluva lot like voodoo to me." Zach turned back to Eleanor, his exasperation obvious. "Dammit, Eleanor—"

"Don't you see, Zachary," she interrupted earnestly, "Rosa can tell us what happened to Anna."

The two men exchanged weary, resigned looks. Zach raked his hand through his jet hair and cursed softly in the Acadian French, that during his childhood years, had been the only language spoken in his bayou home.

"Eleanor," Averill said softly. Gently. "It's been twenty-four years since Robbie and Melanie were…" He paused, selecting his words carefully. "Since Anna disappeared," he said, instead. "Don't you think it's time you gave it up?"

"I promised Robbie I'd find Anna. Since I never broke a promise to my son while he was alive, I'll be damned if I start with this one."

"I'm only suggesting a few days in the hospital," Averill said. "For tests. And some well-deserved rest. After all, you need to be in tip-top shape to keep up your search. If that's what you insist on doing."

"It is." But Eleanor's determined expression wavered. Her gaze went to the table, where they'd been so close to contacting the nanny.

"It won't hurt to have a checkup before we leave for the Paris shows next month," Zachary pointed out with the unwavering logic she'd always admired.

In so many ways Zach reminded Eleanor of her dear James. Granted, their backgrounds were vastly different. But even discounting her late husband's family wealth, both James Lord and Zachary Deveraux were quintessential self-made men.

Zachary had been her personal discovery. Eleanor had watched his meteoric progress with a certain secret pride. And although he didn't yet know it, she was grooming him to take over the reins of the Lord's chain when she retired.

Upon her death, this man she'd come to think of as a son would receive enough of the family stock to ensure control of The Lord's Group. But included in her will was a provision for Anna to receive the bulk of Eleanor's personal estate.

"All right. Three days," Eleanor said finally, ignoring Clara's frustrated huff. "Then if you won't release me, I'm checking myself out."

Although Eleanor knew Zach was more than capable of handling business, she insisted on remaining a vital part of Lord's. She'd seen too many of her male colleagues retire, only to drop dead of a heart attack six months later. Eleanor had no intention of joining their ranks.

"Three days," Averill agreed. "That's all I'm asking."

"And I want Clara to have a bed in my room."

"Impossible," Zach ground out before Averill could respond. His rugged face could have been chiseled from granite. "There's no way you're going to get any rest with Sybil the Soothsayer hovering over you like one of Macbeth's damned witches."

Clara's scowl darkened. She crossed her arms over her abundant bosom and glared at him. "Has anyone ever told you that you have a very negative aura, Mr. Deveraux?"

"All the time," he snapped.

"Eleanor—" Averill deftly entered the debate "—Zach's right. You need rest. Time away from all this." He waved his hand, encompassing the accumulation of mystical accoutrements that had taken over the house.

Eleanor held her ground. "Those are my terms, Averill. Take them or leave them."

Professional demeanor was abandoned as he allowed his frustration to show. "There are times when I can't decide whether you are the most obstinate woman I've ever met or simply crazy," he muttered, picking up the receiver to make the arrangements.

If she was insulted, Eleanor didn't reveal it. "That's precisely the reason I'm going to find Anna."

Chapter Five

Two days later, Miranda Lord Baptista Smythe burst into Eleanor's hospital room. She was fashionably thin and sported a sleek blond hairdo that was as much a signature of her British Ascot class as her accent. Although she was in her midforties, her complexion, thanks to a benevolent British climate and the clever hand of her plastic surgeon, was as smooth and unlined as that of a girl in her twenties.

"Dear, dear Aunt Eleanor," she greeted the older woman with a brush of powdered cheek. "I rushed over from London on the Concorde as soon as I heard! Honestly, I don't understand how you could have let that horrid old witch get you so upset!"

"Clara doesn't upset me, Miranda," Eleanor said mildly.

"She gave you a heart attack."

"It was a flutter. And Clara had nothing to do with it."

Miranda took a cigarette from her Gucci bag and

was prepared to light it when she caught sight of the No Smoking—Oxygen in Use sign posted beside Eleanor's hospital bed.

"Those things already killed your mother," Eleanor pointed out knowingly.

"Living like some over-the-hill party girl, squandering her inheritance from my father, instead of putting it somewhere safe such as blue-chip stocks or bonds, is what killed my mother," Miranda said. "Why, if it weren't for all the money she threw away on those damned gigolos, I wouldn't be fighting to keep the wolves away from the door."

Lawrence Lord, James's younger brother and business partner, and Miranda's father, had been an avid tennis fan and nationally ranked amateur player. Forty-six years ago, when he'd returned from a trip to Wimbledon with news that he had fallen in love with the genteel daughter of an impoverished viscount, James had established a Lord's in London and made his brother president of the new European branch, where Miranda now worked as a style consultant.

"You're far from destitute, dear," Eleanor reminded Miranda. "Your salary is generous. And you still have your stock."

"That's another thing." Miranda began to pace, the skirt of her emerald silk YSL dress rustling with each long stride. "My barrister assures me the prenuptial agreement will be upheld, but in the meantime, Martin is demanding a share of London Lord's."

Eleanor frowned. She knew Miranda's latest marriage—to a London bond trader—was in the process of ending, as had her marriage to a Brazilian polo player before it, in divorce. But she hadn't been informed of this unfortunate legal development.

"Well, we certainly can't have that," she said.

"I'd shoot Martin through his black heart with one of his antique shotguns before I let him get his greedy, aristocratic hands on the family business," Miranda agreed grimly.

"I believe we can defuse this little problem without resorting to violence," Eleanor murmured. "Why don't I ask Zach to meet with your attorney? Or even with Martin himself? Zachary can be very persuasive." Eleanor knew from personal experience that Lord's president also wasn't above employing street-fighter skills when necessary.

Frown lines etched their way into Miranda's smooth forehead. "If you think it will help. Although I still prefer the idea of shooting the bastard. Or perhaps putting poison in his sherry."

As if aware of how unpleasant she sounded, she said, "But enough about my petty problems. Let me arrange your pillows, Auntie. You need your rest."

Her niece's pretense of concern grated. Before Miranda's dramatic entrance, Eleanor had overheard her talking with Averill outside the room.

Averill had spoken gently, in the reassuring way doctors had. Although with proper care she probably had many years left, if Eleanor's heart did fail, Miranda would be able to glean comfort from the fact that her aunt had had a full life. And though she would be missed, all that Eleanor had done would remain as a memorial.

Averill had reminded Eleanor of a man rehearsing

a eulogy. The unctuous testimonial had made her mad enough to want to spit nails.

"The rumors of my impending death have been greatly exaggerated," she paraphrased Mark Twain now.

"Of course, Auntie," Miranda agreed quickly. Too quickly, Eleanor mused. "We all know you're going to live forever."

Well, maybe not forever. But if Averill or Miranda thought she was going to die anytime soon, they had another think coming. Because Eleanor refused to leave this world until Anna was back home again. Where she belonged.

"Miranda, dear, would you do me a favor?"

"Of course."

"Would you please find Clara? I believe she's in the cafeteria."

Miranda's forced smile revealed her distaste for Clara, but she held her tongue. "Of course."

"Oh, and Miranda?"

She turned in the doorway. "Yes?"

"Ask her to bring her tarot cards. I had a dream about Anna when I dozed off earlier. I think a reading is in order."

A nerve twitched at the corner of Miranda's red lips. "Whatever you say, Aunt Eleanor."

Zach sat in a corner of the hospital cafeteria, drinking coffee from a brown-and-white cardboard cup and eating a ham-and-Swiss-cheese sandwich. The coffee tasted like battery acid, the cheese was processed, the dark rye bread stale.

His mind was not on his unsavory meal. It was on

what he was going to do about Eleanor. Every morning, when he went to work, he was in charge of millions of dollars and thousands of Lord's employees. He was intelligent, capable and clever. So why the hell couldn't he figure out what to do about Eleanor's unwavering efforts to locate her missing granddaughter? A granddaughter who'd likely been dead for twenty-four years.

Zach polished off the thick, unappetizing coffee and lost in thought, began methodically tearing the cardboard cup to pieces. On some level, he was vaguely aware of a growing commotion nearby. But since this was a hospital and there was always some tragedy occurring, he paid the raised voices no heed.

Last year Eleanor had been convinced she'd discovered Anna. The woman, a blackjack dealer in a Las Vegas casino, had been an obvious impostor. It was also obvious she'd been put up to the charade by her boyfriend, a low-level gangster.

But when Zach had argued that the things the woman professed to remember about the Montecito house and the family could be found in newspaper morgues and style magazines, Eleanor, her steely logic fogged by unrelenting desire, had refused to listen.

Ignoring Zach's protests, Eleanor had moved the woman and her boyfriend into her home, treating them like family. Nothing, absolutely nothing, was too good for her darling "Anna." On one memorable day, Zach had arrived in Santa Barbara with the quarterly reports just as Eleanor and "Anna" returned home laden down with resort clothes, dresses, and elegant evening gowns—suitable for all the parties Anna would be attending, Eleanor had pointed out. Later that same af-

ternoon, a red Corvette from a local Chevrolet dealer
had been delivered.

Although Zach detested anything resembling a lie,
he had reminded himself that what Eleanor was seeking was family. That being the case, did it really matter
all that much if this newly discovered family member
was not really tied by blood?

It did.

Six weeks after their arrival at Eleanor's door, the
unsavory pair absconded with all the gifts Eleanor had
bestowed upon the woman she'd believed to be her
granddaughter, along with several thousand dollars
from the household expenses checking account, a tea
set crafted by Paul Revere that had been in the family
for two hundred years, and a stunning diamond-and-
pearl necklace set in platinum that James had given
Eleanor on the occasion of their son Robert's birth.

Had it not been for the necklace, Eleanor, horribly
embarrassed by her uncharacteristic mistake in judgment, undoubtedly would have let the matter go. But
the sentimental value of that jewelry overrode any fear
of public humiliation.

She'd pressed charges, and two weeks later, the couple was discovered celebrating their good fortune in
Cancun. Well aware that what he was doing was bribery, Zach traveled to Mexico with an attaché case filled
with American dollars to grease the normally slow-
moving machinery of Mexican justice.

He was successful. The fugitives were extradited to
California, charged and convicted.

Although still slightly bothered by the way he'd
skated along the razor's edge of principle—bribery
and veiled threats were not his usual method of doing

business—Zach did not for a single moment regret his actions.

The son of an impoverished Louisiana trapper and sugarcane farmer, Zach had come up the hard way and was immensely proud of his white-collar status. He also understood that it was not that great a distance between wearing a starched shirt and suit in his executive suite to his early days laboring in a sweat-stained T-shirt on the loading dock of the New Orleans Lord's.

Eleanor Lord had offered Zach wealth, security and the opportunity to prove himself. There was nothing he wouldn't do for her.

The voices in the cafeteria grew louder, infiltrating their way into his thoughts. When he recognized Clara's voice, he looked over to see what the witch was up to now.

She was engaged in an argument with another woman whom Zach recognized as Eleanor's niece. Eleanor kept a crystal-framed photo of Miranda Lord, smiling up at her first husband, the dashing, unfaithful Brazilian polo player, on her desk.

Deciding he'd better intervene before the two women started pulling hair, Zach cursed and pushed himself to his feet.

Clara's pudgy face was as crimson as today's turban, while equally bright color stained Miranda's cheekbones.

"Excuse me," he murmured, from behind Miranda's shoulder, "but you ladies are drawing a crowd."

Miranda spun around. "Who the bloody hell do you think you are?"

Her green eyes were flashing like emeralds and her complexion reminded him of the Devonshire cream he'd sampled the time Eleanor, intent on teaching him manners, had taken him to afternoon tea at the Biltmore.

"If you do not mind, Mr. Deveraux," Clara said, giving him her usual glare, "we are having a discussion."

"Sounded more like an argument to me."

"Mr. Deveraux?" One perfectly shaped blond brow lifted. The fury faded from her bright eyes, replaced by blatant feminine interest. "*You're* Aunt Eleanor's famous Zachary?"

Miranda Lord was reminiscent of an F. Scott Fitzgerald heroine. One of those bright, shining people, like Daisy from *The Great Gatsby*. Zach felt a burst of masculine pride that she knew of him. "Not all that famous."

"On the contrary." Her lips curved, and he was reminded of a cat regarding a succulent saucer of cream. "You're practically all Auntie talks about. And although I knew you were a change from those old fogies who usually sit on the board, I don't know why she never mentioned how—" she allowed her eyes to sweep slowly over him "—substantial you are."

When her gaze lingered a heartbeat too long on his thighs, Zach knew he was being expertly, seductively summed up.

Her openly predatory gaze returned to his face. "I'm so sorry," she cooed. "All this has been so upsetting that I've completely forgotten my manners." She held out a slim, perfectly manicured hand. "I'm Miranda Lord. Soon to be the former Lady, or Mrs. Martin-the-bastard-Smythe." Her silvery, breathless voice, a voice Judy Holliday had invented and Marilyn Monroe had perfected, carried an unmistakable British upper class tinge.

"I heard about your divorce." Her hand felt soft and smooth. "I'm sorry."

"Oh, you shouldn't be," Miranda insisted. "Personally, I look on divorce as not so much of an ending, as a new beginning."

She gave him a suggestive smile before turning back to Clara. "My aunt wishes to see you. Oh, and she wants you to bring your tarot cards."

"Well, why didn't you say so in the first place?" Clara huffed. Gathering up her immense shoulder bag, she waddled from the bustling cafeteria.

"Do you suppose," Miranda suggested, "that if we threw water on Clara, she might melt?"

Zach threw back his head and laughed. A rich, booming release of sound that eased the tension. "It's definitely worth a try."

"Why don't we discuss the logistics? Over coffee." She glanced disparagingly around the room. "I'm absolutely exhausted from traveling. But I doubt the chef at this bleak establishment knows how to brew a proper pot of tea."

"No problem. I know just the place."

Placing a palm at her elbow, he led her out of the hospital.

Ten minutes later, they were sitting in the Biltmore's La Sala lounge. The lounge, with its wealth of polished stonework, luxuriant greenery and comfortable, overstuffed sofas and armchairs, was the most gracious in the city.

"I really am so horribly worried about Aunt Eleanor," Miranda said over porcelain cups of impeccably brewed Earl Grey tea. Her heady, exotic scent bloomed in the warmth of the room, mingling with the aroma of cedar from the fireplace.

"Join the club," Zach said. "If it's any consolation, there's no sign of senile dementia."

"You actually considered that possibility?"

"Of course. Your aunt's a logical, pragmatic woman—"

"Except when it comes to her darling Anna."

"Except when it comes to Anna," Zach agreed. "But although she's admittedly driven and obsessive when it comes to finding her granddaughter, it's only been these last few months that she's decided to try the spirit world."

"That is so bizarre," Miranda murmured. "I had my barrister retain a private detective when Clara moved into the house with Aunt Eleanor." She frowned. "Did you know she's a widow? Three times over? And that all her husbands have been wealthy?"

"I had her checked out, too." Zach knew Eleanor would hit the roof if she found out about his investigation, but that didn't stop him from wanting to protect her. "One of her neighbors insists Clara poisoned her husbands with her herbs."

"How horrible!"

"It would be if it was true. But the police lieutenant I spoke with said that same neighbor calls up after 'Crime Stoppers' reports on the news to say she's seen the criminal lurking around her neighborhood. He also assured me that there was no evidence of foul play in any of Clara's husbands' deaths."

"Are you telling me you believe she's innocent?"

Zach shrugged. "At the moment, I can only conclude

that Clara Kowalski simply seems to have better luck with her plants than with her husbands. But I'm keeping an eye on her."

Miranda leaned forward and placed a hand on his arm. "You've no idea how that relieves my mind, Zachary. To know that someone besides me cares what happens to Aunt Eleanor."

Sitting back again, she spread some frothy cream atop a scone, added a dab of dark red currant jam and took a bite. "Sublime," she said on a soft, pleased sigh. "You have marvelous tastes in restaurants, Mr. Deveraux."

Her lips left a red mark like a crescent moon on the scone; a dab of cream remained at the corner of her mouth. When she licked it away, Zach felt his body harden.

"Thanks." He took a long swallow of tea and wished it was Scotch.

"From your disapproval of Auntie's foray into the spirit realm, I take it you don't believe in things that go bump in the night?"

"No. Although I grew up surrounded by voodoo, I've never bought into the spirit world."

"Voodoo?" Miranda leaned forward, every muscle in her body taut with interest. Once again she reminded Zach of Fitzgerald's Daisy. Her voice suggested moonlight and starshine and champagne; her eyes were dazzling jewels.

"I grew up in Louisiana," Zach revealed. "While it's not nearly as prevalent as it once was, voodoo still lives on in local superstitions and medicines."

"Louisiana," Miranda mused reflectively. Zach watched the wheels turning inside that gorgeous blond head. "But of course," she said, clapping her hands. "That explains the accent I keep hearing. You're a Cajun!"

She was looking at him with the overt fascination one might give to a newly discovered species of animal. "Is it true what they say about your people?"

"What do they say?"

Zach braced himself for the usual stereotypical description of fire-eating swamp dwellers who communicated in an archaic French only they could understand and who had yet to join the nineteenth century, let alone the twentieth.

"That your motto is *Laissez les bons temps rouler?*"

"Let the good times roll?" Zach smiled. "Absolutely." He tried to remember the last time in his own life recently that the *bons temps* had *rouler*ed and came up blank.

"I'm so relieved." Her silky voice caressed, like sensually delicate fingers, making Zach consider suggesting they walk to the lobby check-in and get a room.

"So often the most wonderful things you hear turn out to be an exaggeration. And a crashing disappointment." Miranda's expression revealed that she was finding Zach anything but a disappointment.

"It must be difficult," Miranda mused, "trying to run the business while Aunt Eleanor's locked away in the library with that horrid old witch conducting séances."

"I'm managing," Zach said.

Some inner instinct warned him that Eleanor's niece might have a hidden agenda. The board needed Miranda's vote at this year's annual meeting. Zach wasn't about to give her any hint that the chain's future was not as sound as ever. Which it was. He wouldn't allow it to be otherwise.

"Perhaps things will get better for you," she suggested.

Zach would have had to have been deaf to miss the invitation in her tone. When she smiled at him over the rim of her teacup, he felt another slow pull deep in his groin.

"Perhaps they will," he agreed.

She inclined her head charmingly. Then, recrossing her legs with an erotic swish of silk, she gave him an enticing flash of lacy garter and smooth thigh.

It had begun to rain; a steady drizzle that streamed down the windows and made the line between ocean and sky blur.

"I'm afraid I must confess I don't really keep up on the details of the American end of the business," she admitted. "I have enough to keep me busy with the London store. And, of course, my ongoing effort to increase the chain's couture lines.

"But I do know that Lord's headquarters are in Los Angeles. Before Auntie's unfortunate attack, had you come here to Santa Barbara on business? Or pleasure?"

This morning he would have answered business. But since there was no mistaking her signals, Zach answered, "A bit of both."

"I've always admired a man who knows how to play as hard as he works." She took another sip of tea and eyed him expectantly from under the silken fringe of her expertly dyed lashes. Leaning forward, she placed her hand on his knee and looked him directly in the eye. "Now that you've done your duty and provided me with much needed sustenance, I suppose we should return to the hospital. Heaven knows what that horrid woman has done to Aunt Eleanor's blood pressure."

Her demeanor, as they left the lounge and waited for the valet to bring Zach's Mercedes, revealed that returning to the hospital was definitely not her first choice.

"I have some business to discuss with Eleanor. And then you'll probably want to visit with her again," Zach said ten minutes later as he pulled into the hospital parking area.

"Aunt Eleanor and I have a great deal of catching up to do," Miranda agreed.

"I thought you might. After your visit, I'll take you back to the house."

"I'd appreciate that. If you're certain I won't be intruding on your busy schedule."

She was. But Zach didn't care. *Laissez les bons temps rouler.* His mind was practically writhing with erotic images. "I'll shuffle things around while you're with Eleanor." He cut the engine and pocketed the key.

"That's very kind of you."

"And then, after you get settled in at the house, we'll go out to dinner."

"It sounds positively delightful," Miranda said.

Unable to resist the creamy lure of her skin another minute, Zach ran the back of his hand down her cheek.

"And then, after dinner, you'll spend the night with me," he declared in a firm, deep voice that brooked not a single argument. "All night. In my room. In my bed."

Miranda's lips curved in a slow, seductive smile that burned as hot as an Olympic flame. "Yes."

Chapter Six

Paris

Alex's days, weeks and months flowed into each other like long ocean swells as she labored under Debord's watchful, unrelenting eye.

The designer continued to closely monitor her work, brutally subtracting a flounce here, dispensing with what she considered marvelously sexy feathered trim there, all the while treating her to a dizzying array of seemingly casual touches and intimate smiles that left her weak in the knees.

His personal attention to his new protégée did not go unnoticed by the other assistant designers. Jealousy, that ugly emotion rampant in the fashion business, reared its green head on an almost daily basis.

More than once Alex arrived at work only to find that the "cleaning woman" had mistakenly tossed out yesterday's sketches. Or a colleague "accidentally" spilled coffee over designs she'd labored past midnight to finish. Even her beloved pencils disappeared, fortuitously discovered buried beneath some discarded towels in the change room.

Although the others steadfastly refused to accept her, nothing could banish the joy Alex felt every time she entered the studio.

Four months after her promotion, Debord invited Alex out to dinner. Refusing to play coy, she immediately accepted.

They dined at the Café le Flore, a place that remained unchanged from the days when Picasso had made it his unofficial salon and Jean-Paul Sartre and Simone de Beauvoir had sat out the German occupation at a table in the back.

But Alex's mind was not on the past but the future. The immediate future, to be exact. She wore one of her own creations, which had been designed to capture and hold a man's attention. Created of tissue lamé, the strapless dress dipped to her waist in the back. The sparkling gold fabric duplicated the lightest strands in her multihued hair; layers of black net petticoat peeked enticingly from beneath the billowy skirt.

Glittery gold stockings, ridiculously impractical backless high heels and gold chandelier earrings that dusted her shoulders completed the festive look.

"Did I tell you that I plan to include two of your designs in the fall line?" Debord asked.

"No!" Pleasure surged through her. "Which ones?"

"The silk dinner suit with the sarong-style skirt, for one. It should work up nicely in smoke."

Her tawny eyebrows crashed down toward her nose. "Gray?"

"Purple is inappropriate."

Momentarily putting aside her excitement that the master had chosen her work, Alex crossed her legs with a quick, irritated rustle of ebony petticoats. "It's not purple. It's amethyst. Jewel-toned." Alex had intended to press to have it also offered in ruby, emerald and sapphire.

"More women can wear gray than purple. The suit will be offered in smoke. And, of course, black."

Of course, Alex thought. Although she knew she should be thrilled, she felt like a mother who'd just handed over her only child to the Gypsies.

"What other design did you like?"

Although asking Alex to hold her tongue was a little like asking her to stop breathing, she was clever enough to know that getting into an argument with Debord over the line that would ultimately bear his name would prove a fatal mistake.

Patience, she reminded herself for the umpteenth time in months.

"The velvet evening dress with the gold braid."

"Oh, that's one of my favorites." After the brutal change he was making to her dinner suit, Alex could hardly believe he'd actually selected her most flamboyant and sexy design. "I'm surprised you like it," she admitted.

He lifted an amused brow. "Because it is cut to showcase a woman's curves?"

"Well, yes, actually. I know you usually prefer to design for a thinner female shape."

Debord's gaze moved over her, taking in the softly feminine curves displayed by her gilt dress.

"Although I will not take back what I said about men

preferring their wives to dress like ladies, I will admit that you are definitely correct about one thing, *chérie*."

His voice lowered, becoming deep and intimate. His gaze caressed her breasts, causing her nipples to harden into little points that pressed painfully against the gold tissue lamé.

Alex swallowed. "What's that?"

"A man tires of fashionably bone-thin women."

His unwavering gaze was rife with sexual promise. A woman could drown in those eyes, Alex mused. And this man wouldn't lift a finger to save her. Such thoughts, which should have frightened her away, strangely only made her want this passionate, talented man all the more.

Conversation lulled as they sat close enough for their thighs to touch on the red banquette, exchanging glances that grew longer and more heated as the evening progressed.

When she suggested they have their after-dinner drinks at her apartment, Alex was only following her heart, bringing things to their natural conclusion.

Their lovemaking, she told herself as they stood side by side in the slow, creaky elevator, had always been inevitable. With the single-mindedness that had allowed her to achieve, at the relatively young age of twenty-six, so much of her dream, she couldn't put aside her belief that she and Debord were destined to be together. In every way. The elevator finally reached her floor. The ornate brass door opened. Alex walked with Debord down the hall, her full skirt swaying.

When she went to open her apartment door, the key stubbornly stuck in the lock. She twisted it viciously. Nothing.

"Allow me." Alex could have wept with relief when Debord took over. The door opened, as if by magic.

"Would you like something to drink?" Suddenly horrendously nervous, Alex found her arsenal of feminine allure had mysteriously deserted her. "Some wine? Cognac? Coffee?"

"Cognac will be fine."

"Cognac it is." Although it cost far more than she could comfortably afford, Alex had purchased the expensive Rémy Martin that afternoon. Just in case.

She poured the dark brandy into two balloon glasses, handing one to Debord. His fingers, as they curved around the glass, were long and tapered. The thought of those fingers stroking her body sent a jolt of desire surging through her.

As they sipped their drinks, a pregnant silence settled over them. Debord was the first to break it. He put down his glass on the table in front of him, took hers from her nerveless fingers and placed it beside his. Then he turned toward her.

"You are beautiful, Alexandra Lyons." He trailed his fingers up her throat. "And so very talented."

They were precisely the words she'd been hoping—longing—to hear. "Do you really, honestly think so?" she whispered.

His hands were warm and strong and gentle as they cradled her head. His smile warmed her to the core. *"Bien sûr."*

Desire clouded her mind even as his words thrilled her. Warmth seemed to leave his fingertips and enter her bloodstream, flowing through her, down her legs, through her arms to her fingertips, waves of shimmering, silvery light.

His lips captured hers in a devastatingly long, deliriously deep kiss that left her drugged. She felt hot. Feverish. She wanted to melt into him, she wanted to feel his naked body next to hers, she wanted to immerse herself in the scent of his flesh. Never had Alex known such need! She pressed herself against him. She felt his hardness and wanted him deep inside her.

He stood up and looked down at her for a heartstoppingly long time, his expression unfathomable. When he finally extended his hand, she took it, allowing him to pull her to her feet.

Very slowly, he unzipped her dress. It fell to the floor in a gilt-and-jet puddle at her feet. Alex stepped out of it.

She was wearing a lace-trimmed, strapless, gold satin teddy, and a pair of thigh-high gold stockings. As he carried her into the adjoining bedroom, Alex clung to him mindlessly, eager to go wherever he took her.

She didn't question how her underclothes were whisked from her. She only knew that they disappeared, as if by magic.

And then Debord's clothes were gone, as well. He stood beside the bed, blatantly aroused. The ancient bedsprings creaked as he lay down beside her. "You are so voluptuous, *ma cocotte*." His fingers closed over her full, aching breasts. "So hot." His tongue laved her burning flesh.

He touched her, kissed her, licked her all over—her neck, her breasts, the backs of her knees, her stomach, on the insides of her thighs, in the furrow between her buttocks, even her toes.

He lay bare all her feminine secrets, all the while

murmuring seductive suggestions in French that thrilled her.

It was torment. Torment mingled with escalating pleasure. The exciting, feverish floating feelings built even higher. Her body flushed strawberry pink.

"Please." Alex wanted him wildly. Madly. She begged him to take her. "I don't think...I need..." She could stand this no longer.

But he taunted her with his control, stripping away her defenses layer by layer, leaving her raw and vulnerable.

And then finally he took her. As the passion rose, furiously like a wind before a thunderstorm, Alex clung to Debord, surrendering to the rhythm. To him.

The designer arched his back for a long, charged moment, every gleaming muscle in his body cast into sharp relief. Heat flooded through Alex's body, echoing his primal cry. It was as if the flame of their passion had ignited into a blinding fireball, searing them together for all time.

Forever, she thought as she lay in the strong protective circle of his arms, her lips curved in a secret womanly smile. The final phase of her life's plan had blessedly come true. Just as she'd always dreamed. She and Debord were now inexorably linked—creative minds, spirits and bodies. *Forever.*

London

Located in the heart of modern London, The City, as it was known, was considered by many to be the wealthiest square mile on earth. It was also synonymous with power. Roman legions had once camped on

land now taken over by towering high-rise office buildings, medieval guilds had plied their trades here, and
swashbuckling capitalists—men who financed wars
and countries—had transacted million-pound deals on
the strength of a gentleman's handshake.

These days, Americans and Japanese were rushing
into The City in droves, clutching stuffed briefcases
and folded editions of the *Financial Times*. The deals
now made in The City tended to be about French films,
Arab oil imports and shopping centers.

"You've come a long way from the bayou, boy,"
Zach murmured as he watched a flock of pigeons circling the dome of St. Paul's Cathedral.

"You talking to me?" the taxi driver asked, looking
at his fare in the rearview mirror.

"No. Just thinking out loud."

The driver shrugged and concentrated on making
his way through the crush of traffic.

The business day was coming to a close. Workers
poured forth from the buildings, headed toward the Underground which would take them back to their homes
in Knightsbridge and Mayfair. Buses forged their way
through the crowded streets.

Tomorrow morning the same people would all rush
back, talking fast, working hard, coming up with innovative new ways to make dizzying amounts of money.
Because one thing that never changed was that money
remained the lifeblood of The City.

Just as money was the reason for Zach's being in
London. He'd come here on Lord's business. Or at least
that was what he'd been trying to tell himself.

But the minute Miranda's butler opened the door,
Zach knew that the overriding reason he'd flown across

a continent and an ocean was to be with the woman he'd not been able to get out of his mind for the past three weeks.

He knew he was behaving uncharacteristically. He couldn't remember a time, even during his horny teen-age years, when he'd been so obsessed with sex. Of course, he'd never met a woman like Miranda Lord before, either, Zach mused as he followed the dark-suited butler into the drawing room.

"It's done," he greeted her without preamble.

"Done?" She stubbed out her cigarette in a Lalique ashtray and crossed the room on a swish of crimson silk. "Do you mean…"

Feeling like a knight returning after a success-ful Crusade, he set his briefcase on a priceless Louis Quinze table and extracted a single piece of paper.

"Lord Smythe deeply regrets having caused you emotional distress. As proof of his willingness to ac-cept full blame in the breakup of your marriage, not only has he dropped all claims against your assets, but he insists on paying all legal fees having to do not only with his attempt to acquire your Lord's stock, but the divorce, as well."

"Surely you jest!" She grasped the piece of paper from his hand, her avid eyes eating up the lines of text. "You darling, wonderful man." Her voice was a low, satisfied purr. She pressed her hand against his chest, moving it lower. Then lower still. "How ever can I thank you?"

There was nothing subtle about her stroking fingers or the invitation gleaming in her eyes. Zach had come to the conclusion that directness was one of Miranda's greatest charms.

"I'm sure you'll think of something," he said amiably.

Much, much later, Zach telephoned Eleanor from Miranda's antique bed and amazed his employer by announcing that he was taking five rare days off.

Since they couldn't make love twenty-four hours a day, Zach and Miranda managed to leave the bed from time to time. Miranda proved an enthusiastic tour guide as she took Zach to all the attractions. Hyde Park, the Tower of London, Kensington Gardens.

She also took him to the London Lord's. For a man in charge of a chain of department stores, Zach was an anomaly in that he'd always hated shopping. But unable to resist Miranda's polished charms, he spent an afternoon following her through the big store, and while he couldn't get excited about the aisles of china and linen, he had to admit that the cashmere sweater she selected for him was quite comfortable.

One evening they attended a concert at Albert Hall, immortalized by the Beatles in their *Sergeant Pepper* album. "Did you know," Miranda offered, as they climbed into the back seat of the Daimler limousine that was waiting to take them back to her town house after the concert, "when Tom Jones played here, women actually threw their underwear onto the stage?"

Zach arched a brow. "Surely not proper English women," he said with feigned shock.

Miranda nodded. "So I've been told."

Her eyes glittered like the diamonds she wore at her ears and throat. Her gown was little more than a slip, which clung to every curve of her body, outlining the pert upthrust of her breasts and rounded buttocks in a shimmer of silver satin. It was obvious she was wearing nothing underneath it.

"Sounds like I'm in the wrong business," Zach said. It had begun to rain; the steady drizzle diffused the streetlights and made the streets glisten like black glass.

Miranda's sultry laugh promised myriad sensual pleasures. "You have absolutely nothing to worry about in the bedroom department." She pushed the button that caused the thick, tinted glass to rise between the front and back seats.

Kneeling in front of Zach, she unzipped his slacks, then bent her head, draping his groin in a curtain of blond silk as she lowered her glossy lips over him. With every pull of her mouth, Zach came closer to exploding. When he didn't think he could hold back another moment, he yanked her back up onto the seat, arranging her so that she was lying across his lap.

She sprawled wantonly across him, her silver kid shoes on the seat, her skirt riding high on thighs, which, illuminated by the glow of the streetlights, gleamed like porcelain.

He trailed his fingers up her thighs in a seductive pattern that left her trembling. When he caressed her mound and played with the pale blond hair covering it, Miranda squirmed and arched her back, pressing against his hand.

Threading his fingers through the soft pubic curls, he began stroking her moist vaginal lips. "Tell me what you want," he ordered, crazed to hear it. He'd never had an acquisitive streak. But from the first minute he'd seen her, he'd wanted Miranda. During these past five days, he'd discovered he was a greedy man. The more he had, the more he wanted.

"You, dammit," she complained on a low moan that had nothing to do with surrender. "I want you."

Zach kissed her deeply, tasting himself on her lips. Then he turned her in his arms, his hands spanning her waist, and with one swift, strong movement, lowered her onto him.

Naked flesh seared naked flesh as Miranda met his challenge; her pelvis ground into his, her white teeth nipped at his neck.

The ripe scent of passion filled the car; their bodies were hot and slick with it. Zach's fingers dug into her skin, he suckled greedily on her breasts, and she felt a corresponding tightening deep within her.

She rode him relentlessly, up and down, harder and faster, demanding more and more until they crossed the finish line together. Exhausted, she collapsed against him.

They stayed together for a long time, neither having the inclination nor the energy to move. The only sound was their heavy, ragged breathing and the soft patter of rain on the roof of the limousine.

"I believe I've made a decision," Miranda murmured against his chest.

"What's that?"

She tilted her head back and smiled up at him. "After the Paris shows, I believe I'll take a holiday in America."

"How long a holiday?"

"I was thinking a fortnight. That would also give me an opportunity to examine all the new things you and Aunt Eleanor have been doing with the American stores. I'm always on the lookout for new ideas for the London Lord's."

Zach had already discovered that underneath Miranda's patina of steamy sexual appeal lay a quicksilver brain. She'd been a driving force behind Lord's couture boutiques, and although the deal with Debord had fallen through, she'd been lobbying Eleanor nonstop to give the *avant-garde* designer yet another chance.

"New ideas are the lifeblood of retailing," he agreed mildly.

"And then, of course, there's Auntie's unfortunate friendship with Mrs. Kowalski. Someone has to help you keep an eye on her."

Seeing through Miranda's flimsy excuses, Zach enjoyed the idea that this unbelievably sexy creature was willing to cross an ocean for him—a former bayou brat who hadn't worn shoes until he'd gone to school.

"I think," he said, as he felt himself growing hard again, "that's an excellent idea."

Chapter Seven

Paris

Debord's fall show took place late on a cold, rainy evening in July. Instead of the traditional runway, a huge wooden platform had been constructed over the Olympic-size pool at the Ritz Hotel. Seated around the pool, looking like so many judges at a diving competition, the world's fashion herd had gathered to see if they would be writing the former wunderkind's obituary. Like locusts, the rich and famous, along with thousands of buyers and thousands of fashion reporters, had winged their way to Paris. By the time the last model had twirled her way down the platform, these arbiters of society chic would either praise or bury the king of fashion.

They were, as always, prepared to do either.

No attempt had been made to protect celebrities from the omnipresent paparazzi. Seated in the front rows as many were, they were obvious targets, forced to put up with the hordes of photographers who ambushed them at point-blank range, camera shutters sounding like rain on a tin roof.

"Over here, Bianca," they called out to the former Mrs. Jagger, hidden behind a pair of wraparound sunglasses. "Look this way!... Hey, Ivana, how about giving us one of those million-dollar smiles!" This too, was part of the ambience. The razzle-dazzle game of couture.

Also on hand were a trio of Saudi Arabian wives, properly draped in black for the occasion and accompanied by a phalanx of turbaned, grim-faced bodyguards who'd caused a stir when they'd refused to give up their daggers. From time to time the men's hands would slip inside their dark jackets, ensuring that their automatic pistols were still nestled in their shoulder holsters.

In the pit around the platform the photographers stood on their camera cases for a better view. One enterprising photographer from the *Baltimore Sun* had brought along her own folding stepladder. When the trophy wife of a Wall Street trader continued to loudly complain that a photographer from a big Texas daily was blocking her view, he merely flashed her a snappy salute with his stubby middle finger and kept snapping away.

In the midst of all this sat Miranda and Eleanor Lord. Although one of the prized gilt chairs had also been reserved for Zach, he preferred to watch the show from the back of the crowd.

Backstage, chaos reigned supreme.

Trying to do ten things at once, Alex thought the hectic scene resembled the worst of Lewis Carroll's Wonderland. The surrealistic Mad Hatter's Tea Party, perhaps. Models in various stages of undress raced about like tardy white rabbits, hotly pursued by hairdressers who teased and spritzed, and dressers who tortured them into clothing no normal body could wear even as makeup artists wielded false eyelashes and stubby red pencils and complained that absolutely no one, dear heart, was holding still long enough to draw in a decent lipline!

Debord paced, barked orders and chain-smoked.

"Dammit, Alexandra," he snapped, "you have put the wrong earrings on Monique! She is to wear the crystal teardrops with that gown. Not the tourmalines!"

He viciously yanked the offensive jewelry from the model's earlobes, making both Alex and the model glad they were clip-ons. "*Merde.* Foolish girl! What am I paying you for?"

"Sorry," she murmured, changing the earrings without pointing out that indeed, Debord himself had specified the green tourmalines. Three times.

On the other side of the curtain, their performances timed with stopwatch precision, sleek, sloe-eyed models glided across the platform beneath the unforgiving glare of arc lights.

"*Numéro cinq,* number five…Place des Vosges," a voice announced as a trio of towering mannequins, clad in trousers and smoking jackets, done up in Debord's signature black and gray, marched past the onlookers.

"*Numéro treize,* number thirteen…Jardins du Luxembourg." This season Debord had chosen to name his collection after familiar Paris landmarks.

"*Numéro vingt,* number twenty…Palais-Royal…."

It was soon apparent to all assembled that this collection was more eclectic than usual. One of the smoking jackets boasted wide gold lapels, and a pair of jet trousers were shown with an eye-catching, beaded tuxedo jacket.

No one knew, of course, that the glittery additions had been Alex's contribution. Since a couture line bore the name of the designer, assistants' efforts routinely went unrewarded.

Alex had finally talked Debord into trying her silk dinner suit in some other hue besides black and gray. Although he'd steadfastly refused to make it up in her beloved amethyst, the burst of applause the suit received when shown in the rich ruby made her heart swell with pride.

"Turn for me, baby," the male photographers called out, whistling flirtatiously as the model spun and twirled.

The familiar ponchos from last season returned, along with huge shawls flung over the shoulder and allowed to hang on the ground. Several of the shawls were fringed; many were offered in graduated colors, from misty mauve through dark heather to the deep, rich, royal purple Alex had been denied in the suit.

The applause grew more enthusiastic with each number. Indeed, editors from *Vogue* and *Bazaar* stood up to salute Alex's other effort—a voluptuous velvet evening gown shown in a stunning pimento-red that added a flare of fire to the collection. From her viewing spot behind the curtain, Alex was certain she saw Grace Mirabella wipe away a tear with the knuckle of an index finger.

By the time the show ended with the traditional wedding gown, this one white satin and studded with seed pearls, the verdict was clear. Surrounded by television lights, Debord joined a dozen models on the stage as the crowd bravoed wildly.

Within moments his unshaven jaw was smeared with the lipstick of his admirers. He had successfully reclaimed his place at the uppermost tier of the fashion pack; he was, everyone agreed, a genius!

"Well," Eleanor said, raising her voice to be heard over the enthusiastic applause, "that was quite inspiring. I do believe it's time to invite Debord into our corporate family."

"The show certainly seems to be a success," Zach said. He'd left the back of the room and joined the two women.

"I told you the man was worth his weight in gold to Lord's," Miranda said. Her face had the kind of beatific expression Zach usually associated with religious paintings.

Neither Zach nor Eleanor brought up Debord's earlier disaster. After today's triumph, there was no need.

"No point in trying to talk business with the guy now," Zach decided, eyeing the crowd of women surrounding the designer.

"Tomorrow will be soon enough," Eleanor agreed.

She was suddenly more tired than she cared to admit. But the way Zachary had been hovering over her like an overprotective guard dog ever since that silly heart flutter she'd experienced during the séance, she knew that if she confessed the slightest fatigue, he'd rush her immediately to the Hôpital Américain.

Zach turned to Miranda. "Ready for dinner?"

"If you don't mind, darling, I think I'll stay and schedule my fittings with Marie Hélène."

"Now?" Zach's expression revealed that he damn

well did mind. He'd been looking forward to ravishing her in the suite's hedonistic marble tub.

"You know what they say." Miranda's smile reminded Zach of a sleek, pampered cat. "Never put off until tomorrow what you can do today."

She linked her arms around his neck and brought his mouth down to hers, apparently oblivious to their audience and the whirring sound of camera motor drives freezing the heated kiss on film.

"I won't be long," she murmured caressingly. Her pelvis pressed against his groin in a blatantly sexual promise. "I promise. After all, we can't miss Debord's party."

As her wet tongue insinuated itself between his firmly set lips, Zach relented, as he'd known all along he would.

The private party celebrating Debord's triumph was held in a converted Catholic Church in the first *arrondissement*. The gilded altar and carved oak pews had been replaced by three balconies, five bars, a giant video screen and three dance floors.

The guests were a mix of high society, artists, models, and the occasional Grand Prix driver and soccer star; the music was just as eclectic, ranging from the tango and bossa nova to fifties' and sixties' rock and roll.

Alex was standing on the edge of the crowd beneath a towering white Gothic pillar—one of many holding up an arched, gilded ceiling emblazoned with chubby cherubs—sipping champagne and watching the frenzied activity when Debord materialized beside her.

"Are you ready to leave *mon petit chou?*"

She looked up at him, surprised. "So soon? Don't you want to celebrate?"

"That's precisely what I had in mind." He plucked her glass from her hand and placed it on the tray of a passing waiter.

He put his arm around her, ushering her through the throng of merrymakers, pausing now and again to accept glittering accolades.

Anticipation shimmered in the close interior of his Lamborghini. He reached over and slid his hand beneath the hem of her dress. Few women possessing such bright hair would dare wear the scintillating pink hue; confident in her unerring sense of style, Alex resembled a brilliant candle.

"It was a good day, *non?*"

His caressing touch on her leg was making her melt. "A wonderful day," she breathed.

"And it will be an even better night." His fingers tightened, squeezing her thigh so that she knew he would leave a bruise. It would not be the first mark of passion he'd inflicted during these past weeks together, and if his husky tone was a promise of things to come, it would not be the last.

He returned his hand to the steering wheel and continued driving. "I received good news tonight," he told her. "From Lady Smythe."

Alex had seen him talking to the British heiress. She hadn't recognized Miranda's escort, a tall, handsome man who'd literally stood head and shoulders above the other guests.

"She bought your entire collection," Alex guessed.

"Better. Eleanor Lord has finally seen the light."

Alex remembered the call she'd interrupted the day

months ago when she'd shown Debord her sketches. The call canceling Lord's proposed collaboration with the designer. "Do you mean—"

"There will soon be an Yves Debord collection in every Lord's store in America," he revealed with not a little satisfaction. "And, of course, London."

"That's wonderful! I'm so happy for you!" She waited for him to mention her own small contribution to his successful line.

"It is about time that old woman recognized my genius," he said instead.

Reminding herself that without his oversize ego, Debord would not be the man she'd fallen in love with, Alex tried not to be hurt by his dismissal of her efforts. She realized he could not acknowledge her publicly. But it would have been nice if at least privately, he'd given her a smidgen of credit.

Trying to look on the bright side, that some of the richest women in the world would soon be wearing her designs, Alex reminded herself how lucky she was.

Here she was in Paris, the most romantic city in the world, about to make love to the man who'd played a starring role in her romantic fantasies for years. She would not ruin the moment by wishing for more than Debord was prepared to give.

As they passed the magnificent église du Dome, Napoléon's final resting place, Alex realized that Debord was taking her to his home. It was the first time he had. Her heart soaring, Alex took the gesture as an important shift in their relationship.

"Welcome to my little *maisonette*," he said as they entered his *hôtel particulier*.

Unlike the stark modernism of his *atelier*, where she

knew she could work for a hundred years and never feel comfortable, Alex found Debord's Paris residence charming.

He'd decorated it in the colors of eighteenth-century France—sunny golds, flame reds, rich browns. The walls were expertly lacquered and trimmed with marblized bases and moldings. Small, skirted tables were adorned with candid photographs of the designer with Nancy Reagan, Placido Domingo, Princess Grace, all testaments to Debord's high-gloss life.

As Debord led Alex up the stairway to his bedroom, she caught a fleeting glimpse of the art lining the walls, and although she was no expert, she did recognize a Dali giraffe woman, a Monet Gypsy and a Picasso sketch.

They entered the bedroom. Outside the window, a white, unbelievably large full moon looked as if it had been pasted onto the midnight black sky.

She held her arms out toward this man she loved, anticipating his kiss. But he turned away to light the fire some unseen servant had laid. "Take off your clothes," he commanded brusquely.

Although it was not the romantic approach she would have wished for on this special night, Alex obliged. But by the time she'd dispensed with the final scrap of silk and lace, the heat that his dark gaze could always instill in her had begun to cool.

His expression remained inscrutable, his eyes devoid of warmth. She stood there, hands by her sides, firelight gleaming over her nude body, growing more and more uneasy.

His dark eyes continued to hold her wary gaze with the sheer strength of his not inconsiderable will as took off his own clothing. When he put his arm around her and led her to the bed, Alex's heart leapt. Now would come the tenderness, the love, she'd been yearning for.

But instead of kissing her, as she'd expected, after drawing her down onto the smooth Egyptian-cotton sheets, Debord's teeth closed sharply on her earlobe.

"What are you doing?" Shocked, she touched her stinging lobe, startled to see the drop of crimson on her fingertip.

Once more, his eyes locked on hers as he took her finger between his lips and licked the faint drop of blood from it. There was a menace in his gaze that frightened her.

"Making love to you, Alexandra, of course. What did you think?"

"I don't want this." A dark shadow moved across the ghostly moon. Another moved over her heart. Her earlobe throbbed; the warmth between her thighs went cold.

Alex tried to turn her head away, but his fingers grasped her chin and forced her face back to his.

"Of course you do," he said. "You want me to penetrate you, to possess you."

"Yves, please. Let me go."

"You know that's not what you want."

When she tried to pull away, he tightened his hold. His eyes glittered dangerously, and for a moment Alex thought he was going to hit her. Afraid, but unwilling to show it, she held her ground, refusing to flinch.

He obviously mistook her silence for consent. His lips curved in a cruel, unfamiliar smile. "I promise to make this a night you will remember always."

Before Alex could determine whether to take his

words as a promise or a threat, Debord pinned her wrists above her head and thrust into her dryness, smothering her startled cry with his mouth.

At first she fought him, but she was no match for his superior strength. A vicious, backhanded blow cracked across her face like a gunshot.

He took her with a savage, relentless, animal ferocity. Finally, when she didn't think she could stand the searing pain another moment, he collapsed on top of her, his passion spent.

The moon reemerged from behind the cloud. Alex lay bathed in its cold white light, feeling cruelly violated and sadder than she'd ever felt in her life. He shifted onto his side, his elbow resting on the rumpled sheet, his head propped on his hand, and looked down at her. Unwilling to meet his gaze, Alex covered her eyes with her forearm. She heard the bedroom door open. Surprised, since she could feel Debord still lying beside her, watching her with his unwavering intensity, she removed her arm and looked up.

The newcomer was Marie Hélène. The woman was standing over them, clad only in a crotch-length strand of pearls. For the first time since Alex had known her, she was smiling.

"Ah, *ma chère*." As if nothing unusual had happened, as if it were commonplace for his sister to arrive unannounced and undressed in his bedroom, Debord rose and drew the nude woman into his arms, showing her the tenderness he'd denied Alex.

"Your timing is perfect," he murmured when their long, openmouthed kiss finally ended. He looked down at Alex. "Isn't it, *chérie?*"

As they smiled down on her with benevolent, expectant lust in their eyes, Alex realized that this was not the first time the brother and sister had engaged in such activities.

Self-awareness came crashing down on her like a bomb. She'd thought she was oh, so sophisticated, with her darling little Paris apartment and her fancy couture career and her French lover!

Now she realized that deep down inside, where it really counted, she was just a country bumpkin who'd come to the big city and lost her heart. The trick was to escape before she also lost her soul.

Although every muscle in her body was screaming, she managed to push herself to her feet. Her nose was running. Wiping it, she saw the bright blood on her hand.

"Speaking of timing, I think it's past time that I went home." She managed, with effort, to push the words past the sob that was lodged in her throat.

She looked frantically around the room, searching for her wispy panties and stockings. When she couldn't spot them, she reminded herself that the important thing was to escape this nightmare.

"Surely you do not intend to leave now?" Debord questioned with an arched, mocking brow. "Not when the celebration is just getting started?"

Vomit rose in Alex's throat. She swallowed it back down again. "If you think I'm going to—" her voice was muffled by the dress she was pulling over her head "—play musical beds with you and Morticia here, you're sadly mistaken."

"Alexandra." Debord caught her arm and shook his head in mock chagrin. "I have spent these past weeks patiently introducing you to a world of erotic pleasures.

I've taught you passion. I've taught you to set free your darkest, most innermost emotions."

That much was true. Some of the things he'd asked Alex to do in the name of love had made her grateful that her bedroom was usually so dark he couldn't see her blush. Many of them she hadn't enjoyed. But he obviously had. And at the time, to her, making Debord happy had been the important thing.

"A *ménage à trois* with Marie Hélène is simply the next step in your education."

Her blood was like ice in her veins; it pounded behind her eyes like a jackhammer. "You're both disgusting." What the hell had happened to her shoes?

"I warned you about Americans," Marie Hélène sniffed, slanting a knowing glance at her brother.

"I thought you were turning into a sophisticate," Debord told Alex. His fingers tightened painfully on her upper arm. "But *non,* my sister was right about you. You are merely a silly schoolgirl with dreams of Prince Charming on a white charger."

Something that felt horribly like hysteria began to bubble up inside Alex. She struggled for dignity, vowing she would not let them see her cry.

"You're certainly entitled to your opinion."

Shaking free of his possessive touch, she marched barefoot toward the door with an amazing amount of contemptuous disdain for a woman whose lifelong dream had just been shattered.

She paused in the bedroom doorway, raked her gaze over the unholy coven of two and said, "Oh, and by the way. I quit."

Debord revealed not a scintilla of surprise. He nodded

his head even as he wrapped his arm around Marie Hélène's nude waist, drawing his sister tightly to his side.

"That is your choice. Just remember, Alexandra, any designs you created while employed by the House of Debord belong to me. If you attempt to take them elsewhere, I will make certain that you never work again."

After what he'd done tonight to her body, not to mention her pride and self-esteem, this threat seemed nothing. Less than nothing. Indeed, rather than frighten her, his words turned her into a towering pillar of wrath.

"You're fucking welcome to them," Alex shouted with renewed bravado. "Since they're the only decent thing in your new line."

She slammed the door behind her, feeling a faint satisfaction when she heard a painting fall from the wall. Running back down the stairs, as if the devil himself were on her heels, she left the house.

The street was dark and empty. Numb as she was, the only way she knew she was still walking was that the stone sidewalk felt cold and wet and rough against her bare feet.

Finally, blessedly, a taxi appeared. She flagged it down, grateful when the bulky, mustachioed man displayed no interest in the fact that she was alone on the street at this time of night without any shoes.

Her head was splitting by the time she reached her apartment, but her nose, for the time being, had stopped bleeding. The elevator, naturally, had chosen this night to stop working, forcing her to climb the stairs. Each step proved an effort.

In a delayed reaction to the events of the past hour, as soon as she entered the safety of her apartment, Alex began to shake. She barely made it to the small cubbyhole masquerading as a bathroom before throwing up all the champagne and caviar she'd had at the party celebrating Debord's brilliant showing. She flushed the toilet, longed to wash her face, but was too tired to stand up again. So she remained there on the tile floor, her back against the wall, knees drawn up to her chest, arms wrapped around her legs. Resting her sore cheek against her knees, Alex finally allowed herself to cry.

A long time later, after she'd run out of tears, she brushed her teeth, then took a shower, scrubbing herself viciously in a futile attempt to wash tonight out of her mind, to rid her body of Debord's touch. His scent. His seed.

The hot water turned tepid. Then cold. Alex rubbed her reddened skin dry, pulled on the most sexless, oversize pair of sweats she owned, then dragged herself back out into the hall to the pay phone.

With trembling fingers, she managed to place a collect call to the States.

The following morning, she piled suitcases filled with her clothing, sketch pads and her pencils into the back of a taxi.

Turning her back on the city that had for so long represented her most heartfelt dream, Alex was on her way to California, determined to begin a new life.

In the luxurious first-class section of the Air France jet winging its way over the Atlantic, Eleanor, Miranda and Zach sipped champagne and orange juice cocktails, and toasted Miranda's newest discovery.

Twenty-six rows back, Alex was shoved between a woman with a crying baby and a portly businessman who'd made two passes before the plane had even taxied down the runway.

How had she been so stupid to allow herself to fall under the spell of such a horrible, self-indulgent man as Debord?

The answer came to her as the jet chased the waning moon across the night-black sky. The truth, as unpalatable as it might be, was that she'd closed her eyes to any faults her idol might possess. She'd seen in the designer only what she'd wanted to see. Flattering images born in a teenage girl's romantic fantasies.

And now, because of her foolishness, the dream that had sustained her for years, the dream that had fed her soul during those long periods of personal struggle, had disintegrated like a puff of smoke from a Left Bank chimney.

Chapter Eight

Los Angeles

Wallowing in self-pity had never been Alex's style. By the time her flight landed at LAX, she'd roused herself out of the abyss and managed to regain most of her usual bravado. Her experience with Debord, as exhilarating, fulfilling and ultimately horrendous as it had been, was over.

And now, Alex vowed, as the flight attendant bid her *adieu* with a professional smile, there would be no looking back.

Sophie Friedman was waiting for Alex at the door of the jetway. Her admiring gaze swept over Alex, clad in a scoop-necked cotton peasant dress. Embroidered pink flowers bloomed on the billowy mint-green skirt, appearing like Queen Anne's lace on an Alpine meadow. Impractical for traveling, the outfit was one of Alex's favorites. She'd worn it hoping it would raise her spirits. It hadn't.

"Lord, child, you remind me of a half-wild Tyrolean shepherdess. Hell, if I had any sense, I'd turn in my producer's card, become an agent, drive you straight to the nearest studio, negotiate a multipicture, multimillion-dollar deal, then sit by my swimming pool and wait for the bucks to roll in." Before Alex could insist she had no theatrical ambitions, Sophie was filling her in on the latest episode in her divorce, which she dubbed "The Hundred Years' War."

Sophie didn't stop talking the entire time it took to collect Alex's luggage. Although she interrupted herself constantly, from what Alex could discern, this latest skirmish had begun over custody of Prince Andrew, more familiarly known as Randy Andy, a champion Yorkshire terrier who'd been declared Stud of the Year by the American Kennel Club. Or perhaps it was Sophie's estranged producer husband who was the stud. Alex wasn't quite sure. Alex's depression momentarily lifted when she saw the white car purring beside the curb outside the terminal. "A limo?"

"Just the usual star treatment."

"I'm hardly a star," Alex murmured as the dark-suited driver swept open the passenger door.

"Not yet. But stick with me, kid, and you will be."

The seats were wide and white and smelled of leather balm. After they settled in, Sophie leaned forward and gave Alex a very intense look. "Is that an example of Debord's handiwork?"

Alex's hand went instinctively to her cheek, covering the bruise she thought she'd successfully hidden with concealer and makeup. "I don't want to talk about it." She was still too embarrassed to admit to such a horrid lapse in judgment.

"I was thinking about getting Prince Andrew neutered. To keep my rat of a husband from getting any stud fees," Sophie revealed. "But I've got a better idea. Why don't we take the nut cutters and do a snip job on a certain French designer?"

Alex smiled in spite of herself. "He's not worth the jail time. But thanks, anyway."

"Men," Sophie muttered. "Just because God gave them a set of balls, they think they rule the fucking world.

"Do you believe in fate?" Sophie changed the subject suddenly as the limousine eased into the bumper-to-bumper, circling and suicidal lane changing that was standard driving procedure at the nation's third-busiest airport.

Alex cringed as a white Jaguar abruptly cut off a blue BMW, earning a blast of a horn and an expansive hand gesture from the BMW's driver. "Not really."

"Neither did I." Sophie took a bottle of Dom Pérignon from a bucket filled with ice and poured the sparkling wine into two glasses. "Having come up the hard way, I always figured if you wanted to get ahead, you needed to make your own luck."

Murmuring her thanks, Alex accepted the proffered flute. "That's pretty much what I've always thought."

She certainly hadn't waited for fate to secure her a job with Debord. Alex frowned as she thought about the treacherous, amoral designer.

Sophie observed Alex's scowl without comment. "But," she revealed, "since meeting you, I've changed my mind."

"Oh?" Alex took a sip of the champagne, enjoying the way the tiny bubbles exploded on her tongue.

"I was getting ready to call you when you telephoned."

"About designing for your daytime soaps?"

"Not exactly."

"Oh?" Surely Sophie wouldn't have invited her to Hollywood and met her at the airport with a stretch limousine to tell her she'd changed her mind, would she?

Alex didn't believe Sophie capable of such behavior, but she'd recently discovered that when everything seemed to be coming up roses, it was prudent to watch out for thorns.

"Last month I got an invitation to lunch from this network honcho. Seems they did a market study with some focus groups, and my soaps blew away all the competition."

"I'm not surprised. They're wonderfully written."

"Bless the girl!" Sophie lifted her expressive eyes heavenward. "She didn't even tack on the usual 'for soaps.'

"Anyway," she continued, "although it hasn't been announced yet, I just signed to create a weekly nighttime television drama with a continuing storyline. A prime-time soap, so to speak."

"Like 'Dallas'?" Alex had seen the show in Paris. Although it seemed strange watching Larry Hagman and Victoria Principal speaking French, soon she, like the rest of the world, was addicted to the story revolving around the wealthy Texas oil family.

"Like 'Dallas,'" Sophie confirmed. "But the network guys want more glitz and glamour than the Ewing family. More sex and sin."

She refilled their glasses. "Which naturally made me think of you. Well, your designs, anyway. Whatever sex and sin you have in your private life is your own business."

Alex's expression remained outwardly calm even as Sophie's reference to sex made her hands turn to ice. "I'm flattered."

"Don't be. I told you I thought your creative vision was cinematic. Which was why I couldn't understand why you'd want to hide all that creative light beneath Yves Debord's barrel."

Alex didn't want to talk about Debord. "Tell me about the story line."

"Well, it's still in the planning stages, but the plot revolves around a fiftyish New Orleans oil baron and the three women in his life—his conniving ex-wife, who has maintained a chunk of the business and is always trying to finagle more, his saintly current wife who does her best to make his mansion a home, and his young, ambitious mistress, a dancer working on Bourbon Street. I want to set a hot, steamy atmosphere. Sort of a cross between Tennessee Williams and Harold Robbins."

Such disparate personalities would offer myriad design opportunities, Alex mused. "That sounds like a challenge."

"Don't worry. We've got plenty of time. The network wants an extravagant look to 'Blue Bayou' and I didn't want to be rushed into putting a sloppy show on the air, so I worked a deal allowing us to spend the entire upcoming season creating story lines, getting actors under contract, designing sets and wardrobes. Then the show's going to premiere as a miniseries over three consecutive nights during Sweeps week. We've got a twenty-six-week guarantee, which is double the norm for new show contracts."

"Twenty-six weeks. That's a lot of wardrobe."

"I plan to use enough beadwork to keep an entire village in India working overtime."

"That won't be inexpensive," Alex felt obliged to warn.

"Not to worry. The network brass is behind us all the way. We're going to do a lot of shooting on location, and as for wardrobe, the sky's the limit."

The woman's enthusiasm was contagious. Alex felt a slow smile spread across her own face. "It sounds wonderful."

"Doesn't it?" Sophie lifted her glass in a salute. "To 'Blue Bayou.' And the lady who's going to make it shine."

"To 'Blue Bayou,'" Alex agreed absently.

She was relieved to discover that although he may have stripped her of a dream, Debord hadn't killed her optimism. Rich colors and fabrics were already spinning around in her mind, changing and tilting like the facets of a kaleidoscope.

Professing a desire to clinch the deal over lunch, Sophie whisked Alex off to the famed Bullocks Wilshire Tearoom, high atop the landmark 1929 Art Deco store. The restaurant, a longtime Los Angeles tradition, boasted a high-domed ceiling and, Sophie claimed, the best Caesar salad in town.

As she leaned back in the comfortable chair and watched the lanky models from the department store sashay around the room, Alex found herself sharing Sophie's belief that perhaps there was something to be said for fate, after all.

* * *

While Alex and Sophie celebrated their new artistic collaboration, Miranda was entering an office building on Sunset Boulevard, not far from Frederick's famed purple lingerie palace.

The sign on the glass door said Galbraith and Bailey. Though Jonathon Bailey had been dead for more than a quarter century, Theodore Galbraith had not removed his former law partner's name from the door. He was a man comfortable with tradition. A man of principle. Principles Miranda had every intent of testing.

She'd dressed carefully for this meeting, in a black silk Geoffrey Beene dress that set off her pale skin and displayed an intriguing bit of décolletage. She'd pulled her blond hair back into a society-girl style at the nape of her neck, held with a black satin bow. Her Italian pumps boasted four-inch heels that made her silk-clad legs look as if they went all the way up to her neck.

"Dear, dear Teddy," she greeted the attorney with a warm smile that suggested secrets to share. "It's been too long! How kind of you to make time for me in your busy schedule."

Theodore Galbraith rose quickly and went around his partner's desk to greet her. "When a beautiful woman invites an old fogie like me to lunch, I not only make time, my dear," he responded with a twinkle, "I clear my calendar for the day."

Galbraith was a balding, rumpled man in his late sixties. A contemporary of James and Eleanor Lord, he'd been their lawyer since the beginning, when James had opened his first store. Unlike the new wave of trendy L.A. attorneys, who favored silk Bijan blazers, linen trousers and sockless loafers, Galbraith was not overly concerned with outward appearances.

But Miranda knew the man's aging Savile Row suit, the frayed cuffs on his monogrammed white shirt, the half glasses purchased from a rack at the Walgreens drugstore down the street, all belied a brilliant legal mind.

"Shame on you for talking that way," she scolded lightly. "Why, you're not at all old, Teddy." She took hold of both his hands, allowing her slender white ones to rest in his blue-veined ones slightly longer than necessary. Arthritis had swollen his knuckles, but his grip remained firm and sure. "On the contrary, you are just reaching your prime."

A pleased flush rose from his white collar. "That's a vast exaggeration, Miranda," he said, "but since, like most men, I plead guilty to being highly susceptible to feminine flattery, I won't argue with you."

"It isn't flattery at all. It's true," she lied deftly. "And I know it's very naughty of me to call you on such late notice, but I must be returning to London soon, and I'm so very concerned about Aunt Eleanor."

He frowned. "I do hope she hasn't had another occurrence of that heart problem."

"Oh, no, nothing like that, thank goodness," Miranda hastened to assure him. "But she has been behaving quite strangely lately. I felt it prudent to obtain advice."

His fuzzy white eyebrows lifted above the rim of his reading glasses. "Legal advice?"

"Not really." She lowered her eyes to the faded carpet, as if trying to frame her answer. "Actually," she murmured as she met his waiting gaze again, "I came to you, Teddy, because you're her dearest friend. And I'm terribly afraid Aunt Eleanor is going to need all the friends she can get."

"Oh, my. This does sound ominous."

"Wait until you hear the entire story."

They lunched at the Polo Lounge, where it was apparent that the attorney enjoyed being seen in the company of a much younger, attractive woman. Miranda knew he'd been widowed for nearly as long as he'd been running the office without a partner. Her spies had also told her that for the past decade, he'd been living a scholarly, celibate existence more suited to a Trappist monk than a rich attorney in Lotus Land.

Well, that would soon change. Teddy Galbraith didn't know it, she thought with an inward smile as she refilled their glasses from a second bottle of Tattinger champagne, but he was about to get lucky.

They were both slightly tipsy when her driver finally returned them to his office. Teddy more than her. But she'd been careful that he hadn't gotten too drunk. She definitely hadn't wanted to render the elderly attorney impotent.

"I can't believe Eleanor's involved in the mumbo jumbo spirit world," he said for the umpteenth time. He'd been upset by Miranda's description of the séances, not to mention the suspicious circumstances surrounding the deaths of Clara Kowalski's former husbands. "She's always been such a sensible woman."

"I know. That's what makes her behavior all the more bizarre," Miranda agreed earnestly.

It was late afternoon. His secretary had gone for the day, leaving them alone in the office. Miranda sat down on the leather sofa and crossed her legs.

For a moment he seemed tempted to join her on the couch. She smiled to herself as he overcame the temptation and chose the high-backed chair behind his desk, instead. If he thought that wide expanse of oak was going to protect him, she mused wickedly, the old dear was sadly mistaken.

"I do wish there was something, anything, we could do," she murmured.

He ran a hand over his head, ruffling his wispy white hair, torn between dual loyalties. "I agree this is worrisome, Miranda." Unaccustomed to drinking in the middle of the day, his tongue felt thick and awkward, forcing him to speak slowly.

"But as I've already explained, what you've told me this afternoon, as upsetting as it admittedly is, is simply not enough for a judge to rule in your favor."

She leaned forward, giving him an unrestricted view of her cleavage. "But what if that horrid Mrs. Kowalski has convinced Aunt Eleanor to change her will? What if Eleanor's going to give the old witch control of Lord's? What if Clara is plotting to kill my aunt?"

Sexual feelings he'd successfully locked away in cold storage long ago stirred. With obvious effort, he dragged his gaze from those perfect white globes.

"Miranda, I'm sorry." His voice was strained. Even with the extra effort, he knew he was slurring his words. "You know I can't discuss your aunt's will."

"I understand all about attorney/client privilege." She rose and crossed the room with a smooth, panther-like stride. "But you have to understand how very, very important this is to me, Teddy."

She knelt beside his chair, wrapping him in a cloak of

obsession as she gazed up into his round, red-cheeked face, her green eyes gleaming with implied sex.

"If I could only have a teensy little peek." She ran a seashell pink fingernail up his leg. "To reassure myself."

"Miranda, dear." His voice was rough, choked. "I'd like to help you, but I truly can't."

"I'd be ever so grateful." Her stroking touch grazed the fly of his very un-Californian chalk-striped trousers, kindling embers he'd thought long dead. Her eyes locked on his as she deliberately unfastened his belt. "You've no idea how extremely grateful I can be." Her tongue slid wetly over her glossy lips.

She slowly lowered the zipper. When her palm brushed against the front of his baggy, old-fashioned boxer shorts, he jumped as if she'd touched a hot wire to his flesh.

"I can't," he tried again, clearly torn between dual needs. "It would be a breach of ethics."

"I promise no one will ever know." When she began stroking the flaccid flesh beneath the white cotton fly, he leaned his head against the back of his chair and closed his eyes.

"Miranda…" He wanted her to stop. He wanted her never to stop. His head spun, his body burned.

With a deft, practiced touch, she freed his semierect penis. "Just a glimpse, Teddy." She bent her blond head and kissed it lightly, making him groan. "That's all I want." Her tongue darted catlike across the tip.

"Oh, God." It had been years since he'd known a woman's touch, and Theodore Galbraith was loath to stop the glorious feeling flowing through his veins, like a hot, wet summer storm after a long season of drought.

His arthritic hands curled around the wooden arms of his executive chair. He thought he'd burst into tears when she suddenly stopped her sweet torment.

"I'll make you a deal, Teddy."

"What kind of deal?" he croaked.

His head spun, his body throbbed, and at that moment he would have done anything she asked. He would have crawled naked to Bel Air and back over broken glass. He would have betrayed every client he still had. He would have committed murder for such rapturous ecstasy.

"I'll be nice to you." She licked her glossy lips. "And you be nice to me in return. It will be our little secret."

"Our little secret," he echoed, watching her pink tongue with fascination.

It was an astonishing performance. Theodore Galbraith hadn't always been a celibate sixty-eight-year-old man. Indeed, in his salad days he'd sampled some of the best sex Hollywood had to offer.

But never had he experienced anything that equaled Miranda Lord. He'd heard rumors over the years that she was a woman of uninhibited sexual appetites. Those rumors, he was discovering to his delight, were absolutely true.

"I won't whisper a word to anyone." She bent her head and touched her lips to his dry ones, kissing him with little licks and nips that promised so much more. At the same time, she pressed her palm against his throbbing shaft.

Yes, a truly remarkable performance, he thought. And ultimately irresistible. "You'll have to read it here."

His surrender was rewarded with a satisfied, feline

smile that told the attorney she'd never expected any other outcome.

"Whatever you say, Teddy, dear."

She kissed him then. A deep, wet, soul kiss that took his breath away. Although he was trembling with hunger, with need, Theodore grew frustrated when his penis remained only semierect.

That wasn't about to deter Miranda. "Don't worry," she crooned silkily. "I'll take care of everything." She ran her fingers through his thin hair and treated him to a warm, intimate smile. "You just relax, Teddy, dear. And enjoy."

With those confidence-building words ringing in his ears, she went to work, alternating gentle bites and long licks, covering his shaft with saliva, sucking the tip, while massaging his testicles with cleverly wicked fingers.

His blood began pounding in his veins, his ears, his now straining cock. It crossed his mind that although his penis had risen to the challenge, his galloping heart was still that of an old man.

It didn't matter, he decided as she finally placed her wet mouth fully over him, taking him in deeper than any woman ever had. As he bucked furiously, thrusting himself into that glorious, moist cavern, he decided that if this turned out to be his time to die, he couldn't think of a better way to go.

Coherent thought disintegrated, and with one final mighty spasm he exploded.

When he could think again the room was redolent with the raunchy scent of sex and he felt reborn.

Miranda left him sprawled limply in the chair and walked over to the bank of filing cabinets.

She bent down to open the drawer marked *L-M*, giving him a provocative view of shapely buttocks that would have made him hard again if he'd been ten years younger. As it was, he was content to enjoy the view.

She murmured the client names to herself as she flipped through the manila files.

"Aha!" She retrieved one thick file, then turned, flashing him a brilliant smile over her shoulder. "Eureka."

As he watched her green eyes avidly skim through the pages of legalese, Theodore Galbraith's head began to clear.

The mists gradually parted. His body cooled.

Too late he thought of his longtime friend and client, Eleanor Lord. And what he had done.

Chapter Nine

It was healing work, which kept Alex from regretting the loss of her dream of a life in Paris couture. It was exhausting work, which allowed her to fall into a deep and dreamless sleep each night. And it was exciting work, which encouraged her to greet each new morning with optimism.

As for men, the debacle with Debord had made her take a long hard look at her past relationships.

It was her sophomore year at Phoenix's Thunderbird High School that she'd finally—at last!—gotten her period, and her body, as if anxious to make up for lost time, had sprinted into womanhood. Adolescent boys began falling all over themselves, trying to lure this dazzling wonder of femininity into the backseats of their Dodge Chargers and Ford Mustangs.

Alex had found their juvenile, unsubtle seduction attempts admittedly flattering. She liked them buzzing so intently around her, like a hive of drones around their queen bee.

However, wise beyond her years, she realized they only saw her attractive packaging. Those boys had absolutely no interest in who she was inside, in her hopes and dreams and goals. That being the case, while she might permit a bit of heavy breathing and some harmless groping in the back row of the movie theater, she steadfastly refused to "go all the way."

It was during her first year at the Fashion Institute that she willingly surrendered her virginity to a fashion photographer twenty-five years her senior who'd come to L.A. to shoot a spread for *Vogue* and had agreed as a favor for a friend—an instructor at the institute—to give a lecture while in town.

Alex had not been surprised when he asked her to dinner that night. Nor was she surprised when dinner melded into breakfast. She was ready to make love; she'd only been waiting for the right man.

Max Jones had been funny and kind and sexy, and when he returned to Manhattan, as she'd known all along he must, Alex had not harbored a single regret.

A pattern she hadn't even realized she'd been setting continued. Indeed, if Alex possessed a fatal flaw, it was her unfortunate habit of getting involved with domineering older men.

Her last lover before leaving for Paris had been a Seventh Avenue district sales representative nearly twice her age. But unlike the man to whom she'd joyfully given her virginity, Herb Stein was overbearing and possessive.

Which was why, when he began employing every emotional trick in the book to keep her from going to Paris, she'd broken off the affair and concentrated on making her mother's last days as comfortable as possible.

Irene Lyons, outspoken to the end, had always argued against Alex's romantic choices. "Of course, you don't need to be Freud," she'd say, whenever Alex returned from dinner with one of these cookie-cutter characters, "to realize that you're looking for a father figure, Alexandra, dear."

And although she'd steadfastly denied her mother's claim, Alex's experience with Debord had stripped the blinders from her eyes, forcing her to face a bitter truth about herself.

Her mother had been right. All her lovers had been cut from the same cloth. Such an unpalatable revelation made her realize it was time for a drastic change.

Other women may have vowed simply to modify the self-destructive pattern by turning toward men their own age. Not Alex. Never one to do anything in half measures, with a determination a Carmelite nun might have envied, she vowed not to even think about sex.

With the same tenacity she'd used to gain employment in Paris, Alex set about changing her image, too. Although it was not easy, she purposefully dimmed the glowing aura of vibrant energy in which she usually moved. She narrowed her normally animated gestures and muted her voice. She even went so far as to eschew her usual flamboyant colors, opting instead for more somber hues.

"We waited for you," Sophie complained late one November afternoon, "until the turkey turned as dry as shoe leather."

Sophie had invited her to Thanksgiving dinner with a group of friends. "I'm sorry. I really intended to come…."

"But you got sidetracked. Again."

Alex's answering smile was sheepishly apologetic. "I thought of a new idea for Tiffany's wedding gown."

A newly devised plot twist now had the stripper marrying the oil tycoon's son while continuing her affair with her groom's father. A perfectionist by nature, Alex had discarded three gown ideas Sophie had found delightful.

"By the time I was satisfied with the sketch, it was too late to call."

"Peter was disappointed."

Peter Collins was an Australian actor who'd come to the States and gotten his start in Sophie's daytime drama, "The Edge of Tomorrow." Since the stunningly profitable release of his first major adventure film three months ago, he'd shot like a comet to the top of the A-list of every hostess in town.

"I'm sure he'll survive," Alex murmured dryly. She had no interest in meeting any man. Even one who was being touted as an Australian Harrison Ford.

"Besides," she argued, "didn't I see his picture on the cover of *People* with Debra Winger? The caption said they were about to become engaged."

"That was a publicity date for their new picture. Peter doesn't date actresses. He believes they're too self-involved."

The older woman frowned with well-meaning concern. "You know, darling, as much as I appreciate your devotion to 'Blue Bayou,' you're in danger of becoming an workaholic."

"This from a woman who's been known to sleep in her office to save the commute time," Alex said. "Besides, you don't have to worry about me. I'm happier than I've ever been in my life."

Despite Alex's profession of happiness, it had not escaped Sophie's notice that the light that had shone so brightly in her eyes in Paris had been snuffed out like a candle in an icy wind. Sophie had remained quiet the past five months, waiting for Alex to come to her for a heart-to-heart talk. She realized, with her unerring ability to get beneath the surface of a character, that Alex's metamorphosis had been purposefully planned and executed.

But what Alex didn't realize, Sophie mused now, was that her subterfuge wasn't working. Because all she had to do was walk into a room and it was instantly illuminated by her talent, her independence, and her natural beauty of face and spirit.

Although she was willing to grant Alex her secrets, Sophie had not reached such high echelons in a male-dominated business without being persistent. "You say you're happy. Even so, how do you know Peter wouldn't be the icing on the cake?"

Unwilling to discuss her love life, or lack of it, even with this woman who'd become her best friend, Alex decided it was time to change the subject. "Don't you want to see what I was working on?"

She handed Sophie the sketches. The diversion proved successful. As the producer oohed and aahed over the billowy white vision of crystal-studded tulle and lace, ideas of matchmaking were immediately forgotten.

After convincing Eleanor she should be given the job of organizing the Yves Debord boutiques in all the Lord's stores—after all, who knew the designer's genius better than she?—Miranda threw herself into the task, traveling all over the United States. Although her work was time-consuming, she was careful to fit in regular trips to California.

She and Zach spent Thanksgiving in Santa Barbara with Eleanor. Although Miranda was far from pleased that Clara was still in residence, after reading her aunt's will, she did not feel as threatened by the witch's presence. Especially after paying another visit to Theodore Galbraith, ensuring his promise to notify her if Eleanor decided to revise her will.

The day after Thanksgiving, they returned to Zach's Los Angeles apartment. And to his bed, where they proceeded to ravish one another with a hunger that had not lessened since that first electrifying meeting. Two days later, they were still there.

"Have I ever told you how magnificent you are?" Miranda purred with satisfaction. Her head rested on his damp chest, her fingers playing in the pelt of hair, and her long legs were entwined with his.

"I believe you've mentioned it," Zach murmured drowsily. After two days of ravenous and near-continuous sex, he was finally satiated. "Occasionally." On this late November day, it was still warm enough for air-conditioning. When the cool breeze blew over their sweat-moistened flesh, he pulled the sheet up to cover them. "But it's always nice to hear."

Miranda smiled at him. "I've never met a man like you."

Zach returned the smile with a lazy, satisfied one of his own. "Nor I a woman like you." It was the truth. From the first moment he'd seen Miranda, he'd wanted her. And the need, rather than abating, grew stronger each time they were together this way.

Although he hated to admit to any weakness, Zach realized that somehow, when he hadn't been looking, he'd crossed the line between merely wanting Miranda and needing her. As other men were addicted to the bottle, or gambling, Zach had been lured into obsession with the sultry siren call of sex.

Their work for Lord's kept them apart for days, even weeks, at a time. But whenever the need grew unmanageable, which it always did, one of them would pick up the phone and call the other, and within hours they'd be in bed, driving one another mad.

Miranda was, quite simply, Zach's weakness. The only thing that kept him from denying it was that his need was not one-sided. In fact, although he hadn't really been keeping score, it had not escaped Zach's notice that Miranda had been the one to initiate the majority of these stolen interludes.

"Deborah Langley asked me again when we were going to make an announcement," Miranda said. The society matron had been Averill's companion at Eleanor's holiday dinner party.

"An announcement?" His body soothed, Zach's mind had wandered to a vexsome zoning problem regarding a planned underground parking garage at the new Atlanta Lord's.

"It's embarrassing, this going steady like a pair of teenagers."

He glanced at her, surprised. He'd never received any sign that Miranda gave a damn what anyone thought.

"I'd hardly call it going steady," he said, "since we're hardly ever seen in public."

And then only at the glitzy functions Miranda insisted were *de rigueur* for making and keeping business-society contacts. Although Zach hated any event that forced him into a dinner jacket, he had to admit that couture and jewelry sales inevitably rose after such an appearance.

"It is difficult," Miranda agreed on a sigh. "Our schedules keep us apart so much that when we do get together I don't want to share you with anyone."

Zach knew that feeling all too well.

"But that doesn't mean people don't know we're what the society columnists call an *item*," she tacked on.

Screw the columnists, Zach wanted to say. "Does our affair really embarrass you?" he asked, instead.

"Do you want the truth?"

Having always been honest with Miranda, it had never occurred to Zach that she might not have been equally forthright with him. "Of course."

She gazed up at him through smoky lashes. "Yes, it does embarrass me when I hear people whispering that you don't care enough about me to make our relationship official."

"By official, I assume you're talking about marriage."

"Yes."

On the rare occasion Zach thought about life beyond work, he imagined that if and when he did marry, the union would be based on respect and trust and shared dreams. Having witnessed the wealth of love his parents had shown one another, he'd expected to share that same closeness of mind and spirit with his wife.

All he and Miranda seemed to share were their bodies. And, of course, Lord's.

As if reading his mind, Miranda framed his frowning face with her palms and gave him a slow, reassuring smile.

"Darling Zachary," she murmured on a voice that was half smoke, half honey, "there's no reason to look so grim. I'm not some silly young girl looking for a mythical Grand Love."

Her lips plucked at his enticingly. "What we have together is quite enough." Her fingers trailed down his chest. "More than enough."

Zach had always prided himself on his rational, decision-making abilities. He inevitably weighed every bit of evidence, analyzed all data, lined up facts and figures on a mental ledger. That was exactly what he did now.

On the plus side of the ledger, Miranda was a charming companion. She was a willing, enthusiastic, demanding and amazingly inventive lover. Even after all these months together, knowing that she found him sexually irresistible continued to be a potent aphrodisiac.

On the negative side, she had the irritating habit of showing him off to her jet-setting friends in a way that made Zach feel like an Angus bull on display at a stock show.

Once, when he'd complained about her behavior, she'd broken into hysterical tears, asserting between choking sobs that she was sorry if she'd made him angry. It was just that she was so marvelously proud of him and adored him so that it was hard to hide her happiness. By the time he'd managed to calm her down, Zach had felt like an unappreciative ass.

Miranda was more than a little emotional, not to mention maddeningly complicated, but she was also stunningly beautiful and highly intelligent. And when it came to Lord's, she'd surprised him by being every bit as driven as he.

There was also the inescapable fact that she was a highly sexed animal. If she couldn't satisfy her innate lust with him, her need would drive her into the arms— and the beds—of others. Just the thought of another man tasting that fragrant warm flesh made a red mist billow in front of Zach's eyes.

But marriage?

There were various ways of dealing with a Gordian knot. You could try to untie it, dooming yourself to failure. If you were Alexander the Great, you could simply say to hell with ancient prophesies and cut it.

Or, Zach considered thoughtfully, as he gazed down into Miranda's intense, glittering eyes, you could just accept it the way it was, enjoying the intricacy of its workmanship.

Pushing lingering misgivings into the farthest corner of his mind, with one deft, strong move, he lifted her onto his newly aroused body, claiming possession.

"I think," he said, as Miranda fitted him tightly inside her and began to ride, "it's time I made an honest woman of you."

Chapter Ten

Zach and Miranda's wedding, held three days before Christmas, was the highlight of the Santa Barbara social season.

The bride was beautiful in a Geoffrey Beene cocktail suit of ivory peau de soie, with which she wore a cream, wide-brimmed hat and the pearls Zach had given her for an engagement present.

The groom was handsome in a dark suit, but to the amusement of all gathered, appeared uncharacteristically nervous. The flowers were from Eleanor's greenhouse, the champagne was from France, and the wedding gifts came in blue Tiffany boxes.

After the ceremony, the happy couple flew to Brazil for their holiday honeymoon. Rio de Janeiro had a beat and a beauty all its own. The Cariocas' renowned zest for living was so evident that first-time visitors could be excused for half expecting pedestrians walking along the pink-tiled sidewalks to break into a samba.

Miranda couldn't remember when she'd felt so

grand. Even the light afternoon rain couldn't dampen her spirits. Here she was, in the sexiest, most uninhibited city in the world, lying in bed next to a handsome husband whose lust equaled her own.

Last night, she'd talked Zach into visiting a club in Copacabana, where for a small cover charge, they were given an eye-opening glimpse of Rio in the raw. The motto of the underground nightclub seemed to be Anything Goes. Men danced with men, women with women, in pairs, sometimes threesomes, and if there was a lot more than dancing going on in the dark corners, the management turned a blind eye.

Although Zach had professed distaste for the more blatantly outrageous displays, after returning to their hotel at dawn, he'd taken her with a savage passion that definitely belied his earlier condemnation.

But it was more than great sex that had Miranda floating on air. By becoming Mrs. Zachary Deveraux, she'd pulled off the coup of a lifetime.

At first she'd been furious to discover that Eleanor was leaving control of Lord's to Zach. There was, unsurprisingly, the obligatory bequest to Anna, whom everyone knew was dead. Any good attorney could break that clause.

It wasn't that Miranda had been disinherited. On the contrary, Eleanor had bequeathed her a lump sum of two million dollars and several exquisite pieces of jewelry, including an incomparable jaguar pin once worn by the Duchess of Windsor.

Along with the jewelry, Miranda was to receive the oversize Caravaggio of St. Matthew the tax collector that hung in a gold frame on the library wall, the Cézanne still life from the dining room and a valuable scale model of the London Lord's, complete with Gothic ornaments and flying buttresses.

But the one thing Miranda wasn't going to gain by her aunt's death was the one thing she most wanted: power.

Undaunted, after an initial outburst of rage that had required her to apologize profusely to Teddy Galbraith and to replace the shattered Waterford globe he'd used for thirty years as paperweight, Miranda had devised a new plan.

If she couldn't inherit control of Lord's, she'd earn it the old-fashioned way: by marriage.

Miranda glanced at her sleeping husband. Deciding she deserved a reward for devising such a brilliant solution, she slipped out of bed, dressed and took a taxi to Mesbla, Rio's answer to Macy's.

The department store was bustling. Miranda strolled idly past the fragrant cosmetics counters, past innumerable alligator belts and leather purses, and through the shoe department. She took the escalator to all eleven floors, perusing everything from lingerie to linens to pots and pans. But she could find nothing that shouted, *Choose Me!*

Finally she returned to the main floor and stood by the displays of costume jewelry. Across the aisle, behind the locked glass-topped counter displaying fine jewelry, a salesclerk with coffee-dark eyes and thick hair that fell to her waist was busily trying to convince a covey of young Japanese tourists that they couldn't leave Brazil without a pair of pink tourmaline earrings.

Nearby, a teenage girl, squeezed seductively into a flowered dress a samba dancer would have lusted after, tried on necklace after necklace, looking for the perfect accessory to her beauty.

Miranda plucked a pair of gold hoops from the costume-jewelery display and held them up to her earlobes, examining herself in the round mirror on the counter. They were regretfully common.

She returned them to the rack, choosing instead a pair of pearls surrounded by Austrian crystals. The cultured pearls definitely lacked luster. The faux rubies were too muddy, the sapphires too blue.

And then she saw them. A pair of glittering green stones set in gold. She clipped them on and smiled at her reflection.

Perfect. She looked over at the salesclerk, who had moved on to pushing aquamarines. Satisfied with her choice, Miranda took off the earrings and, with one last casual glance around, slipped them into her crocodile Hermès bag.

Excitement surged through her. She was heady with it. Her blood pounding, she walked quickly back the way she had come.

She'd just made it to the heavy glass doors, when an overweight, middle-aged man, wearing the dark blue uniform of authority the world over, stepped in front of her.

"Excuse me, Madame," he said in heavily accented English. He put a beefy hand on the sleeve of her black silk dress. "If you would please come with me?"

Displaying her usual flair for extravagance, Sophie arranged to transport the entire cast and crew of her three daytime soaps to Colorado for a week on the slopes during that unproductive time between Christ-

mas and New Year's. Also along for the celebration
were several actors and actresses she'd pegged to star
in "Blue Bayou," and the new writers, many of whom
she'd hired away from other daytime productions.

In the beginning, Alex had tried to beg off.

"There's still so much to do," she complained, frustrated by Sophie's tendency to continually tinker with
the script, expunging story lines, adding others, creating havoc with Alex's costuming plans.

"Don't you worry about a thing," Sophie said
blithely. She smiled, thinking about the surprise she
had waiting for this workaholic young woman who had
come to mean so much to her. "Things will all work
out fine. They always do."

"I have a feeling you won't be so sanguine when
Tiffany doesn't have a thing to wear for the opening
scene when the show debuts."

"Tiffany has a body that won't quit. Just having her
play her part in the buff would probably send ratings
through the roof."

Alex laughed and caved in.

While Alex was growing up, her mother, seemingly
possessed with wanderlust, had constantly moved their
small family from town to town, state to state. Although they'd spent nearly a year in Durango, Alex
had never visited Aspen. The former mining town did
not disappoint.

From her first glimpse, the snow-clad valley reminded Alex of a Currier and Ives print. She found
the Victorian architecture and quaint shops charming,
the scenery inspiring, and the people friendlier than
she'd imagined.

Of course, Alex allowed, part of her instant acceptance into Aspen's lofty social stratum was undoubtedly because her hostess was a driving force in the alpine community.

Sophie's ski chalet, which she had wrested from her husband during the bitter divorce negotiations, was nestled at the base of Buttermilk Mountain, two miles from the village center. The enormous house had walls made up almost entirely of triple-paned glass, offering an extraordinary panorama of blue sky, craggy mountains and deep drifts of blindingly white powder snow. In nearly every room of the house, fires blazed merrily away in stone fireplaces.

In the living room, a fifteen-foot Christmas tree, decorated with Western and Native American ornaments, towered above the assembled guests, reaching for the lofty, cantilevered ceiling. Outside the sliding glass doors, steam rose high in the crisp, dry mountain air from a huge hot tub.

On the third night of her visit, Alex was sitting at the pine desk in her room, her bright head bent over her sketchbook.

"Knock, knock" came a voice from the open door.

She glanced up. It was Stone Michaels, signed to play Tiffany's former high school sweetheart, a jazz saxophonist. When she'd first seen the attractive couple together, Alex had thought they looked like Ken and Barbie.

"I've been searching the entire house for you."

With an inward sigh, she put down the royal-blue pencil. Stone was Sophie's latest attempt at matchmaking. After discovering the aspiring actor/musician pumping gas at the Arco station on Sunset, the producer had set her sights on casting him as the man in Alex's life.

"I'm sorry," she said. "I was taking a shower and this thought occurred to me, and—"

"And you just couldn't rest until you got it down on paper," Stone finished. He entered the room on a long, loose-hipped stride reminiscent of James Dean. He was carrying a glass of white wine in each hand. He held one out to Alex.

She accepted the glass. "Guilty."

"I'm the same way when I'm working on a character sketch."

Alex smiled up at him as she took a sip of the wine. "This is great. Thanks."

"My pleasure." He glanced down, trying to catch a glimpse of her newest design.

Alex turned the pad over. A perfectionist by nature, she didn't like anyone seeing her work until she'd completed it to her satisfaction.

Tilting his sun-streaked head, he sipped his wine and studied her. "I thought you were going to soak your aching bones in the hot tub."

At Sophie's urging, she'd spent the day taking ski lessons from a gorgeous hunk who talked like Arnold Schwarzenegger, looked like Robert Redford and skied like Phil Mahre. After several humbling hours struggling to learn the logistics of schussing, herringbone and snowplows, after tumbling again and again into drifts of thick white powder, every muscle in her body was screaming in protest.

Which was why, when she'd returned to the house, Alex had allowed Stone to talk her into joining the gregarious group in the spa. At the time, the idea of all those jets of hot water massaging her aching body sounded like Nirvana.

But then, as so often happened, while she was standing beneath the pelting shower, a new design for a velvet-and-lace cocktail suit popped into her mind, and she'd rushed to get the thought onto paper.

"You know," Stone said when she didn't immediately answer, "if I didn't have the obligatory Hollywood stud superego, I'd think you were ignoring me." His friendly smile took the whine from his accusation.

"That's not true." Alex sipped a little more of her drink. "I seem to remember going into town with you just last night."

"With five other people acting as chaperones," he reminded her. "And you only stayed long enough to dance a couple of numbers. Hell, Alex, you were back here by nine."

Stone was nice. But pushy. She wished he'd hit on someone else. Like Brenda, a writer who hadn't tried to hide her crush on him.

"I'm sorry." Alex brushed his hand away when he began toying with her earring. "But I was exhausted. My body hasn't adjusted to this altitude."

He gave her a chiding look over the rim of his glass. "You're making this awfully hard, Alex."

"This?"

"You." He took her hand. "Me." Brushed his lips over her knuckles. "Us."

Tired and sore, she was not up to playing games. He'd been tossing these sexual innuendos her way since they'd boarded the private train in L.A. Not wanting to get into an argument, she'd tried to ignore them.

Which had been, Alex decided, a mistake. "There

isn't going to be any us," she insisted firmly, tugging her hand free.

"Are you so sure about that?"

"Positive." Alex could feel her temper beginning to fray. "I'm sorry, Stone. I think you're a nice guy. And I like you."

"I like you, too." Encouraged, he tugged on the ends of her hair.

Once again, she brushed his intimate touch away. "I like you as a friend. A 'Blue Bayou' colleague. But right now my work is so demanding I don't have time for a relationship."

"That's okay by me." This time his grin was blatantly suggestive. "I'd settle for a holiday fling."

Why was it, Alex wondered, that the gorgeous ones were inevitably so damn dense? Reminding herself they'd be working on the same program and it wouldn't do to antagonize him, she put her glass down on the desk, stood up, placed both her hands on his broad shoulders and looked him straight in the eye.

"Stone, listen to me. I am not in the market for an affair or a holiday fling. I came up here to relax. Which is very hard to do when you keep trying to get me horizontal."

He stared at her for a long time like someone who couldn't quite comprehend the language. "You really mean that, don't you?" he asked finally with obvious surprise.

"I really, really mean it."

When he raked his long fingers through his gilt hair, looking strangely hurt and definitely confused, Alex's heart softened. "I really should get back to work. Why don't you take Brenda a glass of wine?"

"Brenda?"

"The new writer Sophie stole away from 'The Guiding Light.' You know, the redhead."

"The tall, skinny one?"

Alex's frustrated sigh ruffled her bangs. "Willowy, Stone. The term is willowy. And in case you didn't notice, she's got dynamite legs."

"I was too busy chasing you to notice anyone else." His Paul Newman blue eyes turned thoughtful. "It probably wouldn't be a bad idea to get to know her," he mused aloud. "If she's a writer, she might like my input on my character."

She might also be inclined to pad the part, Alex tacked on silently what he hadn't bothered to say. Stone Michaels might be dense. But he wasn't stupid.

"I think that's an excellent idea." She flashed him a bright, encouraging grin. "Good luck."

"Thanks, Alex. You're a peach." He bent his head, gave her a brief unthreatening kiss, then headed toward the door, stopping momentarily in front of the mirror. After finger combing his wavy, collar-length hair to his satisfaction, he left the room whistling.

Alex laughed, grateful she'd withdrawn from the romance sweepstakes. Then, shaking her head, she turned the sketch pad over again and began reworking the suit's lace-trimmed lapels.

Although Rio was a bustling metropolis by day, by night it truly came alive. The streets filled with stunningly attractive people and clubs were packed with dancing and singing bodies. Zach and Miranda's luxurious hotel suite boasted a breathtaking view of Guanabara Bay, but at the moment, Zach's attention was not on the lights surrounding the gumdrop shape of Sugarloaf Mountain.

Instead, he was pacing the floor, frustration pounding through every pore.

"I don't understand," he repeated for the umpteenth time. "You have a purse filled with credit cards. Not to mention the five thousand dollars in traveler's checks."

"A little more than that, actually," Miranda said with a calm smile that made him want to shake her.

"So why the hell did you feel the need to lift those earrings?"

When he'd first received the telephone call from the manager of Mesbla, awakening him from a much needed nap, Zach had been certain it must be a mistake. When he arrived at the store's security offices, he'd learned it was all too true. His bride of three days had been caught red-handed stealing a pair of fifty-dollar earrings.

"They weren't even real emeralds, goddammit," he said.

"But they were lovely, nevertheless. For costume jewelry."

"So why didn't you just pay for them? Like everyone else?"

"What fun would that be?"

She sighed prettily as she went over to the bar and retrieved a bottle of champagne. Ignoring his smoldering fury, she expertly opened it. A wisp of vapor followed the cork. She poured the champagne into two flutes.

"Please, darling," she murmured, coaxing him to calm with her expressive eyes, her lush lips, "this is our honeymoon. Let's not spend it fighting."

Resisting an overwhelming urge to punch a hole in the wall, Zach thrust his hands through his hair. "Goddammit, Miranda—"

"Take a sip." She held the glass out to him. Zach grimly decided that Eve must have looked a great deal like Miranda did at this moment when she presented Adam with that shiny red apple to take his mind off that serpent hovering overhead. "It's a very special vintage. The concierge spent a great deal of time locating it. Just for you."

Shaking his head with mute frustration, Zach took a drink. Although the champagne was excellent, for a fleeting moment, he had a sudden urge for a cold beer. A Jax in a long-necked bottle.

You're the one who was so all-fired eager to leave the bayou, he reminded himself. *You're the one who wanted to be a big shot.* He might have grown up without the right name or address. He might have grown up without ever hearing of Chippendale or Baccarat or Royal Doulton.

And his working-class family had not possessed any money at all, let alone the kind of old money—respectable, fuck-you money—that was stashed away in Eleanor Lord's vault.

Unable to count on social contacts, Zachary had gotten where he was on brain and guts and hard work, along with a willingness to take risks.

And it had all paid off. In spades.

He was now the very wealthy president of an international company. He was a registered Republican, despite the fact he usually voted Democratic; he worshipped in the Episcopalian church, though there were times when his mind automatically responded in the

Latin of his altar-boy days. He belonged to all the right clubs, even while secretly considering golf excruciatingly boring.

And last, but definitely not least, he was now married to an unbelievably sexy, stunningly beautiful woman from the gilded, fairy-tale world of the Social Register. So dammit, why did he feel as if something was missing?

Perhaps because he'd just found out that his society bride was also a common, garden-variety shoplifter.

"We have to settle this, Miranda."

"Would it help if I told you that I'm terribly sorry?" Her voice was low and throaty. Her bedroom voice. "And that it will never, ever, happen again?"

She put her hand on his cheek. "It was just one of those crazy urges." Her eyes were wide and guileless. "And you know how impossible it is for me to resist my urges. Please don't be mad at me.

"I'll do anything to make this afternoon up to you, darling," she said breathlessly. When the tip of her tongue touched the top of her glossy red lip, Zach flashed back to this morning. The memory of the incredible things she had done with that tongue was all it took to make him hard. "Absolutely anything."

She was manipulating him, using sex to get what she wanted. But even knowing that didn't make him want her any less.

Reading the reluctant acceptance in her husband's eyes, Miranda put her glass down on a nearby table. And then she began to languidly undress, displaying seductive skills that a striptease artist headlining at the Folies Bergère would have envied.

Her eyes were dark with sex and sin as she unbuttoned her silk dress and allowed it to slide down her body, where it drifted into ebony petals on the plush blue carpet.

Her wispy bra was next. She shrugged out of it, revealing breasts as full as ripe melons. Her nipples were already hard. She stood there, smiling at him, wearing nothing but a sinfully sexy garter belt, black lace-topped stockings and skyscraper-high heels, a statuesque marvel of female perfection.

By the time she'd dispensed with the last bit of satin and lace, Zach's body was throbbing.

Their lovemaking, although quick and frenzied, was as torrid as ever. But unlike all those other times, tonight Zach's explosive orgasm left him feeling strangely unfulfilled.

Chapter Eleven

February 1984

Nineteen months after Alex's return to the States the shooting for "Blue Bayou" began with a bang on location—New Orleans during Mardi Gras. Excited about seeing her designs in action, Alex had accompanied the crew to the city.

Even the knowledge that Debord and his sister would be in town for the opening of the new Lord's department store could not burst her bubble of pleasure.

"I cannot believe you," Mary Beth Olson, the actress who was playing Tiffany, complained on their last afternoon in the city.

Alex glanced up from the skirt she'd been repinning, correcting minuscule flaws in the costuming that had shown up during taping. Although the location shooting had been completed, the costume would be worn again when the inside shots were taped back in California.

"What do you mean?"

"She means," Olivia Drew, who played the oil ty-coon's wife, said, "that you are turning out to be a stick-in-the-mud."

"It's the next-to-last night of Mardi Gras and you still haven't seen a single parade," Mary Beth com-plained.

"I've been working."

"That's all you do. Honestly, girl, you're more in-dustrious than one of Santa's little elves."

"All the taping's been done," Olivia coaxed. Even Sophie had not been fearless enough to attempt to get decent footage on the final two nights of carnival. Fortunately there had been large crowds and several parades during their five days in the city. The New Orleans footage would be mixed with that shot on the sound stage at the Century City studio. "Come out and play."

The idea was appealing. Alex had admittedly been a little envious, watching the cast enjoying themselves while she'd remained behind in the hotel making last-minute changes to the extensive wardrobe.

She'd been working nonstop since her return to the States. And although her intense schedule had been self-imposed, perhaps it was time she had a little fun. As a hard, driving beat filtered up from the crowded French Quarter street below, Alex could feel herself weakening.

"I suppose it wouldn't hurt. For just a little while."

That was all it took. An hour or so later, Alex was standing in front of the mirror, staring at the unfamiliar reflection. The off-the-shoulder dress, in Mardi Gras shades of purple, green and gold, and so diaphanous it skated the very fringes of decency, was one Alex had designed for Tiffany. Her arms were covered in gold bracelets; gold hoops swung from her ears to her bare, polished shoulders.

She looked good. Better than good, Alex decided. What was really surprising was that she felt as alluring as she looked. After having worked so hard to subdue her image these past months since escaping Debord, Alex felt a stirring of the female sexuality she'd locked away deep inside.

"Lord, you look like a very wealthy, very sexy Gypsy," Olivia drawled, putting in her two cents' worth.

For a woman whose role required her to wear Chanel knockoffs as she arranged flowers in Ming vases around the mansion, tonight Olivia had gone for broke with a jet leather mini and halter top, complete with a spiked necklace, over-the-thigh ebony boots and a vicious-looking black riding crop. She looked, Mary Beth had exclaimed, like a biker's wet dream.

No slouch in the costume department herself, after a visit to a shop on Chartres Street, Mary Beth had returned to the hotel dressed like a very sexy Pocahontas, complete with suede bikini and towering feathered headdress.

On this night before Fat Tuesday, Bourbon Street was, unsurprisingly, packed with boisterous merrymakers carrying paper cups filled with Hurricanes, the city's famed and lethal blend of rum and passionfruit punch.

"I think I'm going to go back to the hotel!" Alex shouted to be heard over the din of a Dixieland jazz band two hours later.

"So soon?" Olivia swayed on her high heels and was helpfully steadied by a well-muscled man dressed like the cowboy from the Village People. She was obviously drunk, but so were most of the people in the bar and on the street.

It seemed to Alex as if all restrictions of gender, manners, morals and social status had been dispensed with. Old and young, male and female, rich and poor, seemed to have been mixed together and blended like one of the frothy red Hurricanes.

"I'm getting a headache." She wasn't, though she would be if she stayed out much longer.

"I've got some aspirin," Mary Beth offered, digging through her shoulder bag.

"That's all right. Really."

"Just a minute. I know they're here somewhere." She dumped the entire bag onto the bar, sending coins scattering to the floor along with a crumpled pack of cigarettes and a small pink plastic case. "Oh, my God," she cried drunkenly, "I dropped my diaphragm!"

As three men, one dressed as Marie Antoinette, immediately bent down to retrieve it, the actress dissolved into giggles. She was still laughing when Alex left the bar.

Returning to the hotel was easier said than done. A parade float passed, preceded by musicians dressed as creatures from the sea: pink coral, sea horses, exotic fish and shells, moving with sinuous twists and turns as they played, as if buffeted by undersea currents. Following was the float itself, depicting Odysseus tied to the mast, resisting the Sirens, who stopped their seduction efforts every so often to throw plastic doubloons and strings of beads to the enthusiastic, masked and costumed spectators.

Jazz poured out of every open doorway. Battling her way through the raucous, jostling crowd, Alex had reached the corner of Bourbon and St. Peter's Streets when she suddenly found the sidewalk blocked by three very young and very drunken sailors.

"Well," one of them drawled, eyeing her with lust in his glazed eyes, "if it isn't a little Gypsy fortune-teller."

Alex stepped into the street to move around them. Unfortunately the trio moved, as well. "How about reading my palm, sweetheart?" another sailor suggested.

He held his hand out to her. Alex ignored it, glancing instead over his shoulder, looking for the mounted patrolman she'd seen on this corner earlier.

"If you'll excuse me…" She moved the other way, her unease building as they moved with her.

"Don't be in such a hurry, sugar," the first man said. He took hold of her arm and leaned close enough for her to smell the whiskey on his breath. Anger churned with a growing fear inside her, but when she tried to pull away, his fingers tightened, digging into her flesh.

If these three weren't enough, another man appeared behind her.

"There you are, sweetheart," Zach said to Alex with feigned cheer. "I thought I'd lost you in Ryan's." He'd been returning to his hotel from the new store when he'd spotted the woman in obvious trouble.

Didn't she realize, Zach wondered, that for a woman to appear alone on what was, during this week at least, the most hedonistic street in America, dressed in a ridiculously sexy outfit like that was like waving a red flag in front of a bunch of crazed bulls?

When his arm looped possessively around her shoulder, Alex stiffened.

"Where the hell did you go?" An edge of irritation

crept into Zach's tone. "I came back from the john and you were gone."

Alex was nothing if not quick. Although she had no idea who her rescuer was, she read the reassuring message in his eyes and picked up on the conversation.

"It was so crowded I went out for a breath of fresh air and got swept away with the crowd."

"I was worried." He brushed her gilt bangs from her forehead with a tender, concerned gesture, then turned to the trio who'd begun muttering among themselves.

"Thanks for watching out for the little woman for me," Zach said, acknowledging the trio for the first time. He reached into his pocket and pulled out some folded bills. "Let me buy you a beer for your assistance."

The others, weaving on their feet, eyed the steely determination in Zach's eyes and mumbled their agreement. The one who'd been manhandling Alex was not so malleable.

"We were about to have ourselves a little party."

"Good night for it," Zach agreed. He flashed a smile that failed to reach his eyes. "Have fun." He turned, taking Alex with him and began to walk away, only to have the sailor step belligerently in front of him.

"We were planning to have a party with the little Gypsy."

When Zach felt Alex begin to tremble, he tightened his arm around her shoulder. "I'm afraid there's been a small misunderstanding." His voice was amiable enough, but his dark eyes had turned as hard as obsidian. "This lady's taken. So why don't you boys go find yourself some more-willing companionship. Unless you'd rather talk with the Shore Patrol." Along with the deepened bayou patois, a dangerous edge had crept into his voice.

There was a long, silent moment as both men held their ground. Finally the sailor shrugged. "Hey, man, she's all yours," he muttered. With that he turned and staggered away, his companions following drunkenly behind.

Alex released a long, pent-up breath and was prepared to thank him when he turned on her. "Are you always this reckless, lady? Or are you merely stupid?"

He was standing in front of her in a spread-leg, feet-planted stance that made her think that, instead of that dark suit, he should be wearing a pirate costume. All he was lacking, she thought, was an eye patch and a cutlass.

Alex had already had enough trouble with men to-night; she didn't need any lectures from this one, no matter how well intentioned.

"Are you always this rude?" she countered.

"If you're so concerned about manners, you're definitely in the wrong town at the wrong time. You're just damn lucky I came along when I did. Where are you staying? We'd better get you back to your hotel before some other drunk decides to play king of the Gypsies."

Her palms were still damp from fear. "I'm more than capable of getting back to the hotel on my own."

"Dressed like that, you probably won't make it to the next corner. This isn't exactly a Boy Scout convention going on in town. And you, lady, are a rape just waiting to happen."

"This dress isn't any more seductive than any other costume on the street. And it's a lot less sexy than most." Her eyes, as gold as a buccaneer's doubloons, flashed sparks.

"True enough. But most of the women out here aren't you."

Alex supposed his words could have been taken as a compliment, but there was nothing complimentary about his tone.

"Are you always this charming?" she asked sweetly. "Or does rescuing strange women just bring out the best in you?"

They stood there, toe to toe, face-to-face.

And that's when it happened. Zach smiled. An unexpected smile that changed his features, humanizing the man and making him horrendously, dangerously sexy.

"Hell, I'm sorry," he said with absolute honesty. "I don't suppose it's any excuse that I've had a lousy day and I took out my frustrations on you."

Alex shrugged. "You were probably right about a woman alone in this crowd," she admitted reluctantly. "Although I didn't start out alone."

"Lose your husband somewhere along the way?"

"I'm not married."

"So you were with a date?" he probed with a casualness he was suddenly a long way from feeling.

"Actually, I was with friends. But I wanted to go back to the hotel and they wanted to stay out and party."

"If I apologize for being such a jerk, how about letting me walk you back to your hotel? I'm not quite ready to call it a night," he said, conveniently forgetting that only minutes before he couldn't wait to get back to his suite on the top floor of the Royal Orleans.

Something was happening between them. Something more charged than mere sexual tension. All around Zach and Alex, the Mardi Gras festivities flowed, but the pair remained in the center of the celebratory throng of people, an isolated, private island.

"I'd like that," she said in a perfectly rational voice although her eyes displayed her own suddenly turbulent emotions.

"Terrific." He held out his hand. "By the way, I'm Zachary Deveraux."

"Alexandra Lyons." As she took his outstretched hand, the vibrations the seemingly casual handshake set off hummed inside her like a tuning fork.

The Jean Lafitte Hotel, named for the legendary New Orleans pirate and smuggler, was a restored eighteenth-century town house, a romantic place of courtyards filled with tropical plants and private, wrought-iron balconies, in the heart of the Vieux Carré. The walk to the Jean Lafitte from Bourbon Street normally took no more than five minutes. Tonight, with the crowds, it took almost half an hour.

"Would you like to come in for a drink?" Alex asked. She was unwilling to let him get away so soon.

Zach reminded himself that he was a married man. That these feelings he was experiencing for Alexandra Lyons were not only wrong, but dangerous.

Although his marriage was turning out to be a horrendous mistake, Zach never played around. Not that there weren't always available women, both married and unmarried, who let it be known they would not be adverse to spending a stolen afternoon indulging in illicit pleasures.

But Zach had always considered himself a man of his word, and marriage vows were exactly that. Vows. *For better or for worse.*

"I'd like a drink," he said, ignoring the nagging voice of caution in the back of his mind.

Not surprisingly the Jean Lafitte's All That Jazz bar, along with the l'Escale dining room and the Gazebo Salon were packed.

In for a penny, in for a pound. Telling herself she had no other choice, Alex said, "I suppose we could go upstairs and call room service." As she waited for his answer, Alex realized she'd forgotten how to breathe.

Zach knew it was wrong. He realized he would be treading on very thin ice. But at this moment, on this freewheeling, carnival night, with the sound of Louis Armstrong floating on the breeze, Zach felt his usually dependable self-control slipping away like grains of sand—or strands of her magnificent red-gold hair—between his fingers.

"Sounds great," he heard himself saying before he could come to his senses and change his mind.

While Zach struggled with his conscience, Miranda and a companion strolled arm in arm into a bar near the Mississippi River levee. Tucked away in Miranda's quilted Chanel bag was a lovely pair of suede gloves she'd lifted that afternoon from the Canal Street Maison Blanche.

Although from the outside, the dimly lighted cocktail lounge looked like any other in the historic Vieux Carré, the management catered to a unique clientele. After ordering Sazeracs, Miranda and her escort managed to squeeze, just barely, into a spot on the crowded, postage-stamp-size dance floor.

As she felt Marie Hélène's long slender fingers settle on her waist, Zach's wife smiled with anticipation.

Chapter Twelve

Alex's hotel room was actually a minisuite, with an alcove containing a couch and easy chair adjoining the bedroom, which allowed them to keep their visit on a proper plane even as unspoken feelings swirled around them.

Alex had never met a man who was more easy to talk with. She found herself telling him more about herself than she'd ever told anyone—about growing up with her mother and twin brother, about the way they never stayed in one town or even one state for more than a year, about the pain and loneliness she suffered at first David's, then her mother's death.

It was as if, once she started talking, she couldn't stop. She told him all about her dreams of becoming a designer. And about her time working in New York and more recently in Paris. She told him what she could about "Blue Bayou" without divulging the plotline, which Sophie guarded as ferociously as a mother bear protecting her cubs.

Alex did not mention her affair with Debord. It wasn't that she was ashamed of it. On the contrary, she was rather proud of the way she'd picked herself up, dusted herself off and started over.

She didn't mention it because looking back, it seemed as if the affair and its dreadful conclusion had all happened to some other woman. A far more foolish, more naive woman.

"Gracious," she said, when she finally ran down. "I've been doing all the talking."

Zach refilled their glasses from the bottle of wine they'd ordered from room service. "I like hearing you talk." Her enthusiasm for life was contagious. And although she worked in Tinseltown, it was obvious she hadn't gone Hollywood. She was, he considered, the most natural woman he'd ever met.

The simple compliment shouldn't give her so much pleasure. But it did. "But I don't know anything about you," she protested. "Other than you should be wearing a coat of shining armor instead of that Brooks Brothers suit."

"I didn't own a suit until I graduated from college," he surprised himself by saying. Although he was not ashamed of his humble roots, he was not in the habit of sharing his past. Let alone with someone he'd just met.

"Ah." She curled up in the corner of the couch, tucking her legs beneath her flowing skirt. "A self-made man."

"With a little help from some friends."

Zach told her briefly about his life growing up in Lafourche Parish, of the early years fishing and trapping with his father.

"My father died when I was ten," he said when she asked about his parents. Alex murmured a sound of sympathy. She knew firsthand the pain of losing a parent as an adult. She couldn't imagine how she'd have survived if her mother had died while she and David were still children.

"Was yours a large family?" she asked.

"I was the oldest in a family of eight kids. One boy and seven girls."

"Gracious. You were definitely outnumbered."

"I didn't mind."

Imbued with a deep sense of duty and an even deeper sense of family, Zach had immediately stepped into the role of second parent. When his mother, desperate for additional funds to feed her family, went to work as a domestic in town, Zach took over the household chores, which made him not only an excellent cook, but the only ten-year-old boy in the bayou who could weave a French braid.

"When I was sixteen, I got a summer job working on the loading dock at the New Orleans Lord's," he continued his story. "The old one. A new one just opened today on Canal Street."

Alex nodded. "So I heard." She'd fretted some about running into Debord. When she arrived in town and saw how many thousands of people came to New Orleans during the festival, she realized she'd been foolish to worry. The odds against seeing the horrid man again were astronomical. "I've always liked Lord's. Their buyers have a tremendous sense of style."

"Thanks. I'll pass the word along."

"It's a long way from the loading dock to the executive offices," she prompted, growing more curious about this unique man by the moment. "Are you manager of the new store?"

"Actually, I'm president of the company."

She wasn't all that surprised. Zachary Deveraux radiated power. "I'm impressed."

"I was lucky. I got some breaks along the way."

Alex liked the fact that he didn't have an enormous ego. Actually, she had a feeling this was a man who would succeed at whatever he chose. With or without any breaks along the way.

When she told him what she was thinking, he shrugged. "To tell the truth, my senior year of high school, the loading-dock manager offered me a full-time job after graduation. I wanted to take it."

"But?"

"My mother hit the roof. She wanted me to go to college."

"I think that's every mother's dream for her children. My mother scrimped for years so I could attend the Fashion Institute." She'd also vehemently protested when Alex had dropped out to take care of her.

"It wasn't a common goal in the bayou," Zach revealed. "In my father's day, any young Acadian who considered college was considered lazy. But my folks realized times were changing. They knew my future lay working out among the Americaines."

"Americaines?"

"That's how Cajuns refer to non-Acadian Louisianans."

"Oh." Alex considered that for a moment. "It must have been difficult," she murmured. "When I first arrived in France, I might as well have landed on the moon, things seemed so different from what I was used to."

So she was insightful, as well as beautiful. That made her, Zach considered, even more dangerous.

"I got used to it," he said, purposefully understating what had indeed been a major cultural adjustment.

She took a sip of wine and eyed him with bright interest. "Where did you go to college?"

"I got a football scholarship at Tulane, right here in the city." Which had allowed him to continue to work part-time at Lord's, where he'd been promoted to the sales floor. The money he'd earned he'd sent home to his mother.

She envisioned him wearing shoulder pads and those tight white pants and decided he must have looked magnificent. "Were you any good?"

Zach shrugged. "My sack statistics weren't bad." Actually, they'd been so impressive he'd garnered the pros' attention. "But my junior year I injured my knee in the final game of the season, which quashed my dreams of NFL stardom."

"You must have been terribly disappointed." Alex knew all too well the power of youthful dreams.

"For a while. But if there was one thing life had taught me, it was how to punt."

Another thing they had in common, Alex mused. If she was keeping score. Which she wasn't.

Hell. Of course she was.

"So, to make a long story short, I graduated with degrees in business and marketing—" he didn't mention those degrees had been cum laude "—and moved into

management. In a few months, I went back to business
school for my MBA."

That had been Eleanor's doing. Six months after he'd
begun work full-time, he'd suggested a new inventory
system that had garnered her attention. Recognizing
potential when she saw it, Eleanor offered to pay his
tuition to Harvard Business School.

Although he'd refused her charity, Zach did accept
the money as a loan, payable on installment when he
graduated.

"Then I returned to work at Lord's L.A. headquarters." He spread his hands. "End of story," he said,
leaving out his meteoric rise to vice president and finally president.

Alex suspected there was a great deal more to the
story than he was telling.

"Your wife must be very proud of you," she murmured, wishing she could ignore the gold band on his
left hand.

"I suppose so." His lack of enthusiasm was in direct
contrast to his earlier tone.

"Is she in town with you?"

"Since Miranda's in charge of setting up the Debord
boutiques, she came for the opening." He'd been neither
surprised nor disappointed when his wife had opted to
spend the evening with the designer and his iceberg of
a sister, rather than with her husband.

Since returning from their honeymoon thirteen
months ago, Zach doubted if he and Miranda had spent
more than five consecutive days together. Their work
was demanding. And it required a great deal of travel.
But, he'd asked himself time and time again, if they

truly loved one another, wouldn't they make the time to be together?

Unfortunately whenever his wife did deign to join him at the French Normandy–style manor she'd convinced him to buy in Brentwood, it was as if a dangerous wind had swept into the house, disturbing the calm, predictable routine of his existence.

Alex watched the scowl darken his features. "Your wife is Miranda Smythe?" Try as she might, she could not envision this man married to the mercurial Lady Smythe. She knew the old adage about opposites attracting, but Zachary Deveraux and Miranda Lord Baptista Smythe had to be the mismatch of the millennium.

"That *was* her name," Zach allowed. "Do you know her?"

"I've seen her picture in the magazines." To reveal any more would bring up her time with Debord, and Alex refused to allow that bastard to ruin a wonderful night. As if to remind himself that he was married, Zach spent the next half hour telling Alex what he could about his wife.

He told her about the success of the Debord boutiques. He did not mention Miranda's recreational shoplifting. Hardly a week went by that Zach didn't receive a discreet bill in the mail for some item his wife had not been able to resist taking.

Fortunately, after that experience in Rio, Miranda had stuck to stores where they had an account. Apparently she wasn't willing to risk incarceration over a Hermès scarf or a bottle of Obsession, both of which she could easily afford.

He lauded Miranda's inspired remodeling job at the

London Lord's. He did not mention the glacier that had begun creeping inexorably over their marriage bed after their return from Rio.

Nor did he admit the truth that sex had been the coinage of his and Miranda's odd-couple relationship from the beginning. And now, having just recently celebrated their first anniversary on separate continents, that relationship was already approaching bankruptcy.

He expressed, with honest admiration, his wife's unerring sense of style and her ability to draw British society to the store's special events, thus increasing customer loyalty.

He left unsaid that these days her conversation skills, when she did trouble to speak to him, seemed limited to clothes and parties and race horses, and gossip about face-lifts and tummy tucks and what wife had run off with her karate instructor and what yacht club member of the Newport–Palm Beach crowd was committing adultery with what married princess of some European pocket principality he'd never even heard of.

He also didn't relate his belief that Miranda was so busy going places, seeing and being seen with the right people with the most money, she had precious little time for normal, everyday activities.

Despite his discretion, Alex had no difficulty reading between the lines. From what Zach didn't say about his marriage, she realized that all was not well in the Deveraux household.

Which was, she told herself firmly, none of her business. As attracted to Zach as she was, she had no desire to get involved with a married man. Feeling the pall settle over the room, Zach returned the conversation to Alex's reason for being in New Orleans in the first place. For nearly nineteen months, she'd lived, eaten, slept and dreamed "Blue Bayou." It was, quite literally, the most important thing in her life.

And on this long Mardi Gras night, it didn't take much encouragement for her to talk about the show and, more specifically, her costuming.

Pink fingers of dawn began creeping above the wrought-iron railing when Alex finally ran out of steam.

"I can't believe we've been talking all night," she said.

"Time has a way of flying during Mardi Gras." Zach knew he should get up from his chair, thank her for a lovely evening and return to the Royal Orleans, where just perhaps, his errant wife may have returned by now.

They fell silent, Zach sprawled in the chair, Alex curled up in the corner of the flowered sofa, watching as the rising sun streaked the sky over the courtyard in a dazzling display of gold and ruby rays.

During their hours together, he'd come to realize that Alexandra Lyons was a warm and caring, talented and special woman. Zach found himself unwilling to say goodbye just yet.

The effect she was having on his body was considerable—and not entirely unexpected. After all, he'd been celibate for months, and Alexandra Lyons was a ravishing woman. As a normal, heterosexual male, Zach was not immune to attractive women. What was coming as a distinct surprise was what Alexandra was doing to his mind. He wanted her, he realized. And for a helluva lot more than an adulterous roll in the hay.

Quicksand, Zach warned himself. *Take one more step and you're in deep, deep trouble.*

"My mother's getting married today," he revealed. "I don't suppose you've ever been to a Cajun wedding."

She briefly thought of a time when she'd been foolish enough to think she'd be planning her own Paris wedding. "No. But from what you've said about Cajun parties, I'll bet they're special."

"They are. How would you like to experience one firsthand?"

Yes, yes, her unruly heart called in reply. "With you?" she asked cautiously.

"I'd like your company." Although his tone remained matter-of-fact, his eyes were unnervingly intimate, setting off warning bells.

"What about your wife?" she had to ask.

"Miranda's not going. She's not exactly wild about my humble rural roots."

Before their marriage, Miranda had displayed a burning fascination with everything about Zach: his Louisiana childhood, his family, his hardscrabble, pull-himself-up-by-the-bootstraps success story, his work at Lord's.

These days, she found everything about their life together boring. Santa Barbara was boring. Los Angeles was boring. California. Constant sunshine. All were so, so boring. Even Zach, she'd accused on more than one stormy occasion, screeching at him in a voice high enough to risk shattering her precious collection of crystal, had become bloody, bloody boring! In Miranda's eyes, her husband had committed the cardinal sin.

It hadn't taken Zach long, after they were married,

to discover that he'd never really known Miranda at all. His wife reinvented herself every day in the mirror. Everything Miranda did, everything she said, was another brush stroke in that carefully drawn self-portrait.

If he was disillusioned with his marriage, which he most definitely was, Zach knew that he had no one to blame but himself. He'd understood from the beginning that Miranda led life in the fast lane.

The only problem was that during this past year Zach had begun to feel more and more as if he were standing all alone in the roadway, facing the fatal rush of oncoming traffic.

"If you're worried about not getting any sleep," Zach said, unreasonably unnerved by her hesitation, "the ceremony's not until this evening. I thought I'd return to my hotel, then meet you back here around two or three."

Before putting her feelings on such a restrictive rein, Alex had not been a woman to guide her emotions. More often, she allowed them to guide her. And although such behavior might be considered foolhardy, especially when it led her into the type of trouble she experienced with Debord, in the balance, her life had been rewarding.

She was, quite honestly, weary of trying to live a lie, of pretending to be someone she was not. She was tired of her dark and proper clothing, her subdued behavior. It was as if by donning this bright Gypsy outfit last night, she'd let the genie of her own daring, slightly reckless personality out of the bottle, and Alex didn't know if she'd want to put it back even if she could. And she suspected she couldn't.

Knowing that she was already too attracted to this

very married man and telling herself she should refuse,
Alex took a deep breath, threw caution to the winds
and said, "I'd love to attend your mother's wedding
with you, Zachary."

Chapter Thirteen

Alex felt the change in Zach as they drove away from the city. Soon after they'd crossed the iron bridge spanning the Mississippi River, he tuned the car radio to a station playing an infectious, toe-tapping medley he told her was called zydeco. As "The Lake Arthur Stomp" gave way to "Jolie Blonde," Zach visibly relaxed.

They sped along a highway that spread like a long gray ribbon over swampland, past stretches of sugarcane fields and rice paddies. Blue herons glided soundlessly among magnificent cypress trees, bearded in Spanish moss, which the sun backlit in ghostly gold; nutria and muskrats paddled along, furry shadows in the dark waters.

A silence descended that could be described as companionable, if only the participants hadn't been so studiously avoiding feelings too risky to acknowledge out loud.

"This is so beautiful," Alex said quietly after a while.

"We call it the trembling prairie. Roots sink deep here."

She knew he was not talking about the knobby cypress roots, which rose out of the water. "You must miss it a great deal."

"It's good to get back home," he agreed. "Once the bayou gets into your blood, I don't think you can ever get it out. Even if you want to."

"Which you don't."

"No."

His familiarity with the seemingly unfathomable maze of dirt roads and waterways reminded Alex of what she'd once read about a nomad's ability to find his way home over miles of shifting desert sands. From the fact that he'd risen so quickly in the Lord's organization, it was obvious he possessed an enormous talent for business. But she suspected that it was here, in this misty, mystical land, that Zachary felt truly comfortable.

The wedding, held in Zach's former waterfront home, was a vibrant celebration of family and community. Eve Deveraux, who was marrying a nearby rancher, gave Alex a warm greeting.

"Thank you for celebrating our happiness with us today," she said. Although her smile was sincere, Alex thought she detected a fleeting concern in the dark eyes that so resembled her son's.

A beautiful woman in her fifties, Eve had chosen a royal-blue dress, cut on the bias and falling to just below the knee. Alex decided it definitely suited her.

Zach's paternal grandmother was more outspoken

than her daughter-in-law. After giving Zach a huge hug, she stepped back, gave his companion a long, probing once-over with eyes that reminded Alex of a curious bird and said without preamble, "You have known heartache."

Although startled, Alex kept her smile from slipping. "What woman hasn't?"

The elderly woman didn't respond to Alex's flippant remark. "There will be more to come," she pronounced. "But in the long run, you will find the love you deserve."

"Maman," Eve murmured. "Please..." She slanted Alex an apologetic look.

Zach's grandmother ignored the quiet warning. "As for you, boy," she said, tilting her white head back to look a long, long way up into Zach's face, *"Lâchez pas la patate."*

Zach's answering grin was meant to charm his grandmother, but Alex found herself mesmerized by its warmth. "Why don't you tell me what you really think?" he suggested blandly.

The maternal concern Alex had witnessed earlier in Zach's mother's gaze was back as Eve skillfully led them away to introduce Alex to the rest of the huge Deveraux clan.

The wedding feast was a culinary extravaganza—spicy gumbo, jambalaya, crayfish and filet of alligator topped with Tabasco sauce hot enough to clear Alex's sinuses. The mood was as joyful as the food was lavish; dust from the dancers' feet and smoke from the barbecue grills rose into the cooling air.

More than once Alex was pulled, laughing, into a conga line led by guests dressed in Mardi Gras costumes, and by the time the sun had set over the water, she decided that she must have danced with at least twenty of Zach's cousins.

"I envy you," she murmured when she found herself in Zach's arms for the first time since their arrival hours earlier. As the marsh gas flickered a phosphorous green, the band started interspersing a few ballads in with the livelier dance tunes.

"Why?" Zach asked, his attention distracted by her eyes, which were shining like antique gold in the light of the campfires that had been set.

"You have so many people who care about you. And love you."

"I suppose, where life is hard, family becomes even more important," he said thoughtfully. "I have a photo of Dad and Mom and my sisters and me all picking Grand-mère's sugarcane. Last year, when I became president of Lord's, I had an artist copy it.

"Whenever I start getting cocky, I look at that painting on my office wall and remember where I came from. And what's important."

She was not surprised by the story. Watching Zach with his family and friends had revealed a side of the man she suspected few people were permitted to see. Did his wife know the real Zachary Deveraux? Or had Lady Miranda set her sights only on the high-powered executive?

The fact that Zach had brought her to his mother's wedding, rather than Miranda, provided the answer to that question, she decided.

"Your grandmother's an interesting woman," she murmured.

Zach laughed. A deep rumbling sound Alex found

herself liking too much for safety. "That's one way to describe her. She's stubborn, like all us Deveraux. And she claims to have second sight. Like her own *grand-mère*."

"Do you believe her?"

Zach shrugged. "When I was a kid, I didn't. But one fall when I was thirteen, I couldn't find a deer all season. We really needed the venison to get us through the winter. That's when she told me exactly where to go.

"Deciding I didn't have anything to lose, I took her advice and found an enormous buck standing beside a cypress as if he'd been waiting for me to come and shoot him. After that, I started listening to her more often."

"What about tonight? What did she tell you?"

"Oh, that." Zach knew his grandmother didn't approve of his wife. He also knew she approved of divorce even less. "It's an old Cajun expression—'Don't drop the potato.' Loosely translated, it means 'Hang in there.'"

"Oh." When she felt his body tense, Alex opted against questioning him further.

He danced her away from the others to a hidden place of shadows beneath a grove of trees. They swayed to the sultry romantic ballad, his chin atop her hair, her fingers linked around his neck.

And even when the music stopped, they stood there for a long, immeasurable time, still clasped together, looking into each other's eyes, silently exchanging seductive messages too dangerous to put into words.

"Alexandra." There was a husky poignancy in his voice.

Looking up at him, Alex saw a man who'd just come

to the stark realization that his life has, in the space of a single day, been changed forever. She could recognize the tumultuous emotions because she was feeling the same way.

Alex knew she was playing with fire. She also knew one of them was likely to get burned, and more than likely it would be her. But at this absolutely perfect moment in time, she didn't care.

Zach had spent the entire day valiantly trying to keep his hands off her, but it had been like fighting an undertow. Dammit, he'd never claimed to be bucking for sainthood.

He brushed his fingers down her cheek, following the slow, seductive movement with his eyes. "You are, without a doubt, the most beautiful woman here today."

The soft touch of his fingers made Alex's blood hum. "The bride's the most beautiful woman at her wedding," she argued on a shaky little whisper.

"Maman's always been beautiful." His hand trailed down her throat as he took in the sight of her, clad in a moss-green dress and forest-green suede boots that reminded him of a wood nymph.

Last night, in theatrical makeup, Alexandra had appeared lush and sultry and vampish. Earlier today, with her face flushed from a heady mixture of sun and exertion and pleasure, she'd possessed a bright, breezy type of nonconformist beauty that had reminded him of Audrey Hepburn's Holly Golightly.

Tonight in the moonlight, with a dusting of freckles scattered across the bridge of her nose, Alexandra Lyons seemed delicate and vulnerable.

"But you," he alleged gravely, "are absolutely exquisite."

Slowly, giving her time to read his intention and back away, he framed her face between his large, re-assuring hands and with the utmost deliberation and gravity, lowered his mouth to hers.

With a patience he'd never known he possessed, Zach took his time to kiss her tingling lips from one corner to the other, loving her for a long, delicious time with only his mouth. As his lips tempted, cajoled, ca-ressed, Alex's world was reinvented.

Beguiled, she closed her eyes, twined her arms around his neck and allowed her mind to empty. She melted into his exquisite kiss because at this suspended moment in time, to do otherwise would have been to deny her own feelings. And to deny her emotions would have been contrary to her honest nature.

Caught up in the wonder of Alex, Zach savored her every sigh, each soft moan. As her warm breath shud-dered out of her, he forgot all the reasons why this was wrong; as he heard his name murmured against his mouth he could only think how perfectly Alexandra Lyons fit in his arms.

His lips skimmed over her face, drinking in the tan-talizing taste of her skin before returning to her mouth.

The kiss could have lasted a minute. An hour. An eternity. When it finally ended, Zach was as disoriented as if someone had just informed him that the laws of physics had been suspended, and down was now up, up down, and gravity no longer existed.

Not quite knowing how to tell her what he was feel-ing, he said her name again—"Alexandra"—savoring the pure sweetness of it. The pleasure. The absolute joy. He wound a strand of gleaming hair around his finger into a ringlet; he released it and it immediately sprang back into the mass of riotous waves. Although he knew it was masochistic, Zach imagined what that silky hair would feel like against his naked chest. His thighs.

"This is…" His voice trailed off, and all he could do was shake his head in wonder and frustration.

"Unexpected," Alex filled in for him. "Exciting. Frightening."

"Terrifying," Zach concurred.

The one description neither of them was prepared to resort to was *mistake*.

"I want to be honest with you, Alexandra. I *need* to be honest with you. The problem is, I have the feeling that whatever I say is going to come out wrong."

"This can't go anywhere." Alex's voice was soft and resigned.

He wished she'd argue. Shout. Anything but this quiet acceptance. "Not now. Although you'll probably never believe this, I'm not the type of man who plays around on his wife."

"I believe it. Because I'm not the kind of woman who has affairs with married men."

"I don't want to hurt you."

But he would hurt her, Alex knew. Oh, he wouldn't mean to. But she could see the heartbreak coming, like the headlight of a runaway freight train approaching in a tunnel.

"I was going to ask if you'd let me show you the real Louisiana tomorrow."

Alex could hear the regret in his tone. "But?" she asked softly.

"I received a phone call a while ago," he said, telling her nothing she didn't know. She'd watched him go into his mother's house, wondered if it was his wife calling and noticed his grim expression when he'd emerged several minutes later.

"There was a fire at a Lord's store under construction in Santa Monica. They think it was started by a welder's torch."

"I hope no one was hurt."

"Fortunately, no. But the city fire inspector's going to be on the site first thing in the morning. Since I should be there, I had to change my flight. There's a plane leaving at 4:30 in the morning, which will get me back to L.A. in time."

"Four-thirty." *So soon.*

He heard the soft shimmer of regret in her tone. "I'm sorry."

Alex managed a wobbly smile. "We still have the rest of tonight." The smile moved to her eyes. "I'm going to change my flight so we can return to California together, Zachary. And then I want to dance with you at your mother's wedding."

"And then?" Zach had a feeling he wasn't going to like her answer.

He didn't. "And then," she continued quietly, firmly, "once we land at LAX, you'll return to your life. And I'll go back to mine."

Part of him knew she was right. But then his gaze moved to her mouth—Jesus, her sweet, soft, delectable mouth!—and he found himself wishing she'd suggest they run away together. To some faraway, romantic South Sea island where no one would ever find them and they could spend the rest of their days making love and feeding each other tropical fruit. Passion fruit.

"You can really walk away from whatever's happening between us here? Just like that?" His voice, his eyes, testified to his disbelief.

Unable to speak past the sudden lump in her throat, Alex merely nodded.

Even as she tried to tell herself that these few golden hours together would be enough, as they danced and kissed and whispered and sighed, she felt horribly like Cinderella facing the countdown of that treacherous palace clock. Later, as they drove in heavy silence back along the darkened highway toward New Orleans, Alex half expected Zach's rental car to turn into a pumpkin.

The stolen hours passed all too quickly. Hidden beneath the blue blanket in the first-class section they had all to themselves at this unpalatable hour of the morning, they kissed like lovesick teenagers, their bodies aching with feverish yearning.

Finally the long day caught up with Alex and she fell asleep, her head on Zach's shoulder, her legs curled up beneath her on the seat.

While the plane sped closer and closer to Los Angeles, Zach remained awake. Indulging himself in the pure pleasure of watching Alex undetected, he wished for the impossible. As the plane made its inevitable approach into LAX, the change in engine speed roused Alex from her light slumber. She escaped to the lavatory, dragged a brush through her tangled hair, splashed cold water on her face, took several deep breaths and reminded herself that as wonderful as her romantic interlude with Zach had been, it was time to return to the real world.

Reality was Los Angeles, with its smog and soaring property prices, traffic jams and escalating crime. Reality was Zach returning to his Century City offices. Reality was her continuing her work for Sophie.

Reality was Zach's marriage.

And his wife.

They stood face-to-face, close enough to touch, but not daring to as the bustling early-morning crowd in the terminal surged around them.

Although Zach didn't want to let Alex get away, he couldn't escape the unpalatable fact that he was married. And while he suspected Alex might be willing to meet him for the occasional rendezvous, he could not play with her emotions that way.

Divorce was, of course, an option. But the last time he'd suggested it to Miranda, she'd lost her temper, become hysterical and taken an overdose of Valium. She hadn't taken enough to kill herself, the doctor had assured Zach.

But she had achieved her objective. She'd scared the hell out of her husband.

Looking back on that fateful day when he'd first met Miranda Lord Baptista Smythe, Zach knew he'd been foolishly led with his hormones and not his heart. Or his brain.

And now, the price for the unbridled lust he'd once felt for the woman who was now his wife, for better or for worse, would be to live with the bad bargain he'd made.

"You know, this is a small town, really," he said. "Perhaps we'll run into one another."

"Perhaps." The sheen of moisture in Alex's eyes belied her falsely bright tone.

They both knew it would not happen. They could not allow it to happen. Because the chemistry between them was too potent to allow them to remain merely friends.

Alex was putting on such a goddamn good show of being cheerful and brave. Zach thought this would all be a helluva lot easier if she'd break down and cry. Or shout.

Forsaking all others. The vow he'd willingly taken felt as heavy and burdensome as Jacob Marley's chains.

Unable to resist, he touched her cheek. "Goodbye, Alexandra."

The tender touch threatened to be her undoing. "Goodbye, Zach."

As her eyes filled with hot, frustrated tears, Alex turned and walked away, the heels of her suede boots clicking a rapid staccato on the tile floor.

Zach stood there, his fists shoved deep into the pockets of his slacks, his heart aching. He desperately wanted to call her back, but knew it would only hurt her more if he did.

Chapter Fourteen

Deciding she was a disaster just waiting to happen when it came to romance, Alex threw herself back into the one thing she could control in her life, safe, soothing work.

When she wasn't hard at work, she ran along the packed sand, mile after mile, until her physical pain equaled her emotional pain. And then she ran farther still, until the ocean breeze dried her salty tears and she was too exhausted to dwell on what might have been if she'd only met Zach during that brief window of time when they'd both been in Paris. Before he'd married Miranda.

The first episode of "Blue Bayou" proved a blockbuster hit, outscoring even "The Cosby Show" in the overnight ratings.

The media, unsurprisingly, panned the glitzy soap opera. One particularly harsh critic declared that Americans possessed a limitless desire to identify with the upper classes. That being the case, he'd gone on sarcastically, it was no wonder they'd all tuned in to watch a show where the characters, who changed clothes between the appetizer and soup course, appeared to be the classiest people on television.

Undeterred by the strident criticism, Sophie laughed all the way to the bank.

"Blue Bayou" quickly became not only America's number-one television show, but was also watched by citizens of seventy other countries, including Iceland, Japan and Bangladesh.

And, as Sophie had predicted, Alex's designs made her a rising star in Tinseltown. Even critics who hated the program couldn't resist a positive mention of the dazzling wardrobe.

Her imaginative costuming expressed the basic conflict around which the steamy nighttime drama revolved. Typically the wicked ex-wife would strike a blow with a black crepe cocktail dress trimmed with rhinestones along a plunging neckline, while the saintly current wife would counter with a pink peplum jacket accented by thin silver piping.

Across town the exotic dancer/mistress would go shopping in a sequined blue baseball jacket over a ribbed red silk tank top and tight white shorts.

And every week, without fail, the studio mail room was flooded with letters from fans wanting to know where they could buy those ultraglamorous Hollywood fashions for themselves.

To Sophie's delight and Alex's surprise, Alex was nominated for a coveted Emmy for television costuming. As she dressed for the awards program, Alex said a silent prayer of thanks to whatever fickle fates or gods had led Sophie to Debord's salon that long-ago day.

Television might not be couture. But from the cold dead ashes of that lost dream, like a legendary phoenix, another had risen. One Alex had already determined was a lot more fun.

While Alex sat with her nerves in a tangle amid so many of Tinseltown's glitterati—albeit in the back of the auditorium with the rest of the technical nominees—Eleanor Lord was in the den of her Santa Barbara home, watching the live television broadcast with Clara Kowalski.

Although Clara had yet to contact the nanny, or anyone else on the other side for that matter, Eleanor enjoyed her company and refused to give up hope that someday they would learn the truth about her granddaughter's disappearance.

But tonight Eleanor's mind was not focused on Anna. It was centered, as was so often the case, on business. She never missed an Emmy or Oscar presentation; inevitably, knockoffs of the actresses' evening dresses would begin appearing in the stores almost as soon as the broadcast was over. And Eleanor knew from past experience that customers from Seattle to Miami would expect to find them in their local Lord's.

"Damn," she muttered as Jane Curtin received the Emmy for lead actress in a comedy.

"I like 'Kate and Allie,'" Clara offered.

"It's a nice enough program. And the woman's a fine actress," Eleanor agreed. "But she isn't exactly a fashion celebrity. This isn't going to help sales at all."

Her irritation increased as the awards show progressed. This was definitely turning out not to be a year for glamour, she thought dejectedly, when Tyne Daly won an award for her role as detective in the popular "Cagney and Lacey."

It was during the costume category that Eleanor perked up. On a personal level, she and Clara never missed an episode of "Blue Bayou"; as a retailing executive, she was hoping the dazzling costuming worn on the show would encourage designers to instill more glamour into their distressingly predictable ready-to-wear lines. Anything to bring more women into the stores.

"Clara!" Eleanor pressed her hand against her heart, which had trebled its beat as she watched the young woman going up on stage to accept her award. "Look!"

"Isn't that the most gorgeous dress you've ever seen!" Clara agreed enthusiastically, taking in the gown that was even more special and exciting than the evening's festivities. The fire-engine-red silk mousseline, adorned with several trompe l'oeil necklaces of glittering Austrian crystal beads, fell in a long fluid column to the floor.

"Not the dress!" Eleanor snapped, earning a surprised and injured look from her friend. "The girl, dammit! Look at that girl!"

"She's lovely. And slender enough to get away with such a figure-revealing dress. I wonder if she's wearing anything underneath it," Clara mused. "I can't see any panty lines."

"The hell with panty lines," Eleanor said impatiently. "It's her, Clara. It's my Anna!"

"It can't be!"

"Look at the portrait," Eleanor insisted. "Alexandra Lyons could be me at her age." Clara's gaze went from Eleanor to the television, to the portrait above the fireplace of Eleanor, painted as a young bride, then back to Eleanor. "Perhaps there's a resemblance," she conceded. "But—"

"It's Anna! I know it is." Eleanor picked up the desk phone and dialed the familiar Los Angeles number.

"Do you have the television on?" she demanded, dispensing with any polite greeting when the male voice answered.

"Not at the moment," Zach said. "Miranda's in town, and she's throwing a dinner party for a bunch of Los Angeles anglophiles and expatriated British nobility who claim to be 'languishing away' in lotusland. Why?"

"Because I've seen Anna."

He sighed. "On TV?" Zach half expected to hear Eleanor claim that her missing granddaughter had just popped up as a guest star on "St. Elsewhere."

"On the Emmy broadcast. She just won an award. She's going by the name Alexandra Lyons."

The name rang an instantaneous and painful bell. Hardly a day went by that Zach didn't find himself thinking about Alex with regret. "You're kidding."

"You know I would never kid about a thing like this." Anna's image had faded from the screen, replaced by a car commercial. "It's her, Zachary!"

"Eleanor," Zach said patiently, "that's impossible. I met Alexandra Lyons in New Orleans."

"You never told me that."

"There was nothing to tell." That wasn't true, but his feelings for Alex were no one's business but his own.

"It's her, Zachary," Eleanor repeated stubbornly.

"I'll tell you what," he suggested, "if you promise to calm down, I'll look into it first thing in the morning."

"I want you to check it out now."

"Short of going downtown and crashing the awards ceremony, which will be over by the time I arrive, there isn't a helluva lot I can do tonight," he pointed out reasonably. "But I promise to call the studio as soon as the switchboard opens in the morning. All right?"

"No, it's not all right. But I suppose it'll have to do," Eleanor grumbled.

After reassuring her yet again, Zach hung up, wondering as he did so if Eleanor's obsession would ever fade. After placing a call to Averill and asking the doctor to run by the house and check on the elderly woman, Zach returned to the gilt-trimmed and mirrored dining room, wishing for a party featuring a steaming pot of spicy crayfish, some equally spicy zydeco music and a sweet-smelling, sexy strawberry-blonde to hold in his arms.

All night long.

Two weeks later, Zach was in Santa Barbara, sipping a Scotch as Eleanor read the portfolio the private detective had compiled.

"Alex Lyons was born in Raleigh, North Carolina," he revealed. "Her mother's name was Irene Lyons. Her father was listed as 'unknown' on her birth certificate. It was, by the way, a double birth. She had a fraternal twin brother. David Lyons died in his teens. A drunk driver hit his car late one night."

"How tragic."

"Isn't it?" Zach remembered the pain on Alex's face when she'd told him about her twin's death. "The brother is the key. Even if Irene Lyons was in on

Anna's kidnapping, she couldn't have pulled a boy child the same age out of the air."

Eleanor waved his words away. "Perhaps she already had a son of her own. Perhaps she always wanted a daughter, so she took my Anna."

Zach bit back his frustration and struggled for patience. "The birth certificates for both children list them as twins."

"Birth certificates can be forged."

Zach's jaw tightened as he recalled the debacle with the blackjack dealer. It was happening all over again. "True. But there's no reason to believe these were. Or that she's Anna."

"There's one way to find out for sure."

"You're not going to tell her what you suspect?"

"No. Believe it or not, Zachary, even this old dog can learn a few new tricks. I'm not going to tip my hand. At least not yet."

Zach's relief was short-lived.

"You know," Eleanor mused aloud, "it's been a long time since I had a party."

"I suppose Alexandra Lyons's name is at the top of the invitation list."

Eleanor smiled for the first time since Zach had arrived with the dossier. "Of course."

As he left the estate, though he knew it was wrong, Zach found himself looking forward to seeing Alexandra Lyons again. Oh, there was no way he believed she would ultimately prove to be Anna Lord. But perhaps, he told himself during the drive back to L.A., now that fate was about to throw them together again, he'd discover that his usually faultless memory had merely exaggerated Alexandra's charms.

Perhaps she was nothing more than a romantic, moonlit bayou fantasy.

The hell she was.

"I don't understand you," Sophie complained. "Eleanor Lord is one of the most influential people in the state. Hell, probably the entire country. To be invited to one of her soirees is a coup."

"I know that," Alex mumbled, running her fingernail along the gilt edge of the invitation.

"And it's for a good cause."

"I know that, too." But couldn't she just skip the fundraising party and write out a generous check to the Save the Beaches Foundation?

"So what's the problem?"

Even as Alex continued to vacillate over the next two days, she knew that the real reason for her indecision could be spelled out in two words: Zachary Deveraux. She wanted to see him again, if for no other reason than to prove to herself that the chemistry she remembered was nothing more than the product of a dazzling, crazy Mardi Gras night and a steamy, mystical bayou day.

But another part of her was afraid of what would happen if she did attend the party and discovered that the emotional bond they shared during those long hours together turned out to be real.

It had taken her a long time to expunge Zach from her mind; sometimes entire days went by when she managed not to think of him, yet all she'd have to do was drive past a Lord's store and all those bittersweet memories would come flooding back.

As for the long, lonely nighttime hours, although

she'd throw herself off the top of the "Blue Bayou" billboard towering over Sunset Strip before admitting it, the truth was that Zachary Deveraux continued to play a starring role in far too many of her erotic dreams.

Reminding herself that her mother had brought her up to take risks, after several sleepless nights and anxiety-filled days, during which Sophie nagged incessantly, Alex finally decided to accept Eleanor Lord's invitation.

Uncharacteristically, she dithered over her dress for days, trying on and discarding everything in her closet before moving on to the show's wardrobe department. Claiming it heightened the program's visibility, Sophie enouraged the "Blue Bayou" cast to borrow clothing for personal appearances. She'd made the same offer to Alex, who'd never seriously considered doing so until now.

But even these glamorous gowns weren't quite right. Because Alex wanted something new. Something that was all hers. Something that would knock Zachary Deveraux's socks off.

She stayed up for three nights, draping and stitching, ripping and restitching. The night of the party, as she ran her bath, she tossed in colorful crystals and scented oil from Victoria's Secret into the hot water with the careless abandonment of a teenager preparing for the senior prom.

Which was exactly how she felt, Alex admitted, as she soaked in the perfumed water, sipping a glass of preparty champagne to soothe her tangled nerves.

Chapter Fifteen

Rather than make her guests drive up the coast to her Santa Barbara estate, Eleanor had booked the swank Rex Il Ristorante for the evening. The building, which had once housed the city's most elegant haberdasher, clothier to the Duke of Windsor and the Shah of Iran, among others, had been turned into a lushly romantic place—a tribute to Hollywood in its heyday.

Swathed in soft hues of peach, plum and mauve, the main dining room resembled the grand salon of a luxury liner. Art Deco chairs and cozy love seats were not merely furniture, but curvaceous, sensual pink shells and calla lilies; glass tables appeared to float on crystal bases.

Despite the lingering nervousness she felt from the moment she walked through the etched Lalique doors, Alex was absolutely enchanted.

She'd no sooner entered the room when she was greeted by her hostess. "My dear," Eleanor Lord said, taking both Alex's hands in her beringed ones, "don't you look absolutely stunning!" Her gaze swept approvingly over the short scarlet sarong. Alex had spent hours sewing glittering gold beads onto the strapless bodice. "I assume this marvelous gown is your own design."

"It is," Alex said with a smile.

"With such talent, it's no wonder you won an Emmy. You've no idea how pleased I am you could make our little party."

Although the elderly woman's smile was warm and inviting, there was something about the way Eleanor was looking at her—deep and hard—that made Alex vaguely uneasy.

"I'm honored to be invited."

"It's we who should be honored," Eleanor corrected absently. Her gaze was riveted on Alex's face. "It's not often we're in the company of artistic genius."

Alex laughed at that and managed to relax. Just a little. "That's definitely an exaggeration, but I was taught at a very early age that a proper guest never argues with her hostess."

"That's absolutely right," Eleanor agreed. Something indiscernible flashed in her eyes, something that came and went so quickly Alex nearly missed it. "It sounds as if your mother paid more attention to Emily Post than Dr. Spock." Her voice went up a little on the end, turning the observation into a question, but before Alex could respond, a tall, distinguished, silver-haired man in black tie approached.

"Eleanor, don't tell me you're going to keep this lovely creature to yourself all evening," he complained. "Not when everyone's dying to meet Hollywood's newest celebrity."

The moment for private conversation had passed.

Alex was introduced to a dizzying number of people, most of whom she'd watched on television and movie screens for years.

All the time she remained devastatingly aware of Zach, looking resplendent and too handsome for comfort in black tie. Having practiced her polite, casual greeting all afternoon, she waited for him to approach. An hour later, she was still waiting.

Finally, feeling a need for solitude, Alex climbed the stairway to the circular mezzanine promenade, where intimately arranged conversation areas allowed for private *tête-à-têtes*.

Settling into a comfortable, mauve-and-pink suede seashell, she watched the dancers glide across the black marble floor and found herself picturing a billowy, white tulle dance dress, shimmering with crystal beadwork, the type of dress Ginger Rogers might have worn. The type of dress that would be perfect for the oil man's wife to wear in the season's end cliff-hanger charity ball scene.

"Makes you wish you'd been around for the days of the Coconut Grove and the Copacabana, doesn't it?" an all too familiar voice murmured. Lost in her creative muse, Alex hadn't heard Zach come up beside her.

The deep sound strummed a hundred, a thousand, hidden chords in Alex. Feeling the color rise in her cheeks, she looked up into the ruggedly handsome face she'd tried so hard to forget.

She had to force herself to remember how to breathe. *Inhale.* "I half expect to see Rita Hayworth dancing cheek to cheek with the Ali Khan," she admitted. *Exhale.*

Oh, God. It was happening all over again. What

made her think she could ever forget this man? And the dizzy, terrifying, wonderful way he could make her feel.

"While he whispers sweet nothings in her shell pink ear," Zach said, reminding them both of a time when he'd held her in his arms and told her again and again how beautiful she was. How sweet. How exquisitely unique. He casually flicked a finger at her dangling gold earring. "Hello."

"Hi." *Stop that!* Alex instructed her lips, which had curved into a foolish, adoring teenager's smile. *Inhale.*

"Congratulations on your Emmy."

"Thank you." *Exhale.*

"I'm no expert on women's fashions, but according to my mother, who never misses an episode of 'Blue Bayou,' you were a shoo-in to win."

At the mention of Eve, Alex's smile turned warm and genuine. "How is she?"

"Wonderful." He sat down across from her, close enough that their knees were almost touching. "I visited last month, and she's still glowing like a new bride. I think it must be love."

Alex's soft answering laugh made Zach realize exactly how long it had been since he'd heard that rich, vibrating sound. And how much he'd mourned its absence. "That's sweet," she said.

"I think so, too. She's wild about that dress you made for her, by the way. It was a very nice thing to do."

"I had such a marvelous time at her wedding, I wanted to find some way to repay her." Alex couldn't believe she'd actually brought up that magic, romantic night. *Stupid, stupid, stupid!*

Zach had spent the past hour nursing a single drink

while he made polite small talk. Sipping and smiling and chatting, all the time watching Alex. And now, as she crossed her legs, clad in shimmering stockings that reminded him of stardust, he had an urge to whisk her out of there and take her for a midnight stroll on the beach. Just the two of them. Alone, with only the full, benevolent moon and sparkling stars to keep them company.

"It was a good time, wasn't it?"

Not wanting to lie, but unwilling to admit it had been the best time of her life, Alex lowered her gaze so he wouldn't see the dangerous yearnings that had leapt into her heart.

She was wearing her hair the same way she'd worn it for the Emmy broadcast, piled high atop her head in wild, sexy disarray and looking as if it might tumble down over her bare shoulders with the slightest provocation. She'd precariously secured the bright concoction with a trio of jeweled combs. Zach had a perverse urge to pluck those combs loose so he could watch the gilt waves cascade free.

He reached out and brushed away an errant curl that had escaped to tumble down her cheek. At the feathery feel of his fingertip against her skin, Alex's mind emptied.

"I'm glad you came," Zach said.

"I almost didn't."

Another silence settled. They exchanged a long look rife with sensual temptations. Alex felt as if she were standing on a precipice and it would take only the slightest nudge to send her toppling over the edge.

Dragging her gaze from his, Alex glanced around

with a casualness she was a long way from feeling. "Where's your wife?"

The question spoke volumes. Zach wondered if Alex actually thought he was coming on to her because Miranda was out of the country.

That wasn't the case, even though he admittedly wasn't as upstanding a husband as he'd been when he'd first met Alex. A few months after Mardi Gras, in a futile attempt to convince himself that what he'd felt for Alexandra Lyons could be felt for any intelligent, beautiful woman, he'd entered into a discreet, noncompromising, brief and emotionless affair with a local and very married television anchorwoman, which had left him feeling guilty and even lonelier than before.

"We need to talk."

"I don't think that's a very good idea." Remembering where they were, and who they were, she glanced around to make certain no one was standing within hearing distance. "I'm sorry, Zach. But I'm not into sneaking around."

"Dammit, I'm not asking you to—"

"I know." She put her hand on his arm and felt the muscle tense. "You want to talk. But we both know it wouldn't stop at that, and eventually, although we wouldn't mean to, we'd end up hurting everyone."

Did she think he wasn't hurting now? Hell, just being close to her without being able to touch her, to kiss her, was ripping his heart to ribbons. He was surprised that the mauve carpeting wasn't soaked red with his blood.

"Do you have any idea," he said roughly, "how much I've missed you?" The hell with protecting his male ego.

"Yes. Because not a day has gone by since New Orleans that I haven't wondered if I did the right thing walking away from you."

On the table in front of them a crystal Art Deco vase held a single pink rose. Unreasonably nervous, Alex began plucking unconsciously at the velvety petals. "But I know that I did. Because it's obvious that your relationship with Miranda—" there, she'd said her rival's name without choking "—is important enough to keep you in your marriage."

"Dammit, Alexandra, you don't understand."

"That's where you're wrong, Zach," she said softly. "I understand only too well."

The fact, as much as she wished otherwise, was that Zach was married. That was all she needed to know. End of story.

At least it should have been. But although she'd tried her best to avoid thinking about Zach, tried to convince herself that he'd been nothing more than a Mardi Gras fling, she now realized that their time together in New Orleans had left behind some smoldering embers that only needed the slightest breath of air, the most fleeting touch of a match, to ignite.

Miranda arrived late at the gala party. The first thing she did when she entered the room was grab a flute of Mumm champagne from a passing tray. Sipping the bubbly liquid, she began idly looking around the room, trying to locate her aunt's newest folly.

She spotted the interloper talking to, of all people, Zachary. And from the look on his face, Miranda realized that Eleanor wasn't the only one intrigued with Alexandra Lyons.

She tossed down the champagne, following it with

two more in rapid succession. Then, fortified for battle, she crossed the room with long, purposeful strides.

"Darling!" she gushed, ignoring Alex completely as she captured Zach's face between her palms and gave him a long, inappropriately intimate, openmouthed kiss.

"I would have been here sooner," she said when they finally came up for air. "But my plane was stacked up for hours over LAX. I barely had time to throw on a decent dress and redo my face."

"You look lovely as always," Zach said on cue, wiping the scarlet lipstick from his mouth with his handkerchief.

He recognized the long, sinuous, skintight black gown as being from Yves Debord's latest collection. Even with her generous discount, the evening dress had been outrageously expensive. Although she'd assured him that the design was the very height of fashion, Zach thought the dress, with its layers of jet sequins, made Miranda resemble a snake. Or an eel.

"And you always say the right thing. I suppose that's only one of the reasons I adore you so." She gave him another wet kiss that stained his cheek and made Zach wonder what the hell his wife was up to now. He couldn't remember the last time Miranda had shown him even a scintilla of affection.

As if noticing Zach's companion for the first time, Miranda cast wide, expectant, green eyes Alex's way. "Zachary, darling," she cooed, "you're forgetting your manners. Aren't you going to introduce me to your friend?"

Of course, Zach realized. Miranda was staking her claim, on the Lord's empire, as well as on her husband. He could practically feel *No Trespassing* being stamped on his chest.

"Miranda, Alexandra Lyons. Alexandra, this is Miranda." There was a brief, all too noticeable pause. "My wife."

"Not *the* Alexandra Lyons!" Miranda looked at Alex as if admiring a newly cut precious stone. "The Emmy-winning costume designer the entire city is abuzz about?"

Miranda's photographs, which had graced the glossy pages of last month's *Town and Country,* had not begun to do her justice. Her blond hair swung in sleek, polished wings; there was an innate superiority in the way she dressed, the way she moved, the absolute perfection of face and figure. Zach's wife was a dazzling blend of glacial beauty and smoldering sexuality.

Alex hated her on sight.

"I'm not sure the entire city is abuzz," she said mildly, steadfastly ignoring the apologetic look Zach was trying to send her way. "But yes, I did just win an Emmy."

"I knew it!" Miranda clapped her hands. A diamond the size of the Taj Mahal glittered coldly on the ring finger of her left hand. "Of course I'm much too busy to watch the telly, but my dear Aunt Eleanor would never miss an episode of your little show. I do believe she's hooked," Miranda confided in a conspiratorial tone.

"Along with much of the television-viewing world," Zach broke in, determined to somehow spare Alex his wife's whip of a tongue. Although their marriage bed had become as arid as the Sahara, for some reason he could not understand, Miranda was an insanely jealous woman.

OFFICIAL OPINION POLL

Dear Reader,

Since you are a book enthusiast, we would like to know what you think.

Inside you will find a short Opinion Poll. Please participate in our poll by sharing your opinion on 3 subjects that are very important to all of us.

To thank you for your participation, we would like to send you **2 FREE BOOKS** and **2 FREE GIFTS!**

Please enjoy them with our compliments.

Sincerely,

Pam Powers

YOUR OPINION POLL
THANK-YOU FREE GIFTS INCLUDE:

▶ **2 ROMANCE BOOKS**

▶ **2 LOVELY SURPRISE GIFTS**

OFFICIAL OPINION POLL

YOUR OPINION COUNTS!
Please check TRUE or FALSE below to express your opinion about the following statements:

Q1 Do you believe in "true love"?

"TRUE LOVE HAPPENS ONLY ONCE IN A LIFETIME."
○ TRUE
○ FALSE

Q2 Do you think marriage has any value in today's world?

"YOU CAN BE TOTALLY COMMITTED TO SOMEONE WITHOUT BEING MARRIED."
○ TRUE
○ FALSE

Q3 What kind of books do you enjoy?

"A GREAT NOVEL MUST HAVE A HAPPY ENDING."
○ TRUE
○ FALSE

YES! I have placed my sticker in the space provided below. Please send me the **2 FREE books** and **2 FREE gifts** for which I qualify. I understand that I am under no obligation to purchase anything further, as explained on the back of this card.

194/394 MDL FV45

FIRST NAME	LAST NAME

ADDRESS

APT.#	CITY

STATE/PROV.	ZIP/POSTAL CODE

⊕ HARLEQUIN® READER SERVICE—Here's How It Works:

Accepting your 2 free books and 2 free gifts (gifts valued at approximately $10.00) places you under no obligation to buy anything. You may keep the books and gifts and return the shipping statement marked "cancel." If you do not cancel, about a month later we'll send you 4 additional books and bill you just $5.99 each in the U.S. or $6.49 each in Canada. That is a savings of at least 25% off the cover price. It's quite a bargain! Shipping and handling is just 50¢ per book in the U.S. and 75¢ per book in Canada.* You may cancel at any time, but if you choose to continue, every month we'll send you 4 more books, which you may either purchase at the discount price or return to us and cancel your subscription.

*Terms and prices subject to change without notice. Prices do not include applicable taxes. Sales tax applicable in N.Y. Canadian residents will be charged applicable taxes. Offer not valid in Quebec. Books received may not be as shown. All orders subject to credit approval. Credit or debit balances in a customer's account(s) may be offset by any other outstanding balance owed by or to the customer. Please allow 4 to 6 weeks for delivery. Offer available while quantities last.

Woe to the female who was caught talking to him alone, double woe to the woman who dared to smile at him, even in passing. And woe, woe, triple woe to the poor unsuspecting female who might display even the faintest interest in Miranda Lord Baptista Smythe Deveraux's latest husband.

As she returned Miranda's predator smile with a bland, polite one of her own, Alex found herself grateful for the woman's interruption.

She could not—would not!—let herself fall in love with Zach. No way. Absolutely not. Only fools fell in love with married men, Alex reminded herself. Fools or women with strong suicidal streaks.

"Well, it's certainly been wonderful meeting both of you," she said. All right, so it was a lie. But only a little white one. Besides, from the dangerous, possessive glint in Miranda's gem-bright eyes, Alex knew better than to admit she and Zach had met before. "But I'm afraid I must be going."

"Oh?" Miranda's glossy lips formed into a perfect, pouty *O* of regret. "So soon? We've barely had time to get acquainted."

"I'm sorry. But we're taping early tomorrow morning."

"I'll walk you out," Zach said. As he'd feared, his casual remark drew a dark, fatal glance from his wife.

Lord, if looks could kill, Alex thought, Zachary Deveraux would be six feet under. "Thank you," she said, declining his offer firmly, "but that really isn't necessary."

Alex prided herself on getting through the obligatory parting conversation with Eleanor Lord, making her way back downstairs and remembering to tip the liveried parking valet.

It was only when she was all alone in the privacy of the new red Porsche that Friedman Television Productions had leased for her as a reward for winning the Emmy, driving through the darkened Los Angeles streets back to Venice, that Alex finally allowed herself to weep.

Chapter Sixteen

Lord's executive offices were located in Century City, built on land that had once been 20th Century Fox's back lot and had housed Sunnybrook Farm, Peyton Place and Boot Hill. Before that, the valuable Los Angeles real estate had been cowboy star Tom Mix's ranch.

The day after the party, Zach sat in his office in one of the two towers, which had so altered the Los Angeles skyline, going over the monthly sales figures with Eleanor.

He found it difficult to keep his mind on the report. Because he knew that just across the way, in the vast network entertainment center on the other side of the sculpture garden, "Blue Bayou" was taping.

The memory of those stolen, magical hours with Alex in Louisiana flickered seductively through his mind, teasing him with sensual memories and erotic wishes.

"What about the Texas Fashion House acquisition?" Eleanor asked, leafing through the thick sheaf of papers.

Since opportunities for new stores nationwide were limited, expansion-minded chains like Lord's were forced to seek market share by acquiring existing stores in other cities. Zach was currently negotiating to purchase a small chain of boutiques in San Antonio, Houston and Dallas.

Known throughout the retail industry for sales growth, Lord's was adding floor space at a faster rate than any other chain in the country. Expansion under Zach's leadership had fueled a thirty-three percent sales gain during the past five-year period.

Still, unlike so many of his contemporaries, who were leveraged up to their eyebrows, Zach was a conservative businessman. He slept easily each night knowing that under his leadership, The Lord's Group would survive—indeed, thrive—when the inevitable down cycle did occur.

"They've turned out to be more heavily leveraged than we first thought," he revealed. "However, since our debt-to-capital ratio is down considerably since last quarter, that shouldn't prove a problem."

"Good. Neiman-Marcus is opening a new store in Dallas. I don't want to lose market share there."

"I'll see that we don't." What was Alex doing right now?

Eleanor knew that on a lesser man, such innate confidence would have sounded like arrogance. On Zach it was an understatement. "I have every faith in you, Zachary."

She put the Texas figures aside. "By the way, did you receive my memo about the boutique lighting?"

"About dividing the various departments with neon signs?"

"That's the one. Clara and I went shopping yesterday in the Rodeo Drive store and were met with a distressing phalanx of dress racks."

"Well, it is a dress store," Zach said. Was Alex standing at a window in that twin tower, perhaps, looking out across the complex, thinking of him and wondering if he was thinking of her?

"True. But the store seemed boring."

"I believe the term you and the decorator agreed on last year during all those months of planning the remodeling was 'sophisticated and timeless,'" Zach reminded her.

"I liked the plans on paper," Eleanor conceded grumpily. "But in reality, there's just no *pow*. We need to liven things up."

"Don't tell me you want to hire perfume terrorists like they have at some stores."

During his last trip to Manhattan, on the way to a first-floor escalator in a major department store, he'd gotten attacked by a frighteningly aggressive young woman who'd leapt out from behind a counter and sprayed Polo cologne on him. Zach had spent the rest of the afternoon yearning for a shower.

"Nothing that drastic," she assured him. "But these are exciting, fast-moving times, Zach. And our stores should reflect that. The minute a customer enters Lord's, she should experience a sensual overload that gives her an immediate sense of something going on. A happening."

"I think happenings went out with the sixties."

"Don't be difficult. You know what I mean. Neon is bright and lively, and I think we ought to implement it in the Rodeo Drive store. If it works the way I think it will, we can take it nationwide."

"I'll get work started on the designs." He'd learned not to argue with Eleanor's innate sense of marketing.

"Good. While you're at it, have the design staff add some spotlights to brighten up our more special merchandise, as if they were on stage. Center stage."

"Spotlights," he murmured, jotting it down, along with a note to have the construction department ensure there would be enough capacity for the increased electrical demand. One thing they didn't need was another fire.

They were momentarily interrupted by his secretary, who arrived with the latest sales figures. Last quarter Zach had installed a much envied management information and control system that provided hourly updates on sales and inventory in every department of every store in the country.

Such a state-of-the-art computer system allowed Lord's buyers to recognize both the dogs and the hot sellers quickly. It also revealed regional trends; what sold well in Dallas or Los Angeles didn't necessarily work in Peoria or Buffalo.

He gave a copy of the report to Eleanor, keeping one for himself. "Debord's sales are still slipping," he pointed out unnecessarily.

"I know." Eleanor's lips drew down in a frown. It was not often she made a judgment in error. But when she did she characteristically made a quick correction. "Do you happen to know what it would cost us to buy out the last year of his contract?"

Zach had anticipated that question.

"You're always one step ahead of me," she complained when he answered quickly off the top of his head. In truth, she wanted it no other way. "I don't understand what happened," she mused. "The line we saw in Paris, when we signed him to that contract, was wonderfully energetic. I thought it would leap out of the stores."

"Which it did. First-quarter sales were unprecedented."

"And have been going downhill ever since. Just like his fashions. Oh, well." She shook her bright head. "We'll just pay the man off and be done with it."

"You know," Zach said, "although I'll agree with you that his designs lack something, it isn't completely Debord's fault. All the designer lines, as well as the store brand names in other chains, have experienced slippage this past year."

"I know. I've been giving that some thought and have decided that clothing has become so ubiquitous that we department stores are living our own version of every chic woman's private nightmare. Every store in every mall in every city has the exact same clothes...."

"We need something new. A look that says, Only Available Here."

Zach's attention had wandered again, across the sculpture garden, over the landscaped plaza, to Alex. "I suppose you have something in mind," he murmured absently.

"You know me so well." Eleanor sat back in her chair, crossed her legs and said, "Here's my plan."

Her next words, spoken in that brook-no-argument tone he'd learned to respect, brought Zach back to reality with a resounding crash.

* * *

Alex was sitting on the porch of her rented home in Venice, watching the waves roll relentlessly onto the packed sand. The sun had sliced its way through the smog, splintering the sky with shafts of pure gold. The clarity of the light intensified the landscape, making the water sparkle like crystal beneath the gleaming sapphire sky.

Like so many residents of the City of Angels, Alex knew she was guilty of taking the benevolent weather for granted. It took mornings like this to make one stop and bask in the pure glory of California sunshine.

Unfortunately she was not to be given that luxury today. Because in a few short hours she was scheduled to have lunch with Eleanor Lord. And Zachary Deveraux.

Six days had passed since she'd encountered Zach at Eleanor's fundraising party. Six long days and six equally long and restless nights. In trying to keep up with Sophie's demands that "Blue Bayou" remain the glitziest, most dazzling show on television, along with struggling to live up to her own design reputation, which seemed to be ballooning into the stratosphere since the Emmy, Alex's work required her undivided attention.

So why the hell couldn't she stop thinking about Zach?

Although she'd fought it, he'd infiltrated her thoughts. Which she must not allow! A lifetime of experience had taught her that everything was transitory—here today, gone tomorrow. Homes, schools, work, relationships.

Nothing was forever.

Especially relationships.

With a sigh, she went back into the house. She stood under the shower, head back, allowing the water to sluice over her, willing it to dampen her desire for a man she had no business thinking about.

He was married, for God's sake, she reminded herself firmly as she rubbed herself dry with enough vigor to practically scrape away a layer of skin. And she'd seen enough women badly burned by unhappy experiences with married men to vow that she'd never make that mistake herself. Even if the man in question caused her pulse to jump with a single glance, or her heart to turn somersaults with a mere touch.

The company dining room in the Lord's Century City office complex was, as Alex would have expected, exquisitely decorated. Dove-gray silk walls blended quietly with the soft blue sky outside the tall windows, which wrapped the room in nonstop views.

Rosewood gleamed, glazed pale pewter tile glimmered underfoot. Oriental vases claimed space in arched wall niches, while special-effects lighting illuminated priceless Impressionist paintings.

Although she'd been nervous about this meeting, Alex tried to relax as Eleanor greeted her warmly and congratulated her again on her Emmy, then complimented her work, the dress she'd worn to the party, the outfit she'd chosen to wear today.

Other than greeting her politely, Zach remained silent. But as she exchanged preluncheon small talk with the department store owner, Alex was all too aware of him leaning back in his chair, his nonchalant pose doing nothing to soften his innate power.

The lunch, a fresh Alaska king crab and shrimp

salad topped with raspberry vinaigrette and served by a blue-suited butler, was a superb example of California cuisine. The polite conversation continued over lunch as they discussed the weather, the Lakers and, of course, "Blue Bayou," the plot line of which Alex knew, but could not reveal.

And still Alex had no idea why she'd been invited here today.

The plates were cleared. Finally, after a dessert of pears poached in California champagne, Eleanor said, "I have a proposition for you, Alexandra."

"A proposition?"

"I'd like you to adapt your glamorous television designs for Lord's ready-to-wear market."

The Limoges cup filled with coffee was halfway to her lips. Alex slowly lowered it back to the table. "Like your Lady Lord's line?"

"Not at all," Eleanor corrected quickly. "Actually, I always had my personal doubts about Lady Lord's. The only reason we initiated the line was it seemed like a good idea at the time. After all, everyone else was establishing private-label clothes. But there was a problem we didn't foresee."

"The latest focus-group study revealed customers view private labels as knockoffs," Zach said, entering the conversation. "Which was Eleanor's concern all along," he added, giving credence to his employer's instincts.

"Actually, the report said customers perceive private labels as the kind of frumpy, cheap stuff you'd see on the first floor," Eleanor revealed. "Store brands are, unfortunately, viewed as the bottom of the line. Which is definitely not where we would position your designs.

"We'd insist on exclusivity, of course. But we are willing to pay for that privilege." The figure she suggested was higher than the deal Debord had reportedly cut with the chain. "And, naturally, we would work out a generous commission schedule," Eleanor tacked on matter-of-factly.

Alex was, quite literally, stunned. The idea was intriguing, the money being offered staggering. But the deal also came with a definite downside. And that was that if she agreed, she would undoubtedly be forced into frequent contact with the very man she'd vowed to stay away from.

That brought up another even more unpalatable thought. What if this had been all Zach's idea? What if he was willing to spend Lord's money to force her into an intimate relationship?

Eleanor misunderstood Alex's hesitation. "I realize that couture gets all the headlines. But perhaps you've heard of something Prince Matchabelli once said: 'When customers come to you in Rolls-Royces, you go home on the subway—"

"When customers come to you on the subway, you go home in a Rolls-Royce," Alex filled in the rest of the quote. She shot Zach a sharp look, earning only a bland one in return.

"Exactly." Eleanor smiled her approval. "Besides," she said, "you wouldn't be designing clothing for Kmart, Alexandra. Lord's is decidedly upscale. And as I was telling Zach just the other day, with all the department store chains now carrying the same designers, fashion has grown boring.

"It will give Lord's extra clout to have its own line.

You've a remarkable gift, Alexandra, dear. Together we could bring that gift to women all across America."

"How would it be displayed?" Alex asked, intrigued in spite of herself.

"Oh, I'm so glad you asked that question."

Eleanor reached into the leather-bound portfolio on the chair beside her and pulled out a series of sketches, which she handed across the table to Alex. "I took the liberty of commissioning these specifically for this meeting."

Alex stared in wonder at the dazzling artist's renderings of an in-store boutique featuring the Alexandra Lyons Blue Bayou collection. Exclusively at Lord's.

The drawings were incredibly detailed, making Alex wonder if Eleanor always worked at such warp speed. She glanced at Zach, who merely shrugged, revealing his own surprise with the artwork.

"I've always wanted to have my name up in lights," Alex murmured, half in truth, half in jest.

"Blue neon," Eleanor agreed robustly. "And now I think it's time to relinquish the floor to Lord's brilliant president."

Zach pushed himself to his feet, trying, as he had been for the past hour, to keep focused on the conversation at hand. Ever since Alex had arrived, bright and brazen in a red blazer and sinfully short, pleated white skirt that made her look like a nubile cheerleader, he'd been fighting a losing battle to keep his mind on work.

"'Blue Bayou' is the number-one show in the world," he said, telling Alex nothing she didn't already know. "Our research shows that an extraordinary number of women want an opportunity to wear your glamorous

Hollywood fashions. And men want to buy the intimate apparel for their wives or lovers."

"The studio does receive a lot of mail from fans," Alex agreed. She wondered if Zach's research had also revealed the transvestites and professional female impersonators who'd professed a desire to own the sexy fashions.

He pulled out a stack of colorful computer-generated charts depicting wholesale and retail costs of producing the line, the estimated potential sales, profit, loss, her share, until her head was whirling with numbers, which made it even more difficult to keep her mind on business.

Because try as she might, and as irritated as she was at him, as Alex watched Zach pointing out the various statistics, she kept focusing on his strong dark hands rather than the numbers depicted, remembering with vivid, painful detail how they had been capable of creating such warmth. Such pleasure. Such deep and aching need.

"I'm overwhelmed," she said quietly.

Eleanor would've had to be deaf to miss the hesitation in Alex's tone. "But?" she coaxed.

"I'm not certain my contract allows me to enter into outside agreements."

"Your contract with Friedman Television Production Company gives you sole ownership of your designs," Zach assured her. "There's no conflict."

Alex was not surprised that Zach would know the details of her two-page contract with Sophie. He would not have invited her to this business meeting *without* knowing.

"I'm sure your producer would enjoy the additional promotion for her program," Eleanor said.

Alex knew she was being offered a once-in-a-lifetime opportunity. She wanted the chance so badly she could taste it. But she was worried about her unruly feelings for Zachary, and angry that he'd manipulated her into this uncomfortable situation in the first place.

"I'd like to give you a decision, but my horoscope said I shouldn't enter into any business agreements until Jupiter aligns with Mars."

"When will that be?" Impatience surrounded Eleanor like a shimmering life force.

"I don't know," Alex said, regretting the flippant answer the moment it left her lips. "I'm sorry, I was just kidding. I never read my horoscope." Actually she did. But she only chose to believe the positive messages. "But I would like a few days to think it over."

"How many days?" Eleanor's earlier restraint began to slip.

Zach put a calming hand on the older woman's arm. "Take all the time you need," he told Alex.

After promising Eleanor that she would make her decision within the next few days, Alex left the suite of offices, relieved when Zach allowed her to walk away without a word.

She was in the parking garage, congratulating herself on escaping without incident, when he caught up with her.

"Go away." Alex marched toward her Porsche, her heels clattering on the concrete floor.

"You're angry at me," he diagnosed.

She spun around, her color rising. "You're damn right I am!"

Zach wasn't all that bothered by her flare of temper. An angry woman was not an indifferent one. Although he would have preferred some other response—such as her throwing herself into his arms—at this point he was willing to take whatever he could get.

"I hadn't realized you'd consider the chance to have your name become a household word an insult."

"It's not the offer. It's the way you manipulated things just to throw us together again that I'm furious about."

He rocked back on his heels and regarded her, his eyes shuttered. "I'm not in the habit of manipulating women into my bed. Nor have I ever paid for a woman's favors. The offer is only for your work, Alex. Not your body."

"Are you saying this wasn't your idea?"

"Actually, I argued against it."

That statement, calmly spoken and so obviously the truth, took some of the wind out of her sails. "Don't you like my work?"

"Why do I get the feeling I'm in a no-win conversation?" Alex could hear the dry humor in his voice.

"Beats me," she retorted, refusing to let him see he'd hurt her feelings. When she turned to walk away, he caught hold of her hand.

"Alex." It was just her name. But uttered with such depth of emotion it had the power to stop her in her tracks.

She shook her head. "I have to go."

"I know." He stroked the back of her hand, leaving an unsettling trail of heat in its path.

Their gazes met and held. And Alex felt a strange little jolt in her heart.

"I'm sorry you thought I was trying to manipulate you."

She shrugged and tried to look away. But she couldn't. "I shouldn't have jumped to conclusions."

"Would it make you feel any better if I told you I'm very impressed with your talent? And that if you were any other designer, any other woman, I would have been beating your door down trying to get your signature on the dotted line?"

They were standing a discreet distance apart, linked by eyes and hands. "It should," she admitted quietly.

"But it doesn't." They were courting disaster. Even knowing that, Zach could not let go of her hand.

"I really ought to leave."

"Not yet." He drew her closer.

"We can't do this," she insisted shakily. It was only a whisper, but easily heard in the cavernous stillness of subterranean garage.

"You know that." He lifted her hand to his lips. "And I know that."

He observed her solemnly, almost sadly, over the top of their linked hands. "So do you want to tell me why the idea feels so right?"

There were reasons. Alex knew there had to be reasons—hundreds of them, thousands, millions of logical, sensible reasons. But heaven help her, with his lips burning her hand and his eyes looking so deeply into hers, as if he could see all the way to her soul, she couldn't think of a single one. "Zach—"

"I love the way you say my name." The thumb of his free hand brushed against her lips, his touch as light as goose down. "Say it again."

"I can't." She pulled her hand away and was appalled

to realize she was trembling. Her mind was turning cartwheels; it was a struggle to think straight.

"I have a picture of you. Of us."

"You do?" She had her own pictures, of course. Hundreds of them. Wonderful, romantic, sexy portraits, all in her mind, popping up at the most inopportune times to torment her.

"It's a snapshot taken by one of my brothers-in-law at the wedding. I keep it in my wallet." When she backed away, running up against the driver's door of the red Porsche, Zach moved toward her, closing the distance once more between them.

"We're dancing." He stroked her hair. "There's not a day that goes by that I don't take it out and look at it and think of how right you look, how right you felt, in my arms."

Alex longed for Zach's touch. His kiss. She ached for him. What she craved was wrong, forbidden, and a mortal sin in probably every major religion of the world.

She knew that. But she couldn't help herself.

The need to touch him was overpowering. Just an innocent touch. What could it hurt?

She lifted her hand to his cheek. "I think about you, too. Far too often," she admitted softly. To herself she admitted there was nothing innocent about what was happening here.

"Ah, Alex." He closed his eyes, as if the touch of her fingertips was just the balm he needed. "Do you have any idea—"

"Yes." She pressed her fingertips against his lips, cutting off the words. It was as if once he said the words out loud, once he told her how much he wanted to make love with her, she would be helpless to prevent it. "I do."

She bit her lip and wished her mother had not brought her up to feel responsible for the consequences of her own behavior. "But we can't."

"I know." Zach cursed softly. "And that's what makes this all so damn hard." He took in a deep, shuddering breath. "But I promise not to let my personal feelings stand in the way of your future.

"Eleanor's right. You're extremely talented, and the Blue Bayou collection would be a boon for our bottom line. We need you, Alex. And I think at this point in your career, you could use us, too."

"Of course I could." The opportunity would establish her as a top name in design. Like Cher's sexy television costuming did for Bob Mackie in the seventies. "But do you really think you could keep things on a business level?" she asked doubtfully. If her own feelings were anything to go by, they were sunk.

"I'll do my damnedest."

It was, she allowed, all she could ask for. If she was absolutely honest, she would have to admit it wasn't really what she wanted.

What she wanted, she realized with little surprise, was for Zach to take matters into his own hands. She wanted him to free her of all responsibility. She wanted him to drag her to the floor—all right, perhaps the back seat of the nearest car—and wildly ravish her until neither one of them could move.

But she knew that wasn't going to happen. When and if she decided to make love with Zachary Deveraux, Alex knew, she'd have to be willing to accept the consequences.

"Tell Eleanor I'll seriously consider her offer."

He studied Alex for one final, painful minute. "I will."

He stepped back, giving her room to open the car door. He stood there, silent and watchful as she fastened her seat belt and put the key in the ignition.

And then he watched her drive away.

Alex lectured herself all the way back to the "Blue Bayou" offices. He's married, she reminded herself.

Unhappily married, an argumentative little voice piped up.

That doesn't matter. Unhappily married is still married.

Everyone knows his wife fools around. Since meeting Zach, Alex had developed an almost unhealthy obsession with jet-set gossip. Especially that concerning Miranda Deveraux.

So, if everyone jumped off the roof, she remembered her mother saying, that wouldn't give you permission to jump off, too.

Lord, when had she become so willing to justify bad behavior?

When she'd fallen in love with a married man.

The bottom line was that Zachary Deveraux was married. And that made him off-limits.

Sophie was, unsurprisingly, ecstatic. "This is absolutely fantastic! The high-profile visibility Eleanor Lord is offering will definitely translate into big bucks at syndication time." Watching Sophie's smile, Alex could practically see the dollar signs dancing in her head.

"Not to mention your designs being sold in every major city in the country. My God, girl, do you know what this means?"

"Of course," Alex murmured. Her sketch pad was covered with lopsided stars, proof of her inability to concentrate these days.

Sophie's hands were splayed on her silk-draped hips. "As long as I've known you, I've never seen you as indecisive as you've been these past couple of weeks. First you didn't want to go to Eleanor Lord's party, and now you're hesitating about working with her. What do you have against the woman?"

"Nothing at all," Alex answered honestly, switching to rectangles.

"It's a very good opportunity, Alex."

"It's a terrific opportunity," Alex agreed.

"So what the hell is the problem?"

"I don't know." Not wanting to discuss anything so personal as her feelings for Zach, even with this woman who was both friend and benefactress, Alex laughed off her indecision.

One week later, still worried she was stepping into quicksand, she picked up the telephone.

"I've made a decision."

Her answer shouldn't mean so damn much, Zach told himself. It shouldn't. But it did.

"I'm glad to hear that," he replied mildly.

How was it that even his voice, coming across the wires, could create that now familiar, enervating flood of desire? What was she doing?

She should hang up. Now! Before she found herself in very hot water. Over her head.

She took a deep breath.

"You can draw up the papers."

Chapter Seventeen

The Irish pub, located in, of all places, Pasadena, would definitely not have been Miranda's first choice for an intimate rendezvous. The single thing the out-of-the-way watering hole had going for it, she decided, was that she did not have to worry about running into anyone she knew.

Or more importantly, anyone who knew Zach.

She was on her second martini when the man she'd been waiting for finally showed up.

"You're late."

Mickey O'Rourke shrugged uncaringly as he waved to a pair of uniformed cops seated nearby. From what she'd already determined during her irritating wait, the Hibernian watering hole was a favorite with the police. "Something came up."

She frowned at him over the rim of the iced glass. When he sat down across the table, she caught the unmistakable scent of cheap drugstore cologne. "If you must meet me reeking of other women, I would prefer you find a bedmate with better taste in perfume."

He grinned unrepentantly. "Don't tell me you're jealous."

"Hardly."

The grin widened, a cocky flash of white in his freckled face. He tilted the wooden chair on its back legs and laced his fingers behind his head. The gesture, which she had no doubt was meant to impress, caused his biceps to swell against the sleeves of his navy blue polo shirt.

"You sure about that?" Lines crinkled outward from his boyish blue eyes.

"Absolutely. I was merely pointing out that I am not paying you two hundred dollars a day—"

"Two hundred dollars a day, plus expenses," he reminded her helpfully.

"Plus expenses," she agreed, "to waste time screwing."

"Could have fooled me." He lowered the chair to all four legs again and leaned across the small wooden table toward Miranda. "My balls still ache from our marathon fuckarama in Bungalow Five of the Beverly Hills Hotel last week."

"Must you be so crude?"

"Don't get up on your high horse with me, sweetheart." He ran his hand up her leg beneath the table. His thick square fingers slipped beneath her emerald silk skirt, exploring the soft skin above her stocking top. "I remember you liking it crude." His fingers tightened. "And hard.

"In fact, how about you and I moving this meeting somewhere else. Somewhere more private."

Mickey O'Rourke was everything Miranda despised. He was uneducated, horridly common and, thanks to an unfortunate habit of playing the ponies at Santa Anita racetrack, he was also, despite his hefty fees, always skating on the brink of poverty.

She had no doubt that while her civilized ancestors had been drinking tea and playing polo, his people had amused themselves by painting their naked bodies blue and leaping out of trees.

He showed her no respect. Not in their business meetings or in bed. But, she allowed, the man was hung like a Brahma bull and could keep it up all night. He also had access to something she wanted. Something that made her willing to hang around places like this waiting for him to show up.

"What have you discovered?"

"I'll give you the rundown in a minute. Soon as I get a drink." He signaled the bartender, calling out an order for something called a Black Marble.

"Okay. The information your husband's private cop came up with checks out," he revealed, proving finally that he could, when required, get down to business. "Alex Lyons was born in Raleigh. She had a twin brother who was killed when he was still a kid. There's no record of any father."

"I already know that," Miranda said on a frustrated huff of breath.

"Yeah, but did you know that the mother seemed to have an incurable case of wanderlust?"

Damn. Miranda wondered if O'Rourke was going to turn out to be a waste of money, after all. "The papers I found in my husband's home safe reveal that the family moved a great deal."

"Every year, like clockwork," he agreed. The waitress delivered his drink to the table. He took a taste and nodded his satisfaction.

"You know, Wambaugh invented this drink," he informed Miranda. "Stolichnaya on the rocks with an orange peel and a black olive."

"It sounds absolutely delightful." Her acid tone said otherwise. "Who is Wambaugh?"

"Joseph Wambaugh. The writer," he elaborated at her blank look. "He used to be a cop. Now he writes books about cops."

"Ah. A kindred spirit." Her voice was tinged with sarcasm, letting him know she was fully aware that he'd been dismissed from the LAPD for various infractions, among them allegations of illegal gambling and citizen complaints of police brutality.

His open Irish face closed up. Storm clouds gathered in his blue eyes, reminding Miranda that despite his seeming Celtic charm, O'Rourke could be a very dangerous man. "Christ, you can be a bitch."

"True enough." She took another sip of her martini. Her green eyes turned as frosty as the Beefeater gin. "But let us not forget that I happen to be a very wealthy bitch. Who has thus far paid you a great deal of money for nothing."

"Not exactly for nothing. What would you say if I told you that the Lyons family happened to move hearth and home each spring?"

"Spring?"

"April to be exact." He leaned back in the chair, took another drink and waited.

It did not take long for comprehension to click in. "That's the anniversary of the murders and kidnapping. It's also the same month Eleanor runs her annual newspaper advertisements seeking information concerning Anna."

"Bingo. Interesting coincidence, isn't it?"

"But not proof."

"True enough. But it's a start."

"Yes." She sipped thoughtfully.

"You know, if this Lyons chick does turn out to be Anna Lord, it wouldn't be that difficult to arrange an accident."

"An accident?" The idea, which she honestly hadn't considered, proved surprisingly appealing. "Surely that would be extremely dangerous."

He shrugged again. His shoulders, thickly muscled from daily workouts at Gold's Gym, strained the shirt seams. "Not really." He lifted his glass in a pantomimed farewell to the cops as they left the pub to return to their black-and-white cruiser parked outside.

"Don't forget," rogue cop Mickey O'Rourke reminded Miranda, "I've got a lot of friends in high places."

Miranda toyed with the green plastic toothpick from her drink as she thought about Eleanor Lord's will leaving the bulk of her vast empire to Anna. She thought about the irritating design deal Eleanor had offered Alexandra Lyons.

Then she thought about the way Zachary had been looking at Alex the night of Eleanor's party. From his intense expression, she'd suspected the pair had not been discussing business.

Whether or not Alex Lyons was, indeed, Anna Lord, Miranda realized that the woman still represented a very real threat.

"Let's cross that unsavory little bridge when we come to it," she advised. "In the meantime, I've something else I want you to do."

Reaching into her handbag, she pulled out a photograph. The candid snapshot of Zach had been taken on Ipanema Beach during their honeymoon. Before that unfortunate little episode in the Mesbla store. He was wearing the brief black European swimsuit she'd had to coax him into. His hair was ruffled by the ocean breezes and he was smiling into the camera lens. That was, Miranda considered, the last time she could recall Zach smiling at her.

"This is a photograph of my husband."

O'Rourke nodded in recognition. "Zachary Deveraux. The department-store honcho."

"Yes. I wish to know every time he and Alexandra Lyons are together."

"You got it." He took the snapshot and slipped it into his shirt pocket. "How much coverage do you want? We can do bugs in both their offices and the broad's home, photo stakeouts, around-the-clock surveillance—"

"I want, as you investigator types put it, the works."

"Gonna be expensive."

"I've always believed one gets what one pays for."

"A lady after my own heart." He tossed back his drink, popped the fat black olive into his mouth and slipped his clever hand beneath the table again. "Is this meeting over?"

A familiar warmth that had nothing to do with the two martinis she'd drunk began to flow through Miranda's bloodstream. "I believe so."

"Good." He snapped her garter. "What would you say to a little afternoon delight?"

She'd been planning a brief trip to Saks. A few days ago, while comparison checking their couture lines, she'd seen a silk Chanel scarf she'd found particularly appealing. Miranda weighed the equally attractive choices; both shoplifting and sex always gave her a rush. Then, remembering that long, lust-filled afternoon at the Beverly Hills Hotel last week, she made her decision.

"It will have to be off the clock." She absolutely refused to pay for what was so readily available for free. "You're good, Mr. O'Rourke. But not that good."

"Why don't you withhold judgment on that?" The rogue grin was back. "Until you've seen what I can do with my handcuffs."

That idea, Miranda admitted privately as they left the pub, had definite possibilities.

Chapter Eighteen

With "Blue Bayou" on hiatus and Eleanor's optimistic and energetic plan to launch the retail line in a mere six months, Alex turned all her attention to creating her retail designs.

She was not working in a vacuum. In order to work with Alex on the design concept—and to observe her closely—Eleanor began to spend more and more time in Los Angeles, staying at her bungalow at the Beverly Hills Hotel. Worried that perhaps she'd bitten off a bit more than she could comfortably chew, Alex found the canny retailer's assistance invaluable.

As the first television product licensing venture ever aimed at upper-middle-class adults, the Alexandra Lyons Blue Bayou collection was staking out new retailing territory. The trick was adapting Alex's ultraglamorous costumes into equally alluring, reasonably affordable clothing.

Remembering what Debord had said about knowing exactly who you were designing for before she put pencil to sketch pad, Alex spent hours staking out Lord's stores to get a true fix on her clientele. The quintessential Lord's woman, she determined, was a woman with charm and sophistication and beauty. She was intelligent and successful and as a rule preferred sensual, rather than overtly sexy, clothing.

It was decided from the start that Alex's clothes would not bear any outer labels linking them with the popular television program. After all, Eleanor pointed out succinctly, a Lord's customer was independent and self-confident. She would never purchase anything that might label her as a fashion victim.

"As you can see, I modified certain outfits," Alex explained during a meeting with Eleanor in Zach's vast corner office. She'd been relieved to learn Zach wouldn't be sitting in on the design portion of the meeting. "What works on television doesn't always translate into real life."

Eleanor nodded thoughtfully, comparing the actual still photographs of the actresses wearing the various dresses and suits during taping and the colorful sketches depicting Alex's adaptations.

"That's true," she agreed with a regretful little sigh that suggested her retail marketing sense was warring with her feminine side. "Most women aren't going to put on big, veiled hats to go to the market or the office. More's the pity," she murmured as her gaze lingered a long time on an ultraglamorous, but oh, so huge red hat draped in black flowered lace.

"Oh, I like this." She held up a sketch of a pastel pink gingham dress with a full, gathered skirt. The model in the drawing was holding a prim little handbag and sporting a beribboned straw boater. "It reminds me of

Leslie Caron in *Gigi,* with a touch of Brigitte Bardot in *Babette Goes to War.*"

"That's the idea," Alex admitted with a quick, only slightly sheepish grin. "Those films were on late-night cable back-to-back the night I was trying to come up with a design for Tiffany to wear back home to the bayou for her sister's wedding."

Sophie had devised that plot twist after Alex, needing to talk about Zach with someone, had told her about that long ago day.

"The day she got pregnant with her old high-school sweetheart's baby," Eleanor remembered. "Gracious, that was a hot scene! The night Clara and I watched that episode, I half expected their lovemaking to set off the smoke detector."

She grinned and fanned herself dramatically with the sketch; for not the first time since they'd begun working together, Alex found it difficult to believe that Eleanor was actually in her seventies. Her appearance, along with her unwavering zest for life, made her seem decades younger.

"The contrast between that sexy scene and that sweet fifties-style dress was brilliant," Eleanor said, unstinting as always with her praise.

Alex returned the warm smile. "Thanks."

At the time, Sophie had worried that the dress wasn't as blatantly obvious as the rest of Tiffany's wardrobe. But Alex had argued that the exaggeratedly innocent gingham would work. And it had, better than she could have hoped.

"The Tiffany wardrobe is certainly different from what we usually feature at Lord's," Eleanor mused, flipping through the sketches for the umpteenth time.

Eleanor's careful study of the sketches reminded Alex of the time Debord had first examined her portfolio. Back then, she'd felt certain she would die from anxiety. Now she had more confidence, and while she admittedly worried that the older woman might reject her suggested designs, she knew such a rejection was not the end of the world.

"It is a slightly younger look," Alex said carefully.

She'd been worried about that ever since Zach's demographics had revealed the average Lord's charge-card customer was nearly a decade older than the Bourbon Street stripper character. But conversely, letters from younger viewers made up a large proportion of "Blue Bayou's" fan mail.

And although she'd never claim to be a retailer, from a purely practical viewpoint, Alex thought it foolish to ignore such sales potential.

"Definitely younger," Eleanor agreed. Her gaze lingered on a blue-and-green plaid pleated skirt and white blouse reminiscent of a Catholic school uniform. The only difference was that the skirt was scandalously short and shot with gleaming gold threads, and the blouse was created from diaphanous silk organza. *Schoolgirl sex.*

"What you've done is wonderful, Alex. It's about time Lord's had an infusion of new blood."

As she dug into her portfolio for the lingerie collection, Alex released a breath she'd been unaware of holding.

"I realize that marketing really isn't my field," Alex said, distracted momentarily by Zach's arrival. Knowing he kept a very close eye—and an equally tight fist—on the Lord's bankbook, Alex had been expecting him.

Today they were going to discuss factories, and she had a very good idea that she and Zachary Deveraux were about to have their first serious disagreement.

"But," she continued, returning her attention to Eleanor, "an idea occurred to me I want to share with you."

"What idea is that?"

"I thought you might want to consider having actual customers appear in some of the print advertising."

"Like those mink ads?"

"Exactly. Except they always use famous faces. I thought it might be fun to show that any woman can be a star wearing clothing from the Blue Bayou collection."

A curtain of silence settled over the room. Alex could practically see the wheels turning inside Eleanor's head.

"I love it." She clapped her hands together and gave Alex a look that reminded her of the gold stars teachers used to put on her papers. "You definitely have a flair for retailing."

A genetic flare, Eleanor decided, exchanging a brief, I-told-you-so look with Zach.

Alex grinned, enjoying the praise and the moment. She'd been admittedly nervous about working with Eleanor. And not only because the job would entail seeing Zach on a regular basis. Stories regarding the elderly retailer's impatient, often curt tongue and short temper were legion; independently minded herself, Alex had worried that she and Eleanor Lord might clash on a regular basis.

But instead, they worked flawlessly together. For

two women of different generations, raised in such disparate lifestyles, she and Eleanor were, Alex had discovered to her surprise, remarkably alike.

As much as Alex enjoyed her work for Lord's, she quickly discovered she'd been right to worry about working so closely with Zach. The truth, as much as she tried to deny it to Sophie, as much as she wished it otherwise, was that she possessed a burning passion for a man she was forced to work with, a man she could only see in public, a man she didn't dare permit herself to be alone with anywhere but in his office.

And even there they tended to keep the door open by mutual unspoken agreement, making Marge, his secretary, or better yet, Eleanor, their chaperone. And on the rare occasion they did find themselves alone, they maintained an inviolate border between personal and business conversations.

"The important thing is to find a factory that will give us low labor costs and efficient delivery," Zach began without preamble when Eleanor turned the meeting over to him. "And right now, from a cost-per-unit criteria, we can get the biggest bang for our bucks in Korea."

Alex had been expecting this. She was also ready for it. "I won't allow the Alexandra Lyons collection to be manufactured by miserably underpaid women in some horrid Seoul workshop."

"*You* won't allow?" He reined in a burst of irritation that was threatening to ignite a temper he thought he'd put away when he'd donned his expensive Brooks Brothers suits.

"That's right."

Alex folded her arms and turned her gaze to the oil

painting on the wall depicting Zach with his parents, sisters and grandmother working the family sugarcane farm. She remembered him telling her how it reminded him of his roots.

"And quite honestly, knowing your background," she added, "I'm amazed that you'd consider exploiting the less fortunate."

Eleanor, watching the exchange with interest, made a slight sound that could have been a cough. Or a smothered laugh.

"I fail to see where giving impoverished citizens honest employment is exploiting the less fortunate."

"Did you actually visit any of those so-called factories?"

Zach had the grace to flush. Alex watched the color rise from his white shirt collar and felt a flicker of hope.

"They're not that bad," he argued. But his voice lacked conviction.

"Not that bad?" She raised her voice, realizing immediately she'd taken the wrong tack when his ebony brows came crashing down toward those midnight dark eyes. "Zach." She lowered her voice. *Patience.* "They're horrible."

"I suppose you've been there?" His normally mild tone was edged with a sarcasm she was unaccustomed to hearing from this man.

"Actually, I have. When I was working on Seventh Avenue, one of the foreign reps had a heart attack, so I was sent in his place."

A cloud moved across her face at the memory of those vile, dark workrooms redolent with the stench of sweat and *kimchi,* where half-naked laborers toiled eighty or more hours a week for a miserly wage.

"The first one I saw had some unpronounceable name, but like all the others I visited, it should have been called Pandemonium."

The capital of Hell in *Paradise Lost*. It was, Zach admitted reluctantly, a deadly accurate description. He'd found the shops as unpalatable as Alex had. But despite his moral misgivings, his first loyalty was, as always, to Lord's.

"Look, Alex, I'll agree that in a perfect world, everyone would live in nice little houses with picket fences surrounding lush green lawns and spreading elm trees. But we're talking about the real world. Where life isn't always fair."

Her exquisite face, which haunted too many of both his sleeping and waking hours, had closed up. Realizing that she wasn't buying this argument, Zach decided to try another tack.

"I don't know if you're aware that The Lord's Group gives a very generous amount of its corporate profits to charity each year," he began slowly, shifting into the same lecturing mode he used when delivering the annual report to the stockholders.

"Which in turn generates a very healthy tax write-off," she countered.

"That's beside the point, dammit! Would you just let me finish?"

"Go right ahead."

"Fine." He gave her a warning look. "My point is, Lord's contributions assist a great many needy people. What moral victory would be achieved if the company went bankrupt and that money stopped flowing into charitable coffers?"

"Lord, talk about false justification," Alex muttered.

"If you truly believe that, Zachary, I'm amazed you get any sleep at night. But since you seem to only understand the bottom line, Mr. President, let me spell things out for you in black and white. In case you've forgotten, my contract with Lord's gives me manufacturing approval."

"I recall that clause." All too well. He'd argued against it, but Eleanor, damn her, had been immovable.

"Fine. Then I'm only going to say this once. Any clothing line with my name on it will not be manufactured in South Korea. Or Taiwan, or Indonesia or Mexico. The clothing will be made here, in the United States, by American workers."

"You sound like a campaign speech," he muttered.

"And you sound like an apologist for Big Business. That's my bottom line, Zach. Take it or leave it. But let me warn you, if you don't agree, I'll take my designs and go home."

"Oh, we wouldn't want you to do that," Eleanor insisted quickly, finally entering into the argument. "Surely we can come up with some compromise."

"There's a garment factory in Brooklyn," Alex said, reaching into her portfolio and taking out a business card, which she held out to Zach. "I've done business with them before. They're efficient, relatively inexpensive, and they don't treat their workers like indentured servants."

There was no point in arguing any longer, Zach decided. He'd investigate Alex's damn factory, and if it wasn't competitive, he was just going to have to make her see the light.

After all, she wasn't designing clothes for her dolls

any longer. Or her mother. This was business. Pure and simple.

He plucked the card from her fingers. "I'll check it out."

She gave him a sweet smile that was only slightly tinged with sarcasm. "Thank you. I'd appreciate that."

"So, have you decided where you're going to debut the collection?" Zach asked Eleanor.

Eleanor frowned. She'd been worrying about that exact question for weeks. "I suppose the Rodeo Drive store would be the most obvious."

"But you've never been one to settle for the obvious," Zach said with a slow, intimate smile that, although focused on Eleanor, managed to warm Alex, who was seated across the small round table from him, to the core.

She dug her nails into her palms, denying the need to reach across that space and touch her hand to his cheek.

"That's what keeps Lord's on top," Eleanor agreed. "There's always Manhattan. We'd ensure a great deal of fashion press that way." Her lack of enthusiasm showed in her flat tone.

"May I make a suggestion?" Zach asked.

"Of course."

"How about Chicago?"

"Chicago?"

"We're opening a new store there next quarter," he reminded her unnecessarily. "It wouldn't be a bad place to showcase the Alexandra Lyons collection."

"Like we did with Debord in New Orleans."

"Like New Orleans," Zach echoed, his words directed toward Eleanor, but his dark eyes on Alex.

Eleanor, caught up in the logistics of Zach's suggestion, failed to notice that her two favorite people had become snared in the silvery strands of an emotionally sticky web.

Zach watched the shared memories shimmer in Alex's remarkable amber eyes. He saw her full lips part ever so slightly, as if she were remembering that night of desperate kisses.

"That's an excellent idea, Zachary." Eleanor's voice shattered the thick tension strung between Zach and Alex. "Women in Los Angeles and Manhattan have grown horribly blasé. What we need is the excitement a wildly enthusiastic Chicago audience can bring to Alex's marvelous clothing."

Alex shook off her lingering desire, as well as the guilt she always experienced when she found herself wishing for a life with Zach, and allowed herself to be swept up by Eleanor's enthusiasm.

"I have another idea," she suggested, as if the thought had just occurred to her. "Along with the professional models, what would you say to having the actual actresses from 'Blue Bayou' take part in the show?"

Eleanor's eyes lighted up like a child getting her first glimpse of a Christmas tree. "That would certainly add Hollywood pizzazz to an already glamorous collection. But do you think Sophie Friedman would agree?"

"In a minute." Alex laughed, thinking of how Sophie's calculator brain had begun clicking away the dollars of free publicity when she'd suggested the idea to the producer over Cobb salads at the Bistro Garden yesterday.

Alex's clear laughter reminded Zach of summer sunshine on an Alpine lake. Desire stirred in him, as unwelcome as distant rumbles signaling a thunderstorm and just as impossible to fend off.

Chapter Nineteen

Moonlight streamed into the room. Candlelight glowed, creating flickering shadows on the wall. A bed, draped in a canopy of gauze netting, dominated the room. A couple lay atop satin sheets, arms and legs entangled. The woman was clad in a clinging white slip. The man was wearing a pair of jeans. His muscled chest was bare.

"You are so beautiful." There was reverent awe in his tone as his hand moved up her thigh, slipping beneath the hem of the slip. "I've been going crazy thinking about you. About us."

The woman smiled, pleased with her feminine power. "Ah've been thinkin' about you, too, sugah." She rolled over on top of him, fitting her lush curves to his hard male angles.

His hands cupped her buttocks, holding her hard against him. "Even while you're making love to your husband?"

"*Especially* while Ah'm makin' love to my husband," she promised on a silvery laugh.

"Cut!" The director's voice shattered the sensual moment. "Dammit, Mary Beth, I'm still seeing panty lines."

"I am not taking off my underwear," the actress countered. "That's the kind of stuff that gets into the *Enquirer*."

"I doubt Tiffany would even wear panties," Stone Michaels suggested helpfully.

Mary Beth Olson turned on him. "You're just trying to figure out a way to get me naked."

"Not me!" The handsome actor held up his hands and glanced toward the control booth, where his bride of six weeks sat following the action on the script she'd fine-tuned just the night before. Since beginning his relationship with Brenda, the show's head writer, Stone's part had, as Alex had predicted, grown considerably.

But he hadn't needed to marry to ensure fame. Not when the show's female audience found him the ultimate hunk. *People* magazine had recently voted him the sexiest man alive, and Helen Gurley Brown was talking to his agent about a *Cosmopolitan* centerfold.

"Why don't we put Mary Beth in a teddy?" Alex, who was standing on the sidelines, suggested.

"It has to be white," the director warned. "White works best with moonlight and candles."

"How about ivory?"

He rubbed his chin. "I suppose that'll do."

"I've got just the thing. I'll be right back."

"Okay, boys and girls! Lunch!" the director shouted.

"Lunch," the assistant director echoed.

Alex turned to leave the soundstage when she suddenly came face-to-face with Zach's wife. "Mrs. Deveraux?"

Miranda nodded. "Ms. Lyons."

"This is a surprise."

Miranda's sharp gaze didn't miss Alex's discomfort. "Not a pleasant one, I take it."

Alex straightened. "I'm sorry if I sounded rude. It's just that this isn't one of my better days." Although the writers stayed the same, directors changed on a regular, sometimes weekly basis.

The one they had now seemed determined to make things difficult. He'd changed the clothing cues innumerable times, keeping her running a marathon back and forth between the soundstage and the costuming department. She wasn't the only one being worn to a frazzle. Alex had heard the hairdresser threaten to do something painful and probably anatomically impossible with her curling iron after he'd had her restyle Olivia's hair three times.

"I can see you're busy," Miranda said agreeably. "So, I'll be brief and to the point." She leaned forward, placing a manicured hand on Alex's arm. Her diamond wedding band glittered. "It's about my husband."

"What about him?"

"I want you to stay away from him."

She was now so close her breath fanned Alex's cheek. Her green eyes had turned flat and cold. Alex felt a chill race up her spine. "Your husband and I work together, Mrs. Deveraux. That's all."

"Don't try to lie to me, because I know what you're up to." Animosity etched vertical furrows next to Miranda's perfectly drawn lips. "First you insinuate yourself into Eleanor's life just like all the others—"

"All the others? What—"

Miranda cut her off with a furious wave of the hand.

"You've wormed your way into my aunt's life. And now you're after my husband."

Her voice was low and controlled, but Alex would have been no more shaken if Miranda had suddenly begun to rant and rave. The fury she saw on Zach's wife's face and in her eyes was more frightening than any display of temper.

Miranda's fingers tightened on Alex's arm. Her nails dug deep into Alex's flesh. "You must understand, I can make things very difficult for you. And for Zach."

Alex knew, without a shadow of a doubt, that Miranda was telling the absolute truth. "I'm not having an affair with your husband, Mrs. Deveraux," she insisted.

"See that you don't." Miranda's deadly smile reminded Alex of a shark. "Unless you wish to suffer the consequences. And believe me, dear," she said with silky menace, "the consequences of crossing me are not at all pretty."

Outraged that Miranda dared to show up at her workplace and threaten her, and concerned that the woman just might resort to physical violence, Alex was turned momentarily speechless.

Tension hummed between them, a living, breathing, thing.

"Alex? Is anything wrong?"

Alex could have kissed Sophie for interrupting.

"Nothing at all," she managed through lips that had gone as dry as dust. "Mrs. Deveraux is just leaving."

"That's right," Miranda agreed with the trademark public smile that had graced the glossy pages of *Town and Country* and *Tattler* on numerous occasions. "I'm already late for a luncheon date with my husband. And you know, Ms. Lyons, how Zachary hates to be kept waiting."

She loosened her death grip on Alex's arm. "I enjoyed our little chat, dear. We must do it again sometime soon."

"What the hell was that all about?" Sophie demanded, hands on her hips, as they watched Miranda Deveraux walk away.

Alex fought a shiver and wiped the dampness from her hands onto her poppy suede skirt. "She thinks I'm sleeping with her husband."

Sophie lifted a brow. "Did she actually threaten you?"

Alex shrugged and tried to tell herself she'd only imagined the fatal threat in Miranda's green eyes. That's what came from hanging around a soap opera all day, she decided. Life started looking like some stormy television drama.

"Not in so many words."

"Then why are you as white as new snow?" Sophie's expression was one of concern. "Perhaps you ought to talk to Zach about setting her straight."

"No." Alex released a deep breath. "I haven't done anything for her to be jealous about. And since I have no intention of having an affair with Zach everything will be okay."

But as she headed off again to retrieve the ivory satin teddy, Alex couldn't quite shake a lingering feeling of unease.

Six hours later, the taping finally completed to the satisfaction of the unrelenting, obsessive-compulsive director, Alex left the nearly deserted studio.

When she reached the Porsche, parked in her reserved spot—the spot with her name clearly stenciled on the concrete curb in bright white lettering—she found all four tires flat.

Alex was admittedly relieved when, as the weeks passed, there were no further incidents.

Immersed in the Blue Bayou collection, along with designing for the show, she worked even harder. After a run on the beach every morning, she'd settle down with a pot of coffee and her sketch pad. Lunch, when she remembered to stop and eat, was more coffee and a sandwich. Dinner often went ignored completely.

She slept little and ate less. Pounds drifted away unnoticed.

"What the hell are you doing to yourself?" Zach asked one rainy afternoon when she arrived at his office for a budget meeting.

He'd been away on a lengthy inspection tour of potential new building sites. She'd been both relieved and disappointed when nearly three weeks passed without seeing him. But now that they were finally alone Alex realized she needn't have worried about Zach trying to seduce her.

On the contrary, he was looking at her with something uncomfortably akin to horror.

"I have no idea what you're talking about." Exhaustion made her tone sharper than usual. A lingering cold she'd not been able to shake made her cough.

"When was the last time you looked in a mirror? You look like shit." Her peaches-and-cream complexion had the unhealthy pallor of paste, her unpainted lips were chalky pale, and her usually remarkable eyes were red-rimmed. Her cashmere cardigan sweater hung on her too-thin frame.

"Gee," she said in a saccharine tone, "thanks a lot. Anyone ever tell you that you're wonderful for a woman's ego?"

She ran a trembling hand over her red wool slacks. She'd worn the trousers with a matching sweater, hoping the vivid color would not only brighten the dreary day but add some color to her cheeks, as well. From Zach's disapproving words and harshly critical look, she guessed her ploy had failed.

"Didn't anyone ever tell you that the pale, consumptive look went out with Camille?"

"Wow, you *are* complimentary," she muttered. "Where's Eleanor?"

"In Santa Barbara. This lousy weather has her arthritis acting up. Averill thought she ought to stay in."

"Oh. So it's just going to be the two of us?"

"Got a problem with that?" he challenged softly.

"None at all," she lied. She thought about suggesting that his wife might, but didn't. "Let's get down to business."

As she struggled to keep her attention focused on the multitude of figures Zach kept flashing at her, Alex considered that there were times when her mind seemed every bit as foggy as the slate-gray day outside the bank of floor-to-ceiling windows.

On more than one occasion lately, she'd walk into a room and forget why she was there. Or she'd dial the phone to ask Zach a question or share with him her latest idea, only to have the thought erased from her mind when his rich, deep, voice came on the line.

They'd be discussing the pricing of the Blue Bayou clothing, when her gaze would suddenly be captured by the sight of his fingers holding the sheet of lettuce-green ledger paper and all the figures would flee her mind, like dry leaves blown away by gale-force autumn winds.

But the past. Ah, Alex considered, as she found herself drowning in the glittering black depths of Zach's gaze, the past was an entirely different story! The past, most specifically her time in Louisiana with Zach, was crystal clear, sparkling with the brilliance of an alpine mountain stream.

She'd hoped time would have dulled her memories. She'd prayed she would forget how his touch made her knees weak, how his arms wrapped around her waist had felt so very right.

But despite her hopes, her prayers, her best intentions, everything about that distant, all too brief and frustratingly unconsummated romance remained etched on her rebellious mind in the same perfect detail as the facets on the Waterford crystal in the Lord's corporate dining room.

Alex's mind was spinning treacherously out of control. As she did too often these days, she found herself thinking terrible, uncharitable thoughts. She hoped for irreconcilable differences in their marriage; she wished that Miranda would run away with one of her many rumored lovers.

Sometimes, late at night, lying in her lonely bed, staring up at the ceiling, though she knew it was unforgivable, she imagined turning on the television news to hear that the Concorde had crashed over the Alps, and although the crew had survived, the sole passenger—socialite and department store heiress Miranda Lord Baptista Smythe Deveraux—had tragically died.

She pictured herself rushing to Zach's side, offer-

ing her heartfelt solace. It was then that he'd tell her
what she'd longed to hear—that he'd never loved Miranda, that the only woman he'd ever loved, would ever
love, was her. And then finally, blissfully, he'd draw
her into his arms.

Sometimes she'd picture them making love on the
beach beneath a full white moon, or in a deep marble
tub filled to overflowing with frothy white bubbles.
Other times she'd imagine him undressing her slowly,
reverently, beside a white-draped canopy bed strewn
with snowy rose petals.

Yet another fantasy had them making love in a warm
Polynesian lagoon behind a thundering waterfall, while
the tropical setting sun turned the water a dazzling,
blinding gold. The location changed, but the words and
the exhilarating feelings were always the same. Alex
knew her fantasies were horribly wrong. Even sinful.
But she couldn't help herself.

"Alex? Are you all right?"

Zach's deep, concerned voice made her realize that
her mind had been drifting again. "I'm fine. Can we
just forget about me and get back to work?"

He frowned, but having already discovered that
Alex's tenacity rivaled even Eleanor's, he decided there
was no point in wasting either time or her obviously
depleted energy by arguing.

"I've decided to use the Brooklyn factory for production."

Such news should have made her ecstatic. All she
could manage was a nod, which she regretted when the
movement sent rocks tumbling around inside her head.
"I'm glad," she said quietly. Too quietly, Zach thought.

"That's about all I have for today," he lied. Actually,

he'd wanted to question her about going over budget again on trim for the lingerie line, but looking at her pale face, he decided any discussions about whether or not she'd really needed all those ostrich feathers could wait.

"Well, that didn't take long."

Alex didn't bother to hide her relief; she'd half expected to receive a reprimand about the gorgeous feathers she'd bought for Tiffany's negligee set. Eager to escape the office before he mentioned her little extravagance, she stood up too fast.

Her head swam; the room began to spin; little dots danced in front of her eyes.

Then the floor tilted and rushed up at her.

Chapter Twenty

Zach was at Alex's side before she reached the plush carpeting. His hands caught her upper arms and he lowered her to the chair.

"Why the hell didn't you tell my secretary you were sick when she scheduled this meeting?" he growled.

As angry as he was at Alex for her blatant disregard for her health, he was even angrier at himself for not having noticed how ill she was. "We could have postponed it until you were feeling better."

"I didn't want to postpone, because we're running out of time as it is. Besides, it's just a cold."

"Colds don't make you faint. And scheduling isn't your problem."

"I thought—"

"You think too damn much." Squatting, he placed the back of his hand against her forehead. "You've got a fever."

Her flesh was raging hot and clammy at the same time. Something alien ripped through Zach, something that felt a great deal like fear. "I'm taking you to the hospital emergency room."

"You're overreacting." Why didn't he just leave her alone? Alex tried to stand and was immediately pushed back down. "It's just a cold," she repeated. "And perhaps a bit too much work."

"How about a lot too much work? When was the last time you had a decent meal?"

"I had spaghetti last night." The noodles and tomato sauce had tasted like the cardboard box they'd come in. She'd thrown away most of the microwave meal. "And I don't want to go to any hospital."

"Tough."

"Dammit, Zach—" Her planned protest was cut off by a deep, racking cough that went on and on.

He swore at her richly. "That's it." With a speed that caused her head to start spinning again, his fingers curved around her shoulders and he hauled her to her feet.

"Don't touch me."

"I've been trying like hell not to touch you for weeks," he retorted. "But thanks to your lack of concern for your own health, we're both just going to have to put up with it." Ignoring her hurt intake of breath, he said, "Do you think you can walk?"

"Of course." She hoped.

"Then come on." He half carried, half dragged her out the office door. "Call Dan Matheson at Presbyterian General," he barked uncharacteristically at his secretary. "Tell him I'm bringing in a patient."

"You don't have to call anyone," Alex countermanded, "because I'm not going to any hospital."

Zach's hold on her tightened. "Shut up." His tone

was brusque and unsympathetic. To his secretary he said, "Tell Matheson we'll be there in ten minutes. Fifteen tops."

With that, Zach hauled Alex into the private elevator from his office suite.

"You can't treat me this way," she complained as he jabbed the button. "I don't work for you. In case you've forgotten, Zachary Deveraux, I'm a privately licensed contractor. That contract I signed with Lord's doesn't give you the right to interfere in my personal life."

He jerked her close against him, literally holding her on her feet. "If you don't quit wasting valuable energy talking, I'm going to have to resort to a left hook to shut you up."

"You wouldn't dare!"

Of course he wouldn't. He'd never in his entire life struck a woman. Not even Miranda, who'd certainly tempted him on enough occasions.

"I wouldn't put it to the test if I were you," he said.

They reached the underground garage. As they exited the elevator, Alex's knees sagged. Zach caught her when she stumbled and scooped her up in his arms.

"I said I could walk," she complained.

"Yeah, you were doing a real great job." He wanted to hold her close against his chest and never let go. He wanted to take care of her. And not just today, but all the days of their lives.

"I don't know what you're so mad about," she grumbled. Succumbing to the irresistible lure of his strong shoulder, she rested her head against the gray wool.

"Stupidity always makes me angry. You should be old enough to take care of yourself without a keeper."

"I've had a lot of work to do."

He managed to unlock the door of his car and deposit her in the passenger seat and buckle her seat belt. "Ever heard of delegating?"

"My name's going to be on the label." When the garage began spinning, she leaned her head against the leather seat back and closed her eyes. "If I want the clothes to be perfect, which I do, I have to take full responsibility."

"Just what the world needs. Another dead overachiever."

"I wish you'd just leave me alone."

"That makes two of us," he snapped. "But in case you haven't been paying attention during all those meetings, The Lord's Group is investing one helluva lot of money in you, Alexandra Lyons. I'm not about to let anything happen to that investment."

"That's what all this is about? Money?"

"What the hell do you think?"

His husky growl sent a warmth flowing through her that Alex feared had nothing to do with her fever. She opened her eyes and found herself looking directly into his. "Dammit, Alex," he said, softening his demeanor and his tone, "don't argue. Not now."

He brushed her cheek with his knuckles in a slow, tender sweep she knew was meant to soothe rather than arouse, but nevertheless created a violent rush of feeling deep inside her.

Dragging her gaze from his, she glanced around the lushly appointed interior, which smelled of leather and wood. "Nice car."

"Thanks. I like it."

As a kid, he'd pored over the pages of his uncle's *Motor Trend* magazines, practically drooling over the dazzling, unaffordable cars. If anyone had ever told him he'd actually own a Jaguar like this one, he'd have wondered just what kind of cigarettes they'd been smoking.

"Looks like you'd need a pilot's license to drive it," she murmured, taking in the multitude of dials on the dash. When those dials began to dance, she leaned her head back again, closed her eyes and allowed her mind to drift as Zach drove through the wet streets.

At her insistence, he allowed her to walk into the hospital, but kept one strong arm around her for support. She was relieved when he didn't declare his intention of accompanying her into the examining room. She wasn't up to another confrontation.

"I don't believe it," she murmured an hour later when they were back in the Jag.

"Neither do I." His expression was as grim as she'd ever seen it; his stony jaw could have been chiseled from granite. "Christ, how the hell could you not notice you had pneumonia?"

"I really wish you'd quit yelling at me," she complained weakly.

"Sorry," he muttered, sounding as if he meant it.

"I thought it was just a cold." Then, in a frail voice so unlike her own usual robust one, she said, "Thank you."

He slanted her a look. "You're welcome."

Alex would have given anything to know what he was thinking, but his gaze was expertly and frustratingly shuttered. Groggy from her fever and light-headed from the injection the doctor had given her, Alex didn't question how Zach knew where she lived.

Nor did she protest when he lifted her from the passenger seat and carried her into the funky pink-and-yellow bungalow on Venice Beach, one of a handful that had managed to evade falling prey to greedy land developers' bulldozers.

Warning bells began to peal when he headed unerringly toward her bedroom, but her mind was too fogged to offer up a single word of complaint.

He sat her down on the edge of the bed. The bits and pieces of fabric and papers scattered over the puffy comforter emblazoned with wildflowers were mute testimony to the fact that she'd been working when she should have been sleeping.

"This is ridiculous," he muttered, gathering up the colorful swatches.

"Wrong. It's Italian silk."

"Cute, Alex. Real cute." He tossed the fabric and sketches onto a nearby wicker table.

"Need any help getting undressed?" he asked with more casualness than he was feeling.

Christ, it was getting harder and harder to be around this woman without wanting her! Even dressed as she was, engulfed in that oversize scarlet sweater, too-baggy slacks and black boots, even with her Rudolph-red nose and her too-pale cheeks, even knowing how sick she was, Zach still had a burning desire to touch her.

He longed to slip his hand beneath the hem of her sweater and caress the flesh he knew would be even softer than the crimson cashmere. These long and frustrating months of working so closely with her, at the same time forcing himself to keep his distance, had taken their emotional toll on him.

"I think I can manage it."

Relief and regret washed over him. It was, Zach

reminded himself, for the best. "I'll wait in the other room. Shout if you need anything."

Although it wasn't easy, he forced himself to cool his heels in her living room, taking the opportunity to study the room that bore her own personal stamp in the same way as her unique designs.

Casual wicker furniture with bright blue-and-yellow sailcloth cushions sat on a bleached oak floor. In the center of the room, colorful hot-air balloons took flight on a sky blue rug. Green plants flourished in brightly flowered ceramic cache pots. Art posters hung on the snow-white walls.

A pair of red shoes with ridiculously high heels rested haphazardly on the rug in front of the wicker sofa, surrounded by more scraps of vivid silks and glowing satins. A small plastic globe rested on a nearby table, the scene inside depicting the New York skyline. Other similar globes displayed the St. Louis arch, the Golden Gate Bridge, the Seattle space needle and the Alamo, making Zach remember her telling him about her youthful Gypsy existence.

One plastic globe in particular captured his attention; he picked it up and turned it over, causing snow to fall on St. Louis Cathedral across the street from New Orleans's Jackson Square.

Zach experienced a pang of bittersweet remembrance and wondered if there were times when Alex held this same toy world in her palms and thought of him.

Sighing, he returned the globe to its place and continued his study of the room, searching for clues about Alex's life. He took special note of the framed photo of a middle-aged gray-haired woman and a smiling, dark-haired boy atop a table painted to resemble a bright yellow sunflower.

Her mother and brother, Zach decided, looking for a resemblance to Alex and finding none.

Perhaps Eleanor was right.

You're letting anxiety about the lady warp your mind, pal. Zach reminded himself that of the eight kids in his family, he and his sister Maggie resembled his mother, Paula and Lorraine resembled their dad, and the other four girls didn't really look like either parent. Or each other.

That being the case, there really wasn't any reason for Alex to look like her mother. And her twin, he reminded himself, was not identical, but fraternal.

He went into the pocket-size, old-fashioned kitchen which, while painted a sunny yellow with a bright blue ceiling and smelling of Christmas due to the pyramid of clove-studded oranges on the creamy ceramic tile, didn't look as if it had changed since the house was built, probably in the thirties. He filled a red enamel kettle with water for tea, then stood at the window, hands jammed into the pockets of his slacks gazing out at the sea, which was draped by the misty rain in a silvery blanket of fog, while his mind was filled, as it was too often these days, with thoughts of Alex.

He'd come to realize that Alexandra Lyons was smart and sweet and dazzlingly talented. Her stunning beauty was only illuminated by the blaze of her fiercely independent ambition, an ambition he clearly recognized, possessing a fair share of that character trait himself.

She was, without a doubt, the most fascinating and

intriguing—and ill, he reminded himself firmly—woman he'd ever met.

His thoughts were shattered by the shrill whistle of the kettle. As he poured the water over a Constant Comment tea bag he'd found in a flowered canister on the open shelf, he glanced up at the whimsical black-and-white cat clock and realized she'd been in the bedroom a very long time. What the hell was she doing? Taking the tea with him, he went back to the bedroom and tapped lightly on the door. Once. Twice, then a third time. When she didn't answer, he decided to risk her ire and go in.

She was sprawled atop the comforter, appearing dead to the world. Zach experienced a momentary panic that was eased when he viewed the slow rise and fall of her chest. Her breathing was shallow and strained, but it was steady.

Bending down, working gently so as not to disturb her, Zach unzipped her knee-length boots and slipped them off. Her red socks, then her slacks followed.

"Oh, hell." Zach groaned when he discovered the scrap of crimson lace cut high on her delicately rounded hips. Trust this woman not to wear nice, safe, white cotton underpants. Although, he considered, his gaze lingering on that soft shadow of femininity between her long legs, Alex could probably make even a nun's drawers look sexy.

Frowning, he set to work on the sweater, unbuttoning it with fingers that were not nearly as steady as they should have been. As he'd feared, her bra matched those ridiculous panties. It was as scarlet as sin.

Standing beside the bed, staring down at the provocative sight, Zach felt like a starving man, his nose pressed against the glass of a bakery, denied even the smallest morsel.

During these past months, Zach had come to the unwilling conclusion that Alex had been designed by the Fates to taunt him, to torment his sleep and drive him crazy with dreams of what he could not—dared not—have. She was a bewitching nymph created solely to teach him that the self-control he'd always prided himself on was nothing more than a well-constructed sham. She was also a bright, intelligent woman who made every other woman he'd ever known pale in comparison.

Exhaling a long sigh, he managed to tuck her beneath the sheets. He bent and touched his lips to hers.

Then, leaving her to sleep, he went into the living room, picked up the receiver of her Mickey Mouse phone and placed a call to Eleanor.

When Alex awoke several hours later, she found herself in the capable hands of the private nurse Zach and Eleanor had hired. When she tried to assure the blond Amazon that she could take care of herself, Inga Nusland simply folded her muscular arms over her ample chest and refused to budge.

By the third day of sinfully hedonistic pampering, during which time the phlegmatic Inga proved herself to be not only a capable nurse but a marvelous cook and baker, Alex decided that perhaps there was something to be said for relaxation, after all.

Chapter Twenty-One

"When are you going to admit she's Anna?" Eleanor demanded.

Zach had come to Santa Barbara to fill the older woman in on Alexandra's recuperation. Although he hadn't returned to that cheerful little bungalow, Inga gave him daily updates, and he'd spoken with her doctor.

"There's still no proof," Zach pointed out as he did every time they had this conversation.

Sometimes, and this was one of them, he almost wished he'd never met Alexandra Lyons, hadn't played Sir Galahad in that long-ago Mardi Gras. But dammit, he had, and now, thanks to him, they were both suffering.

Once, when he was a boy, he'd come across a wild owl struggling impotently to fly with a broken wing. He'd wrapped the crippled bird in his shirt, taken it home, then spent the next two weeks feeding it field mice and nightcrawlers, only to have the ungrateful owl nearly bite off the end of his finger.

No good deed ever goes unpunished, his *grand-mère* had proclaimed. At the time, Zach hadn't known how prophetic her words would prove to be.

"Surely you can see the resemblance?" Eleanor pressed.

"I'll agree she looks a lot like you as a young woman. But that doesn't mean she's your granddaughter. After all, Miranda's your niece, and there's no Lord family resemblance there."

Eleanor scowled at the memory of her niece's call the night before, when she'd asked for a little loan to cover her losses in Monte Carlo. She'd also requested Eleanor not mention the call to Zach, which was bothersome because Eleanor had tried to stay out of the disaster that was Zach and Miranda's marriage.

They were both adults, she'd told herself innumerable times. What they did, or with whom, was their own business. So long as it didn't impact adversely on Lord's.

"Miranda inherited her looks from her mother's gene pool."

Along with, Eleanor worried, her behavior. After marrying Lawrence Lord, Sylvie, the viscount's tennis-playing daughter had proved to be not so genteel, after all. The sad truth was that Sylvie had been a gin-guzzling nymphomaniac.

Zach wished he hadn't brought Miranda up. He didn't want to talk about his wife. He also didn't want to admit that during these months working closely with Alex, he'd noticed things about her that defied any rational explanation.

She possessed certain gestures that he'd witnessed innumerable times in Eleanor herself, along with a stubborn intelligence he couldn't help but admire, even as it frustrated him whenever they found themselves on opposite sides of an issue. Like that damn factory ultimatum.

"Are you planning to share your suspicions with Alex?"

Eleanor sighed. "No. Not yet." From the deep furrows on her brow, Zach suspected she was recalling another time she'd felt so sure she'd found Anna. "Not until after we launch the Blue Bayou collection. But what would be wrong with seeing if we could strike a chord in her memory?"

"Eleanor—"

Eleanor ignored his planned protest. "The poor girl's been working so hard she made herself sick. Even after the doctor pronounces her recovered, she'll still need her rest."

"You're suggesting she recuperate here. In Santa Barbara." It was not a question.

Eleanor's forehead smoothed. "Here," she confirmed. "In the home where she and her father and grandfather were all born."

There was so much to prepare; Eleanor wanted things absolutely perfect when Anna finally returned home.

After ten days of antibiotics, supplemented by biscuits slathered with butter and marmalade, apple strudel, and steaming stews and chicken pies topped with fat, fluffy dumplings, Alex proclaimed herself ready to go back to work.

Her doctor confirmed her self-diagnosis, with the

caveat that she begin with a few hours each day, taking time to work herself back to full throttle.

"You're still too pale," Eleanor complained during a visit to Venice. Although she'd gained back several much needed pounds, Alex's complexion continued to lack its normal healthy hue.

"I'll be fine."

"Of course you will. But we need you well rested, Alexandra. The Chicago debut of the Alexandra Lyons collection is only a month away," she reminded her. "And there's no better place to finish your recuperation than my house."

"You want me to come to Santa Barbara? To stay with you?"

"I'd love to have you as a houseguest."

"But I can't leave town. Zach and I still haven't worked out the problem with the music." She was insisting on live musicians while he argued for a less expensive audio tape, which she in turn countered would sound like elevator music.

"That can wait." Eleanor brushed off Alex's worries. "Zach will solve your little impasse. Believe me, dear, he always accomplishes everything he sets out to achieve. Besides, you couldn't have your meeting now, anyway. He's out of town."

"Oh?" Alex said with careful casualness. Against all common sense, she'd been hoping Zach might visit her. He hadn't.

"He's in Toronto. We're entering into negotiations to open our first Lord's in Canada. But right now things are hush-hush."

"I won't tell a soul," Alex promised, vaguely surprised Eleanor had shared confidential business information with her.

"Why, I never thought you would, dear," Eleanor answered mildly. "Now, let me help you pack."

One thing she'd learned during their months together was that like so many other rich, powerful women, Eleanor Lord was more than a little accustomed to getting her way. Rather than stand up to the silken bulldozer currently plucking clothes from her closet, Alex decided to simply relax and go with the flow.

Miranda was furious. And when Miranda was furious, she paced. Zach stood in front of the upstairs bedroom window, looking out over Eleanor's Santa Barbara estate and tried to ignore the furious energy radiating from his wife's every pore.

"I cannot believe she's invited that bloody little impostor into this house!" She was clenching and unclenching her fists, twisting her rings on her long aristocratic fingers, an outward sign of her tumultuous thoughts.

Miranda was not about to be cut out of her inheritance by any calculating con artist. How dare Alexandra Lyons endanger her happiness, her comfort, her entire livelihood this way! The threat she represented hovered over Miranda like a thick, suffocating cloud of noxious smog.

"Your aunt doesn't believe she's an impostor."

He shouldn't be here, Zach told himself. He should be at his office in L.A. Someone had begun quietly buying up outstanding shares of Lord's stock, and as hard as he'd tried, he had not been able to work his way through the maze of holding companies designed to keep the buyer's identity a secret.

But Eleanor had insisted he be on hand for Alex's arrival, and as much as he hated to admit it, he was curious to see how she'd react to the house.

Miranda continued to wear a path across the needlepoint cabbage-rose rug. Her furious, restless strides reminded Zach of a tigress that hadn't been fed for a week.

"You realize, of course, that the old woman's gone absolutely batty." She stopped long enough to light a cigarette. Puffs of blue smoke rose to the beamed ceiling as if from a smoldering volcano.

"You're exaggerating again."

"The hell I am. Any qualified psychiatrist would declare her incompetent."

He spun around. "I'm warning you, Miranda, if you try it, I'll block you at every turn."

Miranda took in his glittering dark eyes, his threatening stance, the tautly reigned-in violence simmering just beneath the surface. There was a looming menace about him that was palpable. And extremely exciting.

It had been a long time since she'd managed to garner a reaction other than his usual cold disdain. A rush of sexual anticipation rushed through her loins, making her momentarily forget her fury concerning Eleanor's newest protégée.

"Do you know, darling," she said slowly, switching gears with a blink of her gleaming emerald eyes, "that you are frightfully sexy when you're angry?" Deliberately, with regained control, she approached on a slow, hip-swiveling feline glide he'd once found incredibly appealing. Now he just found her obvious seduction attempt depressing.

"It isn't going to work."

She placed her hand against his chest. "Are you so sure about that?" She began toying with the buttons of his shirt. "Do you realize how long it's been since we made love?"

"Made love?" He plucked her hand away. "Is that what you call it?"

"Of course." Refusing to give up, she twined her arms around his neck. "We used to be so good together, Zachary. Remember?" Taking the fact that he hadn't moved away as a sign of encouragement, she pressed her body against his taut, unresisting one.

"Remember that lovely evening in the limousine in London? Remember how we spent the remainder of the night, steeped in sex and sin?" Her voice was a velvety purr; her teeth nipped at his earlobe. "Remember how you told me you'd never met a woman who made you feel the way I did?" She paused and assumed a tragic look. "When did everything go so wrong?"

"How about when you stole those earrings on our honeymoon?"

She sighed prettily. "You never will let me live that down, will you?" Moisture shone in her green eyes. "Perhaps, if we tried again. Perhaps, if I could believe that you truly loved me, no matter what my faults, I could be strong enough to get help for my sickness." On cue, tears began to stream down her face.

She was a remarkable actress, Zach mused distantly. He'd give her that. If he didn't know her so well, he'd actually believe that she regretted the chasm that had grown between them. A gulf as deep and wide as the Grand Canyon.

She went up on her toes and brushed her parted lips against his. "Please, Zachary. Can't we try to put the pieces together again? So we can have a wonderful, heavenly life together?"

She was definitely pulling out all the stops. Her fingers were caressing the back of his neck, her voice was a soft breeze against his mouth and her pelvis was moving seductively against his groin.

She was also out of luck. He didn't need to look down to know that his body was steadfastly refusing to respond.

"And I suppose all I have to do to achieve such Nirvana is help you gain Eleanor's power of attorney and lock her away in some home for addled old ladies."

"Well, you can't deny that she is old," Miranda said. "And even you must admit this latest idea about that little slut of a Hollywood dress designer being her long-lost Anna is proof that she's not completely in her right mind."

"Alexandra Lyons is not a slut." Fed up, he shoved Miranda away with an unexpected force that had her tottling on her high heels. "She just happens to be an extremely talented woman who's overcome a lot of hard knocks by integrity and tenacity and working damn hard."

"So." Miranda's seductive expression turned hard and cold, making her look every bit her age, which just happened to be ten years older than that printed on her California driver's license. "I was right about her all along."

"I don't know what you're talking about." Furious

at himself for rising to her bait, Zach turned his back to her, jammed his hands into his pockets and resumed staring out the window.

She thought about the photographs Mickey O'Rourke had given her. Incriminating photos of Zach carrying Alexandra into her house. Photos that, from the intense, concerned expression the camera lens had frozen on her husband's face, suggested their relationship was much more than a mere business alliance.

Miranda hadn't confronted her husband with the damning evidence. Not yet. Although patience had never been her long suit, she was willing, when necessary, to bide her time. But if the conniving little tart thought she could steal both Miranda's husband and her inheritance, she was going to be in for a very rude awakening!

"I've wondered why you've been so indulgent with Auntie's delusion this time." She was practically biting the words off, one at a time and spitting them at him like stones. "Tell me, Zachary, is she any good in bed?"

"I wouldn't know."

A breath hissed from between Miranda's glossy lips. "Liar," she taunted. "I'll bet you know very well. I'll bet the little chit's been spreading her legs for you for months. All the better to convince you to go along with her little scheme to inherit the Lord millions."

His hands curled into fists. "I'm warning you, Miranda—"

"No, darling," she said, her voice a silken threat, "I'm warning you. If you so much as look at that girl again, let alone fuck her, I'll sell my shares of Lord's stock to Nelson Montague so fast yours and Auntie's heads will spin."

"Nelson Montague?"

"Didn't I mention that I'd run into him in Monte Carlo last month?" She examined her polished nails, dragging the moment out for as long as possible. "He was playing baccarat—winning wonderfully, by the way—and I was doing miserably at roulette."

Her eyes gleamed coldly, like green neon. "Well, generous man that he was, he gave me part of his winnings so I wouldn't have to go over my credit limit." She smiled. "We had a wonderful time."

"I'm so happy for you both," Zach said dryly. "And I suppose sometime during this fun-filled evening he offered to buy your shares."

"No."

"No?" She was enjoying herself immensely, Zach realized grimly, tempted to wring her neck for the way she was dragging this out.

"Actually, it was the next morning, after breakfast, that he brought up the stock." That her eyes gleamed with memories of whatever orgy she and Montague had indulged in didn't faze him. She had long ago lost the power to make him jealous.

But the idea of Nelson Montague getting his grubby Australian raider's hands on any Lord's stock bothered the hell out of him.

A former miner who'd made his first millions when he'd struck a mother lode of gem-quality diamonds on Australia's Kimberly plateau, Montague was a ruthless, take-no-prisoners type of businessman who viewed things like laws and ethics as nothing more than petty annoyances to be overcome.

"You're not going to sell." It was not a suggestion. Nor a request. It was an order, pure and simple.

"Not right now," she agreed. "However, Nelson assures me that before long, if I were to sell, he'd have controlling interest in the company you and Auntie care so much about."

Zach damned her dissolute father for having sold his family stock in the first place. If Lawrence Lord hadn't been such a poor excuse for a man, if he hadn't succumbed to gambling fever, if his luck hadn't always been so bad, the company his brother founded would not be in jeopardy now.

"Actually, to tell the truth, I don't really like the man," Miranda confided. "He's coarse and crude."

"He's also the fifth wealthiest man in the world."

"That does make up for a great many faults," she agreed pragmatically. "And I can't deny that I found much of what he was offering quite attractive. Did I tell you he proposed?"

"I don't believe you mentioned it. Tell me, did you accept?"

That would certainly solve one of his problems, Zach considered. Unfortunately it would also mean that Eleanor would end up losing control of Lord's. Something he would not allow to happen.

Although he was more than capable of starting over, Zach knew exactly how much Lord's meant to Eleanor. The company was, quite simply, her life, second only to her quest for Anna. He didn't think her aging heart could take such a loss.

"Of course not, silly boy. How could I? Since I'm already married to you."

"There's also the little matter of that Aussie thug probably killing any wife who dared even think about playing around."

Rumors of the corporate raider beating a former unfaithful mistress to death had been circulating in the international business community for years. The official report was the depressed young woman had jumped from Montague's penthouse terrace.

"Well, there is that," Miranda agreed. "So," she said with a remarkable amount of cheer, considering the mutual antipathy surrounding the discussion, "we're agreed? You keep your hands off that conniving little fortune hunter and help me get Auntie the help she needs, and in return for your husbandly fidelity, I'll not sell my stock."

"I won't let you do anything to Eleanor. You make one move against your aunt and I'll refuse to cover up for your shoplifting ever again."

Frown lines furrowed her porcelain brow. "Honestly, Zachary, you can be so distressingly unbending." She bit her lip and considered her options. Jail was not one of the prettier ones. "All right. I suppose we've reached a stalemate. So long as you're at the helm of Lord's protecting my investment, I'll allow Auntie her little eccentricities.

"But," she continued, her tone growing hard, "I want that girl gone."

"That isn't my decision to make."

Miranda's eyes turned as flinty as her tone. "Then you'd better figure out something, darling. Because if you won't get rid of Alexandra Lyons, I will."

It was not, Zach feared, an idle threat.

Chapter Twenty-Two

Refusing to allow Alex to make the drive up the coast in her weakened condition, Eleanor sent a limo to fetch her. As the white limousine approached the estate, winding its way through avocado orchards and eucalyptus groves, Alex felt as if she were entering another, more privileged world.

She rode through pastures, where Arabian horses galloped across wildflower-dotted fields, their manes flowing in the breeze. The driver paused momentarily at the palacelike wrought-iron security gate hung with bright pink bougainvillea, where an elderly guard welcomed Alexandra to Casa Contenta. His proprietorial air made Alex suspect he'd worked for Eleanor Lord for a very long time.

Majestic, graceful California oaks flanked the long, curving brick driveway which led through even more acres of brilliantly colored formal gardens in full bloom, accented with cascading fountains. Finally they arrived at the sprawling, Spanish-revival mansion.

The house, if such a magnificent display of architecture could be deemed a mere house, perched atop a gentle rise of luxuriant bluegrass, offered panoramic views of pastures, mountains and sea.

The limo had no sooner glided to a stop beneath the wide red-tiled *porte cochère,* when the towering oak doors opened and Eleanor emerged.

"Welcome, Alexandra dear. I've been waiting for you." As she hugged her guest, kissing her on both cheeks, Eleanor wondered what Alexandra would say if she knew exactly how long.

If she'd thought the drive through the Lord estate was like entering another world, Alex was struck momentarily speechless by the baronial splendor of the home's interior.

Sunlight streamed through a bank of skylights, casting a warm yellow glow over the deep red Spanish tile of a reception galleria that was more spacious than many of the apartments Alex and her mother and brother had lived in during their Gypsy years. The hand-carved wooden posts lining the plaster walls and the massive beams adorning the dizzyingly high ceiling overhead recalled California's earlier era of Spanish *dons* and *doñas.*

"Well, Toto, I don't think we're in Kansas anymore," she murmured.

Eleanor laughed. "I realize it seems a little grand at first sight, but we live quite casually." She patted Alex's arm comfortingly. "Let me introduce you to the others."

One grand room followed the other as she led Alex into what she called the library and what, if the rugs had been taken up from the floor and one didn't worry about all those undoubtedly priceless knickknacks perched atop marble pedestals, was large enough to double as a gymnasium. As in the galleria, wood was abundant—in the heavy Mexican furniture, in the built-in bookcases lining the paneled walls, on the high, elaborately honeycombed wood ceiling. They could have held the NBA finals in this room, Alex mused. And still have room down by the massive see-through stone fireplace at the far end for the concession stand.

A portrait of Eleanor as a young woman hung in a gilt frame above the fireplace. Alex stopped in her tracks, stunned. Except for the fact that the portrait's subject had glossy auburn hair and was wearing a wedding gown, she could have been looking in the mirror.

"That was painted a month after my marriage to James," Eleanor said. "I see you've noticed the resemblance."

"It would be hard not to." Alex wondered why Eleanor had never mentioned this before. "They say everyone has a double, but this is incredible."

"Isn't coincidence a remarkable thing?" an all too familiar, distinctly British voice offered from the other side of the vast room. Alex slowly turned.

They were waiting for her. Zach was wearing the same smooth mask of composure he always donned when forced to rein in his emotions, while Miranda looked as if she'd like to pull Alex's hair out, strand by strand. Before she had time to dwell on Miranda's obvious antipathy, Alex was being introduced to a heavyset woman outrageously clad in a rainbow-striped chiffon caftan and matching turban, and a tall, handsome man in his fifties.

Although he appeared momentarily startled by Alex's appearance, Averill quickly recovered.

"Welcome to Santa Barbara, Alexandra," he greeted her warmly. The laugh lines framing his friendly eyes crinkled attractively. "I've been looking forward to meeting Eleanor's brilliant designer. You know," he said, dropping his tone confidentially, "you're all she talks about these days."

"I'm pleased to meet you, Dr. Brandford."

"Please…call me Averill." His gaze turned momentarily professional as it swept over her face. "Eleanor says you've had pneumonia. How are you feeling?"

"I'm fine. Well, mostly fine," she amended, when she saw the physician's eyes narrow.

"This is an excellent place for R & R," he assured her. "And perhaps, before you leave, you'll let me take you out on my ketch. You do sail, don't you?" he asked with the air of a man who couldn't imagine otherwise.

"Actually, I've never been sailing."

"Then you must. You'll love it, Alexandra." He rubbed his hands together with anticipation. "There's nothing more invigorating than the tang of the salt spray and the sea breeze in your hair."

"It sounds wonderful," Alex agreed, returning his smile.

There was a momentary lull in the conversation. The way they were all suddenly staring at her made Alex feel like a laboratory specimen.

The suspended moment was broken by the arrival of a housemaid with a trolley of steaming tea and fresh-baked pastries. Over the brief repast, Averill entertained Alex with amusing anecdotes of past sailing adventures.

Zach did not enter the conversation. Nor did Miranda, who seemed content to sip her Scotch and glower at Alex. Eleanor, too, remained oddly quiet, watching Alex with a deep, unwavering gaze that reminded Alex of the first time they'd met.

After a time, fatigue from the trip abetted by the strained atmosphere, began to take its toll.

"You've had a long drive," Eleanor said, noticing Alex's slight, stifled yawn. "Why don't we get you settled into your room?"

"Thank you. I am a little tired," Alex admitted.

She followed Eleanor out of the library, up a gracefully curving staircase and down a hall adorned with framed, formally posed portraits of elegantly clad individuals she assumed were Lord ancestors. For some reason she could not explain, she paused momentarily before a closed door.

Watching Alex stop in front of Anna's nursery, Eleanor experienced a burst of pure victorious pleasure. Of course Anna would remember which door it was!

"Your room is right next door, dear," Eleanor said in a mild tone she was a very long way from feeling.

Shaking her head to rid it of a sudden strange, slightly disorienting sensation, Alex entered a room that was both luxurious and cozy at the same time. The bed, ornately carved from the same dark wood that graced the honeycomb ceiling in the library, was draped with a crocheted comforter.

More crocheted and needlepoint pillows had been scattered at the head of the mattress. There was a fireplace in this room, as well, topped by a hand-carved mantel; needlepoint tapestry rugs were scattered over the polished oak flooring.

Ceiling-high windows looked out over the vast green grounds; from this vantage point, Alex could view a

Palladian teahouse, leafy dark green hedges and a red clay tennis court that had been built beside a serene, crystal blue swimming pool.

"It's absolutely lovely," she murmured. "Exquisite, actually."

"I want you to feel at home here, Alex."

She laughed at that. "Never in my wildest dreams could I imagine living in a home like this," she said with her characteristic frankness. "But I know I'll be comfortable," she tacked on quickly in a belated attempt to avoid hurting Eleanor's feelings.

"I do so hope so," Eleanor said fervently. "The bathroom's right through that door. It's stocked with soaps and shampoos and various other items, including a hair dryer, but if you need anything, anything at all, just pick up the phone and dial zero for the housekeeper. She'll be able to get you anything you wish."

"I'll be fine."

"Then I guess I'll leave you to your rest," Eleanor murmured, appearing oddly reluctant to leave.

Something occurred to Alex as the older woman reached the door. "Oh, I could use my suitcase from the limo."

"It's already been brought upstairs," Eleanor assured her. "Maria has already put your things away."

"Maria?"

"Juanita and Jesus's daughter. Juanita is the housekeeper," she explained. "Jesus is our main gardener. He took over after Averill's father, who had the job for years, died. Maria's the upstairs maid."

With that she was gone, leaving Alex to sink onto the bed and stare around at her luxurious surroundings.

"The upstairs maid," she murmured. "Of course."

She began to giggle. "Boy, Mom," she said, flinging herself backward onto the mattress and staring up at the restful garden mural painted on the ceiling. "I sure hope you can see me now."

Although Alex was tired, she found she could not relax. After thirty minutes or so, inexplicably drawn to the room next door, she crept back down the hallway, feeling like a cat burglar.

The room was a lovely flowered bower. Dainty pink rose blossoms bloomed on the cream wallpaper, stuffed animals and exquisitely dressed dolls with porcelain faces and hands lay atop a quilt hand-appliquéd with pink and pastel yellow tulips. Peeking out from beneath the quilt was an eyelet dust ruffle accented with pink grosgrain ribbon; more white eyelet draped a round bedside table and framed the windows. A pine rocking horse painted glossy white and boasting a white yarn mane stood in one corner of the room, while a Victorian dollhouse claimed another corner. Entranced, Alex was examining a beautiful wicker carriage, fit for a princess—or her dolls—when Eleanor, who'd come upstairs to fetch her for dinner, entered the room on silent cat feet.

"This was Anna's room."

The quiet voice behind Alex made her jump. "Anna?" A pink-cheeked, cupid-mouthed doll lay in the wicker carriage; Alex reached down and carefully adjusted the battenberg lace christening gown.

"My granddaughter."

"I didn't know you had a granddaughter." Now that she thought about it, Eleanor had never mentioned any family other than her late husband, James. Alex had assumed the couple had been childless.

"Oh, yes." A shadow moved across the older woman's face. "She was the most beautiful child. With a personality like summer sunshine. Even as a baby, she brightened the room with her sweet smile. Her mother, my son Robbie's wife, always accused me of spoiling her, but I never believed it possible to spoil a child with too much love."

"That's what my mother always said," Alex murmured. Although she may not have possessed Anna Lord's wealth of toys and treasures, Alex had always known that she was much loved. "You said *was,*" she said, as the thought suddenly occurred to her. "Anna isn't—".

"Dead?" Eleanor broke in, saving Alex from having to say the unthinkable. "No." She shook her auburn head. "No, my Anna isn't dead. Unfortunately her parents are. They were murdered," she revealed. "Downstairs, in the library, twenty-eight years ago. When Anna was only two."

"How tragic!"

"It was horrific," Eleanor said. "But quite honestly, it took a long time for Robbie's and Melanie's—that was my daughter-in-law—deaths to sink in because Anna was kidnapped at the same time."

"Kidnapped?" Alex's startled gaze moved slowly around the room.

"She was taken from her bed the night of the murder." Eleanor was watching Alex carefully. "Naturally, I've left the room exactly as it was that night. The only change I've made was to replace the crib with a child's bed, and now this full-sized Shaker.

"Although the police never found my granddaughter,

I've always known Anna will return. I want her room
to be waiting for her."

"It's a beautiful room," Alex murmured. "When I
was little, I used to dream of a room like this."

"Of course you did." When Alex gave her a quick,
puzzled glance, Eleanor hastily added, "Doesn't every
little girl?"

"I think so."

Alex walked over to a glossy white bookshelf and
ran her hands over the leather-bound classics—*Tom
Sawyer, Huckleberry Finn, Robin Hood, Black Beauty,
Treasure Island*—which were far too advanced for the
two-year-old child Anna Lord had been when she disappeared.

"*Black Beauty* was one of my favorite stories." Alex
wondered if Anna's mother had read this book to her
at bedtime, as her own mother had done.

"Anna loved horses." Eleanor's eyes misted at the
memory. "I wanted to get her a pony for her third birthday, but Melanie thought she was too young. Of course,
Papa put me on a horse before I could walk."

The brief flash of temper in Eleanor's eyes suggested that she was recalling the long-ago argument
with her daughter-in-law. "My earliest memory is sitting in front of Papa on Moonglow—his favorite Thor-
oughbred from the family stables—feeling on top of
the world."

Once again Alex noticed Eleanor's casual regard toward such vast family wealth. She'd tossed off the comment about the family stables with the same offhand
attitude she'd mentioned the upstairs maid. When she'd
been younger, during those years when her mother had
struggled to keep a roof over their heads and the wolf

away from the door, there had been innumerable times when Alex had thought that if only they were rich, all their problems would be solved.

After watching some of Debord's customers, not to mention the chronically dissatisfied Miranda Deveraux, along with having a front-row seat for Sophie's bitterly fought divorce and, now, hearing of the tragedy in Eleanor Lord's privileged life, Alex considered that wealth was not all it was cracked up to be.

Oh, it could certainly buy a great many lovely things, such as this house and its exquisite furnishings. And it could ease a great many financial concerns of day-to-day living. But the one thing money couldn't buy was happiness.

Or, she considered, thinking of Zach and Miranda, love.

"Gracious," Eleanor said, breaking into Alex's thoughts with a soft, self-conscious laugh. "I certainly didn't mean to cast a pall over your first night here." She reached out, rubbing away the lines that thoughts of Zach and his wife had etched into Alex's forehead. The maternal gesture seemed perfectly normal.

"We'd better get downstairs," Eleanor suggested, "before Beatrice starts yelling at me for ruining her dinner."

"Beatrice is the cook," Alex guessed, beginning to get a handle on how things worked around this vast estate.

"That's right. And unfortunately, when God was passing out short fuses, Beatrice must have been first in line, then turned around and gone back for seconds.

"She has a temper that could blow us all off the face of the earth," Eleanor said conspiratorially as they descended the stairs. "But one taste of her heavenly *crème brûlée* and you'll understand why I've let her bully me all these years."

Chapter Twenty-Three

Although the food was as delicious as Eleanor had promised, Alex found dinner to be a decidedly strained affair. Averill's queries about her life, her family, her career, were couched politely enough, but she couldn't quite shake the feeling she was being cross-examined.

As for Zach, Alex doubted if he uttered two words during the entire meal. Miranda also remained silent, although it would have been impossible to miss the cold fury directed Zach's way. That they had quarreled recently was more than a little obvious.

Eleanor, on the other hand, was as charming as usual, entertaining Alex with stories of her colorful family.

Her father's family, Alex learned over a rich salmon bisque, had been the Philadelphia Longworths, business people, leading players in the world cotton market and patrons of the arts. One of Eleanor's Longworth ancestors had established the Longworth Philadelphia Trust Bank, a leading financier of the American Revolution. Another had been on the board of directors of the Pennsylvania Railroad, which, in the City of Brotherly Love, established one as an undisputed member of the city's aristocracy.

Over hearts-of-palm salad, Eleanor told Alex that her mother's family were New Yorkers, whose roots, like the Longworths, predated the revolution and whose forebears included a signer of the Declaration of Independence.

Eleanor had grown up in splendid luxury on a cotton plantation outside Atlanta, Georgia, where her father raised and brokered cotton. Clothes for the ladies of the house came from Christian Dior, Chanel and Madame Grés in Paris.

She attended Foxcroft, that very proper Virginia private school, where she achieved the polish required of a young lady of her station. Like so many of her equally privileged classmates, she summered in Europe with her grandparents. She made a stunning debut at her grandparents' home on Long Island, then was sent to Paris to be "finished."

She'd wed when she was twenty, wearing a wedding gown of beaded, handmade alençon lace—the same gown she was wearing in the painting that had so startled Alex—and carrying a white Bible that had been in the Longworth family since the 1600s.

"James's parents tragically went down on the *Lusitania* when he was a boy," Eleanor divulged over the main course, grilled pheasant with lingonberry sauce. "I've always thought that being orphaned helped my husband develop the independent streak that served him so well when he began the Lord's chain."

"Those must have been exciting times," Alex said.

"They were wonderful." Eleanor smiled reminiscently. "Why, when he decided to move to the Deep South shortly after our marriage, the *Wall Street Journal* declared the region hadn't seen such a sweeping campaign since Sherman marched through Georgia."

"And of course there's always the London Lord's," Miranda reminded her aunt. A bit testily, Alex thought.

"Of course," Eleanor said agreeably. She did not add that she'd always found Miranda's father lacking. Although James had defended his younger brother on numerous occasions, it had been obvious to Eleanor from the start that Lawrence did not possess the intelligence, vitality or work ethic of his brother. Given the choice between reading a sales report from a regional manager or playing a set of tennis, Lawrence could always be found on the court.

After the dessert cups had been cleared—Eleanor hadn't exaggerated about the hot-tempered Beatrice's *crème brûlée*—the group moved into the library for brandy and coffee.

It was then that Miranda addressed Alex directly for the first time since she'd come downstairs with Eleanor. "From what Zach and Aunt Eleanor tell me, you're the quintessential workaholic, Alex."

Alex looked for the trap, but couldn't find it. "I like to keep busy."

"So I hear. Imagine working so hard that you'd give yourself pneumonia." She refilled her brandy snifter from a Waterford decanter. "How fortunate that Zachary was with you when you collapsed."

The insinuation hovered over the room, just waiting for Alex to pick up on it. "I was grateful for your husband's assistance."

"I'm sure you were." Miranda smiled first at Alex, then Zach, her eyes glittering with anticipation of impending violence, like a spectator at a prize fight. "My husband can be very helpful when he puts his mind to it."

Those dangerous eyes narrowed, giving Alex the feeling she'd just landed in the center of a very deadly bull's-eye.

"Tell me, dear," Miranda said in a silken voice that belied the malice in her gaze, "how do you make time for men in such a busy, allegedly fulfilling life?"

"I manage."

Actually she didn't. Not that there was a shortage of candidates. Actors, agents, heirs to old California fortunes, even a rising young culinary star, whose trendy new Beverly Hills restaurant had Hollywood insiders actually willing to stand in line for a table, had all repeatedly asked Alex out. But she wasn't interested in any of these contenders for her heart.

Because she'd given it to Zach on that magical starkissed bayou night. And her feelings hadn't changed. She still found Zach fascinating; she still wanted him. He was still married.

"I have the most scintillating idea!" Clara, clad tonight in royal purple, clapped her pudgy hands. "Let's have a séance!"

"No!" Zach and Averill shouted in unison.

"I was speaking to Eleanor." Alex found Clara's waspish tone a direct contrast to her soft, pink features.

All eyes turned to their hostess, who, Alex thought, suddenly looked every day of her seventy-plus years.

"I think," Eleanor said slowly, "that perhaps Alexandra should be given time to settle in before we expose her to the supernatural, Clara, dear."

Out of the corner of her eye, Alex saw Zach and Averill visibly relax. "A séance sounds fascinating," she told Clara not quite truthfully. Although she didn't believe in ghosts, Alex was not all that eager to go dabbling in the afterlife. "Perhaps some other time."

Slightly mollified, Clara spent the next half hour regaling Alex with tales of supernatural manifestations, and although Alex had no desire to insult Eleanor's elderly friend, she was relieved when the dinner party finally broke up.

After extracting a promise from Alex to go sailing soon, Averill left. Zach was next, accompanied upstairs by Miranda who, after several glasses of brandy appeared none too steady on her feet.

Alex rose to go upstairs as well, pausing briefly to wish the two elderly women good-night and to give Eleanor a quick peck on the cheek. Although she realized such behavior was unprofessional, for some reason, in this house at this time, it seemed right.

As she entered the comfortable guest room, Alex realized she was exhausted. Her head ached and she felt both cold and hot at the same time, just as she had in Zach's office. Worried that she might be in danger of a relapse, she poured a glass of water from the crystal carafe that had appeared as if by magic on her bedside table, took two aspirins, then, on second thought, swallowed a third.

"All you need is a good night's sleep," she told herself as she slipped beneath the perfumed sheets.

Unfortunately sleep proved a frustratingly elusive target. Alex tossed and turned, twisting the Egyptian cotton sheets into a restless tangle. The house was dark and silent, with only the occasional creaks as it settled for the night, as old homes seem to do.

It was after two in the morning before she finally drifted off.

Sometime later, awareness filtered slowly into Alex's subconscious mind. Something feathered against her cheek. She groggily brushed it away.

"Go home," a low, deep voice intoned.

Murmuring a protest, Alex rolled over.

"You should not have come."

Alex was emerging from the depths of what she thought to be a dream. The room had gone cold. Alex had curled up in a tight ball in an attempt to keep warm. She felt rather than saw the movement above her. She blinked slowly, trying to focus in the darkness. A strangely familiar, musty scent teased her nostrils.

A gauzy figure was standing over her. As she watched, momentarily transfixed, it began to lower a fluffy down pillow over her face.

She came to full alertness as if a bucket of ice water had been thrown on her. Arms flailing, she struck out wildly at the white-draped figure. Her bloodcurdling screams awakened the entire household.

They all rushed in—Eleanor, Clara, Zach and Miranda—and found her standing beside the bed, shaking like a leaf.

"Alex?" Although her own eyes were wide with lingering fright from being roused so abruptly, Eleanor placed a calming hand on Alex's shoulder. Alex flinched. "What's wrong?"

"Someone was in here." One of them had turned

on the light upon entering. She blinked against the brightness.

"Who, dear?"

"Three guesses," Miranda drawled. She shot a blistering glare Zach's way. "And the first two don't count."

Alex was still shaking. She was as white as the pillow lying on the floor by the window. Seeing her in such obvious distress made Zach want to take her in his arms, to hold her until the color returned to her cheeks, to stroke her hair until her fright was vanquished.

"Shut up, Miranda," he said equably. He picked up an afghan from the foot of the bed and draped it over Alex's trembling shoulders. Her turquoise nightshirt ended high on her thighs. Drenched with sweat as it was, it clung to her body. "Are you all right?"

"I—I—I think so." Alex's confused gaze circled the room, taking in the quartet of faces watching her with varying levels of intensity. "I thought I saw someone. Standing over my bed. And then..." She was hit with violent tremors.

Knowing he'd pay for this later, Zach dared Miranda's wrath and put his arm around her. She was as taut as a wire. He could practically feel her nerves crackling.

"And then?" he prompted with a gentleness that had Miranda grinding her teeth and Eleanor looking at him with sharp interest.

She felt so safe in his embrace. So protected. Alex knew she should move away. But she didn't. "I thought he was going to suffocate me. With that pillow."

"The one by the window?"

Alex followed his gaze to the floor below the open

window, where the pillow had landed when she'd wildly knocked it out of the intruder's grasp.

"I think so." The entire experience was taking on the surrealistic sensation of a nightmare.

"Ghosts," Clara declared knowingly. She'd wrapped her ample body into a silk kimono embroidered with a fire-breathing dragon. The purple and red rollers in her hair made her look as if she were trying to pick up satellite signals from space. "Perhaps Rosa has finally made contact. Your aura, Alexandra, dear," she confided, "is very strong."

"I rather doubt that Alexandra's midnight visitor was a ghost," Eleanor murmured. She'd long ago given up on Clara's psychic abilities. Especially since her own explanation was so much simpler. It was not lost souls who'd plagued Alex in the lonely dark night, Eleanor surmised. But memories. Memories, perhaps, of a child's last night in this house. The night her mother and father had been murdered.

"Well, the answer is obvious," Miranda said scathingly. Her black silk robe billowed out behind her as she marched across the room and shut the window. "The wind made the white lace curtains billow," she said. "Which to Alex's overactive imagination must have looked like a ghost. That's all there is to it. So, now that the gothic mystery is solved, can we all go back to bed?"

"I'm sorry to have bothered you all," Alex said. She glanced at the window. She could have sworn she'd closed it earlier. "Miranda's right. The curtain makes the most sense. Or a nightmare."

"It was a ghost," Clara repeated with surprising cheer considering the circumstances.

"Good night, Mrs. Kowalski," Zach said firmly.

"But—"

"Come along, Clara." Eleanor seconded Zach's order. "Let's let Alexandra get back to sleep." She kissed Alex on the cheek, gave her a fond look and practically dragged the robust woman from the bedroom.

Miranda folded her arms. "Coming, Zach?"

He knew he should go. But he couldn't. "Go on to bed, Miranda," he instructed, knowing he was further risking her ire, but feeling an even stronger pull to ensure himself that Alex was truly all right. "I'll be along in a minute."

Miranda surprised both Zach and Alex. "Whatever you say," she said sweetly. "Good night, Alex. Sweet dreams."

Her friendly smile matched her pleasant tone. So why, Alex wondered, did she hear a threat behind those sugarcoated words?

"How are you, really?" Zach asked when they were alone.

"Fine." Her voice was frail. "I'm fine," she repeated more firmly this time. "Actually, I'm more embarrassed than frightened."

His hands were stroking her arms, soothing her lingering distress and creating another even more vital. "Do you think it was a dream?"

"What else could it have been?"

"I don't know."

Surely Miranda wouldn't have… No! Zach assured himself. His wife was admittedly a pathologically jealous woman. But even Miranda was not capable of murder.

"It was a dream," she said.

Unable to think of any other plausible solution, Zach murmured an agreement. He drew her against him and ran his hands up and down her back, soothing and stimulating her at the same time.

"You should go."

He brushed his lips against her hair, inhaling its fresh, sunshine scent. "In a minute."

She closed her eyes and rested her cheek against his chest. Alex knew she should send him back to his wife, back to the bed they shared. But she couldn't. Not yet.

"A minute," she breathed. She wrapped her arms around his waist and clung. He was wearing the jeans he'd hurriedly tugged on when awakened by Alex's screams. His chest was bare. And so, so enticing. In a warm haze of need, Alex brushed her lips over his shoulder. His chest.

"Alexandra," he moaned. Her mouth was searing his skin with every breathy kiss.

"Shh." She smiled against his warm flesh. "Just a little more."

Half-blind with need, Zach grasped a handful of fragrant hair and tilted her head back, lifting her gaze to his. "More." His lips hovered inches above hers. His voice was rough and husky.

And then he closed the distance.

A soft, yielding sigh slipped from between her lips to his. She went up on her toes, twining her arms around his neck, clinging tightly. The afghan slipped unnoticed to the floor.

Her body strained against his. Her hot, avid mouth was as urgent and impatient as his. He stroked her through the nightshirt, delighting in the sensuous movements of her body beneath the silk. Beneath his hands. He slipped his hands under the hem and discovered that her flesh, so icy just minutes ago, had warmed.

Fear disintegrated. Her earlier shock dissolved. At this suspended moment in time there was only now. Only Zach.

Through her dazed senses, she could hear him whispering to her, intimate soft words, crazy, wonderful promises.

Zach knew it was foolhardy, allowing the reins on his tautly held hunger to slip here, and now, with the house filled with people and his wife just next door.

He knew it was dangerous. Knew it was wrong. But, God help him, he was only human and she was so soft and so sweet and he'd been so terrified when he'd heard her scream, so relieved when he'd discovered she was all right, that all he could do, dammit, was feel.

Oh, yes! This was what she'd been wanting. Alex had been longing for the taste of his firm lips, dying to feel those strong bold hands against her flesh. She wanted him with a need that bordered on insanity, which is why she didn't back away, even as she knew that what she and Zach were doing was madness.

He pushed the turquoise silk up, giving his lips access to her breasts. As he breathed on the hot flesh, kissed it, licked it, a direct line of fire shot from her taut, tingling nipples to the center of her legs.

She moaned deep in her throat. Her fingers dug into his hips. If this was, indeed, madness, Alex welcomed it with open arms.

With trembling fingers she unsnapped his jeans.

But when she reached for him, desperate to drive him as crazy as he was driving her, he caught her wrists.

"Alex, sweetheart." He steadied himself by drawing in deep drafts of air. "We have to stop."

She shook her head, sending her hair out in a shimmering arc. "Not yet."

His body was throbbing, reaching for the touch she was trying to bestow. Zach's head was swimming, and although he wanted nothing more than to drag her to the bed, strip off that scrap of turquoise silk and bury himself deep inside her welcoming heat, he knew that the risk would be too great.

Besides, a nagging little voice of conscience reminded him, only moments ago she'd been terrified. What if her response had been born only out of the need to be comforted? If he went to bed with her now, wouldn't that be taking advantage of her atypical fragility?

And, first and foremost, his agonized, convoluted thought process returned as it always did to the simple fact that he couldn't offer her anything beyond the moment. And to Zach's mind, that was offering her nothing at all.

Alex was looking up at him, her heart shining in her wide, luminous eyes. Then she took a deep shuddering breath, glanced around and belatedly remembered where she was, where they were.

"Thank you."

"For what?" His voice was rough.

"For having the good sense to stop." She combed her fingers through her hair. "If your wife had walked in…"

There was no need to finish the sentence. They both

knew the scene that Miranda was capable of creating would not be pretty.

As their gazes met and clung, Alex shivered.

"You're cold." Zach reached for the afghan again.

Alex wrapped her arms around herself in an unconscious gesture of self-protection. "No, not cold. Scared."

He glanced over at the window. "It's closed now. And locked."

She shook her head. "That's not what I'm afraid of. I'm afraid of you."

"Me?" She couldn't have said anything that hurt more.

"Of the way you make me feel."

Zach closed his eyes and dragged his hand down over his face. "Don't feel like the Lone Ranger."

He smiled a crooked, self-deprecating smile as he trailed his fingertips down the side of her somber face, tracing the full shape of her lips before continuing along her jaw and down her throat. Then, heaving a deep sigh of regret, he dropped his hand.

"Do you think you can sleep now?"

"Yes." It was the only lie she'd ever told him. How did he think she could sleep when every pore in her body ached for his touch? Just when she thought she was going to burst into frustrated tears of unfulfillment, humor rose to rescue her. "After a cold shower."

He chuckled at that, as she'd meant him to. "At least Eleanor won't have to worry about running out of hot water with the two of us stuck together under the same roof."

He ran a hand down her hair, gave her a long look overbrimming with emotion. "Good night."

Her smile wobbled, her eyes misted. "Night."

And then he was gone.

Dammit, women slept with married men every day, Alex told herself. And husbands fooled around. Afternoon talk shows routinely discussed the advantages of open marriages, and movies and novels depicting infidelity were becoming so common it seemed that recreational adultery between consenting adults was becoming almost chic.

As she climbed back into bed and pulled the sheets over her head, Alex found herself wishing that her mother had imbued her children with less scruples.

Or that Eve Deveraux had raised a less honorable son.

Chapter Twenty-Four

"Good morning!" Clara greeted Alex the next morning.

"Morning." Alex had come downstairs in desperate need of a cup of coffee. "Good morning, Eleanor."

"Good morning, dear. How are you feeling?"

"Fine." Actually, a maniac was pounding away with a hammer inside her head, but Alex decided a polite white lie was in order. She went over to the antique sideboard and poured a cup of coffee from a silver samovar.

"I was concerned you might have another nightmare," Eleanor said.

Alex stirred in a teaspoon of sugar. "I slept like a baby." Another lie. Beside the samovar were silver bowls of fresh berries and a damask-lined basket of fresh breads and pastries. Alex plucked a blueberry muffin from the basket, put it on a plate and sat down at the table.

"Beatrice will be happy to make whatever else you'd

like," Eleanor said. "Some hotcakes, perhaps? French toast? An omelet?"

"This is fine. I'm not much of a breakfast eater."

"You need to get your strength back," Eleanor reminded her.

"I also need to fit into the dress I'm making for the Chicago debut. Thanks to Inga, I've gained at least ten pounds."

"Thank goodness," Eleanor countered. "You were looking far too thin before your collapse."

Alex shrugged. "You know what they say. A woman can never be too rich or too thin."

"I knew the Duchess of Windsor," Eleanor revealed. A wicked light danced in her eyes. "And she might be right about the money, dear. But believe me, the woman looked like a corpse."

"I've always found men prefer curvaceous women," Clara declared robustly. "At least my three husbands did." Her dimpled arms reached out of today's billowy green sleeves and plucked a buttery *croissant* from the basket. Two bran muffins and a cinnamon roll joined the *croissant* on her plate.

"You know, Alex," Clara said around a mouthful of muffin, "I've been thinking about your visitor last night."

"It was a nightmare," Alex demurred. "Or a trick of moonlight."

"That's your logical mind speaking," Clara insisted. "Last night you were operating in your intuitive realm. Tell me, have you ever heard of Resurrection Mary?"

"No, but—"

"She was a beautiful young girl, captivating, with blue eyes and the palest, prettiest flaxen hair. And Lord, she loved to dance! One night she died in an automobile accident going home from a ballroom. That was nearly fifty years ago, yet there are still tales of her rising from her grave in Resurrection Cemetery to go dancing with handsome single men at that same ballroom."

"Really, Clara," Eleanor complained, "I have difficulty believing any single young man would care to dance with a fifty-year-old corpse."

"But she looks just the way she did the night she died," Clara explained. "Of course, the men do report that she seems aloof. Cold."

"I would think she'd be cold," Eleanor snorted.

Clara frowned, obviously piqued that she wasn't being taken seriously. "My point is that there have been so many reportings of Mary, a song was written about her. And there's the young maid who hanged herself in Chicago in 1915 and still haunts the Victorian house where she worked, and the young bride in St. Paul, Minnesota, and—"

"I believe you were making a point?" Eleanor interrupted.

"Well, yes." Clara nodded emphatically, starting her several chins jiggling. "I think there's a very good possibility that this house is being haunted. Perhaps by Melanie."

"Dammit, Clara—" Eleanor began.

"But you've told me she was wearing a white evening dress the night she was killed. And Alexandra's apparition was wearing white. Isn't that so?" she demanded of a bemused Alex.

"It was only a nightmare," Alex repeated weakly, wishing the entire humiliating event had never happened.

Clara folded her arms over her ample bosom. "Well, I believe an exorcism is in order."

"Alex is here to rest," Eleanor said briskly. "There will be no exorcism." She rose and placed her folded napkin on the table. "I have to go over the reports Zach brought up from L.A. yesterday. There are papers that need to be signed."

Her expression softened as she turned to Alex. "I hope you don't mind my abandoning you your first day here."

"Don't worry about me," Alex assured her. "I'll just explore the grounds."

"What a grand idea," Clara agreed robustly after Eleanor had left the dining room. "I'll give you a tour. And of course, you won't want to miss the greenhouse. In fact, you're in luck. I was planning to feed my *Dionaea muscipula* this afternoon. My Venus flytrap," she elaborated at Alex's blank look. "I've a nice fat cricket I've been saving just for this occasion."

The idea of watching a plant devour a helpless insect was not Alex's idea of a fun afternoon. "That sounds quite interesting," she lied yet again, "but I just remembered I promised Sophie Friedman some new sketches."

"It's quite fascinating to watch," Clara coaxed.

"Perhaps next time." Alex stood up, flashed the woman an apologetic smile, then escaped the room.

As the afternoon progressed, Alex experienced strange, periodic feelings of *déjà vu*. It was almost as if she'd been here, in Santa Barbara, in this very house before.

But, of course, she assured herself, that was impossible. As impossible as Clara's insistence about restless spirits.

These unsettling emotions, last night's bad dream, along with her continued feeling of being drawn to Anna's nursery, were nothing more than the product of her imagination. The power of suggestion, Alex reminded herself, could be very strong.

On her third day at the house, Clara confronted Alex in the rose garden.

"There you are, Alexandra. I've been searching the entire house for you," she complained, her pink face even rosier than usual. She was out of breath; her ample chest was heaving as if she'd just run a marathon. Today's caftan was the vivid yellow, orange and crimson hue of the Joseph's Coat blossoms Alex had just been admiring.

It crossed Alex's mind that if Clara were truly clairvoyant, she would have known where she was. "Well, you found me."

"I had a vision."

"Another one?" If the elderly woman was to be believed, psychic revelations were a remarkably common occurrence.

"I was in the library, playing canasta with Eleanor, when I just happened to glance over at the fireplace. That's when I saw it."

"It?"

She leaned toward Alex, lowering her voice to a dramatic stage whisper. "There was a lighthouse in the flames."

Almost against her will, Alex was momentarily intrigued. "You can see things in fires?"

"Of course. Didn't I tell you that I am one-eighth Rom?"

"Rom?"

"Romany—Gypsy. My great-grandmother was a *shuvani*," Clara said haughtily. "A wise woman. When I was a girl, she taught me how to divine fortunes from the flames of the *atchen'tan*—the campfire."

"That's very interesting," Alex murmured politely even as she considered, not for the first time, that Clara's talents were definitely being wasted. With her vivid imagination and penchant for storytelling, she could probably clean up writing horror scripts in Hollywood.

"I haven't done it for ages. This time it was totally unconscious...." She shook her head, as if clearing her mind. "A lighthouse means danger. It was at the top of the fire in the position representing the present. But that wasn't all. At the front of the fire, into the future, I saw a monk."

"A monk?"

"Any Gypsy worth her salt knows that a monk is the symbol of deception and subterfuge."

"I see," Alex said, not really seeing anything at all.

"The monk is a warning of some unpleasant incident connected with a man of power and influence. And that's not all."

It never was with Clara. "Oh?"

Clara placed a pudgy pink hand on Alex's arm. "The warning wasn't for me, Alexandra." Her fingers tightened. "It was for you. You must leave Santa Barbara. Now."

Alex gently shrugged off the older woman's touch. "It's not that I don't appreciate the warning, Clara," she said politely, "because I do. But I think I'll take my chances."

Clara bristled. "Well," she huffed, with an angry

shake of her turbaned head, "don't say I didn't warn you." With that, she turned and stomped away, her silk caftan billowing around her ample frame like a bright sail against a gale-force wind.

The nightmare came before dawn, slinking into Alex's subconscious mind like a black cat on All Hallows' Eve. She was walking through the fog; cold gray mists curled around her bare legs, brushed over her arms, settled damply in her hair. In the distance she could barely make out a huge, forbidding house.

The dark, damp earth beneath her bare feet had a pungent, yeasty smell. She had no idea whether it was day or night; the world had become a skyless realm where the only colors were black and green. The immense quiet of the shadowy forest closed in on her; the black, gesticulating trees curtaining the narrow path seemed to be reaching for her.

A gust of wind from the nearby storm-tossed sea ruffled her hair; a sudden flash of sulfurous lightning illuminated the land in a stuttering white light.

And then she saw it. The blood. It was everywhere— flowing wetly over the ground like a dark red river, splattering over the rocks, staining her flowing white dress, soaking into her wild, unkempt hair.

Locked in the escalating terror, Alex tossed and turned on her sweat-drenched sheets.

She was no longer alone. A cowled monk was coming toward her, the evil glint of a dagger in his hand. Although she couldn't make out his features in the overwhelming darkness, his eyes gleamed like red-hot coals.

He slowly raised the dagger high above his head and brought it down viciously, directly at her heart.

Alex woke with a jolt just in time, rescuing herself from the monk's murderous intent.

As she paced the floor in the predawn darkness, waiting anxiously for morning, Alex tried to tell herself that the nightmare was nothing more than a figment of her imagination, brought on by the strain of preparing for her upcoming design debut, Miranda's ongoing antipathy, the lingering effects of her illness and her strange conversation in the garden with Clara.

But even as she assured herself that her nightmare was nothing more than the product of her creative mind, Alex couldn't quite make herself believe it.

Not when her skin was still chilled from the icy gray mists. Not when the image of that cowled monk lurked threateningly in her mind's eye. And certainly not when the acrid, suffocating odor of blood lingered in her nostrils.

Despite the good deal of common sense Alex possessed, she couldn't quite shake the feeling that the nightmare that had disturbed her sleep for the past ten nights had been all too real.

The nightmare continued, night after restless night. Disjointed, frightening fragments, scenes hidden in a misty fog. Scenes that asked more questions than they revealed.

Each night before retiring, Eleanor brought Alex a cup of lemon verbena tea, touted by Clara as a near-miraculous sedative. When the tea proved ineffectual, Clara followed up with valerian, an unpleasant brew that smelled like dirty sweat socks and did nothing to help Alex sleep.

Hearing of Alex's insomnia, Averill offered to prescribe something to help her sleep. But wary of prescription drugs, Alex declined.

Seeking other means of relaxing, which had been the point of this trip all along, Alex began taking long walks on the cliff behind the estate, where she'd stare out at the vast Pacific Ocean and try to sort through her unsettled emotions.

Part of her discomfort, she knew, was due to Miranda. Although Zach had returned to L.A., Miranda had remained in Santa Barbara, living in the family wing. Jealousy surrounded the woman like a particularly noxious cloud; she seemed determined to make Alex's life miserable with her sly innuendos. The unrelenting hostile behavior made Alex face the unpalatable truth of Miranda's very real existence in Zach's life.

The fact of his wife existed as solidly as one of the boulders forming the cliff upon which she walked. And unfortunately, though it was more than obvious that Zach and Miranda's marriage was less than idyllic, the beautiful, spiteful Mrs. Deveraux had made it all too clear that she was every bit as immovable as those enormous granite rocks.

Deciding that perhaps she ought to return to the city, where she wouldn't be forced to endure Miranda's presence, Alex returned to the house to find Averill waiting for her on the terrace. He was dressed in chinos, a navy polo shirt and white deck shoes. A white billed cap with gold braid was perched jauntily atop his sun-streaked hair.

"I came by to kidnap you," he said to her cheerfully.

Alex went ice cold. Her hands, her mind, her heart.

"Alexandra?" Eleanor, who'd been sitting on a blue-

and-white striped lounge, rose quickly to her feet. "What's wrong?"

"Wrong?" Alex answered through lips that seemed to have turned to stone. What the hell was happening to her these days? She was turning into a hysterical ninny.

"Nothing." She shook her head to clear away the mists, then turned back toward the doctor with a smile. "I must have misunderstood you."

"No." He took off his cap and combed his long, aristocratic fingers through his hair, ruffling a fifty-dollar haircut. "It was my fault. I simply dropped by to invite you sailing. But I should have chosen my words more carefully. Especially since Eleanor has told me that you know about Anna's disappearance."

They were both looking at her as if they expected her either to faint or go screaming off across the manicured lawn at any second. Feeling ridiculously foolish, Alex ignored her lingering disquiet.

"I'd love to go sailing with you, Dr. Brandford."

"Averill," he reminded her with a friendly wink.

He was a very nice, uncomplicated person. And the way he hovered over Eleanor like a dutiful son proved he had a warm and caring nature.

Though she'd vowed never again to get involved with an older man, Alex wondered idly if the good doctor was married. If so, his wife, she decided, was a very lucky woman.

"Averill," she agreed with a smile.

As she ran upstairs to change into a pair of rubber-soled shoes, for the first time since her arrival in Santa Barbara, Alex was feeling almost lighthearted.

Before they left port, Averill gave Alex a brief lesson on the fundamentals of sailing, and while she tried to keep track of the terms, he might as well have been speaking in Sanskrit.

He laughed when she'd admitted her confusion. "I'd be equally lost if you began talking about dress design," he assured her. "I figured out buttons and bra hooks when I was a teenager. Other than that, everything else to do with female clothing remains a mystery."

She knew he was attempting to make her feel less foolish. He succeeded. Alex watched him cast off, maneuvering deftly and confidently around the ropes she knew would have tripped her and sent her flying over the gleaming brass railing.

The sail snapped in the breeze, then billowed, appearing starkly white against the cloudless cerulean sky as he guided the sleek ketch through the channel, out into the sea.

The boat skimmed across the water as Averill followed the jagged shoreline. Up till now, Alexandra's sole boating experience had been a futile attempt to row a cumbersome wooden craft across a Minnesota lake at Girl Scout camp the summer she turned twelve. Back then, all she'd gotten for her laborious efforts were blisters and a lobster-red sunburn.

But this was different. This, she mused, as she leaned back and tilted her face up to the California sun, was like flying.

Averill proved to be a wonderful companion, entertaining her with tales of his sailing experiences, including more than one close call when he'd found himself caught in a sudden squall.

"You don't have to worry," he assured her when he viewed her worried frown after one such story. "Today's going to be clear sailing. All the way."

Like Zachary, he managed to appear supremely self-confident without seeming arrogant or egotistical. Reminding herself that one of the reasons she'd taken Averill up on his offer today was to forget about her problems—including those inherent with being in love with a married man—she turned her attention, instead, to the glorious scenery that could have graced the cover of a brochure put out by the Santa Barbara tourist bureau.

Gulls whirled overhead, their strident cries carried off by the ocean wind. Every so often one of them would go hurling downward, disappearing beneath the water, reappearing moments later with a flash of silver in his beak. Long-billed pelicans and wide-winged cormorants skimmed along the surface of the water; sea lions dozed atop sun-warmed rocks.

Averill steered the boat into a sheltered cove, where they sat on the polished teak deck and shared the lunch of cold chicken, pasta salad and crunchy French bread Eleanor's cook had packed into a wicker basket. The doctor's contribution to the picnic was a bottle of Napa Valley chardonnay.

The outing proved even more relaxing than Averill had promised. Alex thoroughly enjoyed the glorious day, the brisk sail, the congenial company.

"Thank you," she said after they'd returned to the yacht basin. "I had a wonderful time."

"The pleasure was all mine." His smiling eyes swept over her, taking in her face, flushed prettily from the sun, her sunset-bright hair, which had been whipped into an enticing froth by the sea breeze, her long, tanned legs, shown off by her daffodil-yellow denim shorts.

"You know," he said, as he took her hand and helped

her off the gently rocking ketch onto the floating dock, "if I were twenty years younger, I'd prove to you that there's a great deal more to life than work." He shook his head in disbelief. "In my day, a lovely woman like you certainly wouldn't still be running around un-claimed."

Alex had two choices: she could be irritated by his blatantly chauvinistic statement, or she could take his words as a masculine, if slightly dated, compliment and be flattered. She chose the latter.

"I do hope you're not calling me an old maid," she said with a light laugh.

"Not at all." He looked honestly horrified that she might think such a thing.

"Good. That being the case, I should tell you that I don't think you're old at all." Feeling remarkably care-free, she linked her arm through his. "In fact, next time you're in L.A., I insist you let me reciprocate by taking you out on the town."

"I'm speaking at a conference in the city next month. Why don't I come down in the ketch? We can sail to Catalina and I'll let you buy me lunch at Las Casitas."

"It's a date. I've never been to Santa Catalina Is-land."

"You haven't?" He stopped in his tracks and looked down at her as if she'd just sprouted a second head. "My prescription for you, Alexandra Lyons, is regular doses of sun and salt air. And I intend to schedule in regular checkups to ensure you're following orders."

Alex laughed, as she was supposed to. "Yes, Doc-tor."

Chapter Twenty-Five

The lightened mood instilled by the brisk sail disintegrated when the terrifying dream returned that night. To make matters worse, the next morning Zach arrived at the house to discuss the logistics of the Chicago opening with Eleanor.

Watching Zach and Miranda was like watching a Tennessee Williams play. Miranda, who seemed in no hurry to return to her work at the London Lord's, was her typical theatrical self, ensuring her place at center stage, while Zach glowered and remained silent.

As if conjured up by some special-effects department in the sky, a storm front coincided with Zach's arrival, driving away the benevolent sunshine with wind gusts, pelting rain and fog.

When Miranda cursed viciously at yet another servant for some minor imagined transgression, Alex decided that rain or no rain, she had to escape.

She went out to the six-car garage and took the Mercedes two-seater Eleanor had generously made available to her during her stay. She drove past the Montecito Country Club, continuing on through the center of town to the coast, passing by sandy East Beach, where the usual weekend arts-and-crafts show had been rained out.

She passed Stearns Wharf—which Averill had told her was the oldest operating wharf on the West Coast—and the yacht harbor, where she was tempted to stop and see if the doctor was working on his ketch, as he was every other weekend he wasn't sailing. She felt an overwhelming urge for some easy, uncomplicated companionship.

Worried that after his remarks about her lack of dating he might think she'd set her sights on him, Alex stopped, instead, at the breakwater and walked along the half-mile manmade marvel, attempting to work off her anxiety.

She stood at the end of the breakwater for a long time, watching the white-capped waves roll in and thinking of Zach. Sea mist dampened her face and went unnoticed.

For whatever reason—Alex knew it wasn't love—Zach appeared determined to make the best of his marriage. Which meant he was off-limits.

Averill was right about one thing: she'd been living unnaturally. It was time she started dating again, if for no other reason than to get on with her life. She'd come a long way from the naive young acolyte who'd let Debord steal her designs, then throw her away as if she were a stale croissant left over from breakfast.

She was an Emmy-winning designer, dammit! She had a fulfilling, glamorous career, and thanks to Eleanor Lord, she was a businesswoman with her first licensing agreement. The thing to do, Alex told herself firmly, was to quit mooning over a man she could not have and get on with her life. It was time, past time, that she put the man out of her mind!

Which wouldn't be all that easy to do, considering the fact that they still had to work together on the Blue Bayou project. But she'd already accomplished so much, had come so far. Her mother had always assured her that she could do anything she put her mind to. So, from now on, she would simply put her mind to burying whatever feelings she had for Zach deep inside her.

The wind picked up and the temperature dropped, causing Alex to realize she'd been standing out in the rain for a very long time. Shivering, she headed back for the car.

Not yet ready to return to the estate, she continued her drive through the fog-draped Santa Ynez Mountains. With the heater going full blast, she warmed up quickly. She tuned the radio to a rock station; the windshield wipers added a *swish-swish-swish* counterpoint to Bruce Springsteen's driving beat.

For a long time, as she maneuvered the car around the curves, she continued to give herself a stern pep talk. "Zach? Zach who? Oh, Zachary Deveraux, *that* Zach. He's only a business associate. Nothing more."

She could tell herself that all day. And all night. But more than an hour later, after she'd made a U-turn in the middle of the road and headed back down the mountainside toward the Montecito estate, Alex realized it was folly to keep lying to herself.

The frightening truth was that despite all her good intentions and stalwart resolutions, if Zach ever wanted her, she would give herself to him.

Immersed in her tumultuous thoughts, she hadn't noticed that the little sports car had begun to pick up more speed than was prudent, given the slick conditions of the road.

Alex pumped the brake lightly. When it failed to gain purchase, she tried again. Nothing.

Again, harder.

Again, nothing.

Risking putting the car into a deadly skid, she pushed the brake pedal all the way to the floor. Instead of coming to a screeching halt or even slowing down, the car picked up speed.

Trying to remain calm, Alex downshifted, which, considering the steep grade she was descending, proved ineffectual. The engine whined as misty trees sped past the windows.

Now she was scared. Leaning forward, she hung on to the wheel with both hands, trying to steer around the treacherous wet curves. Time slowed. She wondered if her life would begin flashing before her eyes.

Alex sincerely hoped not; seeing through the slanting rain was hard enough without having to watch a rerun of past mistakes.

Unfamiliar with the mountains and having paid scant attention to her surroundings earlier, she had no idea how far she still had to go before reaching level ground. As she sped past a side road leading to a winery, she hoped the wild ride would be over soon.

It was. But not in the way she'd hoped. As the car raced around a snakelike series of curves, the tires hit a particularly wet patch of roadway and began to hydroplane. The rear of the car fishtailed, sending her off the pavement, over an embankment, where the front end of the Mercedes settled with a great sucking sound into the mud.

Alex was thrown forward, but her seat belt held, keeping her safe. Safe, she determined once she could breath again. But lost. And the rain was still coming down.

Cursing in a way that even Miranda might have admired, had Zach's wife been unfortunate enough to be out in such horrid weather, Alex managed to push open the door. And then, as the skies opened up still more she began to walk.

Although the winery tasting room was closed, Alex was fortunate to find an employee taking inventory. The young man let her in, retrieved a handful of paper towels from the restroom and, while she called the house to explain about the accident and to request that one of the servants come retrieve her, poured her a very large and very tasty glass of estate-bottled *pinot noir*.

Since she hadn't eaten anything but a grapefruit and a cup of coffee at breakfast time, which was, she realized, glancing down with surprise at her water-fogged watch, more than eight hours ago, the smooth, ruby red wine went straight to her head, creating a comfortable glow. Indeed, the feeling was so pleasurable, she didn't refuse a refill.

Thirty minutes later, Zach arrived, looking every bit as foreboding and dangerous as the weather.

"I didn't ask Eleanor to send you." Alex blinked with surprise at the sight of Zach practically filling the tasting room doorway.

"I volunteered."

"Oh." While far from drunk, Alex was relaxed enough to be able to ignore his lambent fury. "Well, it was certainly nice of you to come out in the rain this way."

"You can thank me later." He pulled a bill from his wallet and tossed it onto the oak bar.

The young man pushed the money back. "It's on the house. My pleasure."

He was talking to Zach, but his gaze was on Alex.

"Zach, this is Steve," Alex said with remarkable cheer, considering the events of the past hour. "Steve, this is Zachary. My, uh, business associate."

"Nice to meet you," Steve said without so much as a glance Zach's way.

Seeing Alex through the other man's eyes, observing the familiar aching on his young face, irritated the hell out of Zach.

"Mrs. Lord appreciates you helping her houseguest," he muttered. He took hold of Alex's arm and yanked her off the bar stool. He also left the bill where it was.

"Come back some time when you're not in such a hurry," Steve called out after them. Zach knew damn well the irritatingly good-looking Steve was not talking to him.

"Thank you, I'll do that," Alex said. Her sunny smile, as Zach dragged her across the wooden floor, could have banished all the rain clouds overhead.

"Wasn't he nice?" Alex asked as they drove away from the winery in Zach's Jag.

"A real prince," Zach muttered. "You certainly didn't waste any time making another conquest."

"What?" Alex glanced toward his rigid profile. "What are you talking about?"

"First you have Averill practically tripping all over himself to take you sailing, and now your new little friend Steve—the guy reminded me of my old hunting dog, Duke, slobbering over a juicy steak bone. By the time you leave town, you'll probably have every male within a thirty-mile radius of Santa Barbara lusting after you."

Was he actually jealous? The idea was both surprising and encouraging. "That's not a very nice thing to say."

"In case you haven't noticed, sweetheart, I'm not exactly in a very nice mood. Have you noticed how fate keeps decreeing I step in and rescue you from your own stupidity? Kinda makes you wonder what I must've done in a past life to deserve such lousy karma, doesn't it?"

So much for encouraging. The warm glow instilled by the wine was shot to smithereens by his gritty tone and unkind words. Refusing to respond, Alex folded her arms and pretended avid interest in the scenery flashing by the passenger window.

Neither one of them spoke for a long time. Finally Zach said, "I arranged for a tow truck to pick up the Mercedes."

"Thank you," she answered stonily, still refusing to look at him.

"In case you're interested, it's not that banged up."

"Oh, I'm so glad," she said on a burst of honest relief. "I was afraid I'd totaled Eleanor's car."

"If you were so concerned about the damn car, you shouldn't have been driving so fast. Christ, Alex, don't you have any more sense than to speed on a wet highway in the rain?"

"Speeding? You think I was speeding?"

"If you'd been driving at a halfway prudent speed,

you wouldn't have gone off the road," he said with the unwavering logic she usually admired.

She gave an unladylike snort. "Gee, you've got a helluva lot of faith in me."

"You're not exactly a model of restraint, sweetheart."

Alex knew he didn't mean the term as an endearment. "I am, too!"

Didn't he realize how much restraint it had taken her not to pull out all the stops and seduce him?

Most of the time, Alex didn't think it would be all that difficult to lure Zachary into her frustratingly lonely bed; at other times, such as now, she almost got the impression that he didn't like her at all.

And women were supposed to be the changeable ones, she thought darkly. Men might not suffer PMS, but they damn well had their own share of mood swings, nevertheless.

He brought the car to a halt at a four-way stop. "Honey, you wouldn't even know how to spell *restraint*."

That did it. To hear such a disparaging tone from the man she loved was the last straw in a very trying day.

"Go to hell." Unfastening her seat belt with trembling fingers, she opened the door and began walking angrily down the road.

Chapter Twenty-Six

"Goddammit, Alexandra!"

He'd been panic-stricken when her call had come. All during the nerve-racking drive to the winery, thoughts of Alex lying in the roadway, broken and bleeding, had billowed in his mind like dark and deadly smoke from a sugarcane field fire.

Wanting, needing, to get to her as quickly as possible, he'd disregarded personal safety and all state speed statutes, racing into the mountains, planning to take her into his arms, to soothe her, to love her.

But then he'd found her sitting coyly atop that bar stool, sipping wine as if she were in some damn nightclub, flirting with that blond beachboy, who in turn looked as if he'd been struck by lightning, and every one of Zach's good intentions had disintegrated.

He was, admittedly, furious. Furious at her for risking her life, furious at himself for allowing loyalty to Eleanor and responsibility toward Lord's to prevent him from simply saying the hell with the company and his marriage and taking what he wanted.

And what he wanted, dammit, was Alex.

"Dammit, Alexandra," he complained, driving slowly along the edge of the road, "would you quit acting like a spoiled brat and get back into this car?"

She didn't answer; nor did she so much as spare him a glance. She just kept walking, her hooded cardinal slicker brightening the dismal gray day.

"It's another ten miles to the house."

"I run ten miles all the time."

"Not in weather like this."

She turned. "It just so happens that I like walking in the rain. And for your information, Mr. Know-It-All Deveraux, if you check with a mechanic after the tow truck driver pulls the car out of that ditch, you'll discover that the brakes gave out. I wasn't speeding."

"Are you saying the brakes failed?"

"Got it on the first try. I guess the famed German automotive engineering isn't all it's cracked up to be." She turned away and began marching down the road again.

This was ridiculous. He couldn't follow her all the way back to Eleanor's. Muttering a string of pungent curses, he pulled the car over to the side of the deserted roadway.

He moved quickly, planning to drag her, kicking and screaming if necessary, back to the car.

She didn't look back when she heard the car door slam. Nor did she pause as his long, determined strides brought him alongside her.

"Go away. And leave me alone."

"The hell I will," he snarled, his temper approaching boiling point. "You're coming with me."

But he'd no sooner grabbed her arm when Alex surprised them both. Swinging her fist wildly, she connected firmly with his jaw.

"I said, leave me alone!" she shouted, her words whipped away by the driving wind.

"Too late." It was the last straw. Ignoring the surprising pain in his jaw, he grabbed hold of the front of her slicker and pulled her toward him. Water streamed down his furious face.

"I'm sick of this," he shouted. "I'm fed up with this entire fucking charade."

A lesser woman would have been intimidated by the savage gleam glittering in his midnight dark eyes. Alex tilted her head—disregarding her hood as it fell backward, exposing her head to the driving rain—and met his dangerous gaze with a challenging glare of her own.

"What charade?"

"For starters, my sitting in my office, drinking in your scent, trying to keep my mind on facts and figures when all the time I'm wondering what you're wearing beneath those outrageously sexy outfits you insist on wearing, instead of proper little pinstriped dress-for-success business suits.

"I'm sick and tired of spending some of the most miserable nights of my life lying alone in bed, imagining you across town—so near, and yet so impossibly far away—and wondering what you're doing. Or worse yet, who you're doing it with.

"I'm sick of remembering that night, when I held you in my arms and wished that I possessed the power to stop time. I'm sick of going to sleep so horny my balls ache and having to take cold showers every morning to get rid of the goddamn hard-on that comes from dreaming about you.

"And mostly I'm sick of having spent all this time wishing for what might have been and kicking myself for not having made love to you when we had the chance.

"I've wanted you more than I've ever wanted any woman in my life. But because I care about you more than I've ever cared about any woman in my life, I've been killing myself trying to keep from hurting you. And what the hell have all these good and noble intentions gotten me?

"A punch in the jaw from a snotty, stubborn female who doesn't even have enough common sense to come in out of the rain!"

He was definitely on a roll. Alex, who was finally seeing the fire she'd always suspected dwelt beneath that infuriatingly remote exterior, stared up at him in awe. She knew she should find such violent emotion frightening. But knowing that Zach would never actually harm her, she was finding it thrilling.

His head swooped down and Alex cried out as his mouth captured hers in a hard, rapacious kiss.

She began kissing him back, desperately, hungrily.

The rain sluicing over their taut, straining bodies went ignored as they consumed each other with deep kisses. They were caught in the unrelenting grip of something powerful and ageless and primal. Something that could no longer be denied.

"If that wasn't an earthquake," she said breathlessly, "we're in trouble."

"It was no earthquake." His lips skimmed hotly up her face; he pulled her hard against him.

Zach wanted to take her here and now. He wanted to drag her to the side of the road and bury his throbbing shaft in her silken, welcoming warmth. Deep, then deeper still. Until he could touch her womb.

Alexandra wanted him to do exactly that. And more.

"Do you have any idea how long I've wanted you?"

"How long?" Her shaky laugh was half seduction, half promise.

"Forever." His declaration was half wonder, half certainty.

A rush of warmth flooded through her, so deep and hot she was amazed that steam wasn't rising from her skin. She rained kisses, stinging, avid kisses all over his wonderful, handsome face. She continued to kiss him as he carried her back to the car.

He set her down on the backseat, impatiently ripped open her slicker, then covered her body with his. He was hard and aroused, and the movement of her hips against his aching groin created a building pressure that made him feel on the brink of exploding.

One final last voice of conscience, lurking in the far reaches of his mind, struggled to make itself heard. He pushed himself up on his elbows. Her cheeks were flushed the deep, pink hue of the Old Blush blossoms in Eleanor's rose garden, her lips were slightly parted, her hair was a gleaming wet tangle. Her eyes shone with a dazzling gold light.

She was, as always, the most beautiful, alluring woman he'd ever seen. But as his *grand-mère* had always told him, and he'd learned the hard way with Miranda, beauty was only skin-deep. Alex's true beauty, Zach knew, was a deep-seated, inner beauty of heart and spirit that would make her still stunning on her one-hundredth birthday.

"I don't want to hurt you."

Caught up in ancient, primal needs, Alex misunderstood his concern. "You won't."

He decided to try one last time. Then he wouldn't be responsible for the consequences. "I can't give you what you want, Alexandra. What you need."

She smiled at that. A slow, fatally seductive smile that beautiful sirens had been using to lure men to their doom since the dawning of time.

"Oh, I think you're wrong about that," she murmured silkily. Lifting her hips, she rubbed her pelvis against the placket of his jeans.

When her hand moved in the direction of his painful tumescence, Zach grasped it and lifted it to his lips. "That's not what I meant." He kissed the soft, delicate flesh at the center of her palm. "You deserve a man who can promise you a future."

She didn't want to think of that. Not now. Not when every nerve ending in her body felt as if it were on fire. "You talk too much." Dragging her hands through his hair, she pulled his head down and gave him another long, heartfelt kiss.

"I don't want to think about the future," she insisted against his lips. "I only want to think about now. And how much I want you."

For months, he'd fought his feelings. Fought her. And now he wouldn't, couldn't, fight any longer.

Consequences be damned. Zach surrendered to her husky voice trembling with pent-up emotion, the seductive movement of her hips, her lips, plucking so enticingly at his. He surrendered to the inevitable.

He pulled down her jeans, saying something pungent and profane when the wet denim clung to her smooth legs. Today's panties were the bright blue color of cornflowers, tied low on her hips with narrow white satin ribbons. He cupped his palm against her silk-covered mound and elicited a soft, shuddering moan of pleasure.

"Christ." Edging his way beneath the lace-trimmed leg band, he eased a finger deep inside her. Her voluptuous flesh was as hot as hellfire, as wet as her lusciously ripe mouth. "You are so hot," he rasped. "So ready for me." He kissed her again, tasting the rain. Tasting her.

"More than ready." Leaning up on her elbows, she began tearing with urgent frenzy at his zipper. "I want you, Zach." She knew she was begging. But she didn't care. She'd have gotten down on her knees if necessary, if only to end this agonizing torment. "Now. Please." A sob of relief escaped her ravished lips when his penis burst free, as hard and smooth as polished marble, rampant with vitality.

When she stroked it wonderingly, from its base amid its nest of crisp ebony hair to its silken tip, spreading the gleaming bead of cream with an innocently seductive fingertip, reason shattered.

Zach ripped at the satin ribbons and tore away the scrap of blue silk. Their lips fused again as together they fought to pull down his own wet jeans. He plunged into her, taking her with a ravenous hunger he feared could never be quenched.

All thought evaporated. Passion burst from their hot, wet pores. When her body went rigid beneath him, he buried his mouth in her throat and moved his hips in one deep, final thrust. She cried out, clinging to him as they came together, proving to Zach that sometimes fantasies really did come true.

Chapter Twenty-Seven

Alex had known this would happen. Just today, she'd admitted the inevitability of making love with Zach, little suspecting that the opportunity would come so soon.

No, she reminded herself, *this was not making love.* This was sex. Hot, fast and thrilling. But it was not love. At least not on Zach's part.

His passion had been born from anger and jealousy, and perhaps, she conceded, from a fear she'd been injured in her accident. But none of those reasons, as understandable as they were, equaled love.

He was lying on top of her, their legs tangled, their hearts still beating in unison even as the shared rhythm gradually slowed. He lifted his head and looked down into her face, his dark eyes as grave as his expression.

"Alex—"

"No." She caught his hand as it brushed away the tangled damp hairs clinging to her cheek. "If you dare apologize—"

This time it was he who cut her off with a quick,

hard kiss that would have sent her reeling had she not already been lying down.

"I wasn't going to apologize. Well, maybe I was," he allowed when she gave him a knowing look. "But not in the way you think. I'm not at all sorry this happened. But I *am* sorry that when I finally did get around to doing what I've wanted to do for months, for years, what I should have done that first night..."

He frowned and shook his head in obvious self-disgust. He hadn't even bothered taking off her raincoat or sweater.

"Lord, Alexandra, never in my wildest dreams did I envision making love to you in the backseat of a car like some oversexed teenager."

His tender gaze threatened to be her undoing. Afraid that her love for him was written across her face in bold, black script, Alex wiggled out from beneath him and began struggling to locate her clothes.

Her panties had landed atop the back of the front seat; they were, she decided, observing the torn ribbons, a lost cause.

"I'll buy you a new pair."

"That's not necessary." She shoved them into her slicker pocket and started working on turning her jeans right side out.

"I said I'll buy you a new pair."

"Fine. Do whatever you want." She began to struggle into the tight jeans, which wasn't all that easy, from a sitting position, with Zach watching her with those steady, unblinking eyes.

If she kept wiggling her little ass like that, he was going to end up stripping those jeans back off again,

Zach mused, as he felt an all too familiar tightening in his groin.

She'd encased herself in enough ice to cover the North and South poles. Silently working his way through every curse he knew, both in English and the Acadian of his roots, Zach jerked his own pants up and wished he hadn't given up smoking during football training in his freshman year of college.

His renewed frustration gave birth to an urge for a cigarette. Or a drink. Jack Daniel's, straight up, no ice.

"Look," he said, deciding to try again, "I said I was sorry. What else can I say to try and make this right?"

"I told you, you don't have to apologize." To Alex's aghast humiliation, fat hot tears started flowing down her cheeks. "I understand, Zach."

Unable to bear the pity she thought she was reading in his expression, she turned her head away and stared out unseeing into the rain, trying to calm her whirling mind and soothe her aching heart.

"Dammit—"

"We got carried away. It happens sometimes." She took another deep, shuddering breath. "No harm, no foul. Besides—"

"I love you." He ran his hand impotently across her hunched shoulders.

"—you certainly didn't do it all by yourself. You know what they say, it takes two—"

"I love you."

"—to tango. And to tell you the truth, I wanted it every bit as much as you did."

His words, stated so calmly and matter-of-factly, finally sank in. Hope was a hummingbird—no, Alex considered, a giant golden eagle—flapping its wings inside her heart. "Are you saying—"

"What I should have told you a long time ago. I love you, Alexandra Lyons."

She flung her arms around his neck and kissed him deep and hard. "I love you, too, Zachary Deveraux."

"I know."

"Was I that obvious?"

"Not really. In fact, you've been driving me crazy trying to figure out exactly how you felt. Until earlier, when you finally let down your guard."

She'd hoped that, caught up in his own explosive orgasm, he hadn't heard her cry out her heart's most closely guarded secret. But whether loving Zach was wise or prudent, or even particularly moral, given his marital status, love him she did. She'd grown weary of hiding her feelings every time they were together.

"I'm still sorry I was kind of rough. And fast," he tacked on reluctantly.

"Actually," she said with a sassy grin, "I rather liked that part." It had been incredibly exciting. But it had also been more than that. It had been, in its own re-markable way, an epiphany.

As she sat in the backseat of Zach's car, watching the rain stream down the fogged-up windshield, Alex realized that what she'd experienced with Debord had been purely sexual.

It, too, had been exciting. But somehow, she'd al-ways remained detached, as if watching herself per-form for his pleasure. Even at the moment of orgasm, there had been no real emotional connection; instead,

Alex had always been aware of her reaction through Debord's eyes.

But making love to Zach had been so very, very different. It had taught her that sometimes love didn't have to be soft and gentle. It could be hard and even a little frightening. And though she knew it was wrong, the blazing lovemaking she and Zach had just shared had left her wanting more.

Zach was stroking her shoulders and making a futile but endearing attempt to finger-comb her tangled hair. "We need to talk."

She opened her mouth to argue, to assure him it wasn't necessary, then decided there'd already been enough lies and evasions between them. "Yes."

After they returned to the front seat, Zach placed a call to a worried Eleanor from the car phone, assuring her that Alex was safe and sound, but that it was going to take a while for the tow truck to arrive.

That much was the truth. What he didn't tell his employer and friend was that he had no intention of waiting around for the truck. Not when he had more important things to do.

"I don't know about you, but I'm starved," he said after he'd hung up. "I'll admit to having things backward, but I think I owe you dinner."

His smile was that warm, uncensored one she hadn't seen since his mother's wedding. "I'm not exactly dressed to go out." She plucked at her damp sweatshirt and wrinkled damp jeans.

"That wouldn't matter at one of the little hole-in-the-wall seafood places on the pier," he pointed out.

She wasn't eager to have such a long-overdue private conversation in a public setting. Nor was she quite prepared to share Zach with anyone. Not yet.

"We could get takeout," she suggested. "And talk in the car."

"Brilliant." He leaned across the space between their leather seats and kissed her, a brief, feathery meeting of lips that sent warmth shimmering through her. "Takeout it is."

Which was how they came to be parked in a deserted lot overlooking the crashing surf, sharing french fries, Big Macs, cherry turnovers and a bottle of Dom Pérignon Zach had picked up at the liquor store next to McDonald's.

"I always promised myself that the first time we made love, we'd have champagne." He popped the cork with a flair that told Alex he did it often, then poured the sparkling golden wine into two paper cups. "And music." The car radio was tuned to a local jazz-and-blues station. "Unfortunately the liquor store didn't have any candles."

She took a sip of the champagne, enjoying the way the bubbles danced on her tongue. "This is perfect," she said, meaning it.

"Are you always this easy to please?"

"I'm a cheap date," she said on a laugh. "A Big Mac and I'm all yours."

He smiled and refilled her cup. "Next time I think we can do better."

Next time. Alex's yearning heart leapt upon the words, holding them close like a talisman.

They sat there for a long, comfortable time, sipping champagne and watching the waves roll unceasingly onto the shore. The sky was a misty gray curtain; in the distance came the lonely sound of a foghorn, a counterpoint to the voice of Billie Holiday singing of love and heartbreak.

"How long?" she murmured.

"Have I loved you?"

Alex nodded.

"I don't know," he answered honestly. "It snuck up on me over time. I was attracted to you that first night, but to be perfectly honest, I think that might've been my hormones talking."

"Thank God for talkative hormones," she murmured, grateful he hadn't turned down her invitation for that drink.

"Ain't that the truth." He took a sip of champagne and looked thoughtfully out to sea. "I knew I was getting into trouble at my mother's wedding. Because, if it had been just lust, I probably would've done something about it—either that night, or after we got back to L.A., instead of letting you walk out of my life."

"You wanted to keep from hurting me."

"That was the plan. Unfortunately I think all I succeeded in doing was delaying the inevitable."

"Lucky for us, fate threw us back together again."

"I didn't mean what I said earlier." Zach ran the back of his hand down the side of her face in a slow, warming sweep. "About fate and my lousy karma."

"I know.... I think I've loved you from that first night," Alex admitted.

"Why didn't you tell me before now?"

"Did you really not know how I felt?" At times she'd

thought it had been so obvious that everyone in the Lord's offices must have seen it.

Zach shrugged. For the second time in a few hours, he was feeling uncomfortably like a teenager again. *She loves me. She loves me not.* It had been years— aeons—since any woman possessed the power to make him feel so insecure.

"I thought, sometimes, you did. But whenever we'd start to get close, you'd back away."

"You were married."

"I still am," he felt obliged to say.

"I know." She sighed. "But somehow, as horrible as this sounds, back there in the mountains it just didn't matter anymore." Besides, she mused in an effort to justify her behavior, it wasn't as if Zach had a real marriage.

"No," he agreed. "It didn't."

His flat tone worried her. "I hope I didn't complicate things."

He heard the uncharacteristic insecurity in her soft voice and hurried to reassure her. "Things were already complicated before we met." Her hair had dried into a riotous halo of red-gold waves around her lovely, too-somber face. Zach tugged on the bright ends. "You are the best thing that's ever happened to me."

He kissed her again. For a long, glorious, heart-swelling time. "It's not going to be easy," he warned after they could breathe again.

She laughed at that. "It couldn't be any harder than it's been all these months, trying to keep my feelings from showing."

"That's just it." He took her hand and kissed her fingertips, one at a time, with an exquisitely sweet tenderness. "I wasn't exaggerating when I told you that things were complicated," he began slowly, reluctantly.

It wasn't easy admitting he'd made a major mistake in getting involved with an emotionally unstable woman who only wanted to parade him around on a leash in front of her society friends. But after the unintentional pain he'd caused Alex, Zach felt he owed her the truth.

"Miranda's beautiful. And sexy," Alex murmured. "Any man would be attracted to her."

"For a kid who came out of bayou Catholic schools, the kind of uninhibited sex Miranda offered was a definite turn-on," he admitted grimly. "But I guess some of those youthful catechism lessons took, after all. Because it didn't take long to realize that sex without emotional commitment isn't fun at all. It's depressing. And lonely."

"I learned the same lesson," Alex murmured, thinking back on that last, sad night with Debord. "The hard way." She was surprised and relieved to realize the memory no longer hurt. "So, why did you marry Miranda?"

"Because despite my success, I couldn't quite stop thinking of myself as the nearly indigent son of a Louisiana bayou sugarcane farmer. Miranda was beautiful, but more importantly, she was filthy rich. And she had status. And social standing."

"And that was important to you?" Alex was surprised.

He shrugged and wished again for a cigarette. "I thought it was. At the time."

Unable to believe he'd been so shallow, Zach dragged his hand through his hair. "The ugly truth was," he muttered in a voice thick with self-revulsion, "Miranda went on one of her infamous shopping sprees at a time when, as much as I hate to admit it, I'd definitely been for sale."

Alex placed a palm against his cheek and felt the muscle jerk. "You shouldn't be so hard on yourself," she said quietly. "We all have dreams. The problem is that sometimes, when we finally get to where we've always thought we wanted to be, it's an entirely different place from what we'd imagined."

Like her dream of working with Debord, she knew. "Everyone makes mistakes, Zach."

"Yeah, but some mistakes take longer to sort out."

He wasn't exaggerating. Alex listened with a sinking heart to Zach's explanation of the outstanding stock, of the raider who was threatening a takeover, of Miranda's threat to sell her own inherited stock if necessary, to keep Zach away from Alex.

"I knew she suspected we were having an affair," Alex said. "But since there wasn't anything concrete for her to be jealous about…"

"She thinks we've slept together. Which is pretty much the truth now." Once again Zach found himself wishing he'd done things right.

"There'll be other times," Alex assured him, reading the face, the mind, of this man she loved.

"A lifetime," he agreed. He kissed her again, wondering how he could have ever been so lucky to have this dazzling, intelligent, sweet person love him.

"But I'd never be able to live with myself if we

achieved our happiness at Eleanor's expense," Alex murmured.

"You care about her that much?"

"I love her," Alex said simply. "I told you how, when I was little, we moved around a lot."

"I remember you mentioning that." He wondered what Alex would say if she knew he had a thick dossier listing all her addresses from shortly before her third birthday through till today. It was those first two years he'd never been able to uncover; those same missing years that had Eleanor convinced Alex was Anna.

"Whenever I made a friend at school, I'd have to leave her behind. After a while, it was safer not to make any friends."

"I can't imagine you not having friends." Especially boyfriends, Zach thought, shocked at the renewed jolt of jealousy that shot through him at the thought of her swaying in some boy's arms at the spring prom. Or even worse, making out in the backseat of some souped up Chevy after a high-school football game.

"Oh, I always got along with people, but it was easier not to let myself get really close to anyone. My brother, David, was my best friend. And then he died.

"Since then, I've only been close to Sophie. And, of course, you. And Eleanor. I know it sounds strange, but from the first, I've felt a bond with her. Almost like family."

She looked up at Zach, unaware of his reaction to her words. "Do you suppose, because I lost my mother and Eleanor lost her granddaughter, we just naturally gravitated toward one another? To fill some shared emotional need?"

"Makes sense to me," he agreed carefully, even as he wondered what he was going to do about this latest complication. For months he'd been trying to convince himself that his only barrier to a life with Alex was his marriage to Miranda.

But now he was forced to wonder how she would react when she discovered his subterfuge. Would she still love him after learning he'd hired private investigators to delve into every aspect of her life—including her affair with that sicko French designer? Would she still want to build a life with him when she realized he'd been lying to her all these months she'd been working for Lord's?

He hadn't really told her an untruth, but as Sister Mary Joseph, his fourth-grade teacher had always said, a lie of omission was just as much a sin as an out-and-out lie. Zach had the uneasy feeling that when the truth was revealed, Alex would probably agree with the rigid, ruler-wielding nun, who'd spent nine long months terrorizing the ten-year-old boys in her class.

"Well, there's only one thing to do," Alex said, oblivious to Zach's troubled thoughts.

"What's that?" Zach willingly pushed the nagging worries away. There would be, he knew, a price to pay for what he'd done. He just wasn't prepared to face it today.

He wanted, he *needed,* more time. Time to extricate himself from his marriage, time to save Lord's for Eleanor. Time to figure out whether Alex truly was Anna, and how that would affect their future together.

"As hard as it's going to be, we'll have to keep our feelings secret a bit longer," Alex decided aloud. "Until you can ensure that no one can take Lord's away from Eleanor."

"You think I can do that?"

"You're my knight in shining armor, remember?" Alex said, smiling up at him in a way that made him feel even guiltier for all these months of lies. "You can do anything."

As he drew her back into his arms, Zach hoped that she was right.

Chapter Twenty-Eight

Although he longed to take Alex to the nearest hotel where he could make love to her properly all night long, they both knew that wish would have to be postponed.

"We've the rest of our lives," she reminded him as they headed back to the estate.

And although he murmured an agreement, Zach found himself wishing, not for the first time certainly, that life wasn't so damn complicated.

Not surprisingly, their return was met with a great deal of fanfare. Eleanor, pooh-poohing Alex's concerns about the car, was vastly relieved she'd returned safe and sound. Clara, spooky as always, hinted at the possibility of some unseen forces.

"Poltergeist," she declared knowingly. "Or some restless spirit who wants Alexandra out of Santa Barbara."

Although she was no spirit, Miranda fit the description perfectly. She was furious.

"I warned you," she spat out between clenched teeth

once she and Zach were alone in their upstairs bedroom. "I told you what would happen if you slept with that little slut again."

"Although I've always admired your acting skills, Miranda, someone needs to write you a third act," Zach countered. "This dialogue sounds vaguely familiar." He stripped off his sweater, went into the adjoining bathroom and shut the door.

"It's too late for a shower, you two-timing son of a bitch!" Miranda yelled at him when she heard him turn on the water. "Because I already smelled your little whore's perfume on you."

Miranda's temper, which had always been formidable, seemed to be getting worse. And, Zach considered grimly, as the room began to fill with steam, all her hostility was directed toward Alex.

Uneasy about his wife's increasing instability, Zach wanted to avoid doing or saying anything that might give Miranda an excuse to harm Alex.

Knowing he couldn't hide from his wife indefinitely, Zach exited the stall, dried himself, then wrapped a towel around his middle and returned to the bedroom to face Miranda's wrath.

"I've got a suggestion," he said as he took a pair of cotton briefs from the top drawer of the antique mahogany chest.

Miranda eyed him suspiciously. "Why do I think I'm going to hate this?"

"Actually, it's a business proposal."

"Really?" she asked with a show of disinterest. But Zach saw the familiar flash of avarice in her eyes and experienced the hope this might not be as difficult as he'd thought. "What type of business proposal?"

"This marriage has been a farce from the beginning. You're not happy. I'm not happy. So, why don't we just cut our losses? Before we end up hurting one another even more?"

She lighted a cigarette, sat down on the edge of the bed and crossed her legs. Zach remembered when even a glimpse of those smooth, white thighs could make him hard. But that was another time. And sometimes, it seemed, another world.

"The problem is, Zachary, dear, you misunderstand the situation."

"Why don't you explain it to me, then?" he suggested mildly.

"The simple truth is I'm not unhappy. On the contrary, darling, I like being married."

"How can you say that? We hardly see each other. And whenever we are together, all we do is fight."

"There's something that you don't seem to understand," she said patiently, as if speaking to a very slow kindergartner.

Once again Zach realized how superior to him she considered herself. His humble background, which had proved such a source of fascination when they'd first met, was routinely thrown back in his face as proof of his lower status.

"I'm trying to understand," he said.

"The truth, as unpalatable as it may be, is that I am no longer a young woman. And in my world, divorced women of a certain age are often pitied.

"Which is why having a husband—" she exhaled a stream of blue smoke and looked him up and down as if he were livestock she was considering purchasing

"—even an absent one, gives a woman much needed cachet."

"You had two husbands before me," he pointed out. "You'll get married again."

"Perhaps." She stood up, ground out her cigarette in a crystal ashtray and walked across the room to the bureau. "But I'll be the one to decide when and if we get a divorce."

"I could just file. God knows I've got grounds."

"So do I. Don't forget, Zachary, when it comes to adultery, what's sauce for the goose is sauce for the gander. Neither of us has remained faithful to our vows."

She extracted a folded piece of paper from beneath a pile of scented French lingerie. "You may be interested in this."

Curious in spite of his building frustration, Zach snatched the paper from her hand, his heart clenching as he read the three typed paragraphs.

"This is a memo from Nelson Montague."

"To his Hong Kong banker," Miranda agreed with a sly smile that made Zach's flesh crawl. "Revealing his plans for Lord's. After he takes over, of course."

Zach shook his head. "It's insane to think he can turn a thriving upscale chain like Lord's into Walmart."

"More like Loehmans," Miranda corrected. She was smiling like a sleek cat who'd just swallowed a particularly succulent canary. The only thing missing was the yellow feathers sticking out from between those glossy vermilion lips. "Seconds, factory overruns, clothing that didn't sell because the sizes were too large or too small, or just didn't survive the fleeting time span of fashion fads."

"I know the kind of store you mean," Zach countered sharply. "And it damn well doesn't belong on Rodeo Drive."

"Oh, he intends to spin the Beverly Hills store off and sell it to Saks," she informed him, reminding Zach that in her own way, Miranda was no gorgeous blonde bimbo. On the contrary, she had a very good head for business when it suited her.

"As for the others," she revealed, "buyers are already waiting in the wings."

"He intends to dismantle the entire chain?"

Which would, Zach thought, effectively put an end to the Alexandra Lyons Blue Bayou collection.

"That's the plan," she said cheerfully. "But all's well that ends well. The price per share he's offering will make the stockholders very, very rich."

"If they sell."

"Oh, enough will sell, Zachary. There's no limit to what people will do to make a quick profit." Her smile reached all the way to her eyes at the thought of all that lovely money. "Nelson taught me that."

"And did he also send you to me with this memo?" That was the part that didn't make any sense. The Australian raider was not known for tipping his hand.

"Of course not. Actually, I confess to being a bit naughty. I stole it from his briefcase while he was sleeping."

"And now you're selling the information to the highest bidder."

"In a way. This is my trump card, Zachary. We both know I hold the deciding stock. If I vote with you and Aunt Eleanor, Lord's will continue as is. If I choose to vote with Nelson…" She shrugged. "Well, I believe the memo's more than clear as to his plans."

"You realize this would kill your aunt."

"Now who's being overly dramatic? Auntie's a tough old bird. If she could survive the murders and the kidnapping and being widowed, she'd undoubtedly survive losing her beloved company."

"You're sure of that, are you?"

"Actually, I'm that sure of you, darling. As much as you'd love to set up housekeeping with your little chit of a designer, you possess the fatal flaw of loyalty.

"You won't even attempt to divorce me, because if you do, I'll play that trump card. Then we can both see exactly how much dear Auntie's heart can take."

Listening to her hateful words, watching her hard expression, Zach wondered how he could have been so blinded by lust not to have seen that Miranda was more than calculating. She was either very sick or very evil.

That idea sent another shock wave ricocheting through him. "Are you responsible for what happened to Alex today?"

"What are you talking about?" Her surprise appeared genuine.

"Did you have anything to do with that accident?"

"Are you accusing me of tampering with the brakes or something on your lover's borrowed car?"

"You want Alex gone."

"Of course I do. But gracious, Zach, I certainly don't have to stoop to murder to get rid of such an insignificant little problem. Besides," she pointed out, "if I even understood automobile mechanics, which I don't, I'd never risk breaking a nail."

She held out her hands as proof of her innocence,

displaying ten long, perfectly manicured fingernails that sparkled like rubies.

"You could have gotten someone else to do your dirty work."

"But I already have, darling." She came and stood right in front of him and ran one of those ruby nails along the grimly set line of his lips. "I've got you." She pressed a kiss against his hard mouth, then laughing, left the room.

Cursing viciously, Zach crumpled the stolen memo into a ball and flung it across the room. As his Grand-mère Deveraux would have told him, he'd made his thorny bed; now it was up to him to lie in it.

Even if that meant he was destined to spend his nights alone. Thinking of a woman he didn't dare have.

Chapter Twenty-Nine

Although it was difficult, Alex and Zach managed to keep from giving Miranda any reason to sell her stock to the Australian corporate raider. Returning to the rigid self-restraint they'd both exercised for so long, they tried to pretend to be content with stolen kisses behind closed office doors.

They had hoped, in the beginning, that they might steal some private time together, but Alex grew increasingly aware of a man who seemed to be wherever she went. A man who was so unremarkable she might not have noticed him if Zach hadn't warned her that Miranda might hire a private detective.

Well, she obviously had, and although Alex was certain the poor guy must be bored stiff by her uneventful lifestyle, she also had to award this round to Miranda. Because while Miranda might not have any compromising videos or incriminating photographs to look at, she had effectively managed to stop Alex and Zach from making love again.

Alex was in her Venice bungalow, cutting out a piece of brightly flowered silk and singing along with Madonna, who was claiming to be a material girl, when the doorbell rang.

"Damn," she muttered, putting the shears aside. She was working on the dress she planned to wear for the Chicago debut and her mind was constantly filled with design changes. Her outfit had to be absolutely perfect. It had to display her talents, her individuality, her spirit. It had to speak to all those potential buyers, not to mention knocking the socks off the characteristically blasé fashion press.

Which was, Alex admitted as she looked through the peephole at the uniformed man, one helluva lot of responsibility to heap on a yard and a half of silk.

"Ms. Lyons?" he asked when she opened the door.

"Yes."

He handed her an envelope. "If you'll read this, ma'am, I think it should explain what I'm doing here."

Alex recognized Zach's bold scrawl immediately. She skimmed the brief note, which didn't tell her anything except that an emergency had come up and she was to go with the driver.

"What kind of emergency?" she asked.

"I don't know, ma'am. I'm only following orders."

Trusting Zach implicitly and worried enough that she wasn't about to waste time arguing, she grabbed up her purse and followed the driver out to the car.

They drove through the valley to the small Ontario airport, where she found the Lord's executive jet waiting for her. As she entered the cabin, she was surprised not to find Zach waiting aboard. "Isn't Mr. Deveraux joining us?" she asked the steward who welcomed her aboard.

"No, Ms. Lyons. You're our only passenger." He gave her a bright, professional smile and instructed her to fasten her seat belt. "Mr. Deveraux instructed a bottle of champagne to be opened as soon as we're airborne."

"Where are we going?"

"To Phoenix."

A little more than an hour later, Alex was being ushered into a luxurious suite at the five-star Arizona Biltmore Hotel.

"I've been going crazy waiting for you," Zach said in greeting her. His broad hands stroked her face, as his clever lips skimmed her cheek.

As always, her heart took a little leap at the sight of him. "This is a wonderful idea. But is it wise?"

"Miranda's in London."

"But that horrid little man she hired—"

"Is probably posting bail by now."

"Bail?"

"Loitering is against the law," he said. "Seems one of your neighbors got tired of seeing him parked across the street and anonymously called the cops, who weren't very pleased to learn that a guy whose P.I. license had been yanked six months ago was hanging around their jurisdiction with a concealed weapon in his possession."

"How did you know about his license?"

Zach shrugged. "You'd be amazed what you can find out with a computer these days."

"That was very clever of you," she allowed. "But there's just one little problem."

"What's that?"

"Your driver didn't give me time to pack."

His hands shaped her curves from shoulder to thigh. "Don't worry, sweetheart. For the weekend I've got in mind, you're not going to need any clothes."

She laughed and twined her arms around his neck. "Oh, goody."

The first time, when he'd taken her so ruthlessly in his car, all his hunger had come clawing out of him. Now, as he kissed her temple and breathed in her scent, Zach felt the knot in his gut beginning to loosen.

"You have to tell me what you like." He nibbled on her ear as his hands moved up and down her back. "What you want."

His caress was making her bones melt. She closed her eyes and swayed against him. "I want you to kiss me."

He complied, kissing her slowly from one corner of her lips to the other. "Like this?"

"That's an excellent start," she whispered. Her breath was like a soft summer breeze against his mouth.

"That's all it was, baby," he promised. "A start."

His tongue created a ring of fire as it circled her parted lips. A matching warmth flickered between her thighs. "Has anyone ever told you you're a very good kisser, Zachary?"

"Someone has now." He deepened the kiss, keeping it soft and gentle for a long, glorious time.

Entranced by the way he could make her float with only his mouth, Alex felt as if she'd fallen into a bed of feathers. Or clouds.

"Better than good," she declared. "You, Zachary Deveraux, are world-class."

"And you're prejudiced."

Seduced by the slow, deep kisses himself, he lifted her into his arms as tenderly as if she were a piece of Eleanor's precious crystal, rather than a flesh-and-blood woman. No man had ever treated her with such care.

"I won't break," she murmured as he placed her gently on the bed. The mattress sighed as he lay down beside her.

"I know. That's one of the things I love about you." He took off her outer clothing, treating each piece of revealed flesh to a sweet, seductive torment with hands that were heartbreakingly gentle, with a mouth that was warm and sensuous. "You can be strong and soft at the same time. Like steel wrapped in satin."

A delicious time later, he'd worked his way down to her teddy—a brief confection of silk and midnight lace.

And then his clothes were gone, as well, and he held her against him.

Even as her mind became wrapped in a gauzy pleasure, a tiny portion of her brain reminded her that this was supposed to be an activity for two people.

"I want to make love to you." She lifted her hand to his chest.

"Later." With his eyes on her, he kissed her fingertips individually. "This first time is for you, Alex. So relax. And just take."

His hands felt so good, stroking, soothing, calming, that she could not summon the strength to argue. So she closed her eyes and gave herself up to these shimmering sensations and allowed Zach to set the pace.

He tasted her and sent her floating. He savored her and made her fly. He murmured his love for her over and over again and made her melt. Though his hands remained gentle, there was a quiet, unyielding strength beneath his tender touch.

His lips took a slow, erotic journey, hot against her glowing flesh. "Promise me something," he murmured.

As his mouth dampened the ebony silk covering her breasts, Alex writhed in mindless pleasure. "Anything."

The word that shuddered from between her trembling lips was the truth. Alex was willing to do whatever Zach wanted. As the treacherous assault continued, she was willing to go wherever he took her.

"Promise me you'll never quit wearing this sexy underwear." Zach knew, without the faintest shadow of a doubt, that the sight of Alexandra clad in her skimpy French lingerie would still excite him when they were in their nineties.

"I promise," she gasped as his teeth tugged on a nipple.

When his palms pressed against the insides of her quivering legs, she willingly opened to him, knowing, even through the mists clouding her mind, that she'd never been more vulnerable. Not even that horrifying time with Debord.

And yet, as his teeth nipped at the sensitive flesh of her inner thighs, as his tongue soothed away the marks, as his heated breath warmed her feminine core through the silk her desire had already dampened, Alex had never felt safer.

Because Zach loved her. And love, she discovered, was stronger than desire, more powerful than need. It was everything she'd been waiting for without having known she'd been waiting; Zach was everything she'd been yearning for, without having known she'd been yearning.

He peeled the silken barrier down her body with deft, expert hands. The same hands created trails of shimmering pleasure through the downy golden-red curls at the juncture of her thighs. When his mouth settled on her throbbing, swollen clitoris, she felt a blaze of hot pleasure.

Zach slipped a finger inside her and found her warm and wet. "You are so incredibly soft." His words vibrated against the ultrasensitive flesh he was kissing as deeply, as erotically, as he'd kissed her mouth. "And sweet."

Nearly weeping, she arched against him, trusting him implicitly, loving him wholly. Her skin was so sensitized that the mere brush of a fingertip made her burn. Every nerve ending in her body had contracted into one tight, hot ball. As she struggled to fill her lungs with air, the ball imploded, leaving her limp, boneless and dazed.

She's so responsive! Zach thought. *So sweet. And she's mine. All mine!*

He held her trembling body tightly against his. He buried his face in her hair and thanked whatever fates had brought this woman to him.

She remained safely in his arms until the shudders racking her body ceased. She wanted to tell Zach everything she was feeling, but her mind, still numb from such exhilarating pleasure, could not think of the words.

All she could do was show him. She turned in his arms and pressed her lips against the pulse at the base of his throat.

"I love you," she whispered. She slid down his body, her mouth blazing a hot, wet trail that bisected his torso.

"Love you." Her hands slid across his shoulders, down his slick sides. "Love you."

As she had done earlier, Zach willingly surrendered his power, allowing Alex to set the pace. As he had done earlier, she drew it out, reveling in the feel of his steely muscles clenching beneath her exploring hands, his quick intake of breath when she blew a soft, teasing breath across his taut stomach, his ragged groan as her lips embraced his rock-hard shaft.

Heat was thundering through him. Her sensuous tongue was stroking his throbbing cock from balls to tip in a way that threatened to blow whatever self-control he still possessed to smithereens.

"Honey," he groaned, grabbing handfuls of her thick bright hair, "if you don't stop right now, I'm going to… Oh, sweet Christ, Alex…"

He felt the pressure building at the base of his spine. Just in time, he pulled away, yanked her into his arms and held her tightly against him, drinking in deep gulps of breath as he struggled for control. When the storm was successfully, albeit temporarily, banked, Zach rolled her onto her back and braced himself over her. With hands that were far from steady, he pushed the tousled red-gold waves away from her face. "I love you."

He slid into her, heat to heat, flesh to flesh, male to female. With a sigh and a murmur, she opened to him, enfolding him with absolute generosity.

Later, as she lay in his arms, waiting for her heartbeat to return to normal, Alex, who'd sworn to herself she would not complain, murmured, "I wish we could stay like this forever."

"I know." Zach sighed, a deep breath thick with regret and lingering frustration. "Hang in there, sweetheart. I've got a plan. The only problem is it's going to take some time to pull it off."

Having no other choice, Alex trusted him. And waited.

The little girl huddled in the back of the closet, her eyes squeezed tightly shut as if that might keep the monsters that lurked in the dark at bay.

Those same monsters had killed her mommy and her daddy. The memory of all that blood remained riveted in her mind's eye, a dark crimson flag that would not go away.

She'd feared that the monsters would kill her, too, but then Rosa had swept her up and carried her out of the house. Clad only in nightgowns, feet bare, they'd made their escape.

Rosa had cried loudly as the car sped through the black night; Anna had not. The horror of what she'd witnessed had rendered her mute.

And then it was day again and they were hiding in the hotel room, awaiting the telephone call that Rosa assured Anna would fix everything.

But the call never came. Instead, the monsters found them. And then they murdered Rosa, just as they'd killed her parents.

Because they'd locked her away in this dark closet, Anna hadn't seen the monsters kill her nanny, the woman who had always seemed more like a mother to her than her own glamorous one.

But Anna had heard Rosa's desperate pleas. And even putting both hands over her ears had not kept her from hearing Rosa's broken sobs. Or her blood-curdling scream.

And then, finally, even more terrifying, a long, empty silence descended.

The little girl lost all sense of time or place. She only knew, with every fiber of her tense young body, that the monsters—those same ones who'd lurked beneath her bed every night just waiting for Rosa to turn off the light—were still out there.

Just on the other side of the door.

Waiting to eat her, the same way the big bad wolf had gobbled up little Red Riding Hood's grandmother.

And so, unable to do anything else, she hunkered deeper into her fear and waited.

Hours later, Anna was jolted from a restless sleep by the sound of her own screams. At the same time, the closet door was flung opened, flooding the small cubicle with blinding light.

Terrified that the monsters were about to devour her whole, Anna screamed louder and began to kick at the intruder....

"Alex! It's all right. It's only a dream!" Zach shouted.

Immersed in her own horror, Alex couldn't hear him.

"It's all right," he insisted, sucking in a sharp breath as a flailing fist slammed against his ribs. "You're safe, sweetheart. No one's going to hurt you."

The struggle continued for another minute, a time that seemed longer to both Zach and Alex. Finally his soothing voice and gentling touch had their effect.

As his wide hand stroked her hair, Alex looked up at him. Fright still lingered in her expressive eyes.

"I had another nightmare."

"I know." He pressed his lips against her hair. "But it's all right. You're all right."

"Yes." Alex sighed and rested her cheek against his bare chest.

Zach listened to her breathing return to normal. Beneath his stroking hand, her flesh warmed. "Feeling better?"

"Uh-huh." She nodded. "I was dreaming of Anna," she murmured drowsily. Secure in his arms, she had already begun falling back to sleep.

Zach decided he must have misunderstood her. "Anna? You were dreaming about Anna Lord?"

"Mmm." She nestled closer against him. "I was dreaming about when she was kidnapped."

His blood chilled. "Oh?" he asked with a studied calm. "What about it?"

But Alex had fallen asleep again. Leaving Zach to watch her. And wonder.

The following morning, to Zach's secret frustration, Alex could recall nothing of her terrifying nightmare. Which kept him from learning if the dream had only been of things Clara and Eleanor had told her, or something else. Something only Anna Lord would have known.

After croissants and strawberries in bed, and another leisurely session of lovemaking, Alex reluctantly returned to Los Angeles.

As he watched the executive jet take off into the vast, blue Arizona sky, Zach was forced to ponder the possibility that, as amazing as it might seem, there was an outside chance, just perhaps, that Eleanor was right about Alexandra Lyons.

Chapter Thirty

On the day of the Chicago opening, there was more excitement than the time Queen Elizabeth and Nancy Reagan visited the Long Beach Lord's. Behind the scenes, as she made last-minute adjustments to the models' gowns, Alex's heart was beating so hard and so fast she was certain it would leap from her chest.

They'd flown to Chicago the previous day on the Lord's executive jet—Alex, Zach, Eleanor, the actresses and models, and, of course, Sophie. Concerned about the slight angina attack Eleanor had suffered a week prior to the trip, Averill had come along, as well. As had Miranda, who seemed determined to keep her husband away from Alex.

A by-invitation-only fashion show was planned for those valued credit-card holders and the fashion press. Afterward, the public would be allowed into the newest store on Michigan Avenue's Magnificent Mile.

The Blue Bayou boutique was on the sixth floor, set advantageously between designer gowns and fur coats. It was a romantic setting, with soft, piped-in music, tufted blue ottomans and deep-cushioned sofas designed to make a waiting husband or lover as comfortable as possible.

The set for today's fashion show resembled an old plantation; the designer—one of several set designers borrowed from the television show—had twined fragrant pink, red and white flowers around faux Grecian marble pillars. A pair of trees draped in Spanish moss flanked the stage.

A white satin-covered runway bisected the boutique; on either side were gilt chairs; a rose had been placed on each white brocade seat.

"It's absolutely stunning," Alex breathed softly, staring at the boutique above which, as Eleanor had promised, her name appeared in sky-blue neon.

She'd seen the drawings, of course. And she'd been here the previous evening, but although she'd stayed till past midnight, the stage had still been little more than scaffolding, and the flowers had been safely stored in the florist's walk-in cooler.

"Not as stunning as the clothes," Eleanor answered. "I knew you were talented, Alexandra, but you've surpassed even my expectations."

Having discovered exactly how demanding Eleanor Lord could be, Alex took her words as high praise indeed.

Only minutes before the show was to begin, Zach appeared backstage. After some vague and incomprehensible remarks about needing her input on pricing structure, he led her into a nearby dressing room and shut the door.

"Zach," she whispered, "the show's about to begin."

"Not for another five minutes." He played with the ends of her hair. "Have I ever told you that I love your hair?"

"Yes, but—"

"Relax, sweetheart. They haven't even opened the downstairs doors yet…. I do, you know." He ran his hand down the mass of waves. "I love the color. The scent." He kissed the top of her head. "I love the feel of it draped over my chest. My thighs."

His unthreatening touch was a direct contrast to the seductive images his words were currently invoking. She put a hand on his chest, whether to draw him closer or push him away, Alex could not quite decide.

"Dammit, Zach," she complained on a soft, shaky little laugh, "you have rotten timing."

"I know." He lifted her hand from his white dress shirt and began nibbling on the sensitive flesh at the inside of her wrist. "It's my single flaw. But I promise to improve."

When he scraped his teeth against her knuckles, Alex's knees turned to water. "You're driving me crazy."

"That's the idea. Because you've been doing the same thing to me and I refuse to make the trip alone." He folded her fingers and returned her hand, enveloped in his larger one, to his chest. His smiling mouth was a breath away from hers. "I wanted some time alone with you, just the two of us, before you got even richer and more famous."

She looked up at him in surprise. Could he possibly think her financial status would make any difference to her love? "It won't change how I feel."

"I know." His soft sigh was one of pleasure, not regret or sorrow. He lifted his eyes upward, to a heaven that, until Alex, he'd never been totally sure he believed in. "Thank you."

And then he lowered his lips to hers.

The kiss was soft, but deep. The kind of kiss a woman could drown in. The kind that could make a woman float. A soft breath escaped her parted lips as Alex closed her eyes and followed Zach into the mists.

"I love you," he murmured, unwilling to relinquish her lips when the warm, stolen kiss ended.

"I know." She smiled up at him, her heart glowing in her eyes. "And that makes everything worthwhile."

"I'm glad to hear you say that." Reluctantly he released her, smoothing out imaginary wrinkles the embrace might have caused in her bright silk dress. "But I think this is where you're supposed to tell me that you love me, too."

"I love you." She kissed his mouth. "Love you." His chin. "Love you." His throat, above the perfect Windsor knot of his tie. "Love you."

His body was growing hard. Not wanting to face all those waiting women in an aroused state, he laughed and put her a little away from him. "That's all I wanted to hear." Still grinning, he gave her a proprietary once-over. "You look gorgeous."

"Thank you." She gave a quick curtsy. "I thought about wearing something softer hued, to match the set, but red always gives me confidence."

The silk dress, with its deeply scooped neckline and short skirt was emblazoned with huge poppies. The way the material hugged Alex's curves was enough to make any male with blood still flowing through his veins want to pick those bright flowers.

"It suits you." He gave her another proprietary look

and forced himself not to think of what vibrant confections she was wearing beneath the flowered silk. "But something's missing."

"Missing?"

She spun around, studying herself in the three-way mirror. At Eleanor's suggestion, the lighting in the dressing room was a warm and complimentary soft pink, vastly different from the usual color-draining fluorescent. It was lighting designed to make a woman look her best.

"I'm no expert on female fashion, but I think it needs this." He pulled a gray velvet box from his suit-coat pocket.

"Oh, Zach!" Alex gasped as she looked down at the slender chain of hammered gold accented with a diamond heart. "It's spectacular."

"Not as spectacular as you. But they haven't invented a gem that even comes close, so I suppose it'll have to do."

She grinned her pleasure at both his flattering words and his extravagant gift. "Flatterer." Turning around, she lifted her hair, baring her neck. "Would you put it on?"

As he fastened the chain, Zach found himself yearning for the time when such intimacies wouldn't have to take place behind closed doors.

Soon, he told himself as they left the dressing room. If everything worked out according to plan, in a few short weeks he would be a free man.

It had been Eleanor's idea that Alex describe her own designs, insisting it would increase the name recognition of the line. Afraid she'd suffer from stage fright, Alex had reluctantly agreed.

Giving in to Alex's belief that live music would be preferable to taped, but wanting to keep costs from soaring into the stratosphere, Zach had compromised with a jazz quartet. The musicians, who hailed from New Orleans, fit both his and Alex's criteria: they were talented and came cheap. And the music, Eleanor had pointed out with her usual marketing flair, was perfect for the Blue Bayou theme.

The fashion show began with daytime wear: graceful, fluid dresses created from whisper-soft silks printed with impressionistic images of flowers and leaves, seductively draped to enhance any woman's figure. Along with the romantic dresses were narrow little suits reminiscent of the fifties, worn with sequined bustiers or crayon-bright silk camisoles.

"Of course, every woman needs a special dress for an afternoon at the theater," Alex read from her script. She lowered her voice. "Or for that forbidden midday assignation."

There was a ripple of excited recognition as Mary Beth, whom every woman in the room loved to hate as the amoral mistress Tiffany, walked out from behind one of the Grecian pillars.

When she unfolded from her cocoonlike fuchsia stole, displaying the snug minidress embroidered with silk flowers, the audience gasped their surprised pleasure, then applauded.

"When temptation is the name of the game, dare to outdazzle the bright lights of Monte Carlo," Alex read, "in a short, sassy, sparkling evening gown...."

"Wear this and everything stops but the music," she described the strapless floor-length tube of clinging red silk.

"And for your gypsy soul..." A trio of models twirled down the runway, resembling flamenco dancers in their calf-length black, red or gold mousseline dresses cascading with ruffles.

The spontaneous burst of applause for the same design Debord had so harshly rejected made Alex's heart soar. Her nervousness vanished; the remainder of the show passed in a glorious blur.

After she'd taken countless bows, the doors to the newest Lord's store in the diamond-bright chain were flung open to the public with a flourish by white-gloved young men wearing red jackets.

Hordes of women clogged the escalators to the sixth floor. The resulting stampede attested to a pent-up demand created by what had been essentially a weekly, hour-long television commercial for Alexandra Lyons clothes. When the number of shoppers quickly swelled to 20,000, the store's security people—whose idea of an incident might be two women fighting over a cashmere sweater—got nervous and ordered the doors temporarily closed until order could be restored.

Once again Eleanor's instincts proved flawless as shoppers proved thrilled to be able to buy the same mint-green, satin peignoir set the beleaguered wife had been wearing when arrested for murder on the season-ending cliff-hanger. Another popular outfit turned out to be the royal-purple silk suit Tiffany had worn on that same episode when she went to the morgue to identify the body of her much older third husband.

As the cash registers rang up the sales, shoppers revealed both their good and bad sides. According to Zach's up-to-the-minute computer tallies, the saintly wife's classic, yet sexy business suits were the best sellers in the daytime wear, the ex-wife captured the cocktail dress crown, while the mistress won the battle of the underwear, hands down.

Even Zach, who had never understood Miranda's obsession with couture clothes, had to admit that the sight of seven hundred dresses and five hundred peignoirs streaming from the store like the soap's leading character's black gold, was quite a sight. If first-day receipts were any indication, the Alexandra Lyons collection was going to be a smashing success.

By the time the harried security guards shut the doors at the end of the day, Lord's had sold most of the Blue Bayou stock and was into back order. Indeed, any woman who wanted to get married in Tiffany's pearl-and-rhinestone-studded wedding gown would have to postpone her ceremony for several weeks to allow the Brooklyn factory to catch up to demand.

The following morning brought even more good news. During a breakfast meeting prior to the return flight to California, Zach announced that on Wall Street, the opening of Lord's shares had been delayed forty-five minutes after the bell because of the crush of would-be investors clamoring for the stock.

When trading finally did begin, Lord's shares went up considerably. As the company jet crossed over Kansas, the stock had continued to climb and showed no sign of slowing.

It was official. Both the fashion press and the financial media had declared the Alexandra Lyons Blue Bayou collection an unqualified success.

The news came as a vast relief to Alex, who'd harbored a secret fear that perhaps Debord may have been right about her designs not being marketable.

Life would be perfect, she considered as the pilot pointed out the Grand Canyon below, if only for one thing.

If only she could share her happiness with Zach.

Alex was sitting in the richly appointed cabin, lost in thought, idly watching the clouds, when Miranda suddenly appeared in front of her.

"Congratulations. How does it feel to be fashion guru to the middle class?"

Zach's wife's words were not meant, Alex realized, as a compliment. "I'm pleased people like my work."

"Isn't that nice." Miranda lifted the crystal old-fashioned glass to her lips. From the way she was swaying ever so slightly on her Charles Jourdan high heels, Alex suspected it was not mineral water Miranda was drinking. "It's not going to work, you know."

"What isn't going to work?"

"This little act you have going." She waved her arm, splashing vodka onto Alex's white jeans.

Alex pulled a tissue from her purse and began dabbing at the moisture. "Act?"

"You're nothing but a scheming little opportunist," Miranda spat, pointing a scarlet fingernail into Alex's face. "Or are you going to deny you slept with Debord to get that job in Paris?"

Alex's first thought was surprise that Miranda knew about her affair with the designer. Her second thought was that Zach's wife had garnered the attention of everyone on board.

"You've got your facts wrong, Miranda," Alex managed to reply calmly.

"That's what you say." She leaned forward, her red

lips twisted into an ugly sneer. "You're not only a conniving slut—you're a liar."

Zach, who'd been in the cockpit with the pilot, returned just in time to hear his wife's poisonous accusation. "You've had too much to drink, Miranda." He
took hold of her arm and tried to take the glass from
her hand, but she pulled away.

"That's where you're wrong, darling. Because I
haven't had nearly enough to get the taste of your little trollop out of my mouth." Throwing back her blond
head, she finished off the rest of the drink. "I know
you're sleeping with my husband," she hissed at Alex.
"I also know why. Because you're using him to infil-
trate yourself into my aunt's life."

Miranda glanced around, her daggerlike eyes sweeping the room to settle momentarily on Eleanor before
returning to Alex.

"Just because Aunt Eleanor believes you're her long-
lost granddaughter, don't think for a minute that anyone else is that gullible."

Alex knew she shouldn't respond to such outrageous, drunken accusations, but she couldn't let that
one pass. "That's ridiculous."

"I agree it's ridiculous to think you're Auntie's dear
departed little Anna," Miranda agreed. "But it's not
the first time she's been made a fool of by a scheming
little swindler. Just ask your lover."

Her sleek blond hair flew out like a shimmering
fan as she tossed her head in Zach's direction. "One of
my husband's corporate duties is investigating all the
fraudulent Annas.

"And you should see," Miranda said wickedly, lowering her voice to a conspiratorial tone, "the fat, juicy file he's compiled on you."

No! It couldn't be true. It was merely a delusion born in the murky reaches of Miranda's vengeful, alcohol-sodden mind.

Miranda had never liked her. And she had threatened to make trouble. This was just Zach's wife's latest volley in their ongoing war.

After all, Alex assured herself, Zach loved her. He wouldn't lie. He wouldn't pretend. He wouldn't make a fool out of her. He couldn't. *He loves me!*

Alex looked up at Zach, willing him to tell her that his wife's hateful words were a lie.

Her blood chilled as she read the answer in the stony set of his jaw, the unrelenting bleakness in his dark eyes. For a long, suspended moment, nothing seemed to function—her mind, her heart, her lungs.

Then she felt her heart splinter into a million pieces as Alex realized that, for once, Miranda was telling the truth.

Chapter Thirty-One

The cabin had gone deathly still. The strained silence was palpable; Alex could practically feel it ricocheting around her, like machine-gun bullets against the walls of a dark, cold cave.

Not now, dammit! Zach thought, more furious at Miranda than he'd ever been. But he should have expected such treachery from his wife. Up till this horrible moment, it had been Alex's day of triumph. Miranda had never been willing to cede center stage.

"It's not the way it sounds," he said finally.

Dear God, how she wished that were true! But his expression proclaimed his guilt every bit as loudly as if he'd shouted it on a bullhorn.

He started toward her, but was brought up short when her hands whipped out. "Just tell me one thing," she said through lips that had turned to stone. Could that really be her voice? It sounded so thin. So cold. "Did you investigate me?"

He dragged his hands through his hair in a frustrated gesture she'd come to recognize. "Yes. But—"

Trapped in the icy pain of shock, Alex pressed a hand to her stomach as if to ward off a killing blow. "Because you thought I was some kind of swindler?"

She couldn't believe it. She'd loved him. He'd told her he loved her. How could he think her capable of stealing money from an old woman?

"No, he didn't," Eleanor answered for Zach.

Alex spun around in her seat, prepared to turn on the elderly woman. The pained expression on the lined face took a bit of the furious wind out of Alex's sails.

Eleanor rose unsteadily from her place at the front of the cabin. Her left hand, laden with diamonds, clutched the back of the seat. "Zachary never thought you were a swindler, Alexandra, dear. You must believe that.

"And whatever he did, he did out of loyalty to me. Because I truly believed you were my missing Anna."

"Why didn't you say anything?" Alex's composure was cracking. It was imperative she keep her anger cold. Controlled. She had to think clearly. *Think, not feel.*

"I knew you were my granddaughter when I saw you on television," Eleanor alleged. "But Zachary counseled restraint—"

"Oh, Zachary's always been a virtual pillar of restraint," Alex broke in, shooting him a sharp, bitter look.

She'd trusted him, dammit! She'd believed in him. She'd opened her heart, her body, to this man. How many times was she going to have to stick her hand into the damn flame before she learned not to do it anymore?

"You have to understand, dear. Miranda is correct about my having made a fool out of myself once before," Eleanor revealed reluctantly. After all these years, it was obvious the mistake still stung her not inconsiderable pride. "Because I ignored Zachary's misgivings. This time I chose to heed his warning."

"Makes sense to me," Alex agreed bitterly. "Why make a fool of yourself when you can all make a fool out of me, instead?" Her words hit their mark. The color drained from the elderly woman's face.

"I'm sorry," Alex mumbled when Eleanor took a deep, shuddering breath. "But you should have told me."

Averill, his somber expression revealing both professional and personal concern, took hold of the elderly woman's arm. "Eleanor," he coaxed gently, "please, sit down."

Looking frail and old, Eleanor sank onto a seat across the aisle from Alex. Averill's fingers were on her wrist, taking her pulse even as he gave Alex a warning look.

The plane began its descent into LAX.

"You're right, of course," Eleanor agreed after she'd regained her composure. "We should have given more thought to how you would feel when we broke the news to you about your true identity."

There were so many questions Alex wanted to ask. So many accusations she wanted to fling at Zach. But Eleanor's pallor was frightening. "There's something important you're overlooking," Alex said, gentling her tone and her expression.

"What's that, dear?"

"I understand your need to find your missing grand-daughter. But I'm not her. I'm not Anna."

"Of course you are," Eleanor returned patiently.

"Eleanor—"

"There is one way to find out," Averill suggested.

"What's that?" Zach asked, ignoring the icy looks directed his way by both his wife and the woman he loved.

"A DNA test."

"I've read about that," Eleanor said. The idea seemed to perk her up a bit. "Isn't it also known as genetic fingerprinting?"

"That's right. It's a controversial procedure in the courtroom, but there have been documented cases of DNA matching being used to determine paternity. It's also very expensive."

Renewed color returned to Eleanor's ashen cheeks. "Whatever it costs, the money will be well spent." She reached out across the aisle, took both Alex's hands in hers and said, in a pleading tone that wavered with age and emotion, "Please, Alexandra, say you'll take the test."

This was impossible! She knew who she was. She was Alexandra Lyons. She'd been Alexandra Lyons all her life. Such a test would be a waste of time, money and emotional energy.

But if it freed Eleanor of this obsession… "What would I have to do?" she asked Averill.

"Not that much. We can get sufficient DNA from a simple blood sample."

"I hate to even bring this up," Alex said with a worried, sideways glance at Eleanor, "but how would you obtain DNA samples from Robert and Melanie?"

"Those should be available from the police. The files were never closed."

Alex found the idea of digging through moldy police files for old blood samples from murder victims almost too morbid to contemplate.

"I'll have to think about it," Alex said as the jet's landing wheels touched down.

"Of course, dear," Eleanor replied generously.

Having come to know the woman well, Alex realized such patience did not come easily to her.

Refusing the offer of the Lord's limousine, Alex headed in the direction of the taxi stand. Zach followed directly on her heels.

"Go away!" she shouted. The icy shock had worn off. Her eyes glittered with tears of anger. Tears of betrayal.

He put a hand on her shoulder. "You have to let me explain."

"There's nothing to explain." She shook off his touch. "Unfortunately I understand all too well. Eleanor believed I was a missing heiress, and since you're always so concerned about saving Lord's precious money, you investigated me to prove that I was just another in a long line of fraudulent claimants."

"I never thought you were a swindler, goddamn it." He tried to find a way around the hurt. The lies. "I just didn't think you were Anna."

"But Eleanor did."

Fighting desperation, he shoved his hands into his pockets to keep from touching her again. To keep from dragging her against him and kissing her senseless until she could see, until she could feel, how much he loved her. "Yes."

"And everyone knows you'd do anything for Eleanor Lord. Even prostitute yourself."

Frustration soared, mingling with his own flare of anger. "What the hell are you talking about?"

"You slept with me."

"Because I love you, dammit. What happened between us had nothing to do with Eleanor's belief you were Anna."

"It had everything to do with it. But believe it or not, I can't help admiring your loyalty, Zachary, even while I despise your methods."

She stopped long enough to look up at him, her misty eyes dark with pain. "It was all a lie, wasn't it? New Orleans, your mother's wedding. Everything."

His betrayal cut so fatally deep, Alex could no longer even believe that Zach had loved her. She felt tired. And used.

She was looking at him as if he were something that had just crawled out from beneath a rock. Her anger he could handle. Lord knows he'd had enough experience with Miranda. But Zach had no way of knowing how to cope with Alex's despair.

"I never lied to you, Alex."

"You didn't tell me the truth. And in my book, Zachary Deveraux, that's the same thing."

As she walked away, head held high, spine as straight as a rod of steel, it crossed Zach's mind that Alexandra Lyons and that unbending arbiter of veracity, Sister Mary Joseph, had a lot in common.

The following morning, after a restless night, Alex reluctantly agreed to Averill's DNA test.

She met him in a laboratory at the UCLA medical school, where a white-smocked technician pricked the end of her right index finger, drawing a bright red bead of blood.

And then the waiting began.

Chapter Thirty-Two

Not only was DNA testing expensive, it was, Alex learned, time-consuming. Days passed. Fifteen long days and even longer nights, which Alex spent reliving every event of her life.

She was barely able to sleep. Which was, in its own way, a blessing, because whenever she did drift off, the nightmares would return, more terrifying, more ominous than ever.

This time she could see the house, which had been draped in mist in her earlier dreams, clearly. It was Casa Contenta.

And when the monk raised the glittering knife to strike her, his brown cowl fell back, and in the slanting light of a full moon, Alex found herself staring directly into Zach's traitorous face.

She couldn't eat. Time, which was reputed to heal all wounds, did nothing to ease either her anger or her grief. She'd never been a woman of ambivalent feelings. During her life she'd felt love and hate.

Not until Zach's betrayal had she realized it was possible to feel both at the same time.

Just as she'd done when she'd set out to learn about Eleanor's will, Miranda dressed for her late-afternoon visit to Averill with extreme care.

She was wearing a new Valentino cream suit with gold piping that showed off the golden tan recently acquired in a Beverly Hills salon. Although a dread of wrinkles had already made her eschew the sun, Miranda knew that Averill preferred women who appeared to glow with good health.

"As if skin cancer could ever be healthy," she muttered as she pulled her Rolls into the office parking lot.

Peeking between the lapels of her fitted suit jacket was the lace top of her camisole. Her ivory-hued, lace-topped stockings ended at midthigh. She'd spent two hours this morning having her blond hair whipped into a frothy, windblown cloud. Diorissimo had been smoothed and spritzed over every inch of her supple, well-toned body.

She judiciously checked her reflection in the mirror, applied a bit more peach lip gloss and smiled her satisfaction.

Averill's office nurse had no sooner announced her than the door to the doctor's sanctum sanctorum opened.

"Miranda," he said with his trademark smile, "what a pleasant surprise."

"I was in the neighborhod—" she slipped her creamed and manicured hands into both his outstretched ones "—and thought I'd drop in."

"I'm glad you did." He hugged her briefly. "You smell like springtime."

Her smile was as dazzling as the diamonds surrounding the pearls gleaming at her earlobes. "Aren't you sweet."

She allowed her body to stay against his for a heartbeat too long. "I do hope I'm not interrupting anything important."

"Not at all. As a matter of fact, your timing's perfect. My last patient of the day just left." He glanced at his nurse. "In fact, Terri, if you'd like you can take off early."

The nurse did not hesitate. She grabbed her bag and was out the door, leaving Averill and Miranda alone in the office.

Just as Miranda had planned.

"Would you like a drink?" Averill offered as he ushered her into his inner office. "I've a variety of hard liquor here in the office, but if you'd rather have a glass of wine, we can go down the street to the Biltmore."

"Perhaps later." She sat down on his sofa and crossed her legs in a way that allowed an enticing glimpse of the lacy top of her stocking. And the smooth thigh above it.

She watched the good doctor watching her and felt a glow of female satisfaction. Men were such fools for sex, she thought. Which wasn't so bad, really. Not when it made them so easy to manipulate.

"Actually, I came here to talk with you, Averill. About Alexandra's DNA test."

"Oh?"

He folded his hands atop his desk. His expression turned professionally inscrutable. "What about it?"

"I'm sure you can understand that I'm not exactly a disinterested party."

He nodded. And waited for her to continue.

"After all, I do care a great deal for Aunt Eleanor. And I'm so worried that finding out Alex is not Anna—which we all know is the way that test is going to turn out—will come as quite a blow."

"She's pretty convinced the test will back up her beliefs," Averill said.

"I know." Her soft intake of breath made her breasts swell enticingly. "Well, I thought that if perhaps I could have advance warning, I could make certain I'm at the house. To prepare Auntie."

Averill leaned back in the chair. His intelligent blue eyes studied her for a long moment. "Are you suggesting I give you the results of the test before I tell anyone else?"

She met his gaze with a level one of her own. "That's exactly what I'm suggesting." She recrossed her legs with a swish of silk. "I promise you, Averill, I will be very grateful."

He pressed his fingers together and smiled at her over the tent of his hands. "You know, Miranda, I've always admired you."

"As I've admired you," she said silkily.

He nodded. "I've always admired your beauty and your drive. And your unrelenting avarice."

She stiffened. "Excuse me?"

"You've got balls, lady," Averill allowed. "And although I have no doubt that what you're offering would be world class, I'm afraid I'm going to have to pass."

"Pass?" Her voice rose. Her eyes glittered dangerously. "Are you saying you refuse to cooperate with me?"

"Actually, I'm saying that I can't betray my medical principles, Miranda. Not even for the fuck of a lifetime."

"You're going to be very sorry, Averill."

He looked up at her heaving breasts, flushed cheeks, her glossy, parted peach lips, and sighed heavily.

"Believe me, sweetheart," he said, his voice thick with regret, "I already am.

"But—" he held up his hand to forestall her intended renewed effort "—I'm still not going to give you first crack at Alexandra's test results."

Unaccustomed to rejection, Miranda slapped him. Hard. Then she stormed out of his office, slamming first the inner door, then the outer door behind her.

As he heard the framed diplomas on the waiting-room wall fall to the floor, Averill shook his head and wondered idly if Hippocrates had ever faced a similar ethical dilemma.

"You know," Sophie said, studying Alex's shadowed eyes and pale cheeks, "you look as if you're getting ready to audition for a remake of *Night of the Living Dead*."

"Thanks for the compliment," Alex muttered. They were sitting in Alex's kitchen, the box of doughnuts Sophie had brought with her between them.

"I'm worried about you."

"I'm fine."

"Like hell." Sophie licked the glaze from her fingers. "Call the man, Alex."

Alex opened her mouth to insist there'd be snowball fights in hell first when her telephone rang.

"The machine'll get it."

Immediately upon their return to Los Angeles, Zach had called several times a day, first begging, then, as his frustration obviously built, demanding to talk with her.

But she'd steadfastly refused to pick up the phone, leaving him no choice but to leave a series of messages on her recorder.

Two days ago the calls had stopped. Alex had taken the sudden silence as a sign that Zach had given up.

"Alex?" The masculine voice was smooth and cultured and unthreatening. "It's Averill. I just wanted you to know that I've got the test results back—"

Alex dived for the phone. "Averill, hi. It's me."

"Well, hello, Alex. How are you?"

"Fine, thanks," she lied. "And you?"

"Never been better. The reason I called—"

"I know. The test."

"Yes." He cleared his throat. "What are your plans for this afternoon?"

"Actually I don't have any." Other than avoiding Zach.

"Good, good," he said absently. There was a moment's silence, then Alex heard him talking with someone apparently in the room with him. "Sorry, Alexandra," he said when he came back onto the line, "but my nurse needed me to sign some prescription forms."

"That's okay." Alex took a deep breath. "Well? Was I right? Did your test prove Eleanor wrong?"

He cleared his throat again, revealing atypical discomfort. "Actually, Alex, if you don't mind, I'd prefer to discuss this with both you and Eleanor at the same time."

"You want me to come up to Santa Barbara? Today?"

"I thought that might be best. The strain of waiting has been hard on Eleanor. I'd rather she not make the trip to L.A."

"I'll leave within the hour, Averill."

"Thank you, dear. I'll tell Eleanor you're coming. The news will please her, I know."

"Well?" Sophie demanded after Alex had hung up.

"He wants to break the news to both of us at the same time." Alex sighed. "Poor Eleanor. You know, I really want to be angry at her, but I keep thinking how desperate she must have been all these years."

"You never know," Sophie suggested. "Eleanor Lord may get her wish today. And you may become one of the youngest millionaires in the country."

"Right. And pigs will begin flying all over Los Angeles."

London

Zach had known that the hunch he'd come here to play was a long shot. But he'd played it to win, and it had paid off.

He'd spent the past six hours locked in deliberation with the governor of the Bank of England, the chairman of Lloyd's and the publisher of the *Times,* enough royalty to fill several pages of *Burke's Peerage* and several members of Margaret Thatcher's egalitarian meritocracy.

And now, business concluded, he had one last matter to take care of before he could return home to Los Angeles. And Alex.

He knew it wasn't going to be easy breaching her seemingly concrete parapets. But breach them he would. Zach had not achieved such a high level of success by taking no for an answer.

Typically, for London, it was raining. The sky was a gloomy pewter, the streets were gray, the stone buildings were draped in a slate mist. But the dismal weather could not dampen Zach's enthusiasm. All during today's meeting, it had taken every bit of self-control he possessed to keep from thinking about how, in a few short hours, he would be making love to Alex.

Miranda's town house was located in Belgrave Square. Formerly Elysian Fields, where sheep had once placidly grazed, Belgravia, as it had come to be known, was an oasis between the feverish shopping streets of Knightsbridge and traffic-congested Picadilly.

"You can wait," Zach instructed the driver as the taxi pulled up in front of the Regency London building. "I won't be long."

"Whatever suits you," the driver said with a shrug as he turned off the engine and plucked a racing form from the floor of the front seat.

Zach let himself in with his key. The town house was dark. Hushed. The only sound was the steady *tick-tick* of the mantel clock.

The bedroom was dark, as well, but the adjacent bathroom was illuminated with the flickering glow of candles.

"Miranda?"

Zach stopped in the open doorway, struck momentarily mute by the sight of his wife and Marie Hélène

Debord lying together in the old-fashioned, claw-footed bathtub. The Frenchwoman's hand was on Miranda's naked breast, Miranda's firm thigh was twined around her companion's hip.

"Zach!" Miranda stared up at him. Marie Hélène, Zach noted through his shock, merely curled her lips in her cool, trademark superior smile.

He'd always known his wife had taken lovers. That being the case, he supposed the sex of those bed partners really didn't make a helluva lot of difference.

"Get dressed." He yanked a thick towel down from the heated rack and tossed it at her. "There's something we need to discuss."

Feeling amazingly calm under the circumstances, Zach went back into the living room, poured two fingers of single malt Scotch into a glass, reconsidered, and added a healthy splash more.

He'd no sooner polished it off when Miranda appeared, clad in an emerald silk robe, looking flushed and guilty.

"If you're going to drop in like this, Zachary, it would be nice if you had the decency to telephone first."

"So I don't interrupt when you're entertaining your lovers?"

"Well, it was an unpleasant surprise." She rubbed the nape of her neck. "I suppose you're going to lecture me again."

"Personally, I don't care what you do, or who you do it with, Miranda. I haven't for a very long time. Which is why it's time we put an end to this farce of a marriage that should have been declared dead at the altar."

"You can't divorce me." Her expression turned hard, making her face ugly. "Don't forget, if you even try to leave me for Alexandra Lyons, or anyone else for that matter, I'll sell my stock so fast your uncivilized, barbaric backwoods Cajun head will spin."

"Threats aren't going to work today. It's over."

"I'll call Nelson Montague."

"Go right ahead."

She paused, her hand on the telephone receiver. "You realize this will give him control of Lord's."

"There is no way that pirate will ever gain control of Lord's. I've seen to that."

"What the bloody hell are you talking about?" Her eyes remained as hard as emeralds, but her peaches-and-cream English complexion turned as white as the papers he had brought for her to sign.

"Eleanor and I have just purchased all the outstanding stock belonging to the British consortium. Which leaves you and your Aussie pirate out in the cold."

"That's a lie! They promised that stock to Nelson. I saw the preliminary agreement!"

"That was before they knew about his true plans for the company. I have you to thank for that, Miranda. If you hadn't stolen that memo, I wouldn't have had such an effective weapon.

"As it turns out, the London group is big on tradition." It was what he'd been counting on. "And though they'd decided to finally sell their stock and take a hefty profit, none of them wanted to be responsible for turning an upscale, fifty-year-old department store chain into the five-and-dime."

"Damn you!" Furious, she slapped him, the sound of her palm hitting his cheek like a gunshot.

"If you want to blame someone," Zach said calmly, ignoring her outburst, "I'd suggest you blame your father. If he hadn't sold his stock to pay his gambling debts, it would have remained under family control."

He pulled an envelope from the inside breast pocket of his suit jacket. "Here's a check for your outstanding shares, made out for twenty percent above today's market closing price."

"What makes you think I would sell my stock to you?"

"In the first place, I'm offering you an extremely generous profit. Then there's always the fact that your social cachet might plummet if all your society pals find out about your little playmate." He tilted his head toward the bathroom door.

When he'd come here today, he'd hoped to use Miranda's deep-seated greed to convince her to sign; he hadn't expected her to give him a more powerful weapon.

"That's bloody fucking blackmail."

"You'd be the one to know," he drawled sapiently. "Having used the tactic yourself so many times."

"I'll kill myself if you leave me." It was a last-ditch effort that had succeeded before. This time it failed.

"That threat may have worked once," Zach allowed. "But don't forget, baby, we hadn't been married long. I hadn't seen through your slickly applied veneer yet.

"Besides, you'd never do it," Zach said. "You're too narcissistic to ever hurt yourself." He pulled another check from his pocket. "And to sweeten the pot, Eleanor's willing to give you your inheritance up front."

"I can't believe you actually went to Eleanor with this."

"Lord's is her company," he reminded Miranda. "She was entitled to the opportunity to save it. Face it, sweetheart," he said as she snatched both checks from his fingers, studying them with avid green eyes, "this deal is as good as it's going to get.

"In fact, the offer for your shares automatically drops ten percent per minute." He glanced down at his gold watch. "Beginning now."

He placed the deed of transfer on the nineteenth-century partner's desk he remembered her unearthing at an antique store on Bleecker Street during his first visit to the city and held out his pen.

"You bastard." She took the gold pen from his outstretched hand and signed her name in a furious scrawl far removed from her usual stylish script.

"My lawyer will be contacting yours in the morning to work out the details for the divorce."

At her mumbled obscenity, his eyes hardened to black stones. "I wouldn't advise your stalling on this one, Miranda. Unless you want to see exactly how uncivilized we barbaric backwoods Cajuns can be."

"Bastard," she repeated through clenched teeth.

"Goodbye, Miranda." Zach folded the transfer agreement and returned it to his pocket. "It's been interesting."

Feeling remarkably lighthearted and blessedly free—free!—he walked away, not pausing when the porcelain Ming vase shattered against the doorjamb only inches from his head.

As he returned to the waiting taxi, Zach was whistling.

Chapter Thirty-Three

Though Alex knew Eleanor was about to be proved wrong, she could not rein in her anxiety as she drove up the coast to Casa Contenta. By the time she entered the mansion, her nerves were screaming.

"My dear," Eleanor said, "thank you so very much for coming." She took both Alex's unnaturally icy hands in hers. "I had tea and cakes prepared. Will you join me?"

"Of course." They were both skirting around the real reason for her being there. Which was, of course, like ignoring a dead elephant in your living room.

Averill was waiting for the women in the solarium. After greeting the doctor politely, Alex glanced down at the white, wrought-iron table, relieved to find it set for only three.

Eleanor did not miss Alex's surreptitious study of the table settings. "Zachary is in London. He's returning to L.A. this morning."

"If you don't mind, Eleanor," Alex said, her voice as

tight as the fist that gripped her heart, "I'd rather not discuss Zach." There. She'd done it. Said his name without choking. Alex figured that was progress of sorts.

"Whatever you wish, dear." There would be time, Eleanor assured herself, for the young people to iron out their difficulties.

Alex was forced to wait while Eleanor poured the tea neither of them really wanted.

"I suspect you ladies have been on pins and needles, these past weeks," Averill said as he accepted a raisin-studded scone from the plate Eleanor passed him. "So, shall we get to it?"

At that moment, Alex could have kissed him. He met her eyes and smiled his understanding of her impatience.

He reached into the alligator briefcase on the chair beside him and pulled out a thick sheaf of papers. On the top page was a colorful graph resembling the bar code scanned for supermarket prices.

"As I said, it's a complicated test," he began. "You'll recall that human beings have forty-six pairs of chromosomes, each chromosome consisting of a long string of genes that are, in turn, composed of strands of deoxyribonucleic acid, which is a chemical that carries the, uh, computer programming codes, I suppose you could call them—"

"Averill." Eleanor lifted her hand. "Alexandra and I have both taken high-school biology. We know what chromosomes are and we also understand, as well as any layperson needs to, what genes do. So, do you think you could just skip the lecture and cut to the chase?"

"Of course," he said. "I'm sorry if I bored you."

"We're just a little anxious," Alex said quickly.

"You don't have to apologize, Alexandra," Eleanor countered. "Averill is quite accustomed to my bad manners. Aren't you?"

"I wouldn't touch that line with a ten-foot pole," he responded mildly. "Okay. The bottom line is that there's no match."

His words landed in the center of the table like a bomb. Alex would have not been surprised to see the flower-rimmed Royal Doulton tea plates and delicate cups shatter.

"Are you saying Alexandra is not my granddaughter?"

"Yes." Averill exchanged a glance with Alex and she knew they were thinking the same thing. Neither of them would have willingly harmed Eleanor Lord. Yet that was what they'd done. "I'm sorry, Eleanor."

"How conclusive is that test?" Eleanor demanded.

"Very conclusive. Alex is a charming, intelligent young woman. And it's more than a little apparent that you and she have a great deal in common. But she is not Anna."

"Well." Eleanor exhaled a deep breath and turned her gaze out over the estate. Outside the windows, the groundskeepers were raking the red clay tennis courts. She was silent for so long that Alex thought the older woman had forgotten their presence until she turned from the window and faced her.

"Fate is a powerful force, Alexandra. It was fate that brought us together—in so many ways that are every bit as twisted and interconnected as those genes Averill says proves we're not related by blood.

"But it doesn't matter," Eleanor insisted, reaching out to cover Alex's hand with her own blue-veined one.

"You could not be any closer to me if you were my own flesh and blood, Alexandra. And that's all that matters."

"Yes." Alex nodded. "That's all that matters." She'd never meant anything more in her life.

For a quarter of a century Eleanor had been obsessed with finding her missing granddaughter. Now, as she embraced Alexandra, she finally gave up the quest.

There were tears. And laughter. Then more tears. Then emotional healing.

"It wasn't Zachary's fault, you know," Eleanor said after they had moved from tea to champagne.

Alex took a long sip of the sparkling wine and tried not to think about the day she and Zach had drunk Dom Pérignon from paper cups. "He lied to me."

"Only to protect me. The man was horribly torn, Alexandra."

"I understand that." Alex leaned forward and refilled her glass. "But if he loved me, really loved me…" Her voice drifted off as she ran a fingernail along the rim of the flute.

"May I ask a question?" Eleanor said.

"Of course."

"Do you love Zach?"

Alex didn't want to. She had tried with every fiber of her being to exorcise him from her mind. Her heart. But she might as well have tried to stop the sun from rising in the east or those waves outside the windows from ebbing and flowing.

"So much it hurts."

"Well, then," Eleanor said with her usual brusque, decisive manner, "that's all that matters, isn't it?"

"I don't know," Alex murmured.

"I've always believed that when your head and your

heart seem at odds, it's best to go with your heart," Eleanor advised gently.

Eleanor wondered if they'd like to get married here, at Casa Contenta, then remembering that this was the scene of Zach's first disastrous wedding, reconsidered. The country club was always nice. Or perhaps the winter home she kept on Kauai.

Kauai, Eleanor decided. Outside, on the lanai overlooking the peaceful blue lagoon, with the scent of Plumeria and bougainvillea drifting on the trade winds. Alexandra would make such a lovely bride. She deserved a wedding fit for a fairy-tale princess, and Eleanor intended to see that the day lived up to her darling Alex's most romantic fantasy.

"Eleanor," Averill murmured, interrupting into her pleasant thoughts. "As much as I hate to break up this party, it's past time for your nap."

"Oh, pooh," she complained. "I do wish you'd stop treating me like an old woman."

"You are an old woman," Averill countered, smiling. "The goal is to keep you healthy so you can get even older."

"But I want to talk with Alexandra some more."

"She'll be here when you wake up. Won't you, Alex?" Before she could answer he suggested, "In fact, why don't you spend the night?"

Alex had intended to return to Los Angeles as soon as she'd learned the results of the DNA test. Truthfully, she didn't want to spend another night upstairs, where she'd suffered those frightening nightmares. But one look at the hope etched blatantly into the deep lines of Eleanor's face and she felt her resolve crumbling.

"I'd love to spend the night."

"Thank you, dear." Eleanor rose from the table and kissed Alex's cheek. "You've made me a very happy woman." That said, she allowed the doctor to escort her upstairs.

Alex took the opportunity to call Sophie and let her know about the negative results. She was still in the solarium, sipping champagne and looking out at the ocean when Averill returned.

"That was very nice of you," he said.

"What?"

"Agreeing to spend the night. I'm sorry, Alex. I was so concerned about Eleanor, I forgot about the nightmares."

"That's all right. They're only dreams."

"Of course."

"And dreams can only hurt if Freddy Krueger's starring in them."

"Freddy Krueger?"

Alex laughed, feeling foolish. "He's a character in a movie. He has horrible long fingernails and slaughters high-school students who dream about him. *Nightmare on Elm Street*."

"I must have missed that one."

The idea of this debonair man sitting in a theater with a bunch of screaming teenagers watching the satanic sandman slashing away at defenseless dreamers made Alex laugh again.

"I have got an idea," he said suddenly. "How would you like to go for a sail?"

"Today?" Alex glanced out at the line of clouds building on the horizon.

"That rain is hours away," Averill assured her as if reading her mind. "We'll only stay out a short time. Just long enough to help you relax so you can sleep without worrying about nocturnal visitors. It's better than pills."

Remembering how her day on the water had calmed her nerves the last time she'd been bothered by the nightmares, Alex made her decision. "I like your prescription, Doctor."

Although Alex trusted Averill's sailing skills implicitly, as the sky grew darker and the water became choppier, she began to feel uneasy.

"Eleanor's probably awake by now," she said. "Perhaps we should go back in. Before she begins to worry."

He turned from trimming the sail. "Eleanor knows you're with me, Alex. She won't worry."

The wind picked up, blowing her hair into a frothy tangle. "Still, with her heart condition and all…"

"Don't tell me you're afraid."

"Of course not," Alex said quickly. A little too quickly. Averill gave her a sharp, knowing look. "All right," she admitted reluctantly. "I am a little nervous."

"Don't you trust me?"

"Of course, but—"

"Alex, Alex." He laughed off her concern. "I've sailed in worse squalls than this. Don't worry, I know what I'm doing."

She tried to relax. She watched him move around the wet and slanting teak deck, as graceful as a cat walking along the top of a fence. He knew what he was doing, she reminded herself, observing his deft skills. He'd never risk his own life.

She told herself that over and over again, but as the sky grew even darker and thunder boomed ominously beyond the thick fog bank blowing in from the horizon, she began to find it more and more difficult to relax.

A frisson of fear skimmed along her nerve endings when she noticed that, instead of turning the ketch back toward the shore, he was actually taking it farther out to sea.

"Please, Averill," she said. "I want to go back now."

"I'm sorry, Alexandra. But I'm afraid that's impossible."

"What do you mean?"

"I mean it's all your fault," he explained. His voice was calm.

A wave hit the side of the ketch, splashing her. She dragged her hand down her face, wiping away the salt water. "What's my fault? Surely not the weather."

"I hoped I wouldn't have to do this." He shook his head with what appeared to be honest regret. "But then you began having those damn nightmares. Over and over again."

"I don't understand. What do my nightmares have to do with anything? We'd agreed they were only dreams." Alex wasn't afraid. Not yet. But she was confused.

"That's what we'd agreed. But you have to understand. I can't take the risk."

"Risk?"

He shook his head. "Everything went wrong that night," he said as if he hadn't heard her. "Melanie wasn't supposed to die, dammit! Only Robert."

Somehow, some way, she'd deal with this, Alex told herself. "I don't understand."

"Robert met Melanie in L.A., when she was under contract to Paramount. But her career was going nowhere and she was tired of struggling to make ends meet, so he seemed like the answer to her prayers.

"But after he brought her to Santa Barbara, it didn't take long for her to get bored. The town," he said unnecessarily, "is not known for its nightlife. And Robbie was trying to lock her away like one of Eleanor's damn hothouse flowers. But Melanie Patterson was a vibrant, exciting woman. So she turned to me for the stimulation she needed so badly in her life."

"You had an affair with Melanie Lord?"

"Not an affair," he retorted. "I loved her. I'd have done anything for her."

"Even kill your best friend?"

Averill didn't directly respond to her question. "I grew up in Robert Lord's shadow," he said, his eyes focused on some unseen horizon. "My father was Eleanor and James's gardener. When we went away to college, Robbie got a Chrysler convertible. I got a job washing dishes in a sorority kitchen.

"After graduation, Robbie got another new car, a Porsche this time, and went to Harvard law school. I managed to swing some financial aid for medical school, but it took me fifteen years to pay off my student loans. Fifteen damn years."

"That must have been hard."

He gave her a long, unfathomable look. "Yes."

"But then you began to make a great deal of money," Alex said. "You were able to buy your Ferrari and this gorgeous ketch—"

"That's not the goddamn point!" he roared as the ketch reeled on the increasing waves.

Alex swallowed. "I'm sorry. I didn't mean to belittle your struggles."

"Everything always came so easily to Robbie. But then, I had something of his. I had his wife."

"Whom you loved," she said, trying to remain calm. The thing to do, she decided, was to keep him talking. Until she figured out a way out of this.

"Love doesn't begin to cover what I felt. Obsession comes close, but it's still not a strong enough word. Which is why, when she began insisting that the only way we could ever be together would be if Robert were dead, I believed her."

Alex didn't know which she found more horrible: the story itself, or the fact that she was beginning to believe it. "Why didn't she just get a divorce?"

"I suggested that. But Melanie pointed out that if we stayed in town, the scandal would damage my reputation. She said we'd have to move away and I'd be forced to start another practice somewhere else.

"She convinced me it was ridiculous that I should have to struggle all over again when I could marry Robert Lord's widow and have the entire Lord fortune at my fingertips."

"I can't imagine you agreeing to that," Alex said truthfully.

"I can't, either. But at the time, Melanie's sexuality, along with the lure of more money than I'd ever dreamed of, proved terribly seductive. The plan was to kill Robbie on a night when everyone would be out at a party at the club.

"I'd given Melanie something to put in Robbie's drink to make him nauseated. When he was unable to go to the party, Eleanor and Melanie left without him. It was a very clever plan."

Averill's normally kind eyes lighted with pride, and he looked at Alex as if expecting praise.

She wasn't about to risk disappointing him. "Very clever."

"It should have gone off like clockwork. I'd shoot Robbie, then mess up the room, making it look as if he'd interrupted a burglary in progress. The only problem was that Robbie had overheard us plotting his murder. That's when he came up with his own plan. A plan to kill the man who'd stolen his wife."

Alex lifted a hand and rubbed her temple. "*Robert Lord* was going to kill *you?*" If it weren't for the bracing salt spray constantly splashing onto her face, she'd have thought this was just another nightmare.

"Robbie was an extremely jealous man. And he'd begun to drink heavily the past six months. Neither Melanie nor I realized that his drinking had been triggered by his finding out about our affair."

Averill shook his wet head. "It was a ridiculous scenario. There we were, lifelong childhood friends, facing one another across the library like two cowboys at the OK Corral.

"The idea of either of us actually committing murder was so ludicrous we both put our guns away. And," Averill said with regret as he raked his hand through his wet hair, "it would have all ended right there if Melanie hadn't returned unexpectedly. She was afraid I'd lose my nerve."

He laughed at that, but the sound held no humor. "As it turned out, she was right. She began taunting Robbie, telling him what a failure he was as a man. She told him that he'd never satisfied her sexually, that she'd only married him for his money. Unfortunately

Robbie was drunk and Melanie, who always knew how to find someone's sore spot, definitely hit the bull's-eye that night.

"When he picked up his revolver from the desk and aimed it at her, I tried to take it away. We wrestled and somehow it went off. The bullet struck Melanie in the throat."

As he described the incident, flashes of Alex's nightmares flickered on the screen of her mind. Her flesh turned an icy cold that had nothing to do with the soaked red sweatshirt and jeans clinging to her skin.

She closed her eyes. A vision, imprinted deep on her subconscious, flashed behind her closed lids. The sound of gunshots reverberated through her head. She began to shake violently.

Then suddenly, shockingly, it all flooded back, distant, horrifying memories locked in a child's subconscious.

"Oh, my God! It was you!" Her eyes flew open and she stared at Averill in horror. "You killed my father."

My father. Those impossible words echoed in her mind like the deep, warning toll of a bell. Her hands tightened around the water-slick brass railing, and she held on for dear life, as if to keep from sliding off the face of the earth. Her life, the entire world as she'd always known it, was spinning dizzyingly around her, tilting dangerously out of control.

"I didn't kill him. After Melanie was shot, the damn gun fell to the floor and fired again. The bullet entered Robbie's chest and struck his heart. He died instantly.

"I was kneeling over Melanie's body when I looked up and saw you standing in the doorway of the library, watching me with an expression of absolute shock. And horror. The same way you're looking at me now.

"You were supposed to be in bed, dammit! Rosa had been well paid to give you a sleeping pill, take one herself and stay in her room. That way, the next morning, she could truthfully tell the police that she'd heard nothing."

Alex wrapped her arms around herself to ward off the chill that had seeped deep into her bones. She wasn't Alexandra Lyons at all. She was Anna Lord. Her entire life had been a lie.

"But what about my mother?" she asked numbly. "I know she loved me. How could she have lied to me all those years?"

"It was precisely Irene's love that put you in this untenable situation in the first place. I met Ruth Black— the woman you knew as your mother—when I was going to medical school in North Carolina.

"I was doing illegal abortions to supplement my income. Ruth, who was unable to earn a living at her dressmaking business, was working as a clerk at the North Carolina state adoption agency. There she saw couples who, for various reasons, couldn't meet the state's rigid adoption requirements. We both realized that we had something to offer one another."

"You had access to pregnant women," Alex said slowly. "My mother knew people willing to pay handsomely for a child."

No. Not her mother. Her mother had been Melanie Lord. A murdered, adulterous actress. And the woman she'd thought all her life to be her mother had been engaged in black-market baby selling. Alex felt sick.

"It seemed a match made in heaven," Averill agreed.

Or hell, Alex thought, devastated. So many lies. Years and years of them. A lifetime.

"When I graduated from Duke and returned to Santa Barbara, I brought another doctor into the scheme so Ruth's income wouldn't drop off."

"How generous of you." Despite her fear and shock, Alex could not keep the sarcasm from her voice.

"She thought so. Only one person knew what happened the night Robbie and Melanie were killed."

"Me."

"Yes. Since Rosa knew of the plot, she'd have to be eliminated, which was, of course, unfortunate, but at the time I couldn't think of any other choice. But you…" He shook his head and his gaze softened. "You were an innocent child. I couldn't have a child killed."

The man was, Alex thought, one helluva humanitarian. She glanced grimly out at the rough sea and ever darkening sky, then back at her captor.

"I called Ruth," he went on, "and without telling her the circumstances, asked if she could place a two-year-old girl. She said she could. That little piece of business out of the way, I warned Rosa she was an accessory to murder and instructed her to take you to Tijuana and wait for Ruth's arrival.

"Finding someone to stage Rosa's suicide was easy. The bars were filled with men willing to do anything for a few hundred pesos.

"Unfortunately Ruth fell instantly in love with you. She called me from Mexico and told me she was keeping you for her own. Then she disappeared. I decided she must have seen the national news coverage of the double murder and kidnapping and changed both your names. After a few years, I felt safe enough to stop looking for you."

"But what about David? What about my brother?"

He shrugged. "I'd heard through the grapevine that Ruth had a son of her own. Obviously, after she brought you back from Mexico, she got new birth certificates for both of you." He rubbed his jaw. "That was clever, actually, I never would have thought to look for twins."

Suddenly a scene flashed in Alex's mind, like one of those black-and-white horror movies shown on cable television at four in the morning.

After hours in the dark, the closet door had finally opened, flooding the small cubicle with blinding light. Terrified that the monsters were about to devour her whole, the little girl screamed and kicked out at the intruder.

"It's going to be all right!" a female voice shouted.

The woman struggled to avoid the child's kicks at the same time her hands attempted to capture the flailing fists. Finally Anna's arms were locked against her sides and she was lying across the woman's lap.

Her pupils were enormous in her frightened amber eyes; her complexion was as white as her lace-trimmed nightgown, and an enormous handprint, a souvenir of the monster's brawny paw, cast a dark shadow across her pale cheek. Her exertion had her breathing heavily; her thin chest rose and fell beneath the cotton gown.

"Shh, baby," the woman crooned in a very unmonsterlike voice. "It's all right." The woman had blond hair, like Anna's mother. And while not as beautiful, she had a kind face and gentle eyes.

Even as she longed to believe this stranger, Anna remembered how convincing the wolf had been when he'd greeted Little Red Riding Hood wearing her granny's ruffled white cap.

Anna squirmed, trying to get away, but the woman's hold tightened. "As soon as you're calm, I'll let you go," she promised with a warm smile that reminded Anna painfully of Rosa. "I can't let you run away, baby. There are too many dangers out there. Too many bad things that could happen to a little girl."

As if anything could be worse than what she'd already been through! Anna knew, with a child's absolute clarity, that she could no longer trust anyone. That being the case, she glared up at the woman, trying to resist the comforting hand that was now brushing her dirty, tousled hair away from her face.

"I'll bet it was scary in that closet," the woman murmured, her gentle touch meant to soothe. "I remember, when I was a little girl just like you, I was afraid there were monsters hiding in my closet, waiting to pounce on me as soon as my mother turned off the light."

Anna refused to answer. But she couldn't keep the truth of her own fears from flooding into her eyes.

The woman nodded knowingly. "You don't have to be afraid anymore, sweetheart. I promise I'll keep all those mean, nasty monsters away from you. They'll never hurt you again."

Anna flinched when the stroking fingers brushed the tender bruise on her cheek.

"I used to have bad dreams sometimes, too," the woman revealed on a soothing, almost hypnotic tone that gradually had Anna relaxing muscle by wire-taut muscle. "Do you ever have bad dreams?"

Not yet ready to trust implicitly, Anna's only response was a slight, almost imperceptible nod of her head.

"It's no wonder. After what those monsters have put you through." There was an edge to her voice, a cold, barely restrained fury that Anna realized was not directed toward her.

"But that's all over now," the woman said. "And you know what? I have an idea that will keep the monsters away. And help you to forget all your bad dreams." She paused. "Would you like to hear it?"

This time Anna's nod was a bit more assertive.

"I thought you might." The woman's smile melted some of the icy fear lingering in Anna. "The problem, the way I see it, is that Anna Lord is the little girl afraid of monsters. It's Anna whose Mommy and Daddy have gone to heaven to live with the angels. And it's Anna who has the nightmares. Isn't that right?"

Anna nodded.

"Poor Anna. She's had a very bad time. So the thing to do," the woman said with authority, "is change your name."

"My name?" Anna asked in a small, frail voice.

"Exactly." The woman rewarded her with a smile. "From now on, your name is Alexandra Lyons. And you are a bright, happy little girl who doesn't have any nightmares."

It was like pretend, Anna thought. She played that all the time. A princess was her favorite, like in the fairy tales her nanna Eleanor read to her every night before bed.

"Who are you?" she finally asked, her voice a little stronger this time.

"Who am I? Why, I'm Irene Lyons," Ruth Black

lied adroitly. The die was cast; regardless of the danger, there would be no turning back. "Alexandra's new mommy."

Anna considered that for a long, thoughtful moment. Then wanting—needing—to put the horror of the past five days behind her, she wrapped her arms around the woman's neck and allowed herself to trust....

Finally it was all so clear. Finally Alex understood why they'd moved so often during her younger years. Obviously she'd been afraid Averill would kill them both to keep his secret safe.

Still not wanting to believe this nightmare, Alex grasped onto one last all important detail. "But the DNA test proved I'm not Eleanor's granddaughter."

"There was no test. I faked the test and the results to convince Eleanor that there was no way you could be Anna. But I knew you were."

She really was Anna Lord! The idea was too enormous to take in all at one time. The sky opened up, the rain pelting down like bullets. Like the bullets that had killed her mother and father.

"So, that's the whole tawdry story," Averill went on. "And it would have ended there, if Eleanor hadn't been watching that damn Emmy broadcast. I was afraid that when you saw the house, you'd remember. But you didn't. So I waited, hoping Eleanor was mistaken again. That you weren't Anna.

"But it became increasingly apparent that you were, and when you started having those nightmares, I knew you were on the brink of remembering. So, as much as I loathe the idea of killing, surely you can understand why I can't let you live."

Panic bubbled up in Alex's throat. "Averill, please,"

she protested, "don't do this. I won't tell anyone what you've told me today. It'll be our secret."

She never had been any good at lying. She knew, as his eyes swept over her face, looking hard and deep, that he wasn't fooled.

"I'm honestly sorry, Alex. But surely you can understand I don't have any other choice."

As he approached her, deadly determination glittering in his steel-blue eyes, there was a deafening crack of lightning directly overhead.

Chapter Thirty-Four

Zach was growing more frustrated by the minute. He'd arrived at Alex's place, laden down with roses and champagne and a ring he had every intention of convincing her to accept, if he had to camp out on her damn doorstep until she finally gave in.

When she wasn't there, he tried the studio, only to learn from Sophie that Alex was spending the night in Santa Barbara. Zach took that news as a sign that perhaps her anger was abating. When Sophie went on to reveal the negative DNA results, Zach was surprised. He'd come to believe that Eleanor had been right this time.

"She still claims to be mad as hell at you," Sophie told him matter-of-factly. "But if you want my opinion, I think it's just injured pride talking."

"I'm going to make it up to her."

"You'd better." Sophie waved her letter opener at him. "Or I'll cut out your heart and feed it to the critics."

With that threat ringing in his ears, Zach drove to

Santa Barbara. He found Eleanor in a state. He'd never seen her like this before. Her eyes were wide and frightened. Her hair was a witch's tangle around her ashen face.

"Thank God you're here!" she cried.

"What's wrong? Your heart?"

"No." She shook her head violently, causing hairpins to scatter onto the tile floor. "It's not my heart. It's Alexandra!

"She and Averill went sailing. When I came downstairs after my nap, they still weren't back. Naturally I was worried, so I called the yacht harbor. Averill's ketch hasn't returned to its slip!"

Zach took one look at the storm pelting the windows and called the Coast Guard.

"She's not Anna, Zachary," Eleanor told him as he hung up the phone and headed toward the front door.

"I know. Sophie told me." He retrieved a squall jacket he kept in the front closet. "But that doesn't matter, does it?"

"No," Eleanor agreed. "I love her, Zach. So much." Tears filled her eyes and slid down her cheeks.

"So do I." He brushed the moisture away with a tender fingertip. "And don't worry." He gave Eleanor a quick kiss on her wet, weathered cheek. "She's going to be all right."

She placed a trembling, beringed hand against the side of his face. "Promise me you'll find her, Zach." Her voice quivered with age and emotion. "Please."

"I promise." With that he was gone. To find Alex. And bring her back home where she belonged.

Although her heart was racing, some detached part of Alex remained calm. She tensed every muscle in her body to keep from trembling. There was a way out of this, she assured herself. She just had to stall long enough to think of it.

"There's something I don't understand."

Averill stopped in his tracks. "What's that?"

"Were you the person who came into my room to frighten me that first night at Casa Contenta?" Although she'd certainly suffered enough bad dreams after that terrifying incident, Alex had never truly believed it had been a nightmare.

"No." He shook his head. "I always figured that was either Miranda or Clara."

Clara, Alex decided. Miranda was too straightforward. Not that she wasn't above threats; she just enjoyed making them directly. Clara, on the other hand, had a motive of sorts. If she could convince everyone of ghostly goings-on at the estate, her position as resident psychic would be strengthened. A scent teased at Alex's memory. The aroma of orrisroot that usually surrounded Clara like a noxious cloud. It had been in her room that night. She'd just been too upset to identify it.

Then later, when she was alone with Zach, her mind had been too clouded with desire to think straight.

"But you did do something to my brakes," she guessed.

"I didn't have any choice. Surely you understand I couldn't allow to you remember what happened that night."

"But I do remember. And what I didn't know, you've told me."

He shrugged. "It doesn't matter anymore."

"Because you're going to kill me."

His lips pulled into a grim line, but he neither confirmed nor denied her accusation. "It's all your fault, Anna. You never should have come back."

The wind was wailing like one of Clara Kowalski's lost spirits. Her wet hair was sticking to her face. Alex shoved it out of her eyes. "You'll never get away with this, Averill."

"Of course I will," he said with that same calm self-confidence she suspected eased innumerable worries in the examining room. "It's too bad, really." He resumed moving toward her, murder on his mind and in his eyes. "Eleanor has already suffered so many misfortunes. It's a pity she has to survive the tragedy of you falling overboard in the storm.

"Of course, I'll tell people how desperately I tried to save you. But the ketch almost capsized, and the deck was so slippery I couldn't get to you in time."

He was inches away. "So you went sliding off into the sea. To your death."

When he began ripping at the fasteners of her orange life jacket, Alex realized her entire life had narrowed down to this one fatal moment.

With a fierce strength she'd not known she possessed, she fought back. Her fingernails tore into the flesh of his tanned face, her fists pounded his chest. But he was so strong! And every bit as determined to kill her as she was determined to remain alive.

Providentially, another drenching wave washed over the railing, causing him to slip just enough that she could break free of his iron grip.

Knowing she had no other choice, Alex closed her eyes and dived headfirst into the whitecapped maelstrom.

And then she began to swim. For her life.

* * *

Zach leaned forward in the copilot's seat, scanning the horizon with a pair of binoculars as the Coast Guard helicopter flew low over the storm-tossed waves.

"The guy's an experienced sailor," Zach complained. "What the hell made him go out in weather like this?"

"Beats me," the pilot said. "Every time we get a storm, we have to launch a search for a few hotshots who think they're invincible."

Zach had seen television news footage of idiotic daredevils being pulled from the surf during a heroic rescue. But Averill Brandford was neither an idiot nor a daredevil.

So what had possessed him to take Alex sailing before a storm that had been forecast for the past forty-eight hours?

"We have to find them, dammit!"

"Hey, there's no point in borrowing trouble. The doctor's boat is not exactly a dinghy. If the guy's as experienced as you say, the chances of them capsizing are slim. Don't worry, pal. They've probably just blown off course."

Zach hoped that was true. But some inner voice was telling him that Alex was in very real danger. And that time was running out.

"Just keep looking," he growled.

"That's what we're doing," the pilot answered with an easy calm that suggested such rescue missions were routine.

The sun, managing only the merest sliver of light through the angry clouds, had almost set into the water. Zach commented uneasily that it would soon be dark.

"That's not as bad as it sounds," the pilot said. "We'll

be able to spot the running lights of the ketch. And on top of that, this baby's fitted for night-vision viewing."

His words did nothing to ease Zach's panic.

"What's that?" he asked suddenly, pointing down at something in the water. Something a great deal smaller than Averill Brandford's sleek white ketch.

"Just a buoy."

"No. That orange speck."

"Probably a piece of driftwood," the pilot guessed. "But we may as well take a look."

He dived lower. "Damned if it isn't a person! Get the ring out," he called out to the third man in the chopper.

Zach was both relieved and terrified at the sight of Alex, clinging to the rocking buoy.

While the man tossed the rescue ring out the open door, Zach shouted out to Alex over the helicopter loudspeaker. His voice cracked with emotion. Taking a deep breath, he cleared his throat and tried again.

Although she'd always considered herself a strong swimmer and she was in a life jacket, Alex had never battled such turbulent waves. She'd shouted instructions to herself in her mind: *Right arm. Left arm. Right. Left. Kick. Kick. Kick, dammit!*

Just when she'd thought she could swim no farther, one particularly violent wave had thrown her against the buoy.

She didn't know how long she'd been clinging to the buoy. But it seemed like forever. Her body, which earlier had been cold, was beginning to turn numb. So numb...

A sound rose over the roar of the surf. It was growing closer. She looked up just as the Coast Guard helicopter flew into view.

She heard a voice, but could not make out the words. When a ring attached to a rope came flying out of the open doorway, she assumed she was supposed to take hold of it. But it landed too far away. And she wasn't about to let go of the violently rocking buoy and swim for it.

The man in the doorway pulled the rescue ring back up and tried again. And then a third time. But each attempt fell short. And when the copter tried to fly lower, the wind from the rotor stirred up the water so badly, she almost disappeared beneath the waves. Alex began to despair.

And then, wondrously, the rope appeared again. But this time a man was riding it down. As he neared, Alex feared that she was hallucinating.

Perhaps, she thought wildly, this was what happened when you died. Perhaps those stories about shining lights and tunnels were wrong. Perhaps your last conscious thought was of the one you loved. Or perhaps the man descending from the sky was an angel who coincidentally resembled the man she loved.

"Alex, it's going to be all right, goddammit!" he shouted. "You're going to be all right."

Although she was definitely no expert on near-death experiences, Alex did not believe any angel worth his wings would use such language.

"Zach?" She stared up at him, strapped into a safety harness, hanging from a steel cable just over her head.

"It's me, sweetheart," he assured her. "And we're getting you out of here." She forgot that only days ago she'd been furious at him for deceiving her. Wanting to cover his wonderful face with kisses, she forced herself to follow instructions, latching the safety belt that would hold her to him and the cable.

Then, finally, wonderfully, she twined her arms around the strong column of his neck and together they were raised higher, then higher still, up to the hovering helicopter, where the copilot helped them into the cockpit.

"We have to stop meeting like this," Zach said as he wrapped her in a heavy blanket.

Her teeth were chattering and she was shaking violently with cold and lingering terror. "Y-y-you won't believe what happened!"

"You can tell me all about it later." Zach put his arm around her and drew her close.

She wanted to tell him everything, in vivid, horrible detail. But her exhaustion was too great. Tears born of relief and sorrow flooded her eyes and streamed down her cheeks.

She put her head on his shoulder, his strong, wonderful shoulder, and closed her eyes. "Zach?"

He kissed the top of her head. "Yeah, honey?"

"Eleanor was right."

"About what?" he answered absently. His thoughts were still on that breath-stealing moment when he'd spotted her hanging on to the buoy in those storm-tossed waters.

"About me." Now that she was safe, fatigue claimed her. Her eyes drifted shut. "I'm Anna."

Epilogue

Santa Barbara
Five years later

The sun shone the day Alexandra Deveraux buried her grandmother.

Beside her, his strong arm around her waist, Zach held four-year-old Ellie's hand, while Alex held the baby, Gabriel—named for Zach's father—in her arms.

"I'm so glad Eleanor lived to see her great-grandchildren," Alex murmured. "I'm grateful we all had the chance to become a real family."

"She never stopped loving you, Alex." Zach bent and brushed a tender, husbandly kiss against her temple. "All those years, she never gave up hope."

"I know it sounds crazy, but I feel as if she's still with us. Even now."

"It's not at all crazy. I can feel her, too." Although Zach had grown up surrounded by a large, loving family, he could not have loved Eleanor more if she'd been his own grandmother. "And her spirit lives on in the kids."

"Do you know what Grand-mère Eve says?" Ellie looked a long, long way up toward her father, her keen young eyes brilliant with golden facets that radiated outward, like the rays of the Santa Barbara sun.

"What does she say?" Zach asked.

"She says that Grand-mère Eleanor is an angel now. And she's watching over me. Like my very own guardian angel." Her voice went up a little on the end, as if seeking reassurance that the comforting words were true.

There were days, and this was one of them, that Zach would drink in the sight of his beautiful daughter and son, and marvel that any man could be so lucky.

Zach would have happily married Alex and never asked God for another thing so long as he lived. These two remarkable children, this vivid, breathing legacy of their love, represented more blessings than he would have ever dared ask for.

"My mother is a very smart lady," Zach assured the little girl. He tousled her marmalade-hued hair that was so like her mother's. "And I think your *grand-mère* Eleanor will make a terrific angel. Don't you agree, darling?" he asked Alex.

"The best." Alex returned his fond smile with a slightly teary one of her own.

She ran her fingers over the marble stone that marked Eleanor's final resting spot, high on the lush wildflower-studded hillside beside her beloved husband, James. Nearby, on the other side of the Lord family plot, Robert and Melanie—the parents Alex still could not remember—were buried.

The horrifying events of that fateful day when she'd learned her true identity and Averill had tried to kill her were blessedly fading from her mind, misty memories she chose not to dwell upon.

When the Coast Guard located the ketch the following morning, Averill had not been on board. Since he was an excellent sailor, Eleanor, Zach and Alex had presumed the doctor had chosen to take his own life, rather than suffer the scandal. Not to mention spending the rest of his life in prison.

"I'll bet Grand-mère Eleanor's up in heaven right now," Ellie said. "Telling all the other angels what to do."

Zach and Alex laughed at the all too accurate notion.

As they returned to the estate, not to mourn Eleanor Lord's death but to celebrate her remarkable life, Alex thought that although she would always consider Irene Lyons—or Ruth Black—and her brother, David, her true family, during these past years with Eleanor, she had also come to feel, in many ways, like a Lord.

But best of all she was Alexandra Deveraux now. She and Zachary had planted the roots of their own dynasty deep into the rich, sun-warmed soil of Southern California.

* * * * *

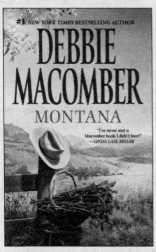

#1 _New York Times_ Bestselling Author

DEBBIE MACOMBER

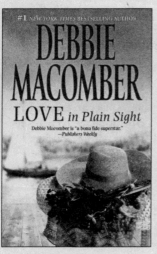

Stephanie Coulter is the assistant to Jonas Lockwood, head of Lockwood Industries. Her boss lives up to his reputation as a tyrant and grouch. But Stephanie's colleagues, romance readers all, decide that he's really the classic lonely hero. What he needs, they say, is "Love 'n' Marriage." And they have just the heroine in mind.

Bethany Stone, on the other hand, is already in love with her boss, Joshua Norris, although their relationship is strictly business. But one day he asks for her help—outside the office. Joshua's ten-year-old daughter, Angie, is coming to live with him and he has no idea how to raise a precocious little girl. Angie might be "Almost an Angel," but she quickly develops a matchmaking plan for her dad—and Bethany!

Available wherever books are sold.

H HARLEQUIN® MIRA®
™ www.Harlequin.com

MDM1413

#1 *New York Times* Bestselling Author

SHERRYL WOODS

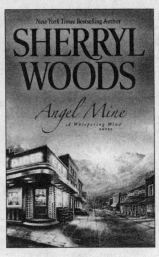

Heather Reed thought she was making the right choice when she decided to raise her daughter, Angel, on her own. But three years later, Heather realizes she needs help. Her career as an actress is faltering, and Angel's more than she can handle alone. It's time to track down Angel's father... Only problem is, he doesn't know Angel exists.

Heather's search leads her to Whispering Wind, Wyoming. If Todd Winston is dismayed to see his old girlfriend, he's shocked when he looks into the angelic eyes of his daughter. Todd flatly refuses to open his life to Angel. Heather flatly refuses to leave town until she finds out why. Amazingly, they discover that through compromise and understanding, lies the road straight to family.

Available wherever books are sold.

HARLEQUIN® MIRA®
™ www.Harlequin.com

MSW1471

New York Times Bestselling Author

SHERRYL WOODS

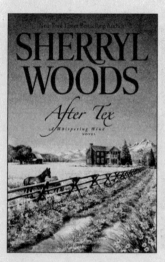

Megan O'Rourke's beloved grandfather had always been determined to lure her out of New York and back to their ranch in Whispering Wind, Wyoming. Now his will makes it impossible for her to refuse. She's named guardian of Tex's daughter—a daughter Megan hadn't known about!

After leaving town years before under a cloud of suspicion, Jake Landers has returned to put down roots. When he comes face-to-face with the woman who shares his troubled past, he hardly recognizes the driven powerhouse Megan has become. Now she has big decisions to make—about life, love and where home really is. Jake's only too happy to help Megan rediscover their old dreams—and maybe this time, fulfill them forever.

Available wherever books are sold.

New York Times Bestselling Author

BRENDA NOVAK

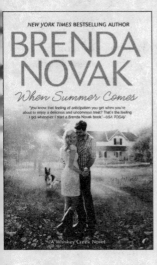

One day, Callie Vanetta receives devastating news...

She needs a liver transplant. But her doctors warn that the chances of finding a compatible donor aren't good.

Determined to spend whatever time she has left on her own terms, she keeps the diagnosis to herself and moves out to her late grandparents' farm. She's always wanted to live there. But the farm hasn't been worked in years and she begins to fear she can't manage it, that she'll have to return to town.

One night, a stranger comes knocking at her door...

He's an attractive and mysterious drifter by the name of Levi McCloud, and he offers to trade work for a few nights' shelter. The arrangement seems ideal until what was supposed to be temporary starts to look more and more permanent. Then Callie realizes she does have something to lose—her heart. And although he doesn't yet know it, Levi stands to lose even more.

Available wherever books are sold.

HARLEQUIN® MIRA®
www.Harlequin.com

MBN1423

New York Times Bestselling Author

JoAnn Ross

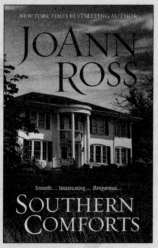

Welcome to Raintree, Georgia—steamy capital of sin, scandal and murder

To her fans, Roxanne Scarbrough is the genteel Southern queen of good taste—she's built an empire around the how-to's of gracious living. To her critics—and there are many—Roxanne is a tyrant. And now somebody wants her dead.

Chelsea Cassidy, Roxanne's official biographer, knows that Roxanne is determined to keep her dark secrets buried, whatever the cost. But when Chelsea begins to unearth the truth about Roxanne's life, her search leads her back into the arms of her college love, Cash Beaudine—a man Roxanne wants for herself. Suddenly Chelsea's investigation takes on a very personal nature—with potentially fatal consequences.

Available wherever books are sold.

HARLEQUIN® MIRA®
www.Harlequin.com

MJR1525

PRAISE FOR PAUL TREMBLAY'S

The Little Sleep

"Well-crafted in a witty voice that doesn't let go, Tremblay's debut is part noir throwback, part medical mystery, part comedy, and thoroughly, wonderfully entertaining. Highly recommended."   —*Library Journal* (starred review)

"*The Little Sleep* is one of the most engaging reads I've come across in a good long while. Tremblay does the near impossible by giving us a new take on the traditional PI tale. Tremblay writes in clear prose that is by turns atmospheric, haunting, and sharply humorous. The mystery is layered but always forward moving, taking us along on a unique journey that features most of the traditional elements of a PI novel, but skewed and twisted into a fresh perspective. You've never read a PI novel like this one before."

—Tom Piccirilli, author of *The Coldest Mile* and *The Cold Spot*

"If Philip K. Dick and Ross Macdonald had collaborated on a mystery novel, they might have come up with something like *The Little Sleep*. . . . I've never used the phrase *new noir* before, but I think I will now. *The Little Sleep* is new noir with panache. Check it out."

—Bill Crider, author of the Sheriff Dan Rhodes mystery series

THE LiTTLE
SLEEP

Also by Paul Tremblay

Survivor Song

Growing Things and Other Stories

The Cabin at the End of the World

Disappearance at Devil's Rock

A Head Full of Ghosts

No Sleep Till Wonderland

PAUL TREMBLAY

THE LITTLE SLEEP

A NOVEL

WILLIAM MORROW
An Imprint of HarperCollinsPublishers

HarperCollins books may be purchased for educational, business, or sales promotional use. For information, please email the Special Markets Department at SPsales@harpercollins.com.

Originally published by Henry Holt and Company in 2009.

FIRST WILLIAM MORROW PAPERBACK PUBLISHED 2021.

Designed by Diahann Sturge

The Library of Congress has catalogued a previous edition as follows:

Tremblay, Paul.
    The little sleep: a novel / Paul Tremblay.—1st ed.
        p.   cm.
    ISBN-13: 978-0-8050-8849-6
    ISBN-10: 0-8050-8849-0
    1. Private investigators—Fiction.   2. South Boston (Boston, Mass.)—Fiction.   3. Narcolepsy—Fiction.   4. Extortion—Fiction.   I. Title.
    PS3620.R445L58   2009
    813'6—dc22

ISBN 978-0-06-299577-3 (pbk.)

21 22 23 24 25 LSC 10 9 8 7 6 5 4 3 2 1

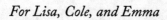

For Lisa, Cole, and Emma

THE LiTTLE SLEEP

ONE

It's about two o'clock in the afternoon, early March. In South Boston that means a cold hard rain that ruins any memories of the sun. Doesn't matter, because I'm in my office, wearing a twenty-year-old thrift-store wool suit. It's brown but not in the brown-is-the-new-black way. My shoes are Doc Martens, black like my socks. I'm not neat and clean or shaved. I am sober but don't feel sober.

There's a woman sitting on the opposite side of my desk. I don't remember her coming in, but I know who she is: Jennifer Times, a flavor-of-the-second local celebrity, singing contestant on *American Star,* daughter of the Suffolk County DA, and she might be older than my suit. Pretty and brunette, lips that are worked out, pumped up. She's tall and her legs go from the north of Maine all the way down to Boston, but she sits like she's small, all compact, a closed book. She wears a white T-shirt and a knee-length skirt. She looks too spring for March, not that I care.

I wear a fedora, trying too hard to be anachronistic or iconoclastic, not sure which. It's dark in my office. The door is closed, the blinds drawn over the bay window. Someone should turn on a light.

I say, "Shouldn't you be in Hollywood? Not that I watch, but the little birdies tell me you're a finalist, and the live competition starts tomorrow night."

She says, "They sent me home to do a promotional shoot at a mall and at my old high school." I like that she talks about her high school as if it were eons removed, instead of mere months.

"Lucky you."

She doesn't smile. Everything is serious. She says, "I need your help, Mr. Genevich," and she pulls her white-gloved hands out of her lap.

I say, "I don't trust hands that wear gloves."

She looks at me like I chose the worst possible words, like I missed the whole point of her story, the story I haven't heard yet. She takes off her right glove and her fingers are individually wrapped in bandages, but it's a bad wrap job, gauze coming undone and sticking out, Christmas presents wrapped in old tissue paper.

She says, "I need you to find out who has my fingers."

I think about opening the shades; maybe some light wouldn't be so bad. I think about clearing my desk of empty soda cans. I think about canceling the Southie lease, too many people double-parking in front of my office/apartment building. I think about the ever-expanding doomed universe. And all of it makes more sense than what she said.

"Say that again."

Her blue eyes stay fixed on me, like she's the one trying to figure out who is telling the truth. She says, "I woke up like this yesterday. Someone stole my fingers and replaced them with these." She holds her hand out to me as if I can take it away from her and inspect it.

"May I?" I gently take her hand, and I lift up the bandage on her index finger and find a ring of angry red stitches. She takes her hand back from me quick, like if I hold on to it too long I might decide to keep those replacement digits of hers.

"Look, Ms. Times, circumstantial evidence to the contrary and all that, but I don't think what you described is exactly possible." I point at her hand. I'm telling her that her hand is impossible. "Granted, my subscription to *Mad Scientist Weekly* did run out. Too many words, not enough pictures."

She says, "It doesn't matter what you think is possible, Mr. Genevich, because I'll only be paying you to find answers to my questions." Her voice is hard as pavement. I get the sense that she isn't used to people telling her no.

I gather the loose papers on my desk, stack them, and then push them over the edge and into the trash can. I want a cigarette but I don't know where I put my pack. "How and why did you find me?" I talk slow. Every letter and syllable has to be in its place.

"Does it matter?" She talks quick and to the point. She wants to tell me more, tell me everything about every thing, but she's holding something back. Or maybe she's just impatient with me, like everyone else.

I say, "I don't do much fieldwork anymore, Ms. Times. Early retirement, so early it happened almost before I got the job. See this computer?" I turn the flat-screen monitor toward her. An infinite network of Escheresque pipes fills the screen-saver pixels. "That's what I do. I research. I do genealogies, find abandoned properties, check the status of out-of-state warrants, and find lost addresses. I search databases and, when desperate, which is all the time, I troll Craigslist and eBay and want ads. I'm no action hero. I find stuff in the Internet ether. Something tells me your fingers won't be in there."

She says, "I'll pay you ten thousand just for trying." She places a check on my desk. I assume it's a check. It's green and rectangular.

"What, no manila envelope bulging with unmarked bills?"

"I'll pay you another fifty thousand if you find out who has my fingers."

I am about to say something sharp and clever about her allowance from Daddy, but I blink my eyes and she is gone.

TWO

Right after I come to is always the worst, when the questions about dreams and reality seem fair game, when I don't know which is which. Jennifer Times is gone and my head is full of murk. I try to push the murk to the corners of my consciousness, but it squeezes out and leaks away, mercury in a closed fist. That murk, it's always there. It's both a threat and a promise. I am narcoleptic.

How long was I asleep? My office is dark, but it's always dark. I have the sense that a lot of time has passed. Or maybe just a little. I have no way of knowing. I generally don't remember to check and set my watch as I'm passing out. Time can't be measured anyway, only guessed at, and my guesses are usually wrong, which doesn't speak well for a guy in my line of work. But I get by.

I paw around my desk and find a pack of cigarettes behind the phone, right where I left them. I light one. It's warm, white, and lethal. I'd like to say that smoking keeps me awake, clears the head, all that good stuff normally associated with nicotine and carcinogens, but it doesn't. Smoking is just something I do to help pass the time in the dark, between sleeps.

On my desk there is no green and rectangular ten-thousand-dollar check. Too bad, I'd quickly grown fond of the little fella. There is a manila envelope, and on my notepad are gouges and scratches in ink, an EKG output of a faulty heart. My notepad is yellow like the warning traffic light.

I lean back in my chair, looking for a new vantage point, a different way to see. My chair complains. The squawking springs tease me and my sedentary existence. No one likes a wiseass. It might be time for a new chair.

Okay, Jennifer Times. I conclude the stuff about her missing fingers was part of a hypnogogic hallucination, which is one of the many pithy symptoms of narcolepsy. It's a vivid dream that occurs when my narcoleptic brain is partially awake, or partially asleep, as if there is a difference.

I pick up the manila envelope and remove its contents: two black-and-white photos, with accompanying negatives.

Photo 1: Jennifer Times sitting on a bed. Shoulder-length hair obscures most of her face. There's a close-lipped smile that peeks through, and it's wary of the camera and, by proxy, me. She's wearing a white T-shirt and a dark-colored pleated skirt. It's hiked above her knees. Her knees have scabs and bruises. Her arms are long and closed in tight, like a mantis.

Photo 2: Jennifer Times sitting on a bed. She's topless and wearing only white panties. She sits on her folded legs, feet under her buttocks, hands resting on her thighs. Her skin is bleached white, and she is folded. Origami. Arms are at her side and they push her small breasts together. Her eyes are closed and head tilted back. A light fixture shines directly above her head, washing her face in white light. Ligature in her neck is visible, as are more than a few ribs. The smile from the first photo has become something else, a grimace maybe.

The photos are curled, a bit washed and faded. They feel old and heavy with passed time. They're imperfect. These photos are like my memories.

I put the photos side by side on my desktop. On the lip of the Coke-can ashtray my cigarette is all ash, burnt down to the filter. I just lit it, but that's how time works for me. My constant enemy, it attacks whenever I'm not looking.

All right. Focus. It's a simple blackmail case. Some entrepreneur wants Jennifer to invest in his private cause or these photos go public and then she gets the gong, the hook, voted off the island on *American Star*.

But why would a blackmailer send the negatives? The photos have likely been digitized and reside on a hard drive or two somewhere. Still, her—and now me—being in possession of the negatives is troubling. There's more here, and less, of course, since I don't remember any of our conversation besides the finger stuff, so I light another cigarette.

The Jennifer in the photos doesn't look exactly like the Jennifer I've seen on TV or the one who visited my office. The difference is hard to describe, but it's there, like the difference in taste between butter and margarine. I look at the photos again. It could be her; the Jennifer from a few years ago, from high school, the Jennifer from before professional makeup teams and personal stylists. Or maybe the photo Jennifer is margarine instead of butter.

I pick up my notepad. There is writing only on that top page. I was dutifully taking notes while asleep. Automatic behavior. Like tying your shoes. Like driving and listening to the radio instead of actually driving, getting there without getting there. Not that I drive anymore.

During micro-sleeps, my narcoleptic brain will keep my body moving, keep it churning through some familiar task, and I won't have any memory of it. These acts belong to my secret life. I've woken up to find e-mails written and sent, soup cans stacked on my desk, peeled wallpaper in my bedroom, pantry items stuffed inside the refrigerator, magazines and books with their covers torn off.

Here's the top page of my notepad:

Most of it is likely junk, including my doodle arrows. The narcoleptic me is rarely accurate in his automatic behavior. The numbers don't add up to any type of phone number or contact information. But there's south shore plaza, Jennifer's public mall appearance. She and I need to talk. I get the hunch that this blackmail case is about as simple as quantum physics.

THREE

All my mornings disappear eventually. Today, some of it disappeared while I was on the phone. I tried to reach Times via her agency. No luck. I couldn't get past the secretary without disclosing too much information, not that I'm in possession of a bucketful of info, and I've always had a hard time with improv.

I did ferret out that my automatic self was wrong about the South Shore Plaza. There's just no trusting that guy. Times's mall meet-and-greet is at Copley Plaza, downtown Boston, this afternoon.

It's later than I wanted it to be, it's still raining, my black coffee is somehow hazelnut, and the line to see Times is longer than the Charles River. I hate hazelnut. The other coffee I'm carrying is loaded with cream and sugar. It's a cup of candy not fit for consumption, which is fine, because I don't intend to drink it.

Copley is cavernous, brightly lit in golden tones and ceramic tile, and caters to the high-end designer consumer. No Dollar Store here, but it's still just a mall, and its speakers pump out

American Star promo ads and tunes sung by Times. I think I prefer the old-school Muzak.

There are kids everywhere. They wait in line and they lean over the railings on the upper levels. Escalators are full in every direction. There's even a pint-sized pack of punks splashing in the fountain, taking other people's dimes and quarters. Everyone screams and waves and takes pictures. They hold up posters and signs, the *i*'s dotted with hearts, *love* spelled *luv*. Times is getting more mall worship than Santa and the Easter Bunny combined.

Because waiting in lines is detrimental to my tenuous conscious state, I walk toward the front. I growl some words that might sound like *Excuse me.*

I'm not a huge guy, but kids and their reluctant parents move out of my way. They do so because I walk with an obvious purpose, with authority. It's an easy trick. A person carrying two coffees has important places to go. Or, just as likely, people let me by because they're afraid of the hairy guy wearing a fedora and trench coat, the guy who's here without a kid and has a voice deeper than the pit of despair. Hey, whatever works.

I'm only ten or so people from the front of the line, far enough away not to be cutting in plain view of the cops and security guards circling Times and her entourage, but close enough that my wait will be mercifully brief. So I stop and step in front of a father-daughter tandem.

The father wears a Bruins hockey jersey and he's built like a puck, so the shirt works for him. His daughter is a mini-puck in jeans and a pink T plastered with Times's cheery face. This will be the greatest moment of her life until she forgets about it tomorrow.

I hold out the second coffee, my do-not-stop-at-go pass, and say, "Ms. Times wanted me to get her a coffee. Thanks, pal." My voice is a receding glacier.

The hockey puck nods and says, "Go ahead," and pulls his daughter against his hip, away from me. At least somebody is thinking of the children.

No one in our immediate vicinity questions my new existence at the front of the line. There are grumbles of disapproval from farther back, but nothing that needs to be addressed. Those grumblers only complain because they're far enough away from me to be safe, to be anonymous. If they were in the puck's shoes, they wouldn't say boo. Most people are cowards.

I sip my coffee and stain my mustache and smell hazelnut. Goddamn hazelnut. I want to light a cigarette and chew on the smoke, scorch that awful taste out of my mouth, but that's not going to fly here. At least the coffee is still hot.

The line moves with its regimented torpor, like all lines do, and my wait won't be long, but my lights are dimming a bit already, an encroaching numbness to the excitement and bustle around me. Thoughts about what I'm going to say to Times can't seem to find a foothold. I cradle the coffees in the crook of an arm, reach inside a pocket, and pinch my thigh. Then I regroup, shake my head, and take another sip of the 'nut. All keep-me-awake tricks that sometimes work and sometimes don't.

I scan the crowd, trying to find a focus. If I lock eyes with someone, they look away quick. Folks around me are think-ing, *If he really got her coffee, why is he waiting in line at all?* It's too late for any kind of revolt, and I'm next. Two bodyguards, each with heads the size of Easter Island statues, flank Times, though they're set back a lunge or two. The background dis-tance is there to encourage a ten-second intimate moment with every fan.

My turn. Maybe she'll John Hancock the brim of my hat, or my hand. I'll never wash it again.

Times sits at a table with stacks of glossy head shots, blue Sharpie in hand, her hair pulled back into a tight ponytail, showing off the crabapple cheekbones. She wears jeans, a long-sleeve Red Sox shirt, and very little makeup. All hints of sexuality have been neutralized; a nonthreatening just-a-sweet-young-American-girl-in-a-mall look.

She's probably not going to be wild about seeing me here. No probably about it. And I'm not exactly sure how I'm going to come out of this impromptu tête-à-tête in a positive light. She is my employer and I'll be admitting, in not so many words, that I was asleep on the job before it even started.

I step up to the plate and extend the candy coffee out to her, a gift from one of the magi, the defective one, the one who's broken. No frankincense or myrrh from this guy.

I say, "Thought you might need a coffee." A good opener for the uncomfortable revelations to come, and it reinforces that I'm willing to work for her.

She opens the curtain on her practiced, polished smile. One thousand watts. It's an egalitarian smile too. Everyone has been getting that flash of teeth and gums. There's not a hint of recognition in her face. Her smile says I'm faceless, like everyone else. She's already a pro at this. I'm the one who's amateur hour.

She says, "I don't drink coffee, but thank you, that's so nice." One of the Easter Island statues moves in and takes the coffee. Maybe he'll analyze it, afraid of death by hazelnut and cream and sugar. I can't think of a worse way to go.

I try to be quiet and discreet, but my voice doesn't have those settings. Check the manual. "Sorry to do this here, you as conquering local hero and all that stuff, but I dropped by because I need your direct phone line. Your agency treated me like a refugee when I tried to call earlier." It isn't smooth. It's bumpy and full of potholes, but I'll explain if she asks.

"Why were you calling my agency?" She looks over both her shoulders. That twin-generator smile has gone, replaced with a help-me look. The giant heads stir, angry pagan gods, awake and looking to smite somebody's ass. They exchange nonverbal communication cues, signs that the muscle-bound and intellectually challenged understand by instinct: puffed-out chests, clenched jaws, tightened fists.

Is Times serious or putting on a public show, acting like she doesn't know me because she's not supposed to know me? Either way, this isn't good. This is already going worse than I imagined.

My head sweats under the hat. Beard and hazelnut mustache itch. Being stressed out won't exactly help me avoid some of my condition's less pleasant symptoms. But I sally forth.

I say, "I was trying to call you because I had some questions about your case, Ms. Times." I use her name in a formal but familiar way, reassuring and reestablishing my professional status.

"Case?"

"Yeah, the case. Your case."

She doesn't say anything.

I lean in to try a conspiratorial whisper, but she slides back in her seat, and it's too loud in here anyway, with all the chattering and screaming. Can't say I practice our culture's celebrity worship, and it's downright inconvenient right now. This place is the monkey house. I lose my cool. "Christ. You know, what was inside that manila envelope you left me certainly wasn't a set of Christmas cards."

All right, I'm not doing well here. Wrong line of questions, no tact. Okay, she clearly doesn't want to talk about it, or talk to me in public. I should've known that.

She says, "I don't understand."

I've been standing here too long. Everyone is staring at us, at me. Nothing is right. We're failing to communicate. It's only a matter of time before someone comes over to break up our verbal clinch.

"Fine. Just sign me a *picture*," I say, and pause, waiting to see if my pointed word has any effect on her. Nothing. She appears to be confused. She appears to be sincere in not knowing who I am. I add, "And I'll leave." It's weak. An after-afterthought.

Her mouth is open and she shrinks into a tightened defensive posture. She looks scared. She looks like the girl in the first photo, the clothed girl. Does she still have those bruises and scabs on her knees?

"My mistake. Sorry to bother you," I say, and reach into my coat for a business card. I'll just leave it on the table and walk away. Yeah, she contacted me first, which means she likely has my number, but I have to do something to save face, to make me feel like something other than a stalker.

I pull out the card between two nicotine-stained fingers and drop it on the table. The statues animate and land their heavy hands on each of my shoulders. There's too much weight and pressure, underlining the banner headline I'M ALREADY FUCK-ING THIS UP COMPLETELY. I've angered the pagan gods with my ineptitude. I don't blame them.

I guess I'm leaving now, and without an autograph. As the statues escort me toward one of Copley's many exits, I have enough leisure time to consider the case and what comes next. A cab ride to my office, more phone calls to Jennifer's agency, Internet searches. A multimedia plan B, whatever that is.

FOUR

Chapter 147: Section 24. Applications; qualifications of applicants

An application for a license to engage in the private detective business or a license to engage in the business of watch, guard, or patrol agency shall be filed with the colonel of the state police on forms furnished by him, and statements of fact therein shall be under oath of the applicant.

George and I dropped out of Curry College together, each with three semesters of criminal justice under our belts. We didn't like where it was going. We spent our last weekend in the dorm skimming the yellow pages, fishing for do-it-yourself career advice. At the end of the weekend, we closed our eyes and made our choices.

I picked private investigation. I figured my mother, Ellen, who would not be pleased about my dropping out, might eventually be receptive given that a PI was somewhat related to my brief collegiate studies. I was right.

Eight years ago I got my license. According to Massachusetts law, having fulfilled the outlined requirements and submitted the fifty-dollar application fee makes me, officially, Mark Genevich, Private Detective.

Such application shall include a certification by each of three reputable citizens of the commonwealth residing in the community in which the applicant resides or has a place of business, or in which the applicant proposes to conduct his business—

Eight years ago I was sitting in the passenger seat of George's van, hurtling back to South Boston from Foxwoods, one of the Connecticut reservation casinos.

George was an upper-middle-class black kid from suburban New Jersey, but he pretended to be from Boston. He wore a Sox hat and talked with a fake accent when we were out at a bar. He played Keno and bought scratch tickets. He told bar patrons that he was from Southie and he was Black Irish. More often than not, people believed him.

George's yellow-pages career was a start-up rug cleaning business. I cleaned rugs for him on the weekends. He had only one machine and its exhaust smelled like wet dog. After getting my private detective's license, I was going to share my Southie office and charge him a ridiculously small rent. I could do that because Ellen owned the building. Still does.

The rug business name was Carpet Warriors. His white van had a pumped-up cartoon version of himself in standard superhero garb: tight red spandex, muscles bulging over other muscles, CW on his chest plate, and a yellow cape. Our buddy Juan-Miguel did the stenciling. George was not really a superhero. He was tall and lanky, his limbs like thin tree branches, always swaying in some breeze. Before getting into his Carpet Warrior van, George would strike a pose in front of his buff superhero doppelgänger and announce, "Never fear, the Carpet Warrior is here," reveling in the innuendo.

George was twenty-two years old. I was twenty-one. At Foxwoods, I played roulette and he played at the tables: blackjack and poker. We lost a shitload of money. In the van, we didn't talk until he said, "We blew ten rugs' worth." We laughed. His laugh was always louder than mine and more infectious. We might've been drunk, we might've been fine.

A tire blew out. I heard it go and felt the sudden drop. The van careened into a drainage ditch and rolled around like a dog trying to pick up a dead squirrel's musk. Everything was dark. I don't remember seeing anything. The seat belt wasn't tight against my chest because I wasn't wearing one. My face broke the passenger's side window and was messed up worse than a Picasso, everything exaggerated and in the wrong spots. Nose and septum pulverized, my flesh as remolded clay that didn't set where it was supposed to.

I broke the window but my body stayed in the van. George's didn't. He went out the windshield, ahead of the van, but he didn't fly far. Like I said, he wasn't a superhero. The van fishtailed sideways, then rolled right over him. George died. I miss him.

—that he has personally known the applicant for at least three years, that he has read the application and believes each of the statements made therein to be true, that he is not related to the applicant by blood or marriage—

After the accident and the surgeries, I grew a beard to hide my damaged face. My left eye is now a little lower than my right, and smaller. I'm always winking at you, but you don't know why. Too bad the beard never covers my eyes. The fedora—I wear it low—comes close.

Postrecovery, I lived with Juan-Miguel and another college buddy in the Southie apartment above my office. My narcolepsy symptoms started as soon as I got back from the hospital, a creeping crawling terror from a bad horror flick. I was Michael Landon turning into the teenage werewolf. I was always tired and had no energy, and I fell asleep while working on the computer or watching TV or eating breakfast or on the phone with potential clients. So I rarely answered the phone and tried to communicate solely by e-mail. I stopped going out unless it was to drink, which made everything worse. I know, hard to believe alcohol didn't make it all better.

Juan-Miguel came home one night to find me half inside the tub, pants down around my ankles, hairy ass in the air. I'd fallen asleep on the toilet and pitched into the tub. I told him I was passed out drunk. Might've been true.

When I was supposed to be sleeping, I didn't sleep well. I had paralyzing nightmares and waking dreams, or I wandered the apartment like the Phantom of the Opera, man turned monster. I emptied the fridge and lit cigarettes I didn't smoke. They left their marks.

Worst of all, I somnambulated into the TV room, freed myself from pants and underwear, lifted up a couch cushion, and let the urine flow. Apparently I wasn't even considerate enough to put the seat down after. I pissed on our couch every other week. I was worse than a goddamn cat.

—and that the applicant is honest and of good moral character.

I denied it all, of course. I wasn't asleep on the couch. If I was, it was because I drank too much. I wasn't doing any of those horrible, crazy things. It wasn't possible. That wasn't me even if my roommates saw me. They were lying to me. They were pulling cruel practical jokes that weren't at all practical. They were leaving lit cigarettes on the kitchen table and on my bedspread. One of them had a cat and they weren't admitting it. The cat was pissing on the couch, not me. I wasn't some animal that wasn't house trained, for chrissakes.

The kicker was that I believed my own denials. The truth was too embarrassing and devastating. I argued with my roommates all the time. Argument became part of my character. Nothing they said was true or right, even the mundane proclamations that had nothing to do with me or my narcoleptic actions. The only way I could consistently deny my new symptoms and odd behavior was to deny everything. I became even more of a recluse, holed up in my room until the asleep me would unleash himself, a midnight, couch-pissin' Kraken. My roommates moved out within the year.

Narcolepsy is not a behavioral disorder. It's neurological. It's physical. Routine helps, but it's no cure. Nothing is. There's no pattern to the symptoms. I tried prescription drugs, but the chemical stimulants resulted in paranoia and wild mood swings. My heart raced like a hummingbird's, and the insomnia worsened. So I stopped. Other than the coffee I'm not supposed to drink and the cigarettes I'm not supposed to smoke, I'm au naturel.

Eight years ago I got my private detective's license and narcolepsy. I now live alone with both.

That said, I'm waking up, and there's someone in my apartment, and that someone is yelling at me.

FIVE

Sleep is heavy. It has mass. Sometimes it has supreme mass. Sleep as a singularity. There's no moving or denying or escaping. Sometimes sleep is light too. I've been able to walk under its weight. It can be light enough to dream through, but more often than not it's the heavy kind. It's the ocean and you're pinned to the bottom of the seafloor.

"... on fire? Jesus Christ! Wake the hell up, Mark!"

The impossible weight lifts away. I resurface too fast and get the bends. Muscles twitch and my heart pushes past my throat and into my head where it doesn't belong, making everything hurt.

It's Ellen, my mother. She stands in the doorway of the living room, wearing frilly blue oversized clown pants and a T that reads LITHUANIA. The shirt is an old favorite of hers, something she wears too often. The clown pants I've never seen before. I hope this means I'm having another hypnogogic hallucination.

I'm sitting on the couch. My mouth is still open because I was asleep with it that way. I blink and mash the back of my hand into my eyes, pushing and squeezing the sleep out. I have my cell phone in my right hand. On my left side is smoke and heat.

The couch is smoking, cigarette and everything. It's a nasty habit the couch can't seem to break. The couch doesn't heed surgeon generals' warnings. Maybe it should try the patch.

I lift my left leg and twist away from the smoke, but the cigarette butt rolls after me, leaving a trail of red ash. In the cushion there's a dime-sized hole, the circumference red and still burning. I'd say it's just one blemish, but the reality is my couch has acne.

I pick up the butt. It's too hot and I drop it on the floor. I pat the couch cushion. Red ashes go black and there's more smoke.

I say, "I wasn't sleeping. I wasn't smoking." Ellen knows what I mean when I'm lying: I don't want to talk about it, and even if I did want to talk about it nothing would change.

She shakes her head and says, "You're gonna burn yourself up one of these days, Mark. I don't know why I bother." Her admonishment is by rote, perfunctory. We can get on with our day, now that it's out of the way.

I make my greeting a subtle dig at her for no good reason other than I'm embarrassed. "Good to see you too, Ellen. Shut the door on the way out." At least this time she didn't find me asleep with my pants around my ankles and an Edward Penishands porno on the TV.

Ellen stays at my apartment a couple of nights a week. If pressed, she maintains she stays here because she wants to play Keno and eat at the Italian American and L Street Diner with her sister and friends. She won't admit to being my de facto caregiver. She's the underwriter of my less-than-successful private detecting business and the landlord who doesn't want her property, the brownstone she inherited from her parents, to burn to the ground. I can't blame her.

Ellen is Southie born and bred and, like every other life-long resident, she knows everything about everybody. Gentrification has toned down the small-town we-are-Southie vibe a bit, but it's still here. She starts right in on some local dirt, mid-story, assuming I know what she's talking about when I don't.

"Davy T said he knew she was lying the whole time. He told me weeks ago. He could just tell she was lying. Do you know when someone's lying, Mark? They say you watch the eyes. Up and left means recall, down and right means they're making stuff up. Or it's the other way around. I don't know. You should take a class in that. You could find a class online, I bet."

Davy T is the centuries-old Greek who owns the pizza joint next door. That's the only part of her monologue that registers with me. I check my cell phone, no messages. It has been a full day since Jennifer's mall appearance.

Ellen says, "Anyway, Davy T knew. It'll be all over the news tonight. They found her out. She was making it all up: the cancer, her foundation, everything. What kind of person does that?" Ellen crosses the room as she talks, her clown pants merrily swishing away. She opens my windows and waves her hands. The smoke obeys and swirls in the fresh air. Magic. Must be the pants. "Maybe you should've been on that case,

Mark. You could've solved that, don't you think? You could've saved folks a lot of money and aggravation."

To avoid discussing my condition or me burning up with the apartment, Ellen defaults into details of already solved cases that presumably I could've tackled; as if I've ever worked on a case that involved anything more than tapping keys in front of my computer or being a ghost at a library or a town hall registrar.

Still patting the couch like I can replace the burned and missing upholstery with my Midas touch, I say, "Sure thing, Ellen." Truth is, my confidence and self-esteem are fighting it out in the subbasement, seeing which can be lower.

Jennifer hasn't returned any of my calls to the agency. I fell asleep up here, waiting for a callback. Waiting for something to get me going, because I have nothing. I don't know how she was contacted by the blackmailer, if the pictures were mailed or left on a doorstop, if there had been earlier contact or contact since. It's kind of hard to start a case without a client, or at least a client that will talk to you.

I say, "So what's with the Bozo the Clown getup?"

Ellen walks into the kitchen. "I was shooting some kid's portrait today and the little bastard wouldn't stop crying until I put the pants on." When Ellen isn't her force-of-nature self in my apartment, she lives in the old family bungalow in Osterville, a small tourist haven on the Cape. In downtown Osterville she has a photography studio and antiques shop. She shoots kids, weddings, graduation pictures. Nothing fancy. She's been doing it since my father died.

"Wouldn't a red nose and a horn get the job done? Maybe one of those flowers that shoots out water. You need to rely on cliché a little more."

"What, you're an expert now? I got the shots." She plays with her clown pants, pulling them up at the knee, making mini circus tents. "I need to change." Ellen abruptly disappears into my bedroom and shuts the door.

I pick up the cigarette butt off the floor and try to tidy things up a bit, putting dirty glasses and dishes in the sink, stacking magazines, moving dust around. I eyeball the couch to make sure it's not still burning.

I check my cell phone again, even though I've already checked for messages. Why wouldn't she call me back? If this is supposed to be some super-special double-secret case, it's not going to work out. The sleeping me should've told her thanks-but-no-thanks when she dumped those pictures on me. The sleeping me is just so irresponsible on my behalf.

Earlier, I did a cursory Web search, reading blogs and message boards, finding no hint or threat of the existence of the photos, or a stalker, or a potential blackmailer. Everything from her camp seems as controlled and wholesome as can be. No one has even posted fake nudes of Jennifer yet, which is usually an instantaneous Internet occurrence once there's a new female celebrity. I don't get the lack of buzz. The irony is that if I posted the pictures, I'd likely be helping her career, but I'm not her agent.

Ellen emerges from the bedroom. Her shoulder-length gray hair is tied up and she has on her black-framed glasses, thick lenses that enlarge her eyes. She's still wearing the clown pants but has on a gray sweatshirt over LITHUANIA.

I say, "Are you going to take my picture later? Maybe tie me up some balloon animals? I want a giraffe, a blue one."

She says, "Everyone at the Lithuanian Club will get a kick out of the pants. And they are comfortable. Nice and roomy." She walks by and punches my shoulder. "So, should we do something for dinner?" Ellen never makes dinner a declarative statement. She's earnest in the illusion of a choice being offered. It's not that I can't say no. I never have a reason to do so.

I say, "Something sounds delicious, Ellen." I have a gut feeling the case is slipping away, and if I let it get away I'll be screwing up something important. This is my shot, my chance to be something more than Ellen's charity-case son who works on glorified have-you-seen-my-lost-puppy cases and sleeps his days away in front of his computer.

So let's skip from plan B down to plan X. I know that Jennifer's father, the DA, grew up in Southie and is around the same age as Ellen. Maybe, a long-shot maybe, she knows something about Jennifer, the first bread crumb in the trail.

I say, "Hey, do you still watch *American Star*?" Plan X: asking Ellen delicate no-I'm-not-working-on-anything-really questions to defibrillate my dying case. I don't have a plan Y or Z.

Ellen looks at me funny, like I stepped in something and she's not sure if she should admit she smells it. She says, "You're kidding, right? I don't miss a show. Never have missed a show in five seasons."

I know that, of course. She's obsessed with *American Star*.

She watched the first two seasons from Osterville and still had me tape all the episodes here.

She says, "Why do you ask? Are you telling me that you're finally watching it too?"

I shrug. Shoulders don't lie. My fedora doesn't hide enough of my hairy face. It's the proverbial only-a-mother-could-love face because the mug was reshuffled partway through the game. Ellen hasn't once suggested that I shave. That means what it means.

I say, "The show is kind of hard to avoid now. I had it on the other night, but I fell asleep." Ellen is waiting for more, so I add, "Been hearing stuff about the local girl. She's the DA's kid, right?"

Ellen smiles. "I might be crazy, but it sounds like you're pumping me for information. If you got something to ask, just come out and ask it. I'll help. You know I want to help."

I can't. I can't let her know that I'm working on a case that potentially involves extensive fieldwork. Leaving the apartment and going out by myself. There will be no dealing with any of that conversation. She wants to be supportive only as long as I'm safe in the apartment.

I say, "Nothing like that. Just having a conversation, Ellen. For someone who wears clown pants, you're tightly wound."

Ellen goes into the kitchen and roots around in the freezer. She says, "Yes, she's his daughter. She's—what, about ten years younger than you?"

Might as well be fifty years younger. "Yeah, I guess so."

Ellen says, "There's nothing good in there," and closes the

freezer. "I didn't have time to pick up anything. We'll have to go out. At least I'm dressed for it, right?"

I stand in the kitchen doorway, holding up the frame. "Isn't DA Times from Southie originally?" A softball question, one I know she can't resist.

"Hell yeah, he's from Southie. He still owns a brownstone at the end of East Broadway. He doesn't stay there anymore, though. He rents it out."

"Do you know him at all?"

"I know him well. Or knew him well, anyway. Billy Times and your father were close, used to pal around as kids. They lived in the same building in Harbor Point."

She hits the softball out of the park. Her answer isn't what I was expecting. Not at all. I talk even slower than normal, making sure I don't mess anything up, stacking the words on the kitchen table like bricks, making a wall; maybe it'll protect me. "Really? You never told me that before."

Ellen says, "Come on. I've told you that before."

"No. You haven't." I'm not offering subterfuge here. I'm more likely to find Spanish doubloons in a handful of loose change than get nuggets of info concerning my father, Tim, from Ellen. She's miserly with it, hoards it all for herself. I stopped asking questions a long time ago.

"That can't be right." Ellen is trying for a light, jovial, fluffy-banter tone, but it's faltering. "You just forgot." She adds that last bit as an afterthought, each word decreasing in volume. The sentence runs out of gas, sputters, and shuts off. The sentence goes to sleep. Everything goes to sleep if you wait long enough.

Now, what she said is not fair. Yeah, I forget stuff all the time, but she can't pass off years of silence and daddy awkwardness on the narcoleptic me like that. I'd call her on the cheap shot, but that's another argument I don't want right now. Need that primed pump to keep spilling. I say, "Cute. So Tim and the DA were BFFs and wore each other's varsity jackets?"

"Yes, actually, they were best friends but no jackets." Ellen laughs, but I'm not quite sure why. Nothing is that funny. "Those two used to be inseparable, always causing trouble. Nothing big, you know, typical Southie boys who thought they were tougher than they were." She waves her hand, like she's clearing the air of more smoke. Further details won't be forthcoming unless I keep pecking away at her.

Okay. This goes a long way toward explaining how Jennifer Times landed in my office with her slide show. Her daddy can't take the case because people talk, word gets out, media sniffing around the DA, especially with his flavor-of-the-minute daughter smiling and primping all over the airwaves. So Daddy DA has Jennifer take her blackmail case, which is as sticky and messy as an ice cream cone on a summer Sunday, to an unknown lower-than-low profile investigator in South Boston, family friend and all that, a schlub willing to do all kinds of favors and keep things quiet with a capital Q, all in the name of his own dear old dad. This makes sense, but the only problem is I don't know any of this. I'm guessing. Maybe I was told a few days ago while the doctor wasn't in. Or maybe I wasn't told anything. Maybe . . .

"Hey, Mark!"

"What?" My body catches itself in mid-slide against the wall. Heavy feet move to get my weight back over them. They're neither graceful nor quiet. They kick a kitchen chair and clap against the hardwood floor. Don't know what my feet have against the floor, but they're always trying to get away.

Ellen is now sitting at the kitchen table, smoking one of my cigarettes. She says, "You were getting ready to go out, Mark." She won't say *sleep*. Not around me.

As difficult as it is to cobble together some dignity after almost falling asleep mid-conversation, I try to patch it up. I've had a lot of practice. I say, "Would the DA recognize the Genevich name, you think?"

"Of course. There's no way he'd forget your father." Ellen leans forward fast, stubs out her cigarette like she's killing a pesky ant. She's adding everything together and doesn't like the sum. She's going to tell me about it too. "Why do you care? What's going on here, Mark? There's something you're not telling me. You better not be messing around with stuff that requires involvement with the DA. Leave that shit to the people who carry guns."

"Relax. There's nothing going on. It's just this all might be useful information. I'm supposed to ask questions for a living, right? Besides, a guy in my line of work having a potential family friend in the big office could help my cause."

Ellen stands up. Chair falls down. She's not buying any of it. "What cause?"

I like that she's so riled up, on edge. She doesn't know for sure I'm working on a case, but even she can sense something big is going on. It's real. It's legit. And thanks to her, I finally have my breadcrumb trail, or at least one crumb. I sit down at the table, take off my hat, run my fingers through my thinning hair.

"I was speaking figuratively, Ellen. My general cause. Or someday, when I have a cause." I wink, which is a mistake. My face doesn't have a wink setting anymore.

"You're being awful strange tonight." She says it to the table. I'm supposed to hear her but not give anything back. Fair enough.

Worry lines march all around Ellen's face, and not in formation. She taps the all-but-empty pack of cigarettes with her wedding ring. Tim Genevich is twenty-five years dead, and Ellen still wears the ring. Does she wear it out of habit, superstition, or true indefinable loss, so the loss is right there in plain sight, her life's pain waving around for anyone to see? The ring as her dead husband, as Tim. My father on her hand.

I lean over and snatch the last cigarette out of the pack. Ellen stops tapping with Tim. I light up and inhale as much smoke as I can, then I take in a little more. Exhale, and then I do some reiterating, just to be clear in our communication.

I say, "Don't worry, Clowny. I have no cause. The DA and I are just gonna get acquainted."

SIX

Tim was a landscaper, caretaker, winterizer of summer cottages, and a handyman, and he died on the job. He was in the basement of someone else's summer home, fighting through cobwebs and checking fuses and the sump pump, when he had an explosion in his brain, an aneurysm. I guess us Genevich boys don't have a lot of luck in the brain department.

Three days passed and no one found him. He didn't keep an appointment book or anything like that, and he left his car at our house and rode his bike to work that morning, so Ellen had no idea where he was. He was an official missing person. Got his name in the paper, and for a few days everyone knew who Tim Genevich was.

The owners of the cottage found him when they came down to the Cape for Memorial Day weekend. The basement bulkhead was open. Tim was lying facedown on the dirt floor. He had a fuse in his hand. I was five years old, and while I'm told I was at the funeral and wake, I don't remember any of it.

I don't remember much of Tim. Memories of him have faded to the edges, where recollection and wish fulfillment blur, or they have been replaced, co-opted by images from pictures. I hate pictures.

Too much time has passed since my own brain-related accident, too many sleeps between. Every time I sleep—doesn't matter how long I'm out—puts more unconscious space between myself and the events I experienced, because every time I wake up it's a new day. Those fraudulent extra days, weeks, years add up. So while my everyday time shrinks, it also gets longer. I'm Billy Pilgrim and Rip Van Winkle at the same time, and Tim died one hundred years ago.

That said, I do have a recurring dream of my father. He's in our backyard in Osterville. He puts tools back in the shed, then emerges with a hand trowel. Tim was shorter than Ellen, a little bent, and he loved flannel. At least, that's what he looks like in my dreams.

Tim won't let me go in the shed. I'm too young. There are too many tools, too many ways to hurt myself. I need to be protected. He gives me a brown paper bag, grocery-sized, and a pat on the head. He encourages me to sing songs while we walk around the yard picking up dog shit. We don't have a dog, but all the neighborhood dogs congregate here. Tim guesses a dog's name every time he picks up some shit. The biggest poops apparently come from a dog named Cleo.

The song I always sing, in my dreams and my memories, is "Take Me Out to the Ball Game." Tim then sings it back to me with different lyrics, mixing in his dog names and poop and words that rhyme with poop. He doesn't say *shit* around the five-year-old me, at least not on purpose. The dream me, the memory me—that kid is the same even if he never really existed, and *that* kid laughs at the silly improvised song but then sings "Ball Game" correctly, restoring balance and harmony to the universe.

Our two-bedroom bungalow is on a hill and the front yard has a noticeable slant, so we have to stand lopsided to keep from falling. We clean the yard, then we walk behind the shed to the cyclone-fenced area of weeds, tall grass, and pricker bushes that gives way to a grove of trees between our property and the next summer home about half a block away. Tim takes the paper bag from me, it's heavy with shit, and he dumps it out, same spot every time. He says "Bombs away" or "Natural fertilizer" or something else that's supposed to make a five-year-old boy laugh.

Then we walk to the shed. Tim opens the doors. Inside are the shiny and sharp tools and machines, teeth everywhere, and I want to touch it all, want to feel the bite. He hangs up the trowel and folds the paper bag. We'll reuse both again, next weekend and in the next dream. Tim stands in the doorway and says, "So, kid, whaddaya think?"

Sometimes I ask for a lemonade or ice cream or soda. Sometimes, if I'm aware I'm in the dream again, I ask him questions. He always answers, and I remember the brief conversation after waking up, but that memory lasts only for a little while, an ice cube melting in a drink. Then it's utterly forgotten, crushed under the weight of all those little sleeps to come.

SEVEN

William "Billy" Times has been the Suffolk County DA for ten years. He's a wildly popular and visible favorite son. All the local news shows are doing spots featuring Billy and his *American Star* daughter. He hosts now-legendary bimonthly Sunday brunch fund-raisers—the proceeds going to homeless shelters—at a restaurant called Amrheins in South Boston. All the local celebs and politicians show their faces at least once a year at the brunches.

Although I am Tim Genevich's kid, I haven't been on the brunch guest list yet. That said, Tim's name did manage to get me a one-on-one audience with DA Times at his office today. What a pal, that Tim.

I fell asleep in the cab. It cost me an extra twenty bucks in drive-around time. I stayed awake long enough to be eventually dumped at 1 Bulfinch Place. Nice government digs for the DA. Location, location, location. It's between the ugly concrete slabs of Government Center and Haymarket T stop, but a short walk from cobblestones, Faneuil Hall Marketplace, and the two-story granite columns and copper dome of Quincy

Market, where you can eat at one of its seventeen overpriced restaurants. It's all very colonial.

Despite naptime, I'm here early when I can't ever be early. Early means being trapped in a waiting room, sitting in plush chairs or couches, anesthetizing Muzak tones washing over me, fluffing my pillow. An embarrassingly large selection of inane and soulless entertainment magazines, magazines filled with fraudulent and beautiful people, is the only proffered stimulus. That environment is enough to put a non-narcoleptic in a coma, so I don't stand a chance. I won't be early.

I stalk around the sidewalk and the pigeons hate me. I don't take it personally, thick skin and all that. I dump some more nicotine and caffeine into my bloodstream. The hope is that filling up with leaded will keep all my pistons firing while in the DA's office. Hope is a desperate man's currency.

I call the DA's secretary and tell her I'm outside the building, enjoying a rare March sunlight appearance, and I ask when the DA will be ready for me. Polite as pudding, she says he's ready for me now. Well, all right. A small victory. A coping adjustment actually working is enough to buoy my spirits. I am doing this. This is going to work, and I will solve this case.

But . . .

There's a swarm of *ifs*, peskier than a cloud of gnats. The ifs: If, as I'm assuming, the DA sent me his daughter and her case, why wouldn't he contact me directly? Again, am I dealing with the ultimate closed-lips case that can't have any of his involvement? If that's right, and I'm supposed to be Mr. Hush Hush, Mr. Not Seen and Not Heard, why am I so easily granted counsel with the public counsel? He certainly seemed eager to meet with me when I called, booking a next-day face-to-face appointment.

There are more ifs, and they're stressing my system. Stress, like time, is a mortal enemy. Stress can be one of my triggers, the grease in the wheel of my more disruptive narcoleptic symptoms. I could use another cigarette or three to choke myself awake, freshen up in the smoke.

I step out of the elevator and walk toward the DA's office. Bright hallways filled with suits of two types: bureaucrats and people carrying guns. The bullets and briefcases in the hallway make me a little edgy.

The DA's waiting area is stark and bright. Modern. Antiseptic. Very we-get-shit-done in its décor. Wooden chairs and glass-topped tables framed in silver metal, and all the window shades are up. No shadows here.

There are two men waiting in the room and they are linebacker big. They wear dark suits and talk on cell phones, the kind that sit inside the cup of your ear. The receiver is literally surrounded by the wearer's flesh; it's almost penetrative. The phones look like blood-swollen robot ticks.

The men are actively not looking at me. Sure, I'm paranoid, but when I enter a room people always look at me. They map out my lopsided features and bushy beard and anachronistic attire. Everyone is my cartographer. I'm not making this up. Even when I display narcoleptic symptoms in public and the cartographers are now truly frightened of me and try not to look, they still look. Furtive glances, stealing and storing final images, completing the map, fodder for their brush-with-unwashed-humanity dinner-party anecdotes. I'm always the punch line.

Instead of the direct path to the secretary's desk, I take the long cut, eyeing the framed citations on the walls, walking past the windows pretending to crane my neck for a better view of Haymarket. Those two guys won't look at me, which means they're here to watch me. I'm already sick of irony.

The secretary says, "Mr. Genevich?"

I've been identified. Tagged.

The two men still don't look up. One guy is shaved bald, though the stubble is thick enough to chew up a razor. The other guy has red hair, cut tight up against his moon-sized brain box. Freckles and craters all over his face. They talk into their phones and listen at alternating intervals like they're speaking to each other, kids with their twenty-first-century can-and-string act.

I say, "That's me." This doesn't bode well for my meeting with the DA. Why does he need Thunder and Thumper to get their eyeful of me?

The secretary says, "The DA is ready for you now." She stays seated behind her desk. She's Ellen's age and wears eye shadow the color of pool-cue chalk. I wonder if she wears clown pants too.

I say, "I guess that's what we'll find out." It feels like the thing to say, but the line lands like a dropped carton of eggs.

His secretary points me past her desk, and I head into an office with an open door. I walk in too fast.

DA William Times sits behind a buffet-style oak desk. The thing spans the width of the room. A twin-engine Cessna could land on top of it. He says, "Mark Genevich. Come on in. Wow, I can't believe it. Tim's kid all grown up. Pleasure to finally meet you." The DA walks out from behind his desk, hand thrust out like a bayonet.

I'm not quite sure of protocol here. How he's supposed to be greeted. What sort of verbal genuflection I'm supposed to give him. I try on, "Thanks for giving me the time, Mr. DA."

DA Times is as big as the two goons in the waiting room. I'm thinking he might've banged out a few hundred push-ups before I came in, just to complete his muscle-beach look. He has on gray slacks and a tight blue dress shirt; both have never seen a wrinkle. His hair is pepper-gray, cut tight and neat. White straight teeth. His whole look screams public opinion and pollsters and handlers. We have so much in common.

We cross the divide of his office and finally shake hands. His grip is a carnival strength test and he rings the bell. He says, "Please, call me Billy, and have a seat."

"Thanks." I don't take off my hat or coat, but I do pull out the manila envelope. I sit. The chair is a soft leather bog, and I sink to a full eye level below the DA and his island-nation desk. I wait as he positions himself. He might need a compass.

He says, "So, how's Ellen doing?"

He's not going to ask about my face, about what happened to me. He's polite and well mannered and makes me feel even more broken. We can play at the small talk, though. That's fine.

Maybe it'll help me get a good foothold before we climb into the uncomfortable stuff. Daddy and his daughter.

I say, "Ellen's fine. She has a good time."

"Do you guys live in Southie again? She still owns that building on the corner of Dorchester and Broadway, right?"

I say, "Yeah, she owns it. I live there, but Ellen part-times Southie now."

"God, I haven't talked to her in years. I have to have you guys down at the next Sunday brunch. I'd love to chat with her."

I'm not quite sure what to say. I come up with, "That'd be just fine, Billy," real slow, and it sounds as awkward as I feel. I'm flummoxed. I was expecting anger on the DA's part, that he'd go all Hulk, you-wouldn't-like-me-when-I'm-angry, yell-scream-bite-scratch and bring in the goons because I wasn't doing my job, wasn't keeping things quiet by showing up at Jennifer's public appearance and now at his office.

He says, "So what can I help you with, Mark?"

Our meeting is young, the conversation still in we're-all-friends-here mode, but I already know he did not contact me. He did not suggest his daughter contact me. He has no idea why I'm here.

Need to play this straight, no funny stuff, no winks and nods. My winks tend to turn into fully shut eyes. "Not sure if you're aware, Billy, but I'm a private investigator."

The DA is still smiling. "Oh, yeah? How long have you been doing that?"

"Eight years, give or take." I pause because I don't know what to say next.

He jumps right in. "No kidding. I probably have a copy of your license somewhere in this building." He laughs. Is that a threat? A harmless attempt at humor? Humor is never harmless.

Maybe this was a mistake. Maybe I'm not ready for this and should've stayed in my apartment behind my desk and forgotten about everything. I'm getting a bad feeling. Not the gut this time. It's more tangible, physical. There's a small hum, a vibration building up, my hands tremble on the envelope a little bit. My system needle is twitching into the red. Danger Will Robinson. It's the same feeling I get before cataplectic attacks.

Cataplexy, like other narcolepsy symptoms, is REM sleep bullying its way into the awake state. Cataplexy is complete and total loss of bodily control. Muscles stop working, I can't even talk, and I melt to the floor, down for the count but not out. I'm not asleep. I'm conscious but can't move and can't speak, paralyzed. Cataplexy is the worst part of my nightmare.

I don't have cataplexy often; the most recent event was that time after Ellen found me asleep in front of a porno. She walked into the apartment and I woke up with my pants around my ankles. She wasn't upset or hiding her face or anything like that, she was laughing. She could've walked in and found me playing with the world's cutest kitten and had the same response, which made it worse, made it seem like she was expecting to find me like that. I was so overwhelmingly embarrassed and ashamed, the emotions were a Category-5 hurricane on my system, and cataplexy hit while I was quickly trying to pull up my pants and put everything away. My strings cut and I dropped to the floor, heavier than a dead body, landing on my cheap came-in-a-box coffee table and smashing it, all my stuff still out and about. Ellen shut off the television without commenting upon a scene involving Edward Penishands and three of his most acrobatic female neighbors. She pulled up my underwear and pants, buttoned my fly, and prepared dinner in the kitchen while I recovered from the attack. Took about twenty minutes to come back completely, to be able to walk into the kitchen under my own power. We ate stir-fry. A little salty but decent, otherwise.

Too much time has passed since the DA last spoke, because his vote-for-me smile is gone and he's leaning on his desk. He says, "Did you bring me something? What's in the envelope, Mark?"

Okay, another new strategy, and yeah, I'm making all this up as I go. If this is going to work, I can't let myself think too much. I'm going to read lines, play a part, and maybe it will keep the emotions from sabotage, keep those symptoms on the bench no matter how much the narcoleptic me wants in the game.

I say, "Your daughter, Jennifer, came into my office the other morning and hired me to solve a little problem." My hands sweat on the envelope, leaving wet marks.

The DA straightens and looks around the room briefly. He

repeats my line back to me. "Jennifer came into your office with a problem." The line sounds good.

"Yup. Left me this package too. She didn't tell you anything about this?"

The DA holds up his hands. "You have me at a loss, Mark, because this is all news to me."

In concert with our everything-is-happy intro conversation, I think he's telling the truth, which complicates matters. Why would Jennifer not tell her DA daddy about the pictures and then come see me, of all PIs? Was it dumb blind luck that landed her in my office? I don't buy it. She and this case were dropped in my sleeping lap for a reason.

I say, "I came here because I had assumed you sent her to see me. To have me, a relation of an old family friend, deal with the situation away from prying public eyes."

"Jesus, Mark, just tell me what you're talking about. Is Jennifer in danger? What's going on?"

If he really hasn't sent Jennifer to me, then I've screwed up, big time. It's going to be very difficult to skip-to-my-Lou out of here without showing him the pictures, and I can't say too much, don't want to put any words into Jennifer's mouth. I don't want the case to be taken away from me.

I say, "I've made a mistake. If you didn't send Jennifer to me, I shouldn't be here. Client confidentiality and all that." I stand up. My legs are water-starved tree roots.

The DA stands and darts around his desk to stop me. He moves fast, and I'm no Artful Dodger. He says, "Wait! You can't come in here and drop a bomb about Jennifer and then just leave."

"Tell it to the goons you have waiting for me outside." I say it, even though I know it doesn't add up. One plus one is three.

"What?" He shakes his head, resetting. "Let's start again. Jennifer. What's wrong? You have to tell me if she's in any danger. You know, I can probably help here." He opens his arms, displaying his office, showing off his grand criminal justice empire.

My system-overload feeling is still there. My hands keep up with their tremors, twitching to some hidden beat, and my mouth is dry. This can't happen now. Not now, can't be now.

I say, "Let's sit again, and you can take a look." I have to sit. At least if I have an attack I'll be sitting.

We sit. The chair is a hug and my body reacts accordingly; the tremors cease but crushing fatigue rolls in like a tide. It's undeniable.

New plan. I don't care that I'm breaking client confidentiality. Given the clientele, I doubt word of my etiquette breach will get out and ruin my little business, taint my street cred. I want to see the DA's reaction. I want to know why she'd drop these photos on my desk and not on Daddy's.

I yawn big, showing off the fillings, sucking in all the air. The DA looks at me like I pissed in the dinner wine. I shrug and say, "Sorry, it's not you, it's me."

I open the envelope and hand him the two photos. Definitely taking a chance on bringing him the originals. I didn't think to make copies; the negatives are in my desk. Anyway, I want to see what his reaction is to the real photos, not copies.

The DA takes the pictures, looks at them, and sinks into his chair. The pictures are a punch to his stonewall stomach. He loses all his air. I feel a little bad for him. Gotta be tough to have someone else's past walk in the door and drop nudie pictures of your kid in your lap.

He holds up both photos side by side and is careful to hold them so that they cover his face. He sees something.

The DA says, "Who gave you these pictures?"

"I told you. Jennifer. Try to stay with me, here."

"Who sent them to her?"

"I don't know yet. That's the case. I'm good, but I do need a little time to work my mojo." I meant to say magic, but it came out mojo.

He says, "Who else has seen these?"

"No idea." This is a rare occasion where telling the truth is easy as Sunday morning.

"Have you shown them to anyone?"

"No, of course not. What kind of private investigator do you think I am?"

He looks at the photos again, then me. The look is a fist cracking knuckles. He says, "I have no idea what's going on here, Mark, but the woman in these pictures is clearly not Jennifer."

Not the response I was looking for. I squirm in my seat,

which is suddenly hot. I'm bacon and someone turned on the griddle. I fight off another yawn and push it down somewhere inside me, but it's still there and will find its way out eventually. I have bigger problems than a yawn. I ask, "What makes you say that?"

"It's not her, Mark." All hint of politics gone from his voice. He's accusing me of something. He's in attack mode, getting ready to lawyer me up. This isn't good.

I say, "It's her. Jennifer was the one who brought me the goddamn photos. Why would she need me if the photos aren't of her?" I'm getting mad, which is not the right response here. Shouldn't be ready to throw a tantrum because someone wants to tell me there's no Tooth Fairy.

The DA focuses. I'm his courtroom. He says, "There are physical inconsistencies. Jennifer has a mole on her collarbone, no mole here—"

I interrupt. "That's easy to Photoshop. You should know that."

He holds up a stop hand. "Her hair is all wrong. In the photo there's too much curl to it, and it doesn't look like a wig. That's not Jennifer's smile; the teeth are too big. This woman is smaller and skinnier than Jennifer. There's a resemblance, but it's clearly not Jennifer, Mark. I'm positive."

All right. What next? I say, "Can I have the photos back?" Christ, I'm asking permission. I'm a pathetic Oliver Twist, begging for table scraps.

The DA doesn't give them to me right away, and my insides

drop into my shoes. I'm not getting the photos back—or my insides. I couldn't possibly have fucked things up any worse if I had a manual and followed the step-by-step instructions on how to screw the pooch.

He does hand the pictures over. I take an eyeful. The hair, her smile, all of it, all wrong. He's right. It's not her. My big mistake is getting bigger. I scratch my beard, then put the photos away. I need an exit strategy.

The DA stands again, walks to his window, then turns toward me, eyebrows arched. Maybe he's really seeing me, the broken man, for the first time. He says, "What are you up to, Mark?"

"I told you what was up, DA. Nothing funny on my end. Can't vouch for your daughter, though."

His hands go from inside his pockets to folded across his chest. He's a statue made of granite. I'm an abandoned rag doll.

"Maybe we should just call Jennifer, then, to straighten everything out," he says, pulling out his cell phone and poking at a few buttons before getting my permission.

"Let's. A fine idea." I yawn, my head getting murky, its natural state. I'm afraid of this phone call. I'll only get to hear his end of the conversation.

He says, "Hi, sweetie. It's Dad. . . . I know, but I need a quick honest answer to a potentially difficult question. . . . I know, great way to start a phone call. . . . So, did you hire a Mark Genevich? . . . Mark Genevich, he's a private detective. . . . He's here in my office, and he claims you went to his Southie office and hired him—says you gave him some photos. . . . What? . . . Oh, he did? . . . Okay, okay, no. . . . Don't worry, Jennifer. Nothing I can't take care of. I have to go. . . . Good luck tonight. You were great last night and I'm sure you'll make it through to next week. . . . Love you too."

I think I need to find my own attack mode. The problem is I'm toothless. I say, "You two have such a swell relationship and all, but if she said she's never met me, she's lying."

"Jennifer said you showed up in the autograph line at Copley the other day, claimed to be working on her case, and left your card."

"I sure did."

"She also said she'd never seen you before Copley."

I yawn again. The DA doesn't like it. There's nothing I can do about that. I say, "I have her signed contract back at my office." Complete bluff. He knows it too.

He walks around to the front of the desk and sits on the top. One leg on the floor, one leg off. A DA flamingo. He says, "Blackmail is a felony, Mark." He drops the hard-guy act momentarily and morphs into pity mode. He holds out his hands as if to say, *Look at you, you're a walking shipwreck, unsalvageable.* "If you need money or help, Mark, I can help you out, but this isn't the way to go about it."

I laugh. It's an ugly sound. "Thanks for the offer, DA, but I get by. And I'm not blackmailing anyone. If I were, would I be dumb enough to do it while sitting in your office? Give me a little credit."

"Okay, okay, but Mark, try to take my point of view here. You are presenting me an odd set of circumstances, to say the least. You come out of nowhere, telling me that my daughter hired you on the basis of photos that aren't of Jennifer. Are we on the same page so far?"

I nod. I yawn. The murk is getting used to my chair. The conversation is getting fuzzy. I need to move around, literally put myself on my toes. I stand up and wander behind the chair, pretending to stretch my back.

He says, "Jennifer denies having ever met you before you showed up at Copley. What is it exactly you want me to believe?"

Good question. I want to hear the answer too. I say, "I don't know what to tell you. Kids lie to their parents all the time, especially when they're in trouble. Maybe she's met some bad people. Maybe she's embarrassed, doesn't want Daddy to know that someone sent her a threat, some nude photos that look a lot like her, enough so that if released into the wild many folks would believe it's her in the pictures." I say it all, but I don't really believe it. There's something missing. What's missing is me. Why am I the one with these pictures?

He says, "No one would believe that woman was Jennifer."

I shrug. "Sure they would. Presented in the proper light; people want to believe the worst."

The DA has his chiseled face in hand, another pose, and says, "I'll have another talk with her later, but right now I believe her, not you."

It's not a shock, but it stings. To be dismissed so easily. I fire back with a double-barrel dose of healthy paranoia. "That's fine. I believe me over both of you. Tell me, DA, how do I know that Jennifer was really the person on the other end of that phone call?"

He rolls his eyes, gets up off the desk, and walks to his office door, holds it open. He says, "Okay, I think our meeting is done. If I hear or see anything more about these photos of yours, don't be surprised if you find me in your Southie office, warrant in hand."

"I guess this means no brunch." I adjust my hat and slip the envelope inside my coat. "I'm only looking out for your daughter's best interests because I was hired to."

There's nothing more to be said. We're all out of words. I walk out of the office. He shuts the door behind me. I tighten my coat, the envelope pressed up against my chest. The secretary has her head down, computer keys clicking.

The goons aren't in the waiting room. Maybe they were never here. Maybe, like Jennifer's mole, they've been Photoshopped out. The room is too empty. No chairs are askew, all the magazines are in a pile, nothing out of place, but it's staged, a crime scene without a body.

I'm alone again, with a client who denies such status and with photos that aren't of her. I'm alone again, with nothing, and I just want to sit and think, but my head is a mess, trying to put together a jigsaw puzzle that's suddenly missing all but a few pieces. I need to call a cab, go back to the office, begin at the beginning, focus on those few pieces I do have, and see if I can't force them to fit together.

EIGHT

After my DA meeting I sat at my office desk and looked at the photos again, searching for clues I might've missed. I didn't see any. In the first photo, the one with the fully clothed Jennifer, there was a bookcase that holds ten books. I couldn't read any of the slimmer titles, but there was one fat hardcover with LIT written big and white across the bottom of the spine. Library book probably. In the second photo, the camera is angled up, and I see only the ceiling and the wall and the topless Jennifer.

I locked the photos with the negatives in my office desk and slept the rest of the afternoon away on my apartment couch. I dreamed my usual Dad-in-the-backyard dream. There was still a lot of shit to clean up. No one called and woke me. No one missed my conscious presence. I'm used to it and don't take it personally anymore.

Now it's two o'clock in the morning. I've been wandering and haunting my own apartment, a ghost without the clanging chains. I can't sleep. I already said I was sick of irony, but it's a narcoleptic's lot.

I turn on the VCR and watch two taped *American Star* episodes, last night's and tonight's, the one I slept through. First show has a disco-night theme. Jennifer Times sings "I Will Survive." She sings well enough, right notes and right key, but she moves stiffly, her hips are rusty hinges and her feet don't want to stay in one spot, a colt walking in a field full of holes. The judges call her on it. The British guy says she was icy and robotic, a mannequin barely come to life. The people in the audience boo the judge even though he's correct. Truth is usually greeted with disdain.

Jennifer doesn't take the criticism well and fires back at the judges. She whines and is rude and short in dismissing the critiques. She turns and tilts her head, rolls her eyes, hands on her hips, stops just short of stomping a foot on the floor. She leaves the stage with, "I thought I was great and they did too," pointing to the audience. She gets a lukewarm cheer.

Jennifer forgot it's not about the song you sing or the words you have to say; it's always about the performance, how you present your public self. She could've come off as a hero if she argued with the judges correctly, mixing self-deprecation, humility, and humor with confidence and determination. Maybe she should've hired me as a coach instead of her PI.

As the vote-off show queues up next on my tape, I fire up my laptop and check out the Internet message boards and blogosphere reaction. Jennifer was universally ripped and often referred to as a privileged brat. There will be no recovering from that. The show's voters agreed with the brat tag, and Jennifer is the first finalist knocked out of *American Star*. A quick THE END to that singing career, I guess. Jennifer doesn't take the news on the vote-off show well either. Instead of gracious smiles and hand-waving, we get the nationally televised equivalent of a kid storming out of her parents' room after a scolding. While I think Jennifer handled her fifteen minutes of fame poorly, I do sympathize with her. Sometimes you just can't win.

Maybe this means she'll return my calls when she gets back to Boston. Maybe she'll apologize for lying to her father, for making my public self appear to be a lunatic. My performance in her daddy's office needed her help, and she threw me tomatoes instead of roses. Or maybe she won't call me and the case is dead, now that she's off the show.

I shut off the VCR and laptop and wander back to bed. Insomnia is there waiting for me. The sheets and comforter feel all wrong, full of points and angles somehow. The pillow is not soft enough; it's too hard. I'm Goldilocks in my own house.

The awake me can't help but rerun everything in my mashed-up head. Yeah, I'm stubborn, but I have to try and see Jennifer one more time, somehow straighten out all that's been bent out of shape and put the case to bed, so to speak.

NINE

The phone rings; it sounds far away, in the next universe. I lift my head off my desk, an incredible feat of strength, and wipe my face. Leftover fried rice trapped in my beard and mustache fall onto the Styrofoam plate that had been my pillow. The rice bounces off and onto the desktop and on my lap. I need to make a note to vacuum later.

It has been two days since my meeting with the DA. My office phone has rung only once. It was Nanning Wok double-checking my order because the woman wasn't sure if I'd said General Gao or Kung Pao. The General, of course, as if there was any question.

I spent those two days getting nowhere with Jennifer's case. Her agency doesn't return my calls, and I don't know when her next public appearance is. I haven't looked at the photos since locking them in my desk. I wanted them to find their own way out, somehow, before I thought about them again. Doing nothing with them couldn't be any worse than my previous attempts at doing something.

The phone is still ringing. Someone insisting that we talk. Fine. Be that way. I pick it up.

I say, "Mark Genevich," my name bubbling up from the depths, sounding worse for the trip.

"Have you found it yet?" A male voice. He sounds older. His voice is deep, heavy with time, like mine.

I'm disappointed. I was really hoping it'd be Jennifer. Instead, it's a client that I've been shirking. I have two abandoned property searches that I've put on hold since the Times case came walking in my door.

I say, "No, I haven't found anything yet. Need more time." I should just hang up and put my face back into the leftover fried rice.

"I don't think we have more time, kid. There's a red car driving around my house. It's been by four times this afternoon already. Fuck!"

Maybe I'm dreaming and I'll wake up on my couch or re-awake with my face in Chinese food to start it all over again. Maybe this is my old buddy Juan-Miguel putting me on, playing a joke. When we lived together he'd call in shit like this. I decide to play along with the caller a bit longer, gather more information before I make a hasty conclusion; it's how I have to live my everyday life. That said, this guy's voice has a kernel of sincerity that's undeniable.

I say, "Relax. Calm down. Red cars won't bother you if you don't bother them."

"There're two people in that red car. They know. They know

about the pictures somehow. Shit! They're driving by again, and they slow down in front of my house every time. You didn't show anyone those pictures yet, did you? You can't until you find—"

I drop the phone, of course. It slides out of my greasy hands and bounces off my foot. Goddamn it! At least I know I'm awake. I'm awake because I'm usually competent in my dreams and hallucinations.

I pick up the phone. "Sorry, dropped you for a second. I'm still here." I stand up, walk across the room, and shut the door to my office. No one's in the hallway, of course, but Ellen could walk in unannounced at any time. "No. I didn't show anyone anything." It's easier to lie because I don't know who I'm talking to.

He says, "I shouldn't have given you those pictures. I don't know what I think I was doing, who I'd be helping. It was dumb. Now we're both fucked. Should've just kept sitting on it like the old hen that I am. This is so screwed up. Shouldn't have done anything. . . ." His words fall into odd rhythms, stops and starts mixed with letters that he holds too long. He slurs his *s*'s. He's been drinking. It's not helping his paranoia—or mine. His voice fades out as he's talking to either himself or someone else in the room with him; the phone must be dropping away from his mouth. I'm losing him. I have to keep him talking, even if it isn't to me.

I say, "Hey, pull it together. It'll be all right once I find"—yeah, find what?—"it." So I'm not so smooth on my end. I pace around my office and look for something that'll help me. Nothing's here. Hopefully he doesn't process my hesitation.

He says, "You need to hurry up. I don't want to say anything more. If they're driving around my house, it probably means they're listening in too, the fuckers."

He and I have seen too many of the same movies. I'm ready to agree with him. I have so many questions to ask this guy, starting with the introductory-level *Who are you?* but I have to pretend I know what's going on.

I say, "All right, all right. But before you hang up, I think we need to talk again. Face-to-face. It'll help us sort all this out, trust me. We'll both feel better about it."

"Not your office. I can't come to Southie again. I'm not going anywhere, not right now. I'm staying here, with my doors locked."

An espresso-like jolt rushes through my system. He's been here before. I say, "Okay, I'll come to you. Give me your address."

He does, but he doesn't give me his name. No matter. Address only. I write it down. Goddamn, he lives on the Cape, in Osterville, not far from where Ellen lives and where my childhood homestead still stands. Now pieces are fitting together where they shouldn't, square pegs in round holes.

I tell him I'll be there tomorrow. He hangs up, and that's it. The office and phone are quiet again. More old fried rice, looking like mouse turds, is on the desk and on the floor. I'm breathing heavy. I pull out a cigarette and start a fire.

I unlock my drawer and take out the photos. I try on a new

set of eyes and look at the girl in the photos. Maybe she's not Times. And the photos: the matte and shading is faded and yellowing in spots. The photos are old, but how old?

Okay, slow down. I know now that Jennifer was never in my office. Even her presence was part and parcel of the whole hypnogogic hallucination. But why would I dream her into my office while asleep during phone guy's little visit? Did I conjure her solely because of the resemblance in the photos? Did her name come up in our initial meeting? Is he just some crazed fan of *American Star*? Maybe he's a would-be blackmailer, but that doesn't feel right. Is he telling the truth about being watched?

He didn't want me to show the pictures to anyone until I found something, and I already showed them to the DA. Oops. Why did phone guy, presumably from Osterville, choose me? Does he know me or Ellen? What am I supposed to find? My note about South Shore Plaza. Red car, Osterville, and a drunk on the Cape.

I think I've falsely harassed Jennifer Times and her DA father. I really don't know anything about this case, and there's still rice in my beard, but at least I have a client now. Yeah, tomorrow I'll make the little road trip to the Cape and then a house call, but I'm not getting paid enough for this.

TEN

I'm in Ellen's little green car. It's fifteen years old. The passenger seat is no longer conducive to my very particular posture, which is somewhere between question mark and Quasimodo. Lower back and legs report extreme discomfort. It's enough to keep me awake, which is miserable because I keep nodding off but not staying asleep.

We're cruising down Route 3 south, headed toward the Cape. It's off-season and the traffic isn't bad, but Ellen maintains a running monologue about how awful the traffic always is and how nobody knows how to drive. Meanwhile, she's tailgating the car in front of us and we're close enough that I can see what radio station he's tuned to.

I still have a driver's license but no car. Renewing the license isn't an issue for me. Driving is. I haven't driven in six years.

Last night I told Ellen that I needed to go to the Osterville library to help with a genealogical search and was pressed for time. She didn't ask for further details. She knew I wouldn't give any. When she picked me up this morning, she didn't ask questions about why all the toilet paper was unrolled and wrapped around my kitchen table—King Tut's table now—and why the apartment door was unlocked but my bedroom door was locked. She knew the narcoleptic me went for an evening stroll with the apartment to himself.

My eyes are closed; we're somewhere between Norwell and Marshfield, I think.

Ellen says, "Are you awake?"

I just want to sit and sleep, or think about what I'm going to say to the mystery client in Osterville. The names associated with the address are Brendan and Janice Sullivan. I was able to ferret out that much online.

I say, "No. I'm asleep and dreaming that you're wearing the clown pants again."

"Stop it. I just didn't want to stuff them into my night bag and get them all wrinkly. Those wrinkles don't come out. You'd think that wouldn't happen with polyester. Anyway, they're comfy driving pants."

I say, "I guess I'm awake then."

She says, "Good. You'll never guess who called me last night."

"You're right."

"Guess."

I pull my fedora farther over my eyes and grind around in my seat, trying to find an impossible position of comfort. I say, "A state lottery commission agent. You've been winning too much on scratch tickets."

"Hardly," she says, and slaps my thigh. "Your new pal Billy Times called."

She might as well have hit me in the groin instead of my thigh. I sit up and crush my fedora between forehead and car ceiling. I resettle and try to play off my fish-caught-on-a-line spasm as a posture adjustment. I say, "Never heard of him."

"Come on, Mark. I know you visited him earlier in the week. He told me."

"Since I'm awake-awake, I might as well be smoking. Mind?"

"Yes. I try not to smoke in the car."

"Good." I light up.

She sighs and opens her window a crack. "I'm a little impressed you went all the way in town to the DA's office." She says it like it was so far away I needed a passport. A condescending cheap shot, but I probably deserve it.

I say, "I had to hire a Sherpa, but I managed."

"I didn't think you were serious the other day with the whole DA-as-family-friend talk." She stops, waiting for me to fill in the blanks. I can't fill those blanks in, not even for myself. She thinks I have something going on. I do, but I'm not going to tell her about it. She wouldn't like it. She certainly wouldn't be transporting me down to the Cape to chat with Sullivan.

I say, "I'm always serious, Ellen." All right, I need to know it all. I need to know why the DA called my mommy. It'll hang over me the whole time I'm in Osterville if I don't ask. "So why'd he call you?"

"Actually, he invited me to one of his Sunday brunches. Isn't that neat?"

"How nice. I'm sure your friends will be excited to hear you've become a socialite. You'll be the talk of Thursday night bingo at the Lithuanian Club." Ellen doesn't say anything, so I add, "Come on, Ellen, you're as bad a liar as I am. What did he want?"

"I'm not lying."

"Ellen. Your clown pants puff out bigger when you're lying. Come on, spill it."

She hits me again. "He did invite me. And, he asked questions about you. Asked if you were okay. He said your meeting was very odd and he got the sense you were struggling."

"Struggling? More proof politicians have no sense."

"Yes, struggling. That's the exact word he used."

"So what'd you tell him?"

Ellen sighs and moves her hands around while talking. Someone should be driving. "I told him you were fine, but I mentioned the accident and how you had narcolepsy now. I stressed that you're doing fine, though." She lilts with each biographical phrase, singing the song of me. It's a dirge she's sung many times before. She performs it well.

"Jesus, Ellen. Thanks a lot. Did you tell him I don't like pickles or ketchup, I pick my nose, and I wet the bed as a kid?"

She says, "What's wrong with you? He was just concerned, that's all. Did you want me to lie or make something up?"

"No. Telling him I was fine would've been enough. He doesn't need to hear my sob story."

"I don't understand why this upsets you."

"If I ever need him for a case, he'll never take me seriously now."

"Of course he will. No one holds narcolepsy against you."

"Come on, Ellen. Everyone does. No one really believes I have anything medically wrong with me. They think I'm lazy or just *odd*, like the DA said." I stop talking but I could go on: most people think I really could keep from falling asleep if I wanted to, if I just focused, like narcolepsy is some algebraic equation I could solve if I worked at it hard enough, did all the homework. I'm a bad joke. A punch line. I'm Beetle Bailey, a cartoon character falling asleep at the switch for laughs. I might as well be wearing her goddamn clown pants.

"I don't think that about you, Mark." She's mad at me and my pity party. I don't blame her.

I inhale the cigarette down to the filter, more ash in my lap than in the ashtray. Yeah, I'm nervous about my meeting with Sullivan, and I'm taking it out on Ellen and myself.

I say, "You're right. I know you don't, Clowny. I'm your *American Star*."

ELEVEN

Ellen drops me at the Osterville Free Library. It's a one-level brick building with white molding, trim, and columns. The Parthenon it's not. Ellen has a couple of family-portrait photo shoots and a meeting with a prospective wedding client, so I have three hours to myself.

I make an appearance inside the small library, wander the stacks for a bit, avoid story time and the children's wing, and check out a slim history of Osterville written and self-published by some local schmoe who probably has more cats than rooms in his house, not that I'm judging anyone. If Ellen comes back to the library before me, I can tell her I went for a read and a stroll. She might believe it or she might not.

The Sullivan house is two miles away from the library according to my Mapquest printout. The old Genevich homestead is on the other side of town, right off Route 28 and closer to downtown, so I'm not very familiar with this section of Osterville. This part of town has larger and pricier homes. No bungalows. No clapboard. These are summer homes for the well-well-to-do, mixed in with slightly more modest houses for folks who live here year-round. According to the map, most of my walk is down Wianno Avenue, left onto Crystal Lake Road, and then a quick right onto Rambler Road. Easy as A, B, and then C.

It's an overcast day with gusty ocean winds. The fedora quivers on my head, thinking about making a break for it. It's a quiet day otherwise. Only a handful of cars pass me on Wianno. None of them are red.

The exercise is good for my head, but the rest of my body thinks it's torture. Cranky knees and ankles carry the scars of the accident too. I walk as slowly as I talk.

While on my little hike, I try to focus on the case. On what it is I'm supposed to find. And it is a *what*, not a *who*. On the phone, Sullivan asked if I had found *it* yet.

Thoughts of the DA and Jennifer Times nag at me. I guess I should call the DA and apologize for the confusion, for thinking he was involved with sending me the photos. Apologize for my mistake. But it hasn't felt exactly like a mistake.

Sullivan's ringing question, *You didn't show the pictures to anyone, did you?*, was the same thing the DA asked me when he first saw the pictures. He didn't come right out with *It's not Jennifer*. He asked if anyone else had seen the pictures. I didn't think anything of it earlier because I'd assumed he didn't want his nude daughter subject to roving packs of prying eyes. Now, I'm not so sure.

Something's not right there. It's why he called Ellen too.

I turn onto Crystal Lake Road, and there are blue and red

lights filtering through the trees ahead, and right there is Rambler Road. It's blocked to traffic by a police car. There are more flashing lights and the occasional chirp of a siren. Sullivan's house. I think the worst. It's easy to think the worst when it always happens. Crystal Lake Road loops around to the other end of Rambler via Barnard Road, but I bet that end is blocked off too.

I stuff my map into a pocket and walk toward the roadblock. There's one cop, leaning on the hood of the car, arms crossed over his chest. He's skinny, a straw that isn't stirring any drink. He wears sunglasses despite the overcast day. I tip my hat. Surprise, surprise, I get to pass without answering his questions three.

Fifty yards or so beyond the roadblock are two more police cars parked on the side of the road. The homes on Rambler don't crowd each other; groves of trees help everyone keep their distance.

The Rambler Road locals must all be at work. There are no rubbernecking neighbors on lawns, dressed in robes and slippers and sipping their home-brewed coffee. There's just me.

My left ankle is swelling up, rebelling against the sock, but I make it to the other cop cars. They're parked next to a black mailbox with *Sullivan* stenciled in golden cursive. The Sullivan home is set back from the road. If it were summer, the place would be difficult to see from the street because of the trees that surround it and flank its L-shaped gravel driveway, but it's March and there are no leaves or blooms. I see everything through the empty branches. The house is big and white, with a two-car garage. The exterior shows signs of wear, missing shingles and peeling paint.

There's a clearing and a small grassy patch at the end of the gravel driveway. Two more cop cars are parked on the grass. An ambulance cozies up to Sullivan's front door with its back doors open. A blue SUV sits in the driveway, the only civilian car on or around the property.

"Can I help you?" Another cop. He suddenly appears next to the mailbox and me. Neat trick. This one is my size and build, but no beard and no mangled face. Nobody's perfect.

I say, "Depends. Can you tell me if Brendan is okay?"

He says, "Sorry, I don't know anything. Move along." He's not wearing sunglasses. He doesn't look at me but past me. I've been dismissed, if considered at all.

He doesn't like me. I can tell. It's okay because the feeling is mutual. I say, "I guess you can't help me, then. I don't suppose you're going to let me walk up there and find someone who will actually, you know, help me?"

He sways on his feet, an impatient boxer listening to the referee's instructions, waiting for me to crawl out of my corner. He lets me get through my slow I'm-running-out-of-batteries spiel. He doesn't interrupt. I guess he deserves an iota of credit for that.

He says, "Why are you still here? Move along."

I hold up my hands. "Just a concerned acquaintance of the Sullivans out for a walk. I saw the lights and figured I'd check in and be neighborly."

Nothing from angry cop.

I say, "Well, you just keep on protecting the people, officer." I consider showing my PI ID and pushing back some more, but it would produce nothing but a migraine headache for me. Whatever happened at the Sullivan house isn't good, and I probably don't want to be connected to it. At least not right now. The last thing I need is to have to answer a bunch of Barney Fife questions *downtown,* and calling Mommy to pick me up at the police station would ruin the whole vibe for everyone involved. I'm more afraid of having to answer Ellen's questions than theirs. She's tougher.

My craven need for information will have to wait. I tell myself that patience will work best here and I'll find out what happened eventually. It's the only play I have right now.

I slowly walk away, exaggerate my limp, maybe give the cop some Keyser Söze thoughts. I'm aimed at the other end of Rambler, figuring to loop around to Wianno Avenue and back to the library. I have the time now, and not having to walk past the same set of cops is a good idea.

Then, through the trees, I see a stretcher brought out of the Sullivan house. It's holding a body with a white sheet over it. The stretcher's metallic legs are like the barren tree branches. They look dead, unfit to carry life and too flimsy to carry any weight.

TWELVE

Back on Wianno and getting physically fatigued fast. Joints tighten and demand that I stop moving. I don't walk this kind of distance regularly—or at all. This is my marathon.

Been waiting and listening for the ambulance and cop cars to pass. Nothing yet. They must've taken a different route.

I might be a half mile from the library now. A car approaches from behind. Its wheels grind salt and sand left over from the winter. The salt and sand have nowhere to go, I suppose. The car slows down and pulls onto the sidewalk ahead of me. It's in my path. It's a red car, something American and muscular, not at all practical, and that tells you all you need to know about the driver of such a thing. Whoever it is has to wait until I drag my limping-for-real ass up to them. Drama and tension happen naturally sometimes.

I mosey up to the car. The front windows are rolled down, engine still on, its idling is somewhere between a growl and a clearing throat. There's a thick arm hanging out the window, tapping the door, tapping to someone's favorite song. Not mine.

The driver says, "Hey there, Genevich. What's that you're

carrying around?" The driver is the redheaded goon from the DA's office. The passenger is his bald buddy. It's sweet how they stick together, even this far from their natural habitat.

I say, "A book. Ever seen one before? Truth be known, I just look at the pictures." I hold it up. I don't have any secrets.

The passenger goon, Baldy, says, "Oh, he's a funny guy. I love funny guys. They make everything more fun."

I say, "That's quite the expressive vocabulary you got there. I can see why your buddy lets you talk." They both have their cell phones in their ears. Maybe they're surgical implants. I point and add, "Those phones will give you cancer. Be careful."

"Thanks for the tip," the redhead says. "What are you doing down on the Cape? For a retard who can't drive, you sure do get around." He laughs. It's forced and goofy.

I don't say anything. The goons go all sit-and-stare on me, dogs pointing at some dead animal floating in the water.

The library is in the visible distance. The clouds part a bit, a tear in the overcast fabric, and the sun shines on the library's white flagpole. I'm on a main road, middle of the day. I convince myself that I'm safe, so I decide to keep up the chatter.

I say, "I like the Cape this time of year. Think I'll play a little mini-golf later. Take advantage of the off-season touristy stuff. Want to play? Five bucks a hole until the windmill. Then it's ten."

Baldy says, "We'll pass, Mushface." He's breathing heavy, practically frothing. His chin juts out, a thick slab of granite, a section of the Great Wall of China. It seems to be growing bigger with each breath.

I say, "Now, now. No need to get personal, boys. This has been fun, but I think I'll continue on my afternoon constitutional, if you don't mind."

I resume my walk. I have goons from the DA's office tailing me in a red car, Sullivan's surveying red car. Nothing is coincidence. Everything is connected.

They follow me. The engine revs, mechanical authority, a thousand angry voices. Clouds of exhaust punctuate the vehicular threats. The roars fill me, then pool in the back of my head. I want to turn to see how close they are, but I won't.

They pull up next to me again, but we all keep moving. Nobody is the leader. The car creeps farther onto the sidewalk, cutting into my path. There's a chest-high stone wall to my left. I might run out of space soon, sandwiched between metal and rock, that proverbial hard place.

Redhead says, "We weren't done talking yet. Leaving us like that was kind of rude, Genevich."

"Yeah, well, Miss Manners I ain't."

Their car edges closer. Heat from the engine block turns loose my sweat. I'm going to keep walking. I won't be the one to flinch in this game of chicken. No way. Not after that retard crack.

Redhead says, "I hope you didn't come all the way down here to talk to Brendan Sullivan."

Baldy finishes the thought. "Yeah, wasted trip, Genevich. He's got nothing to say. Never did."

I'm not safe. I never was. Safety is the big disguise. I keep walking. Straight line. That's what courage is: dumbass perseverance. The library flagpole is my bearing, my shining beacon. I'm done talking. Just walking.

Redhead says, "I can make this simple for you, Genevich. You can make us go away by giving us those photos."

My eyes stay on the flagpole. It's covered in white vines and white roses.

"Yeah, give us the photos, and then you can have a little nap."

"Or a big one."

"It's time to be smart, here."

"We don't play games."

"Ask Brendan."

Baldy says, "Oh, wait a minute, he can't ask Brendan."

The negatives are still in my desk but the manila envelope and photos are inside my jacket. I wanted to make Sullivan look at them again. I wanted to see his eyes seeing the photos. I can't explain what information it would've given me, but it would've been something. Maybe everything.

Redhead says, "Be a smart retard, Genevich. Give us the photos."

I can pretend the photos are inside my library book and, when Redhead reaches for it, smack him in the face with it, knock him silly. Maybe it'll buy me enough time to get to the library. Maybe it won't. I wouldn't mind paying the missing book fee if it worked.

I don't give them anything, feet on pavement, playing it cool when everything is too hot. Their engine revs loud enough to crack the sidewalk under me but I just keep on going. My eyes are locked on the library and its flagpole, the flagpole with vines made of white roses, and those roses are now blooming and growing bigger, just like the smoking and growling threat next to me.

THIRTEEN

I'm falling but not falling. I'm not falling because I am sitting, but I am falling because I am leaning and sliding, sliding down. My right hand shoots out and slaps against wood. It wasn't expecting wood and I wasn't expecting any of this. Adrenaline. Fear. My heart is a trapped rabbit and it frantically kicks the walls with oversized hind legs. Disoriented is a brain comparing short-term memories to what the senses currently report and believing neither.

Goons, the DA's goons. Sitting on a bench. Surgical implants. A bench. Red car. Feet planted in grass. Walking. Falling, sliding. A stone wall. White flagpole on my direct left, and there are no vines or blooming roses. . . .

I blink and stare and look. If I was an owl I'd spin my head like a top and cover all 360 degrees, make sure there're no holes in what I see. Okay. I'm sitting on a bench, the lone bench in front of the library.

My legs hurt. They won't bend at the knee without complaining. I did the walk. Pain is my proof. My next thought is about time. How much I hate it, and how desperate I am to know how much of it has passed.

Here comes Ellen. Her little green car pulls into the library lot. I'll stay here, wait for her, and reboot from my latest system crash, but there'll be files missing. There always are.

I feel inside my jacket. The manila envelope. I peek inside and the photos are still there.

Ellen has mercifully changed out of her clown pants and into old carpenter jeans, faded, like my memories. She also has on a gray sweatshirt, part of her bingo attire. It makes her look older and tired, tired from all the extra years of hands-on mothering. I won't tell her that maybe the clown pants are the way to go.

Ellen says, "Have you been out here long?"

I wonder if she knows how awful a question that is to ask. I could say *not long* and be correct; it's relative. I haven't been out here asleep on this bench for long when you compare it to the amount of time I've existed with narcolepsy, if you compare it to the life span of a galaxy. Or I could say *not long, not long at all, just got here.*

I say, "I don't know."

Ellen ignores my response and its implications. She adjusts her monstrous bag on her right shoulder. She usually complains about that shoulder killing her, but she won't switch the bag over to her left. I don't know anyone else who exclusively uses her right shoulder for load bearing.

She says, "Did you get some work done? Get everything you need?"

I say, "Some work done. Still more to do." Still groggy.

Speaking only in phrases is the ointment. For now, my words are too heavy for complex construction.

"That's good. Though you look a little empty-handed."

I had taken out the little Osterville history book. I check and pat the bench and my coat. It's gone.

Ellen says, "What's the matter?"

Maybe I hit the redheaded goon with the book after all, assuming there were real goons in the first place. I could verify some of my previous extracurricular activities. Go inside and ask if I had checked out that book, but I won't. An answer of *no* would do too much damage to me. I'd rather just believe what I want to believe. It's always easier that way.

I say, "Nothing. I think I left a book inside." I stand up and try not to wince. I'm going to have a hard time walking to the car.

She says, "What's wrong now, Mark?"

Everything. I need to go back to Southie, try to put distance between me, the maybe goons, and whatever happened at the Sullivan house. I also need to give Ellen an answer, an excuse, something that won't lead to a trip full of follow-up questions. "Nothing. My body is protesting another drive in your torture chamber."

"Want me to get your book?"

"No. It wasn't any good."

FOURTEEN

Back home. It's five o'clock. I've been gone for only half a day, but our little excursion to the Cape and back has left me with a weeklong family-vacation-type hangover. I just don't have a cheesy T-shirt, sunburn, and disposable camera full of disposable memories to show for it.

My office phone blinks. A red light. I have a voice-mail message. Let's get right to it.

"Hello—um, Mr. Genevich? This is Jennifer Times. I got your number from your card that you left me?" Her statements are questions. She's unsure of what she's doing. That makes two of us. "I think we need to meet and talk. Please call me back as soon as you can." She leaves her number, and the message ends with a beep.

I won't call her right away. I need the meanings and possibilities to have their way with me for a bit. Just like I need a hot shower to untie my muscles; they're double-knotted.

First I'll check my e-mail. I turn on the computer. The hard drive makes its noises, its crude impersonation of life. The monitor glows, increasing in brightness until the desktop is visible. Same as it was yesterday and the day before. There's no e-mail. Then I do a quick search for any stories about Brendan Sullivan and Osterville and murder. Nothing comes up.

Maybe I should call Sullivan's house. Don't know if that's a good idea. Not sure if I'm ready to have my name popping up on police radar screens, if he was in fact murdered. There's still too much I don't know, too many questions I couldn't answer, but the call is the chance I probably have to take at some point. I should call. Call his house now. Might not have been him I saw being taken out of the house. What I saw might not have even happened.

Screw it. I pick up the phone and dial Jennifer Times instead. Sullivan can wait. The shower can wait. It'll be good to have things to look forward to.

One ring. "Hello?"

"Jennifer, it's Mark Genevich returning your call." I'm all business, even if she's not the client and not in the photos anymore. Let her do the talking. I don't need her. She called me.

"Hi, yeah, thanks for calling me back. So, I was thinking we should meet and talk?" Still with statements that are questions. Maybe being forced from the spotlight has left her withered, without confidence. Maybe it's just my perception. For all I know she's a confident young woman, an aspiring celebrity, and she's only reflecting my constant state of insecurity because I want her to. It's what we all want from our celebrities. We want them to tell us something we don't know about ourselves when they can't.

Suddenly I'm Mr. Popular. I say, "I can do that. You pick

the place." I assume that she doesn't want to come to my office. Otherwise, she would've offered.

"Can we meet for dinner at Amrheins later tonight? Seven p.m.?"

Of course. The DA's pet restaurant. "I can do that too. But make it seven-thirty." I don't need the extra half hour. Sure, it'll give me a safety net, never know when that ever-elusive thief, lost time, might strike, but I said seven-thirty because I want to exert some of my own conscious will upon the situation. For once.

She says, "Okay."

There's silence. It's big enough to span the unknown distance between us. I say, "See you tonight, then, Jennifer." I'm not going to ask why she wants to meet with me or ask her what DA Daddy told her. There'll be plenty of time for the tough questions later. I'm not going to force this. I don't need to. I'm not used to the power position. I'll try not to let it go to my head.

FIFTEEN

A constant stream of traffic passes by like schools of fish, the sheer number of vehicles relentless and numbing. I'm standing on East Broadway, only a block from the Broadway Red Line T stop. Seven-thirty has become seven-forty-five. It's all right. My cigarette is finished. Society always arrives late.

Amrheins is an Irish restaurant. Has its own parking lot, big enough for fifty-plus cars. The lot itself has to be worth a small fortune in real estate. The restaurant is big. It has three sections. Bar section is the middle, dining areas on the left and right. The right side of the restaurant is elevated. Everything is kept suitably dark for the patrons.

I check in with the maître d'. He's a short young guy in a white dress shirt and black pants. The bright ink from his sleeve tattoos is visible through the shirt's thin cloth, their stories hinted at but hidden. He doesn't talk, only motions at the elevated section with his head.

Jennifer is alone, sitting at a table for two tucked away in a corner, as far from the entrance as possible. She sees me and nods. It takes me a dragonfly's life to limp across the restaurant to our table. She has on a jean jacket, open and rolled up to the elbows. Light blue shirt. Her hair is tied up, off her face, and she wears glasses. The glasses are enough to turn her into Clark Kent and successfully disguise her Superman, but I know it's her.

I say, "Sorry I'm late, Jennifer." I try to think of something witty to explain my lateness, but I figure my hangdog reappearance is enough. My clothes look slept in because they are. I never did take that hot shower. I can't even keep appointments with myself.

She says, "That's okay." The tablecloth is green. An unlit tea-light candle floats in a glass bowl. The melted wax makes tentacles. It's a floating inkblot I can't read, a portent for the evening. Maybe I should just sit my ass down. Jennifer sips from a glass of sparkling water, or maybe soda. A person can get lost trying to figure out all the details.

The place is half full, or half empty, the point of view hinging on how our meeting fares. I do sit. My back is turned to the rest of the restaurant. I'm not comfortable with my seating. Don't want my back to Southie because the place is full of goons. One such goon might have red hair, freckles, and a phone in his ear, and he might have a bald buddy. Yeah, it has occurred to me that this dinner could be a setup. I slide my heavy wooden chair loudly toward Jennifer's side of the table.

I say, "I like being able to see what I want to see, which is everything." I'm still fiddling with my chair and position. Jennifer makes a hand gesture and a waiter materializes instantly.

Jennifer orders mango turkey tips with pineapple salsa, then turns to me and says, "Sorry, but I can't stay long. He'll wait while you look at the menu, all right?"

The waiter nods at me. That's all I get from the staff. Head movements.

I suppose I deserve being put on the food spot for being late. I make it easy on everyone and order without looking at the menu. "Shepherd's pie and a coffee, and make sure my mug is always full."

The waiter has his errand, clicks his heels, and returns from whence he came. I say, "So, Ms. Times, here we are." Not exactly the best opening line, but it'll have to do, creepy-older-man vibe notwithstanding.

She says, "I have some questions," then stops. Her spine is telephone-pole straight. It makes me uncomfortable.

I say, "I have many answers. Ask me the questions and we'll see if any of my answers match up."

Her hands are on the table and folded over each other. She could be holding a firefly trapped in her hands or a coin she plans to make disappear. She has all her own fingers, no bandages or scars. Not that I expected differently, of course. She says, "I've never been to your office, Mr. Genevich. Why did you go to my father's office and tell him I hired you?" Her delivery is clinical, rehearsed. She must've practiced her questions with a mirror or with DA Daddy.

Doesn't matter. I tell her. I just flat out tell her everything, the truth along with my mistakes and lies. Can't have truth without lies. First I give an introduction to my wonderful world of narcolepsy. How it started. How it won't stop. Then fast-forward to our supposed meeting in my office. Her missing fingers and the hypnogogic hallucination. She's listening. I'm believing. Believing that if I open up and share my truths, maybe she'll share hers. It's the only chance I have of getting anything meaningful out of this meeting. I give her the highlights from the trip to the DA's minus the photos of her stand-in. She only needs to know I thought she was being blackmailed. Not over what. Finally, I tell her that the real client called me yesterday. I leave out the Cape, red car, and goons. I'm not going to give it all away.

She says, "Well, I'm glad you're admitting that I was never in your office." She unfolds her hands; the firefly is free to go. She reaches for her drink. "But do you know why you hallucinated me into your office?"

"You and *American Star* were impossible to avoid around here. Believe me, I tried. The local rags and news stations pumped out daily features and updates." I stop and Jennifer doesn't say anything. So I add, "That, and I'm your biggest fan. I never missed a show and called in to vote every night, unless I fell asleep first."

I laugh. She doesn't.

She says, "Is it because the woman in the pictures you showed to my father looks like me?"

The questions are piling up fast, adding up, stressing my system again. Not sure if I can keep up. I can keep telling myself I'm in control of this particular situation, but I know better. Luckily, the waiter picks the perfect time to return with my coffee. It's hot enough to melt skin. My belly fills with lava. Perfect.

I say, "So, your father told you about the pictures, I assume. It's nice that you guys can share like that."

She nods. "Did you bring them?"

I don't say anything right away because I don't know what I should say. Experience offers me nothing here because I have none. "I think I have those Kodak moments on me, yeah." The pictures never leave me now. They've taken root inside my coat.

"Will you show them to me?"

I say, "I don't think so. You're not my client." I say that, but I'm going to show them to her. Just want to know how much she'll push.

"I think you owe me. Don't you?" It's the first appearance of that privileged attitude I saw on TV. Can't say I like it. She says it with a face as straight as her spine, which is still as straight as a telephone pole. See, everything is connected.

I say, "No. I don't owe you anything other than a sorry-for-the-inconvenience." My coffee mug is empty despite my explicit instructions. That's inconvenient.

She says, "I want to see her. It's why I called you and it's why I'm here, Mr. Genevich. Nothing else. This is it. Our paths will never cross again after this." Jennifer takes off her glasses and wipes the lenses with her napkin, then puts them back on. Disguise intact. "I would like to see her. Please."

I know the DA put her up to this. It's too obvious. Now I just have to figure out the potential risk/reward of showing her the photos. I smile instead of yawning. It probably comes out all lopsided and crooked, a crack in a glass. I say, "Am I supposed to just pull out the photos here, in the middle of a restaurant?"

She says, "Yeah, why not? There's nobody over here. You're practically sitting in my lap, so it's not like anyone could see."

Hard to argue with that. I open my coat and produce the envelope, which has taken quite a beating. The manila is going all flaky on me, its structural integrity close to being compromised. Nothing lasts forever. I take out the pictures and hand the first one to her, the one with clothes.

Jennifer says, "Wow. She does look like me. Not exactly, but enough to be weird. Aren't there more?" She holds out a hand.

"I'll trade you. New for old."

She rolls her eyes but I don't care. Now I'm the spoiled brat who won't share. I make the international gimme-gimme-gimme sign with my hand and fingers. She gimmes. I put the second picture in her hand.

She says, "What did my father say when he saw these?"

"He said it wasn't you. I asked for proof. He said no mole. Hair and teeth were wrong." I leave out the part where he asked me if anyone else had seen the photos. I'm saving that for myself until I figure out what to do with it.

She says, "She's too skinny to be me. Her breasts are smaller too." Jennifer gives back the photo.

"My girlfriend used to say that all the time." I try to sound nonchalant but come off desperate instead. I rub my beard. It sounds awful loud. Awful and loud.

Jennifer says, "Your girlfriend sounds like a keeper," and gives me a pity smile. Thanks, but no thanks.

I say, "Nah, not really. Barely remember her." I reach for my cigarettes, but then I remember I can't smoke in here. Memory slower than the hand. Back to the beard.

Jennifer says, "But you remember she talked about her small breasts?"

I can't tell how much fun she's having at my expense. Doesn't matter, I suppose. I can pretend I'm out having a harmless conversation. Pretend that I didn't lose my face and then the last eight years of my life to little sleeps. I say, "Yeah. That, and I liked how she read books."

I'm sure Jennifer isn't expecting me to go here, a tangent running wildly into my personal territory, but she plays along. She says, "Should I be afraid to ask?"

"She wrote all over her books. She circled and highlighted words and phrases, drew pictures between the lines, and wrote down descriptions of the emotions she experienced in the margins. So when she went back to reread the book, she only looked at the pictures and the notes."

"That's odd. And certainly memorable."

I say, "I remember it because it's where I live now. In the margins." I don't think Jennifer realizes how honest I am being here. Maybe she does and finds it embarrassing. I'm like a friend admitting some reprehensible bit of behavior that forever warps and taints the relationship. Only I'm not a friend. I think I understand her obvious discomfort. Strangers are supposed to lie.

She steers the conversation back to her turf. "Do you swear no one is trying to use those to blackmail me? If those pictures end up on the Internet somehow, you'll have one pissed-off DA knocking on your door."

I tell her, "You're in the clear," though I don't really believe it. There's some connection. I mean, she's here, in front of me right now. That's more than I can say for any other aspect, potential or otherwise, of this case. An awkward silence has its way.

I say, "Glad we settled that. I can sleep now." I laugh at my own joke. I laugh too hard. It shakes our table. It's a laugh a prisoner might direct at the warden who just made a meal out of the cell key.

"Who do you think it is?" she says.

I stop myself from saying *If I knew, I wouldn't be here with you,* but I don't want her to take it personally. Yeah, that's a bad joke. I know this case is a lot more serious than blackmail and nudie pics, and it scares the hell out of me. I tell her, "Don't know yet."

"So you don't know who's in the pictures and you didn't know who sent the pictures?"

I say, "I know who sent them to me now."

"That's right. The convenient phone call."

"There was nothing convenient about the phone call."

"Still sounds like a tough case."

"Nothing's ever easy. But I'll figure it all out."

"Will you?"

"Yes."

The verbal volley is fast and everything gets returned. I manage to push out every one of my lead-heavy words.

She leans back in her chair, crosses her arms over her chest. "Those pictures felt old to me, like they were taken a long time ago."

"Probably just the black-and-white." She's right, but I don't want to admit it.

Our food arrives. My shepherd's pie is molten. We eat. Our silence becomes a part of the meal, a glass of wine that doesn't add any flavor but doesn't get in the way either.

Then I decide to get in the way. "Sorry you lost, Jennifer."

"Excuse me?"

"Lost. You know, *American Star.* I thought you got screwed, although you probably gave them too much attitude. Nothing wrong with attitude, but you gotta know, the peoples, they want their stars safe, smiling, and happy. At least until they get bored with them."

Oh, she's angry. It's all over her face. The emotion looks exterior, not belonging to her. It's a mask. It's not real. She's giving me what she thinks I expect or want. Maybe I'm projecting again. I don't know anything about this woman, but I did see her on TV surrounded by fans, and we're all conditioned to believe it's validation of her goodness, her worth, even if she was the first loser. Jennifer composes herself, takes off the anger mask.

"Thanks. It's been a tough few days, but I'll be fine. My agent says offers are already coming in."

Sure they are. More local mall appearances to be followed by national anthems at minor league baseball parks, and it only goes downhill from there. Her brief run as a celebrity was a mask too, or a full-body costume, one she rented instead of owned.

Seems the both of us are down, so I won't throw any more kicks her way. But I will throw her an off-speed pitch. "Did you tell your father you'd be meeting with me tonight?"

She says, "No." She doesn't use a knife, just mashes her fork into a turkey tip, splitting it in half. She's lying. That's my assumption until proven otherwise, private detective work as contrapositive.

I say, "Does your father think I'm making this all up? Does he think I'm dangerous? Should I be expecting him and a warrant at my door soon?"

Jennifer shrugs and destroys more turkey. "I don't know. He'll probably forget about it if he doesn't hear from you again. He was pretty pissed about your meeting, though."

"I have that effect on some people." A canned line, one that I regret instantly. "Did he tell you that he and my father were childhood friends?"

Jennifer tilts her head. "No, he didn't. Is that true?"

Could be the old man was just too angry to bother with the cozy nostalgia trip. Could be he didn't tell her for a reason. I say, "As true as eight o'clock." Not sure what that means, but I go with it. "I don't get into the DA's office without the Southie and family-friend bit. They grew up in the Harbor Point projects and palled around. Ask him about it."

Jennifer looks at her watch. I'm the appointment that's supposed to end soon. She says, "I will. Where is your father now?"

"He died when I was five."

"I'm sorry." She looks at me, puts me under glass, and says, "Tell me what narcolepsy is like."

"I can't tell you. I'm in it all the time. No basis for comparison. I might as well ask you what not having narcolepsy is like. I certainly don't remember what I felt like before I had it, before the accident." I stop. She doesn't say anything. She was supposed to. Some dance partner she is. I can't follow if she won't lead.

I say, "Do you remember what you felt like eight years ago?"

"No. I guess I don't."

"Neither do I." I'm getting mad. I shouldn't. If I could be rational for a moment, I should appreciate her interest in the state of the narcoleptic me. Very few people share this interest.

"How often do you fall asleep?"

"Depends on the day. Good days, I can make it through with one or two planned naps. Bad days, I'm falling in and out of sleep as often as some people change channels on their TV. And then bad days become bad nights."

"Is today a good day?"

"I don't have a lot of good days. I guess that makes me a pessimist. I'd care and try to change if I had the energy."

"You can't stop yourself from falling asleep?" Another statement question, one I know everyone thinks but doesn't have the guts to ask.

"Sometimes I can; if I recognize the feelings, I can try to change what I'm doing and fight it off. Coping strategies are hit-or-miss. Usually I'm so used to getting along with my gas tank needle hovering on empty that I don't realize I'm about to go out. And then I'm out. Caught in the little sleep."

"How do you feel right now?"

I say, "Tired. Tired of everything."

Jennifer puts down her fork and stands up slowly, as if afraid a sudden movement would spook me. I'm a frail bird she doesn't want to scare away. Or a cornered and wounded animal she's afraid might attack. She says, "Thanks again for meeting me here, Mr. Genevich. I'm sorry, but I really have to go now."

I make a move to stand up. She says, "Please, stay, finish your meal. It's all taken care of. I've already put it on my father's tab."

"He won't mind?"

"No. I do it all the time." She smiles. It's her first real smile of the evening. It's okay. I've seen worse. She edges away from the table, adjusts her jean jacket and her glasses, and leaves without looking back.

I finish my dinner. How do I feel right now? I feel like I missed something, something important. I always feel that way.

SIXTEEN

I should go straight home and try to find out what, if anything, happened to Brendan Sullivan. But I don't. I stay and take advantage of the tab. I drink three beers, a couple or three shots of whiskey, and two more coffees. At the bar, the townies are on one side and the trendies on the other, and both groups ignore me, use me as their barrier, their Thirty-eighth Parallel.

All right. It's time to go. I'm fine, and I'm taking half the shepherd's pie home with me. It'll make a good breakfast or midnight snack. There's no difference for me.

There's a cabstand down by the Red Line stop, but I'll try and flag a ride in front of the restaurant. It's dark, late, and raining: my perpetual state. I pull up my collar, but that only redirects wind and water into my face and inside my shirt.

I raise the hand that isn't holding a cigarette at a cab, but a black limo cuts it off and pulls into the Amrheins lot, angled, an angry cross-out on a piece of paper, black limo takes the square. Droplets of water on the windshield shine under the streetlamp, making little white holes. Maybe the whiskey shots were overkill.

A rear door opens and the DA thrusts his head out. "I can give you a ride home, Genevich. Jump in."

I know there's no such thing as a free ride, but I take the invite anyway. The door closes and I'm inside the limo with the DA. So are my two friends the goons. I'm not surprised, but it's crowded in here. There are no ashtrays.

I say, "Evening, boys. Have a safe trip up from the Cape?" I blow smoke, smoke and words.

Redhead says, "Hey, retard, remember me?" He's grinning like a manic comic-strip villain, all teeth and split face, flip-top head, a talking Pez dispenser. Ellen still stuffs my Christmas stockings with Pez dispensers, usually superheroes like Spider-Man and the Hulk.

I say, "I missed you most of all." The three of them wear matching blue suits, no wrinkles, and the creases are sharp, dangerous. "Hey, you guys gonna be catering somewhere later? Or maybe you're starting a band. I got a name for you: The Dickheads. Best of luck with that." My anger feels good.

The DA has his legs crossed and hands folded over his knees. If he was any more relaxed he'd be narcoleptic. He says, "I trust you had a nice dinner with Jennifer."

Like I told Jennifer, I'm tired of everything. I knew she was lying to me. There was no appointment she had to keep. Her dinner with the sideshow freak was a little job for Daddy. She set me up, put me on a platter. The only thing missing is an apple in my mouth.

All right. I'm through playing the nice guy, the clueless

schmuck. I'm nobody's fall guy. I'm nobody's cliché. I say, "Nah, the food sucked and she talked too much. I'm glad she lost. The Limey judge was right about her."

The bald goon punches me in the stomach, one for flinching. It doesn't hurt. He says, "Watch your mouth."

"Need to work on that uppercut. Saw it coming from last block," I say. The cigarette hangs off my bottom lip and I'm not controlling it anymore. Whether it's sticking around during a tough time or getting ready to abandon ship, I don't know. "Don't get me wrong, DA. The free beer was great. It'll help me sleep tonight."

Redhead laughs. "We can help you with sleep." His eyes are popping out of his head, showing too much white. He's on something serious. I get the sense that if he throws me a punch, I'll break like a porcelain doll.

The DA furrows his brow. He's so concerned. He says, "You have an odd way of expressing appreciation, Genevich."

I'm not nervous. I'm still on my first ball and nowhere near tilting. I should be nervous, though. The momentum of the evening is not in my favor. Must be the beers and booze helping me out.

I say, "I'll thank you for the ride home if I get there. Unless you're expecting something more. Sorry, but I don't put out on a first date." The interior light is on in the limo but everything is still dark. I think we're headed toward West Broadway.

The DA says, "You should be expressing appreciation for my patience. It wouldn't take more than a phone call and a few computer keystrokes to have you locked up. Or worse." He uncrosses his legs and leans toward me, a spider uncurling itself and readying to sprint down the web.

The goons sitting across from me, they're in the heel position but twitching. Hackles up. Ready to go.

The DA is bluffing. He's all talk and no chalk. Otherwise his threatening little scenario would've already happened. Nothing is going to happen. They're going to drop me at my apartment with another tough-guy act and another warning. Warnings. I'm collecting them now like stamps, or butterflies.

Then again, that's not to say that the DA can't do what he said. It'd be suicide to assume otherwise. I'm going to try this out: "Sounds like you're putting me on double-secret probation. What would my dear old dad say about you harassing his son like this? It's not very Southie of you."

He squints, eyelids putting on a mighty squeeze. I got to him. Not sure how. Can't be just the memory of my father, can it? He says, through a mouthful of teeth, "Your dad isn't around anymore, is he? Hasn't been around for a long time, not sure if you're aware."

"I'm always aware." I sound stupid. He gives me threats and doom, and I give him a self-help life-affirmation aphorism.

He says, "And don't tell me what's Southie, Genevich. You have no idea."

I hold up my hands. The DA is getting too hot. No telling what his goons might do if he starts to smoke. I say, "If you say so. Still not sure why all the fuss here. I'm not in your way now, and I haven't done anything wrong. I'm clean, as in squeaky."

He smiles. "When has that ever mattered?" His regained polished tone and delivery is a gun pointed in my face. It holds that much potential for damage. I have no chance.

The bald goon says, "Let's hurt him."

I say, "Jeez, DA, do your constituents know that you run with this kind of crowd? I'm shocked and more than a little disappointed."

He doesn't go for it. He says, "What do you say you just give me the photos, Genevich. The negatives—and don't look surprised, I know there are negatives—and any copies you might've made, digital or otherwise. Give me everything, and that'll be the end of this and any further unpleasantries."

"Or what? You'll call my mommy again?" Things are happening too fast. I add, "You don't need the photos. I've said my mea culpas. They're not of Jennifer. I told her as much during dinner. She's out of the picture, so to speak. And she's fine with it. You should be too."

The DA and the goons laugh. Apparently I'm funny. He says, "The photos, Genevich. I want them. Now is not soon enough. We can take them by force if necessary. It wouldn't bother me. The funny part is we could hold your hand and take you home, sit on your couch, and just wait for you to fall asleep."

I say nothing. His last line robs me of both cool and machismo. Not that I have any.

The DA says, "Tell our driver to turn left onto D Street, and we'll all just enjoy the ride." Redhead follows through on the instructions.

Might as well lay it all out right here. "So how is our friend Brendan Sullivan these days?"

The goons laugh. I've said something incredibly smart or stupid. Likely both.

Baldy says, "He ain't doing too good right now."

Redhead says, "He did answer our questions though, poor guy."

The DA says, "You don't even know what you're saying half the time, do you, Genevich? I suggest you cut the tough-guy PI act, leave the big-boy stuff to us big boys, and give me the photos."

The limo slows and stops. I look out the tinted window and see a Burger King. We're at the D Street intersection. The D Street projects are on the other side of the street. The buildings look like gravestones.

Baldy slaps my face. I hang on to the cigarette but things go fuzzy. I might just go out now, but I pull it together.

"The patty-cake shit is getting old, goon." I fill my lungs with smoke and it stokes a fire in my chest. I exhale a smoke ring that haloes Baldy's head, and I say, "I buried the photos on Boston Common, under the roots of a sapling. The tree will sprout pictures instead of leaves. Harvest in the fall. Good luck with that."

Baldy tries to slap me again but I catch him by the wrist and stub out my cigarette on the back of his hand. He yells. I pull him into my knee, right in the balls, and then push him over, into Redhead. The DA does nothing. He barely looks interested.

I try the limo door, expecting it to be locked, but it opens and I spill out onto the wet pavement and the other lane. Just ahead is a double-parked and idling cab. It's white with some black checkers on the panels. No driver. He must be inside the fast-food joint taking a leak. I look over my shoulder. Redhead crawls out of the limo after me. A gun is in his hand, big as a smokestack.

There's isn't much time. I scuttle around the cab and jump into the driver's seat. The steering wheel is warm and too big. There're too many places for my hands to go. They don't know what to do. The instruments in the dashboard are all in Japanese.

A bullet spiderwebs the rear passenger window. The glass bleeds and screams. Didn't think they'd shoot at me out in the open like this. Must be a mistake, but one that can't be reversed. A chain of events now set into motion until there's one conclusion: me with extra holes. I fumble for the automatic transmission shift. Goddamn it, it's on the steering wheel. It shouldn't be there. I pull on it but it doesn't move. I don't know its secret.

There are loud and fast footsteps on the pavement. Two footsteps become four and multiply rapidly until there's a whole city of footsteps running at me. Redhead appears at my window. He's yelling some crazy stuff, doesn't make any sense. Maybe he's reading the dashboard labels. The gun barrel snug against the glass doesn't have any problems communicating its message.

I'm pulling as hard as I can and the gearshift finally gives in to my demands, which weren't all that unreasonable. I drop the transmission into drive and squeal the wheels. I'm moving forward and I duck, down beneath the dash; there's another gunshot, this one sending glass snowflakes falling onto my head, and there's . . .

SEVENTEEN

"We're here."

I come to in the back of a cab. I'm still buzzed and my mouth tastes of vomit. I bolt upright like a rake getting stepped on. The Johnny Rotten of headaches lurches and struts around my brain. God save my head.

The cab and me, we're at the corner of Dorchester and Broadway, idling in front of my office and apartment building. I want to go digging back under, into the brine, find me some real sleep, the kind that makes my body glad it's there to support me. But I won't find any in here, and I probably won't find any upstairs in my apartment.

"Don't be sleeping on me now," the cabbie says. His voice is full of *fuck you*, but he really cares about me. I can tell.

I'm awake now. I have no idea how much of the DA, the limo ride, and the goons happened. My left cheek, where Redhead slapped me, is sore and puffy. Maybe I did escape their limo and jump into this cab and then dreamed the rest. I don't know.

The cab's heat is on furnace blast. The muscles in my hands

feel week. I open and close shaky fists. They're empty and tired, like me. The little sleep was and is too hard.

I pull a crumpled bill out of my pocket and throw it at the cabbie. It's not a good throw. "Keep the change." Don't know if it's enough, and don't care. Neither does he apparently.

I open a door, leave without a further exchange, and manage to land standing on the curb. The cab leaves. It was white and had black checkers on the panels. It's late. There aren't any black limos or red cars on the street. It's still dark and raining.

I need time to process the evening: what happened, what didn't happen, what any of it means. I have my keys out, but the front door to my office is open. The door is thick and heavy, probably as old as the brownstone building, and it sways in the wind and rain.

I step inside the front entryway. The stacks of local restaurant menus are all wet and turning to pulp under my feet. This isn't good. I walk into my office. I don't need to turn on a light to see that everything is all wrong, but I turn it on anyway. Never did like surprises.

Someone picked up my office and shook it around like Daddy needed a new pair of shoes and rolled snake eyes. And then the shaker took out his frustration with the undesired result on my fucking office.

Flat-screen computer monitor is not quite flat anymore and is on the floor, where my client chair used to be. That chair is huddled in the corner of the room, licking its wounds. It saw everything and is traumatized. It'll never be the same.

My file cabinet has been stripped of its contents. Its drawers are open, metal tongues saying ah, and the files spread out on the floor. My desk drawers are open and empty too. They didn't want to feel left out. I step on paper and walk over to my desk. My phone is gone. So is the hard drive and backup flash drive. I don't see my yellow notepad, the one with the narcoleptic me notes. It could be buried in here somewhere, but I doubt it. Good goddamn mercy. And Christ, the negatives, they're not in the empty drawers.

I leave the office and walk upstairs in the dark. It occurs to me that the ransackers could still be here, maybe in my apartment, waiting for me, the ransackee, to come home. I don't care. I have no weapons and I'm no brawler, but if there really are goons and they're upstairs, I'll hit as hard as I can give. And then hit them harder.

My apartment got the same treatment. Door is open. This entry was rougher. The door is splintered by the knob and hangs by one hinge. I knock it off its last thread, put it out of its misery. I turn on the lights. I'm alone, I can tell. The TV is gone and so is my laptop. CD towers, bookcases, pictures, lamps, and everything else flipped, kicked, or stomped over. Into the kitchen, and all those drawers are turned out on the floor. The dish didn't run away with the spoon.

I can't face the crime scene waiting for me in the bedroom, so I stumble back to the living room and my couch. I brush off the debris of my life and sit. Cigarette comes out next. Guess I can just use the floor for an ashtray.

I still have the pictures in my coat. I still have my cell phone. I'm going to make one personal call before letting the police know about the sledgehammer tap dance through my building.

I call Jennifer's number. Yeah, I still have that too. She doesn't answer. I wasn't expecting her to. I get her voice mail.

I say, "Hey, thanks for the setup tonight, Jennifer. I hope your dad and his boys had a great time tearing through my place. I knew that was the only reason why you'd eat dinner with me. Tell those guys sorry I didn't have anything good in the fridge for them, and that they had to leave empty-handed."

My voice sounds drunker than I thought. I'm crying too. Practically in full blubber mode, but there's no stopping my message from a bottle.

"So, yeah, I know you were lying to me the whole night. That's okay, because I lied to you too. I said I didn't remember what I felt like before my accident, before I became the narcoleptic me. I remember what it felt like. I was awake, always awake. I didn't miss anything. I could read books for more than a few pages at a time. I didn't smoke. I watched movies from start to finish in real goddamn theaters. Wouldn't even leave my seat to go to the bathroom. I stayed up late on purpose. Woke up and went to sleep when I wanted. Sleep was my pet, something I controlled, scheduled, took for walks. Sit up, roll over, lie down, stay down, give me your fucking paw. Not now. Now there's only me and everything else is on the periphery, just slightly out of reach or out of touch or out of time. I don't have a real career or a real life. Ellen supports me and I sleepwalk through the rest. I'm telling you this because I want you to know who you set up tonight. And there's more. Not done.

Not yet. I remember what it was like to have a regular face, one that folks just glanced at and forgot. There's more. I remember everything I lost. That's what I remember. The loss and loss and loss. . . ."

I stop talking. Too much self-pity, even for me. I'm sure her voice mail stopped recording a long time ago. Who knows how much she got? Who knows what I actually said out loud?

I slouch onto the arm of the couch, cell phone balanced on my head. I'm listening to the digitized silence and it brings an odd comfort. My cigarette slips out of my hand. Hopefully it'll land on something that doesn't take fire personally.

The sleep is coming. I feel it. At least this time, I want it.

EIGHTEEN

The sun shines bright, just like the ones on cereal boxes. Tim and I are in our backyard in Osterville. He's putting tools back in the shed, then emerges with a hand trowel. It's the specialized hand trowel. He locks the shed. I'm still too young to go inside. I wait by the door and receive my brown paper bag and the pat on my head. Good boy. It's time to clean up the yard again. The grass is green but there's more shit than usual to clean up.

The sky is such a light shade of blue, it looks thin, like it could tear at the slightest scratch. I don't feel like singing for Tim today, but I will. I'm a trouper. I give him a round of "Take Me Out to the Ball Game." My bag gets heavy with deposits. He names the dogs. We've all been here before.

We fill three bags' worth of crap and dump it all in the woods behind our property. Each time he dumps the bag, Tim says, "Don't come back."

We walk back to the shed and Tim opens the doors. He says, "So, kid, whaddaya think?"

I twist my foot in the grass and look down. The five-year-old me has something uncomfortable to say. "That friend of yours, Billy Times, he's been a real douche bag to me, Tim."

Tim laughs, bends to one knee, and chucks my chin with his fist.

Aw shucks, Dad.

He says, "He's not all bad." He gets up and locks the shed doors. Tim picks me up and puts me on his shoulders. I'm closer to the cereal-box sun and the paper-thin sky now, close enough to destroy everything if I wanted to.

NINETEEN

The South Boston police know of me like the residents of Sesame Street know of Aloysius Snuffleupagus. They know my name and they tell exaggerated stories of my woe and comic-tragic circumstance, but only some big yellow dope believes I'm real. And I am real.

It's about 11 a.m. The morning after. Two officers, one female and one male, cop A and cop B, walk around my apartment and office. They take notes. They're dressed in their spotless blue uniforms, hats, guns, cuffs, shiny badges, the works.

I wear a hangover. It's three sizes too big. I'd take it back if I could, but it matches my rusty joints and blindingly sore muscles so well.

Okay, I'm still in my own rumpled slept-in-again uniform: work clothes doubling as a lounge-about bathrobe. Everyone should be so lucky.

I sit on home base, the couch, a coffee cup in one hand, a lit cigarette in the other. There's sunlight coming through the naked windows, trapping dust in the rays. I watch the pieces of my apartment floating there in the light. I can't float. I have to squint. I can't squint and think at the same time.

Think, Genevich. First, I decide that yesterday really was only one day. My aching and quivering muscles are proof of my yellow-brick-road jaunt to Sullivan's house. No idea who the body was or, if I'm willing to be completely honest with myself today, if there even was a body. No computer or laptop means, for now, no way to find out what happened. I could call Sullivan's number, but I'm not ready to call yet. I think I can be patient. Play it a little slow, given the current set of circumstances, which is my already broken world breaking at my feet.

Cop A asks for my written statement. I give it to her. It has some stray ashes on it but no burn holes. I grope for the little victories. I told them what's missing and now they have it in writing too. They didn't ask if I thought the break-in was related to one of my cases, which is fine, because I haven't decided how I would answer that question.

More from yesterday's log: The shepherd's-pie doggie bag is on the floor, in front of my bedroom door. It's safe there. My cell phone has my dialed numbers and incoming call history. Proof of my chats with Jennifer right there on the glowing LCD screen, including my late-night soliloquy. She hasn't called back. I don't expect her to.

The police haven't been very chatty or sympathetic. They didn't like that my distress call occurred more than ten hours after the actual break-in. And I think they believed the puke next to the couch and puddle of urine in the corner of the kitchen was somehow my fault. I told them it wasn't. Cop B said I smelled drunk. I said I was drunk, but the puke and piss weren't mine.

The cops leave, finally. My cigarette is dead. I'm left with a trashed office and apartment and more than a few choice items stolen. None of this is circumstantial or coincidence. The DA has a good reason to want those pictures, something more than their chance resemblance to his daughter.

Right about now I'm starting to feel a boulder of guilt roll up onto my shoulders when thinking about Sullivan and his possible or likely fate. Sullivan asked me in a panic if I had shown anyone the pictures yet without finding *it*. I did show them, and I certainly don't have *it*. I took the photos to the DA and then everything that was yesterday happened. I'm that portable Kraken again. Point me in a direction and I unleash my destruction.

"Jesus H. Christ, what happened? Mark, are you in here?"

Ellen. I haven't called her yet. Her voice is on a three-alarm pitch and frequency. It rockets up the stairwell and into my apartment. My hangover appreciates the nuances in its swells of volume.

I shout, "I'm okay and I'm up here, Ellen." I shouldn't be talking, never mind yelling.

Ellen pounds up the stairs, repeating her What-happeneds and sprinkling in some Are-you-all-rights. Maybe I should go into the kitchen and cover the urine puddle with something, but I don't think I can get up.

Ellen stands in the doorway. Her mouth is open as wide as her eyes.

I say, "I know. Friggin' unbelievable mess, isn't it?"

"My God, Mark, what happened? Why the hell didn't you call me?" She looks and sounds hurt. It's not a look I see on her often. I don't like it. It turns that maybe boulder of guilt for Sullivan into the real deal.

I still can't tell her the truth about the case, though. Telling her anything might infect her, put her in more danger than she already is just for being around me. I'm her dark cloud. I'm her walk under a ladder and her broken mirror all in one.

I say, "I went out last night, treated myself to a meal and a few drinks at Amrheins, and found the place like this when I came home. I was a little tipsy and fell asleep on the couch before I could call you or the police. For what it's worth, the police weren't too happy that I didn't call them earlier either."

"You should've called as soon as you woke up." She stands in the doorway with her arms folded across her chest.

"I'm sorry, Ellen. Really, I am." This is getting to be a little too much for me. The edges are blurring again. I put my head in my hands and let slip: "I don't know what I'm going to do."

She says, "About what? Are you in some kind of trouble?" She hikes over the rubble of my existence. There's no path and she has to climb. She makes it, though, sits next to me on the couch, and puts an arm around my shoulder.

I breathe loudly. She waits for me to stop. I say, "No, I'm fine. You know, just how am I going to clean up and get everything going again?"

She says, "We have insurance. I'll get an adjuster here within the hour. We'll get everything fixed up."

We let silence do its thing for a bit. Then I tell her what was stolen. She pulls out a cigarette for both of us. Time passes, whether I want it to or not.

Ellen gets up and says, "I'll call the insurance company, and I'll get somebody to clean this up. You go pack a bag while I make a few phone calls."

I say, "Bag? I'm not going anywhere."

Ellen knows I don't mean it. She says, "You'll stay with me while the place is fixed up. Just a couple of days, right?"

Living at home again for a couple of days. Yeah, Ellen owns this building but it's still my apartment, my place. I promised myself after the accident I'd never live in Osterville, not for day one, because Thomas Wolfe had the whole you-can't-go-home-again thing right.

"Nah, I can stay in a hotel or something."

"Don't be ridiculous, Mark."

I want to say: Look at this place. Look at me. I am ridiculous.

I say, "Couple of days. Okay. Thanks, Ellen. I owe you."

Ellen shakes her head and says, "You don't owe me anything." Her voice is real quiet, not a whisper, but the words have lost all conviction and they are empty.

I get up real slow, then groan and grumble my way to the kitchen. Ellen already has someone on her cell phone. She's a hummingbird of chatter.

Now that I'm up and semimoving, I realize a trip back to

the Cape won't be all bad. Not at all. A couple of days out of Southie might turn down the heat. Maybe I can make another trip to the Sullivan house via the Osterville library. Maybe I'll be safer down there too. Regardless of the maybe goons sighting I had down there, at least I'll be out of the DA's jurisdiction.

Instead of packing a bag, I try to be real quiet while filling the sink with hot water and prying the mop out from under my banana tree, spice rack, and wooden cutlery block. Discreet and mopping up piss generally aren't partners, but I give it my best shot. The job doesn't take long. The puke can be someone else's gig.

Ellen is still on the phone. I go into my bedroom and pack the proverbial bag. When I come out of the room, she's off the phone. I say, "Who were you calling?"

She tells me. Ellen has already rallied the local restaurateurs and some fellow members of the Lithuania Club to set up a nightly neighborhood watch, just like that. Her buddy Sean is going to print T-shirts and window stickers.

I tell her I feel safer already.

She says, "I just have to run to the bank and check in with Millie before we go south, okay?"

I hold out a be-my-guest hand and say, "That's fine. No rush." I'm so magnanimous.

Ellen studies me. I'm the lesson that never gets learned. She says, "Who do you think did this?"

"Terrorists." I adjust the duffel bag on my shoulder, but it's for show. There isn't much in it.

She lights another cigarette but doesn't offer me one. That means I'm in trouble. She says, "When I first came in here I assumed it was local punks. Vandalism and grab-the-new-TV-and-computer type of thing. I know it happens all the time. There was a break-in like this a couple of weeks ago on Gold Street, remember?"

I say, "Yeah," even though I don't.

Ellen walks toward the apartment door but doesn't take her eyes off me.

I say, "I told the police I thought it was vandals."

She says, "Did you?"

"Yeah, Ellen. I did."

She taps the broken front door gently with her foot. The door doesn't move. It's dead. "Is there anything going on that I need to know about, Mark?"

"I got absolutely nothing for you, Ellen." I say it with conviction.

TWENTY

Ellen has been in my apartment twice a week every week for the past eight years, but I don't remember the last time I set foot in the old family bungalow. Was it at Christmas two years ago maybe? No, she had me down for a cookout last summer, I think. I helped her set up her new grill. Isn't that right?

Doesn't matter, the place is the same. It's stuck in time, like me.

There're only five rooms: living room, dining room, kitchen, and two bedrooms with a shared bathroom. There isn't a lot of furniture, and none of it is permanent. Everything is an antique that's in rotation with other unsold antiques from Ellen's store. The rotation usually lasts about six months. Right now, in the dining room there's a waist-high hutch and a wooden table with only two chairs, both pushed in tight, afraid to lose track of the table. A rocking chair sits in the living room with a white wicker couch, its cushion faded and flat. Everything is too hard to sit on, nothing just right.

The most notable aspect of chez Genevich is the army of old black-and-white photos that cover the walls and sit on the hutch and the windowsills and almost anything above the floor with a flat, stable surface. There are photos of buildings in Southie and landscapes from Osterville. There are photos of obscure relatives and friends, or relatives and friends who've become obscure. Those are photos that belonged to Ellen's mother or that Ellen took herself, and mixed in—and likely more than half now—are photos of complete strangers. Ellen continually adds to her photo collection by snatching up random black-and-whites from yard sales and antiques shops.

Whenever I'm here, Ellen gives me a tour of the photos, telling me all their names, or stories if they have no names, and if no stories, then where she bought them. I don't remember any of it.

None of the pictures are labeled. I don't know how she remembers who are our relatives and who are the strangers. Everyone has similar mustaches or hairstyles and they wear the same hats and jackets, T-shirts and skirts. Maybe Ellen forgets everyone and just makes up the stories on the spot, giving them all new secret histories.

I think she moves and switches the pictures around too, just like the rotating furniture. I think the picture of my apartment building was in the kitchen the last time I was here. Now it's in the living room.

Me? I'm in the kitchen. So is Ellen. It's late but not late enough. I smoke. She sits and thinks. We drink tea, and we're surrounded by those old photos and old faces, everyone anonymous to me, everyone probably dead, maybe like Brendan Sullivan.

Ellen stirs her tea with a finger. She's quite the charming hostess. She says, "Feeling okay?"

"I'm peachy." I'm not peachy. I'm not feeling any fruit in particular. The narcoleptic me is taking over more often. The symptoms are getting worse. Dr. Heal-Thyself thinks it's the case and the face-to-faces with the Times clan, the stress of confrontation, that's setting me off. Before the photos landed on my desk like some terrorizing band of Cossacks, I had a hypnogogic hallucination maybe once a month. Now it's daily. I can't go on like this much longer. I need a vacation from the case I don't have.

Ellen adds more honey to her tea and stirs counterclockwise, as if she could reset the tea to its beginning. She licks her finger, and it sounds downright messy.

"Ever hear of a spoon, Ellen? Newest gadget going. Not too expensive, user-friendly too." I shoot smoke at her.

She wipes her hand on a napkin and says, "You don't sound peachy. You seem a little extra frazzled."

"Other than my home and office being put in a blender and set to puree, I'm just fine."

I'm growing more desperate. I'm actually contemplating telling Ellen everything. I'll tell her to avoid the DA and large men with cell phones in their ears. Maybe she could inspect my photos. She's the expert. She'd be able to tease and wiggle something out of the pictures, something I'm not seeing, or at least tell me when the photos were shot, how old they are.

She gets up from the kitchen table. Her chair's legs argue

with the hardwood floors. "There's a picture I want to show you."

"Anyone who had the under on five-minutes-before-the-picture-tour is a winner," I say.

"Don't be a jerk. Come on. It's in the living room."

We walk through the dining room, past the collection of little bits of history, someone else's lost moments. All those forgotten eyes are staring at me, a houseful of Mona Lisas giving me the eye. Christ, I'm a mess. I need some sleep. Some real sleep.

Living room. We walk to one of the front windows. She plucks a photo from the windowsill. She says, "It's the only one I could find with both of them in it," and hands it to me.

Three preteen kids sit on the front stoop of an apartment building, presumably from the Harbor Point projects. It's summer in Southie. The boys have buzz cuts and gaps in their smiles and skinned knees. They all wear white socks and dark-colored sneakers, shoelaces with floppy loops.

The kid in the middle is the biggest, and he has his arms wrapped roughly around the necks of the other two boys. The kid on the right has his head craned away, trying to break out of the hug turned headlock. The kid on the left has his rabbit ears out but didn't get his hand up over his friend quick enough. The one trying to break away is my father, Tim.

I say, "I've probably seen this a hundred times but never really looked at it. That's Tim there, right?"

"That's him. He was a cutie." Ellen is talking about Tim.

A Halley's Comet rare occurrence. "You looked just like him when you were a kid."

That's not true. I looked more like Ellen. Now I look like nobody.

Tim has dark brown hair, almost black. The other two kids have much lighter whiffle stubble and skin. I say, "So that's DA Times in the middle, right?"

"Yup."

Smack in the middle. The ringleader. The hierarchy of neighborhood authority is clear. The other two boys might as well have deputy badges on their T-shirts. Even back then he had his two goons.

The Tim in the picture, the kid so obviously owned by Times, does not jibe with the Tim of my dreams. Tim is a large, confident man in my dreams who can take care of himself and everyone else, especially the kid me, maybe even the narcoleptic me.

I'm embarrassed for this Tim. This is like seeing him with his pants down. This is like finding him sitting and crying in a room by himself. I don't want any part of this Tim, the Tim that DA Times obviously still remembers, given his strong-arm tactics with me.

I say, "Who's the third kid?"

Ellen says, "Brendan Sullivan. For a while there, those boys were never apart. They were practically brothers."

My stomach fills with mutant-sized butterflies. Their wings cut and slash my stomach. Neurons and synapses sputter and fire, and I can actually feel the electricity my body generates amping too high, pumping out too much wattage too soon, and the circuit breaker flips, shutting me off and down. Not a blackout, though. This is worse. I'll be awake and I'll know what's going on. This is cataplexy.

I crumble toward the floor, my head pitching forward and into Ellen's legs. She falls back into the window and sits on the sill, knocking pictures to the floor. I'm going to join them. Nothing works except my thoughts. I can't move or speak. My bulk slides down her legs and I land facedown, my nose pinned against the frame of a picture.

Ellen isn't panicking; she's seen this before. She says, "Are you all right, Mark?" repeatedly, a mantra, something to help her through my attack.

I'm not all right. I'm paralyzed. Maybe this time I won't recover. I'll be stuck like this forever, lying in Ellen's bungalow, facedown, on a photo.

She lifts my head and shoulders off the ground. One of the pictures below my face is of an old guy in a bait-and-tackle shop. I have no idea who it is or if I'm supposed to know. He's likely someone she picked up antiquing. He's been collected by Ellen. He wears a dark-colored winter hat, a turtleneck stretched tight across his chest, suspenders, and hip waders. Maybe he's going clamming, or he already went. He's looking at the camera, looking at me, and holding up something, some bit of unidentifiable fishing gear. It's pointed toward his temple, and from my prone vantage point it looks like a gun. The other picture is the one of my father, DA Times, and Brendan

Sullivan, and I can't look at it without new, cresting waves of panic crashing. I'm in big trouble.

Ellen kicks the pictures away and rolls me onto my back. She feels my cheeks and snaps her fingers in front of my eyes. I see them and hear them, but I can't do anything about them.

All I can do is lie here until the circuits cool and I reboot. Thinking about Tackle Man might help. Why not? He's a ghost, and he can't hurt me or Ellen.

Tim Genevich or Billy Times or Brendan Sullivan, on the other hand? They can hurt us, and they are here now, in the bungalow and in my case.

TWENTY-ONE

Recovery. I'm sitting in the rocking chair, holding the same cup of tea I left in the kitchen. It's warm. Maybe Ellen stirred mine counterclockwise. I hope she used a spoon.

I say, "Can I see that picture of Tim again?" My voice is a cicada's first call after its seventeen-year slumber. After cicadas wake up, they live for only a day or two and then are usually eaten by something.

Ellen sits on the wicker couch with the picture pressed into her lap, protecting it from disaster. She can't protect them. She nods and hands it to me.

I get another good look at the three friends. Tim is part of the case. He has to be. He's why Sullivan sent me the pictures. Times is why Sullivan didn't want me to show the pictures to anyone without finding the *it* first, and yeah, I screwed up that part, just a wee bit. I owe it to Sullivan to see this thing through to the bitter end, probably my own bitter end. I'm going to keep swinging, keep fighting those windmills.

I say, "When did you meet Tim?" I wiggle my toes as a reassurance. For the moment, I'm back behind the controls.

Ellen and I are going to chat about Tim and the boys tonight. We never talk about Tim. He's never been the elephant in our room. He's always been bigger.

Ellen smiles. The smile is lost and far away, lips unsure of their positions. She says, "When he was twelve. Tim and his friends hung around Kelleys on Castle Island, bugging me for free ice cream. I only gave it to Tim. He wasn't as obnoxious as the other two, which wasn't saying much. The three of them were such pains in the ass back then. Hard to believe Billy became a DA."

"Can't disagree with you there." I look at the picture and focus on the Brendan Sullivan kid. Never mind Tackle Man, here's the real ghost—or, at least, the latest model. "These guys all lived in Harbor Point together, right?"

"That's right." Ellen isn't looking at me. Her arms are wound tightly around her chest, a life jacket of arms. I'm interviewing a hostile witness.

I say, "That was a rough neighborhood, right?"

"Roughest in Southie. It's where Whitey Bulger and his boys got their start."

Whitey Bulger. Not crazy about hearing Boston's most notorious—and still on the lam—gangster name getting dropped. I'm not crazy about any of this. Especially since the early-to-mid-seventies time line for Bulger's rise coincides with Tim's teen days. I say, "Did Tim know Whitey at all?"

"Everyone knew of Whitey back then, but no, Tim never talked or bragged about knowing him. Billy, though, he would talk big to all us neighborhood kids, stuff about him helping out and doing little jobs for Bulger. Tim always told me he just liked to talk. He probably hasn't changed a bit," Ellen says, and laughs, but the laugh is sad. It has pity for everyone in it, including herself. She sits on the edge of the couch. She might fall off. She wants the picture back. She's afraid of what I might do to it.

I say, "Was Times really all talk? He wasn't connected at all to Bulger? You know that for sure?"

To her credit, Ellen thinks about it. She doesn't give me the quick, pat answer. "Yes, I'm sure," she says. "There's no way he messed around with Bulger. Tim would've told me. What, you think Billy Times is dirty?" Ellen scowls at me, the idea apparently less believable to her than the shooter on the grassy knoll.

"No. I don't think anything like that."

Whitey Bulger took over the Winter Hill Gang in the mid-to-late seventies. He was smart. He didn't sell the drugs or make the loans or bankroll the bookies. He charged the local urban entrepreneurial types a Bulger fee to stay in business. He later took advantage of FBI protection and contacts to get away with everything, including murder, for decades. The Whitey Bulger name still echoes in South Boston. He's our bogeyman, which means we all know his stories.

This isn't going where I wanted it to. This isn't about Bulger. Ellen still isn't giving me any real information about Tim and his friends.

Then this question bubbles up out of nowhere. I don't like it. The answer might hurt. I say, "Wait a minute. Was this picture taken before you met Tim?"

"Oh, yeah. The boys are like nine or ten, maybe eleven. This is actually the first picture your father ever took. He used a tripod, a timer, and the whole bit. Then his uncle taught him how to develop it."

"Wait, wait, wait." This story is wrong. Ellen is the one with the uncle who taught her to develop pictures, not Tim. I rub my face. My beard resists my fingers. It has grown a year's worth in a matter of days. I feel the house of pictures around me, ready to fall. "You've always told me that you took these pictures, except for the antique buys." I manage a weak gesture at the legion of black-and-white photos that surround us.

There's this look I get all the time from other people, people who don't know me and haven't come close to earning the goddamn right to give me that look. The look is why I stopped talking to Juan-Miguel or any of my old roommates, even when they tried to keep in contact with me.

Ellen has never given me that look, even when seeing or finding me at my worst, but she's giving me that look now. Eyebrows pull down hard like they're planning on taking over her eyelids. Her mouth opens, lip curls. The goddamn look: concern trying to mask or hide scorn. Mashed potatoes spread over the lima beans. You can't hide scorn. Ellen looks at me like I'm wrong, like I'm broken. And nothing will ever be the same.

She says, "You're pulling my leg, right, Mark? Tim took those pictures—"

I jump in, a cannonball dive that'll get everyone wet. "It has been a long day, a long week, a long year, a long goddamn lifetime. I'm not pulling your leg."

She says, "I know, I know. But—"

"What do you mean, Tim took most of these? Tim didn't take pictures. He was a handyman, an odd-job guy, not a photographer. That's you. It's your job. You're the shutterbug. And goddamn it, stop fucking looking at me like that."

It's her turn to put her face in her hands, maybe try to wipe that look off her face. She must feel it. I do. She backs off. "Calm down, Mark, you're just a little confused. Tim was the photographer first, remember? When he died, I took his equipment and started my business. You know all this, Mark, don't you?"

"No. I don't know all this. You assume I know everything about Tim when you never talk about him. You tell me more about these photographs than you do about my father. That's all he is to me, an image. There's nothing there, and it's your fault for not telling me. You've never talked about Tim. Never." It all comes out and it's a mess, just like me. I know it's not fair. It's more likely that me and my broken brain have jumbled everything around, putting the bits and pieces of the past into the wrong but convenient boxes, but I'm not giving in.

I say, "This is not my fault. I did not fuck up my father's past. No one has told me anything. This is not something you can pin on me. No one told me any of this. No one. Not you." Even if it isn't true, repeat the lie enough times and it becomes true.

Ellen holds steady, battens down the hatches, and makes it through my storm. She says, "Okay, okay. I'm sorry. I just assumed you know everything about Tim. You're right, I haven't told you enough about him." She stops short, brakes squealing and coffee spilling. She doesn't believe her own words. We're both liars, trying to get our stories straight.

She lights two cigarettes and gives me one. We're tired and old. She says, "So ask away. What do you want to know?"

"Let's start with telling me about him and you and photography."

She tells me. Despite having no money and living in a project, Tim had a surprising amount of photo and film equipment. Yeah, he might've stolen some of it, but most of it came from locals who swapped their old projectors and cameras for Tim's odd jobs, and he'd scour flea markets and moving sales. He would sell pictures to locals and store owners, not charging much, just enough to buy more film, always black-and-white because it was cheaper, and Tim always insisted it looked nicer. Their first kiss happened in a makeshift darkroom. She only got into photography after they were married. She still has all of Tim's equipment and displays it in her shop. She talked through both of our cigarettes.

I say, "Let's look at more of Tim's pictures." I stand up and my legs are foal-unsteady. I'm learning to walk again.

We go on yet another tour of the pictures, but with a different road map and guide this time. We're walking through Tim's history, which has always been a secret. Ellen starts the tour subdued but gains enthusiasm as we progress. We are progressing. She shows me an aunt who lost a foot and three fingers to diabetes. There's Tackle Man again; he was a great-uncle of Tim's, a fisherman who died at sea. Almost everyone I meet is dead, but they have names.

Ellen keeps going, but I stop and hover at Great-uncle Tackle Man's photo. There's something else there. Three letters: LIT, in the photo's background, written on a small square of paper taped to the glass counter. I've seen those letters before, I think, in another photo, written on the spine of a book.

I'm still holding the photo of Tim and the gang. They're all still there, on the stairs, waiting for me patiently. I look and I look and I look, and there, on the stairs, under Tim's string-skinny legs, written in chalk, the letters are two or three inches high. LIT. I want to open the frame and run my fingers over the scene, feel the chalk.

Ellen stops in the hallway just ahead of me and walks back. "What's up, Mark?"

Trying to remain calm is difficult when my heart is an exploding grenade in my chest. I say, "Just noticing the letters LIT in these two pictures." I should've noticed them earlier. It's a scratch on a new car. It's the mole on somebody's face.

Ellen laughs and says, "That's Tim's signature. He'd hide the letters LIT, for Lithuania, somewhere in the background of almost all his pictures. Your father was never subtle."

I smile. I'm going to check all the pictures, every picture in the house, maybe every picture in Osterville, before I recheck the photos that are burning inside their manila envelope.

I pick up the next picture. It's a shot of a tall-grass meadow with one tree set back, not quite center in framing. I don't see the letters anywhere. I'm frantic looking for them. Maybe in the bark of the tree but the tree is too far away. Time as distance.

Ellen says, "Tim didn't take that one. I bought this last summer. I like how the tree isn't quite centered. Initially it has an amateur look to it, but I think the photographer did it on purpose. Gives it an eccentric feel. I like it."

"Why do you buy these antique pictures, Ellen?"

She doesn't answer right away. She pulls out her lighter but only flips it open and then closed. There's no fire. Ellen isn't comfortable because I'm asking her to be vulnerable.

She gives me time to make up her answer. Either she can't bring herself to throw away or pack up Tim's pictures so she mixes them in with antiques, hiding Tim's work in plain sight, distance by numbers instead of time; or she's pretending that Tim is still around, taking photos, the new ones she buys continuing their silent, unspoken conversation.

Ellen shrugs. "It's hard to explain. It's just a hobby, I guess. I like the way the black-and-white photos look. Aren't most hobbies hard to explain? Can a stamp collector tell you why she collects stamps?"

I say, "I don't know any stamp collectors."

It's all I can do to keep myself from pulling out the manila envelope in front of Ellen, ripping it open, and checking the photos for Tim's signature. I can't do that. I'll have to wait until she goes to bed. The less she knows, the better off she'll be. This case is getting too dangerous; or, to be more accurate, it already was dangerous and I didn't know any better.

Still, my hands vibrate with want. So instead, I snatch the lighter out of her fist and light up a cigarette. The smoke isn't black or white, but gray.

TWENTY-TWO

I'm in my bedroom, sitting at the edge of my bed, manila envelope on the bedspread. The door is shut. Ellen is watching TV. I'd check my closet for monsters, but I'm afraid I'd find one.

I open the envelope. No more monster talk. Now I'm thinking about letters, the molecules of sentences and songs, the bricks of words. Letters, man, letters. They might mean everything or nothing at all.

Letters are everywhere: the DA's waiting room with stacks of magazines and newspapers; the Osterville library, filled with dusty volumes that haven't been read in generations; Southie with its billboards and their screaming ten-feet-tall words; with stenciled script and cursive etchings on pub windows and convenience-store signage; on the unending stream of bills and circulars filling my PO box, and the computer and the Internet and all those sites and search engines and databases and spam e-mails; television; lost pet signs; the tags on my clothing; my yellow notepad that ran away from home.

How many letters are in the whole bungalow, or the town,

or the state, or the country? An infinite sum of letters forming words in every language. Someone at one time or another
wrote all those letters but, unlike their bodies, their armies
of letters live on, like swarms of locusts bearing long-dead
messages of happiness or doom or silliness. And hell, I've
only been thinking about print letters. How many letters do
I speak in a day, then multiply that by a lifetime of days, then
by billions of lifetimes, and add that to our written-letter
count and we're drowning in an uncountable number. We're
the billions of monkeys typing at the billions of typewriters.

Okay. I'm stalling when I don't have time to stall. Let's cut
the infinite number down to three. I'm afraid of three letters.
LIT. I'm afraid I'll see them and afraid that I won't.

First up, the topless photo. I need to reacquaint myself. I
haven't looked at the pictures in days, but with all the little
sleeps between viewings it feels like months. The woman looks
less like Jennifer Times. The photo is now clearly over thirty-
five years old. Perspective makes detective work easy. It's a
hard-earned perspective.

I look. I don't find any letters. The camera is angled up, shot
from a vantage point slightly below the subject. There isn't
much background to the photo. Ceiling, empty wall, tips of
bedposts, the top of the bookcase. The white light above the
woman washes out everything that isn't the woman. I keep
looking, keep staring into the light.

When I come to, I'm horizontal on the bed, legs hanging
off like loose thread on clothing. The photos are on the floor. I

go to the floor, crawl on my hands and knees. Maybe I should check for monsters under my bed, but I'm afraid I'd find one. I'm starting this all over again.

I pick up the fully clothed photo. She's wearing her white T-shirt and skirt. The camera angle is played straight. No ceiling light. There is nothing on the walls behind her, nothing on the bed. There's the bookcase in the left background. It holds books like a good bookcase should.

LIT is there, written on that book, across the bottom of its spine. Tim's signature. Tim's photograph.

The bungalow is quiet, the TV dead. Ellen must be asleep. I don't have a clock in my room. There are no pictures on the walls, only small shelves with assorted knickknacks. I put both photos back in the envelope and go to bed. I shut the light off but I probably won't be able to sleep. There's no one to tuck me in, and there are too many monsters in this room.

TWENTY-THREE

It's morning, I think. The sun is out. Good for the sun. I'm walking down the hallway, the corridor of photos, Tim's memories, everything adding up to a story with some twist ending.

I can't stay here today or for the days after. I have to get out soon, back to Southie. Despite everything I learned last night, agreeing to stay here for the rest of the week is a mistake. I'd rather sleep on the rubble of my life back in Southie than spend another night here. At least then I can be a failure in my own home. And I am going to solve this case if for nothing more than to prove to myself that I can do something, something real, something that has effects, repercussions, something to leave a mark. Mark Genevich was here.

Ellen is in the kitchen sitting with what looks like a week's worth of local newspapers spread out on the table, splashy circulars all mixed in with the black-and-white text. She cradles one steaming coffee mug in her hands, and there're two more full mugs on the counter. I hope one of them is mine.

There's sunlight everywhere in the kitchen, and not enough

shadow. Ellen doesn't look up. "You're not going to believe this."

I say, "Someone is having a sale on clown pants." The coffee is scalding hot, as if it knew exactly when I would be awake. That makes one of us.

Ellen throws a bit of folded-up newspaper at me. I don't catch it and it bounces off my chest.

"Hey! Watch the coffee, crazy lady." The microwave's digital clock has green digits that flash the wrong time. Ellen never sets the thing. Told you she was crazy.

She says, "I was just catching up, reading yesterday's newspaper, and found that."

I pick up the front page of the local rag. Headline: OSTER-VILLE MAN COMMITS SUICIDE. Included is a head shot, and the article identifies the man as Brendan Sullivan, age fifty. I don't see that twelve-year-old I was introduced to last night inside the head shot. This Brendan Sullivan is bald, has jowls a Saint Bernard would envy, and thick glasses, thicker than Ellen's. Apparently, he put a handgun under his chin and pulled the trigger. He leaves behind his wife, Janice; no children. He was an upstanding citizen. Neighbors said he kept to himself, drove tractor trailers, and did a little gardening. Sad story. One that's impossible to believe.

I wish I had a shocked reaction at the ready for Ellen, something I kept like a pet and could let out on command. Instead, I give my honest reaction, a big sigh of relief. Yeah, my buffoon-ery in the DA's office probably killed this man, but now I have confirmation that Sullivan was the body I saw. And what I saw was what I saw, not a hallucination. That counts for something, right?

I say, "Isn't that odd." I've never been very smooth.

Ellen puts down the rest of her newspaper, the afterthought folded and stacked neatly. This might be her moment of epiphany, bells ringing and seraphim floating in her head. Ellen knows there's something going on. She might even think I know more than I know. I'll have to get her on her heels, put some questions out there, keep her from grilling me like a hot dog. I'd crack in record time under her interrogation lamp.

I say, "Did you know that Sullivan was living in Osterville?"

Ellen blinks, loses her train of thought, at least for the moment, and says, "What? No, no. I had no idea. The article says he'd bounced around the Cape, but I never ran into him."

"Strange."

"It gets stranger. I called Aunt Millie to tell her about poor Brendan, and she told me she saw him in Southie last week."

I squeeze the coffee mug and it doesn't squeeze back. "No kidding. Where?"

"She saw him in CVS on West Broadway. She said, 'Hi, Brendan,' and he just said a quick 'Hi' back, but he was in a hurry, left the store, and headed out into that terrible rain last week, remember? She said he started off toward East Broadway."

He was walking toward my office. He was coming to meet me but got the narcoleptic me instead. The narcoleptic me accepted his pictures and wrote down notes on a yellow pad but didn't forward any other pertinent information, especially the promise to not show anyone the photos until I'd found *it*.

I make some toast. Ellen has an old two-slice toaster that burns the sides unevenly. The bell rings and the bread smokes. In the fridge is margarine instead of butter. I hate margarine.

Ellen says, "I'm actually leaving soon because I have a kiddie shoot at eleven. I was going to let you sleep, but now that you're awake, what do you want to do today? Feel like manning the antiques section for a while? I'll open it up if you want."

I haven't been here twenty-four hours and she's already trying to get me to work for her. At least these questions are ones I can answer. I say, "I'll pass on antiquing." Don't know if she noticed, but I have the Sullivan account folded under my arm. I'm taking it with me. "You can drop me at the library again. I've got work I can do there."

She says, "I didn't know you brought any work."

I down the rest of the coffee, scalding my gullet. A ball of warmth radiates in my stomach; it shifts and moves stuff around. "I'm not on vacation, Ellen, and this isn't Disney World. I do have clients who depend on me." I'm so earnest I almost believe it myself, at least until I drop the newspaper. It lands heads with the blazing headline facing up.

Ellen peers over the table. We both stare at the newspaper on the floor as if waiting for it to speak. Maybe it already has. She says, "I think you can take a few days off. Your clients would understand." It sounds angry, accusatory. She knows I'm keeping something from her.

"Sorry, the work—I just can't escape it." I take the toast on a tour of the bungalow. The tour ends where it should, with the photo of Tim, the DA, and Sullivan. Ellen is still inside her newspapers so she doesn't see me lift the photo, frame and all, and slide it inside my coat.

Finally, I have a plan. No more screwing around. The toast approves.

TWENTY-FOUR

I'm tired. I'm always tired; it's part of being me. But this tired is going radioactive. It's being down here in the Cape away from the city. Even when I'm doing nothing in Boston, there's the noise of action, of stuff happening, which helps me push through the tired. Down here, there's nothing but boxes and walls of lost memories.

I don't give Ellen a time to pick me up at the library. I tell her I'm a big boy and I'll make my way downtown eventually. She doesn't argue. Either the fight has momentarily left her or she's relieved to be free of my company. I have that effect on people.

I do an obligatory walk-and-yawn through the library stacks to make sure that I'm seen by the staff, all two of them. It's a weekday, and only moms and their preschoolers are here. The kids stare at me, but their moms won't look.

My cell phone feels like a baseball in my hand, all inert possibility. I have no messages; I knew that before I checked. Then I call Osterville's only off-season cabbie, Steve Brill. He's in the library parking lot two minutes later.

Brill is older than a sand dune and has been eroding for

years. His knuckles are unrolled dice on his fuzzy steering wheel. The cab is an old white station wagon with brown panels and rust, I'm not sure which is which. Duct tape holds together the upholstery, and the interior smells like an egg and cheese sandwich, hold the cheese. A first-class ride.

I say, "Brill, I want you to drive like I'm a tourist."

Although Brill is a regular in Ellen's antiques store and he's met me on a couple of occasions, he isn't much for small talk and gives me nothing but a grunt. Maybe he doesn't like me. Don't know why, as I haven't done anything to him. Yet.

First, we make a quick trip to a florist. Brill waits in the cab with the meter running. I go small and purchase something called the At Peace Bouquet, which is yellow flowers mixed with greens, the sympathy concoction in a small purple vase I can hold in one hand. Me and the peace bouquet hop into the cab.

In the rearview mirror, Brill's eyes are rocks sitting inside a wrinkly bag of skin. The rocks disapprove of something. He says, "What, the big-city PI has a hot date tonight?" Then he cackles. His laughter shakes loose heavy gobs of phlegm in his chest, or maybe chunks of lung. Serves the old bastard right.

I'm nobody's joke. I say, "I have a hot date with your mother."

Brill shuts off the engine but doesn't turn around, just gives me those rocks in the rearview. He says, "I don't care who you think you are, I'm the only one allowed to be an asshole in my cab."

"You're doing a damn fine job of it, Brill. Kudos." I have a fistful of flowers in my hand and I'm talking tough to Rumpelstiltskin. Who am I kidding? I'm everyone's joke.

He says, "I'll throw your ugly ass out of my cab. Don't think I won't. I don't need to give you a ride anywhere."

He's pissing me off, but at least he's getting my juices flowing. I stare at the back of his bald and liver-spotted head. There are wisps of white hair clinging to his scalp, pieces of elderly cotton candy.

I guess he's not going to apply for my personal-driver gig. I have to keep this from escalating. I need his wheels today. "Yeah, I know you can. But you'll give me a ride. Corner of Crystal Lake and Rambler, please."

Brill says nothing. I pull out two cigarettes and offer him one. His nicotine-stained hand snakes behind him, those dice knuckles shaking. He takes the stick and sets it aglow with the dash lighter. He inhales quietly, and the expelled smoke hangs around his head, stays personal.

I say, "Do you know how to get to where I want to go?" I pull out my lighter, flip open the top, and produce my one-inch flame.

Brill says, "I heard you the first time. And no smoking in my cab."

Brill starts up the cab and pulls out of the parking lot. I pocket my cigarette. I won't argue with him. I'm happy to be going somewhere.

Our ride from the florist to Sullivan's house should be short enough that falling asleep isn't really a worry. Knock on wood. The flowers are bothering my eyes and sinuses, though. I try to inhale the secondhand smoke instead. It's stale and spent, just like me and Brill.

He pulls over at the end of Rambler Road, the passenger side of the cab flush up against some bushes. I have to get out on the driver's side, which doesn't feel natural. The old man is screwing with me. He doesn't realize I don't need this shit.

Brill still doesn't turn around. He doesn't have to. He says, "Sad end for that Sullivan fella."

That's interesting. He could be just making small talk, but Brill doesn't do small talk. I'm going to play a hunch here. It sounds like Brill has something to say.

"Ends usually are sad. You know anything about Sullivan?"

Brill shrugs and says, "Maybe."

Even more interesting. I take out a twenty and throw it into the front seat. Brill picks it up quick and stuffs the bill into his front shirt pocket. The shirt is pink. I say, "Talk to me."

Brill says, "He was a quiet, normal guy. I gave him a ride a couple weeks ago to and from Lucky's Auto when his car was on the fritz. He tipped well." He stops. The silence is long enough to communicate some things.

"That's it? That's all you got?" I say it real slow for him, to let him try on the idea that I'm not amused.

He says, "Yeah, that's all I know," then laughs. "It's not my fault if you're playing Mickey Mouse detective."

There's no way this small-town pile of bones is pulling that on me. I may be amateur hour, but I'm not an easy mark. I reach over the bench seat and into his front pocket with my ham-sized fist. It comes back to me with my twenty and interest. I toss the interest back over the seat.

"You motherfucker, stealing from an old man." He still hasn't turned around.

"You know the language, but you wouldn't last a day driving a cab in Boston." It's mean, but it's also true. I add, "You can have the twenty back if you earn it."

He loses some air, deflates behind the wheel. He's a small, shrinking old man, and I don't care. He says, "The day before Sullivan killed himself, he had me pick him up and we just drove around town. I asked him about his car because it was sitting in his driveway, but he brushed me off, seemed agitated, spent most of the time looking out the windows and behind us."

Brill stops again, and he's staring at me. He needs another prompt. I'll provide. "Yeah, and where'd you go?"

"He had me drive by your mother's house. Twice. Second pass he told me to stop, so I did. He was talking low, mumbling stuff."

"What kind of stuff?"

"'Gotta do it yourself, Sullivan,' that kind of thing. He always talked to himself so I didn't pay much attention. He never got out of the cab. I thought he was going to, though. Finally, he told me to take him home. He was all spooked and mumbling the whole way back."

I say, "Did you tell the police any of this?"

"No."

"How about Ellen?"

"No."

"Why not?"

"They didn't ask."

I say, "You mean they didn't gild your lily for the info."

He doesn't say anything. Looking for more bang from my buck, I say, "Kind of strange that he'd be casing her house the day before he offs himself."

Brill shrugs. "I figured Sullivan was cheating on his wife with Ellen. He was acting all paranoid, like a cheat. You know, the cheats are most of my off-season income. I cart them around to their secret lunches and goddamn by-the-hour motels."

Brill paints an alternate scenario in my head, one where Ellen did know Sullivan was living in Osterville and knew him well; secret lunches and other rendezvous. No. That isn't what happened. I dismiss it.

Ellen was genuine in her reaction this morning to the news of Sullivan's Osterville residency and suicide. She has had no contact with him. She wouldn't have shown me the picture of Tim, the DA, and Sullivan if she was playing the other woman with him. Right? I suppose her motivation behind showing me the photo could be a way to introduce me to her new fling, but that's not how it happened, did it? No.

No. The picture was part of her tour, coincidence only. Sullivan came by the bungalow to do his own looking for the fabled *it* because I hadn't come through yet. I have to go on that assumption. It's the only one that fits my case. I don't have the patience or time for curve balls and red herrings.

Still, Brill's cheats spiel shakes me up enough that I'll lie to him. I say, "Ellen doesn't know who Sullivan was. I promise you."

He says, "Maybe. Maybe not. It doesn't matter to me. I don't care what people are up to. I give rides wherever they want to go, and that's it, and everyone knows it. Now give me my twenty bucks, you motherfucker."

I give it to him. Twenty dollars very well spent. I say, "Don't go driving off too far, Brill. I might not be here all that long." I slide across the bench seat and get out. The road is narrow and I'm in its middle, exposed and unprotected.

Brill says, "Are you paying me to wait?"

"No." I pay the fare and add a tip. There's an insistent breeze coming off the nearby water. The individual flowers point in differing directions; they can't agree on anything.

Brill takes my money and doesn't stop to count it. He says, "Then call me later, fuzz face. Maybe I'll answer." Brill spins his rear tires and the station wagon cab speeds away, weaving down Rambler Road. Maybe I didn't tip him enough.

Sullivan's neighborhood is quiet. No one is out. The sun is shining, but it's cold and there are no signs of approaching spring. It's still the long cold winter here. I walk the one hundred feet to Sullivan's house. I have a plan, but I haven't decided what I'm going to do if his wife isn't home.

Looks like I don't have to worry about that. There are three cars in the driveway. One of them is the blue SUV I saw last time. The other two cars are small and of some Japanese make. Neither of them is red.

Okay, Sullivan's wife, Janice, is home but not alone. Alone would've been preferable, but I know such a state isn't likely, given hubby just died. I'm guessing the cars belong to members of the grief squad who swooped in to support her, friends in need and all that.

I walk down the gravel driveway and my feet sound woolly-mammoth heavy. Stones crunch and earth moves under my rumbling weight. I'm the last of some primitive line of prehistoric creatures on his final migration, the one where he dies at the end of the journey, that circle-of-life bullshit that's catchy as a Disney song but ultimately meaningless. Yeah, I'm in a mood.

The house is still white and needs a paint job. I'll try not to bring that up in conversation. I make it to the front door, which is red, and ring the bell. Two chimes. I hold the flowers tight to my chest, playing them close to the vest. This needs to be done right if I'm to learn anything.

When she opens the door, though, I won't take off my hat. No one wants to see that.

TWENTY-FIVE

An old woman answers the door. She might be the same age as Brill the happy cabbie. She's short and hunched, which maximizes her potential for shortness. Her hair is curly and white, so thick it could be a wig.

She says, "Can I help you?" After getting an eyeful of me, she closes the front door a bit, hiding behind the slab of wood. I don't blame her. I don't exactly have a face for the door-to-door gig.

I say, "Yes, hi—um, are you Mrs. Sullivan?"

"No, I'm her Aunt Patty." She wears a light blue dress with white quarter-sized polka dots, and a faux-pearl necklace hangs around her neck. I know the pearls are fake because they're almost as big as cue balls.

Aunt Patty. Doesn't everyone have an Aunty Patty? I give her my best opening statement. "My late father was an old friend of Brendan's. He grew up with Brendan in Southie. When I heard of his passing and the arrangements, saw I wouldn't be able to attend the wake or the funeral, I felt compelled to come down and give my family's condolences in person."

I hope that's enough to win over the jury. I look at her and see conflict. Aunt Patty doesn't know what to do. Aunt Patty keeps looking behind her but there's no one there to talk to, no one to make the decision for her. She's here to cook and clean and help keep the grieving widow safe from interlopers and unwanted distractions. She's here to make sure that grief happens correctly and according to schedule.

I know, because Ellen has been part of so many grief squads in Southie that she might as well register as a professional and rent herself out. Maybe Ellen does it to remember Tim and grieve for him all over again or she's trying to add distance, going through a bunch of little grievings to get over the big one.

I say, "I've come a long way. I won't stay too long, I promise."

That cinches it. Aunt Patty gives me a warm milk smile and says, "Oh, all right, come in. Thank you for coming." She opens the door wide behind her.

I'm in. I say, "You're welcome. Thanks for letting me in. Means a lot. Is Janice doing okay?"

"About as well as can be imagined. She's been very brave." Aunt Patty shuffle-leads me through the dining room, our feet making an odd rhythm on the hardwood floor.

It's dark in here. The shades are drawn over the bay windows. The house is in mourning. It's something I can feel. Sullivan died somewhere in this house. Maybe even the front room. Gun under his chin, bullet into his brain. Coerced or set up or neither, this is serious stuff. I can't screw any of it up.

There are pictures and decorations on the walls, but it's too dark to see them. There are also cardboard boxes on the dining room table. The boxes are brown and sad, both temporary and final.

Aunt Patty limps, favoring her left side, probably a hip. When her hip breaks, she won't make it out of the hospital alive. Yeah, like I said, I'm in a mood.

She says, "What's your name?"

"Mark. Mark Genevich. Nice to meet you, Aunt Patty."

"What nationality?"

"Lithuanian." Maybe I should tell her what I really am: narcoleptic. We narcoleptics have no country and we don't participate in the Olympics. Our status supersedes all notion of nationality. We're neutral, like the Swiss, but they don't trust us with army knives.

She says, "That's nice." My cataloging is a comfort to her. I'm not a stranger anymore; I'm Lithuanian.

The kitchen is big and clean, and bright. The white wallpaper and tile trim has wattage. Flowers fill the island counter. I fight off a sneeze. There are voices, speaking softly to our right. Just off the kitchen is a four-season porch, modestly decorated with a table for four and a large swing seat. Two women sit on the swing seat. The hinges and springs creak faintly in time with the pendulum. One of the women looks just like Aunt Patty, same dress and pool-cue necklace. The other woman does not make three of a kind with the pair of queens.

Patty and I walk onto the porch. The swingers stop swinging; someone turns off the music. The vase of flowers is a dumbbell in my hand.

Aunt Patty says, "That's my twin sister Margaret and, of course, the other beautiful woman is Janice. This is Mark Genevich?" I'm a name and a question. She doesn't remember my opening statement or my purpose. I need to fill in the blanks and fast. I've never been good under pressure.

I open with, "I'm so very sorry for your loss." And then I tell Janice and Aunt Margaret what I told Aunt Patty. Janice is attentive but has a faraway smile. Aunt Margaret seems a bit rougher around the edges than her sister. She sits with her thick arms folded across her chest, nostrils flared. She smells something.

Janice is of medium build and has long straight hair, worn down, parted in the middle, a path through a forest. She looks younger than her front-page husband but has dark, almost purple circles under her eyes. Her recent sleeping habits leaving their scarlet letters. Most people don't like to think about how much damage sleep can do, evidence be damned.

Janice says, "Thank you for coming and for the flowers. It's very thoughtful of you." The dark circles shrink her nose and give it a point.

I give Janice the flowers and nod my head, going for the humble silent exchange of pleasantries. Immediately, I regret the choice. I want her to talk about Brendan but she's not saying anything. Everyone has gone statue and we sit and stare, waiting for the birds to come land on our shoulders and shit all over us.

My heart ratchets its rate up a notch and things are getting tingly, my not-so-subtle spider sense telling me that things aren't good and could quickly become worse. Then I remember I brought the picture, the picture of Brendan and the boys. I focus my forever-dwindling energies on it.

I ask, "Did Brendan ever talk about my father?" For a moment, I panic and think I said something about Brendan and my mother instead. But I didn't say that. I'm fine. I shake it off, rub dirt on it, stay in the game. I reach inside my coat and pull out the photo of Tim, the DA, and Sullivan on the stairs. It's still in the frame. Its spot on Ellen's windowsill is empty. "That's Brendan on the left, my father on the right."

Patty squeezes onto the swing seat, sitting on the outside of her sister. I'm the only one standing now. It's noticeable.

Janice says, "I don't remember your father's name coming up. Brendan and I had only been married for ten years, and he never really talked much about growing up in Southie."

It's getting harder not to be thinking about Ellen and Sullivan sitting in a tree as a slight and gaining maybe. Goddamn Brill. I say, "I understand," even if I don't. It's what I'm supposed to say; a nice-to-see-you after the hello.

Janice sighs heavily; it says, *What am I supposed to do now?* I feel terrible for her. I don't know exactly what happened here with Sullivan, but it was my fault. And this case is far from over. She doesn't know that things could get worse.

Janice fills herself up with air after the devastating sigh, which is admirable but just as sad, and says, "I wish Brendan kept more stuff like this around. Could I ask you for a copy of this picture?"

"Of course, consider it done," I say.

Janice smiles, but it's sad; goddamn it, everything is sad. We both know she's trying to regain something that has already been lost forever.

Aunt Margaret grabs the picture with both hands, and says, "Who's that boy in the middle?"

I say, "That's William Times. Currently he's the Suffolk County district attorney."

Patty clasps her hands together and says, "Oh, his daughter is the singer, right? She's very cute."

"Nah, she's a loser," Margaret says, waving her hand. Case dismissed.

Patty says, "She's not a loser. She sang on national TV. I thought she sang beautifully too."

"She stunk and she was a spoiled brat. That's why they voted her off the show," Margaret says.

Janice, who I assume has been acting as referee for the sisters for as long as they've been at her house, says, "She was a finalist on *American Star*. She's hardly a loser."

Margaret shrugs. "She lost, right? We'll never hear from her again."

The volley between family members is quick, ends quicker, and is more than a little disorienting. It also seems to be the end of the small talk. We're back to staring at each other, looking for an answer that isn't here.

I'm not leaving this house empty-handed, without knowing what the next step is, without having to grill Ellen about a tryst with Sullivan. Hopefully, the photo of the boys has bought me some familiarity chips that I can cash.

I say, "I'm sorry, there's no good way to say this, so I'm just going to come out with it."

Margaret says, "Come out with it already and be done then."

"Good advice." I pull out a business card and my PI ID and hand them to Janice, but Margaret takes them instead. "I'm a small-time, very small-time, private detective in South Boston."

Patty's eyes go saucer-wide and she says, "How exciting!"

It's not warm in here but my head sweats under my hat. I nod at Patty, acknowledging her enthusiasm. At least I'll have one of the three on my side. I say, "Last week your husband, Brendan, came to my office in Southie and hired me."

Janice sinks into her swing seat. Patty covers her mouth. Margaret still has her arms crossed. Janice says, "Hired you? Hired you for what?"

Christ, I probably could've come up with a better way to introduce the subject, but there's no turning back now. As uncomfortable as this is, asking the questions that will haunt Janice for years to come, I owe it to Sullivan to see this through. I owe it to myself too.

I say, "Mind if I sit?" No one says anything. I grab a fold-up chair that's leaning against a wall and wrestle with it for a bit; the wood clacks and bites my fingers. I'm sure I look clumsy, but I'm buying some time so I can figure out what I can and can't tell her. It doesn't work.

I say, "The hard part is that I don't think I can tell you much until I figure it all out for myself."

Margaret says, "He's a crock. This guy is a phony. He's trying to get something out of you, probably money. Let's call the police."

Patty says, "Stop it, he's a real detective."

"How do we know that? How do we know anything about this man? That picture doesn't prove anything. Might not even be Brendan in the picture," Margaret says, building up steam, and a convincing case against me.

Patty is horrified. She says, "Look at his card and ID. He's going to tell us something important, right?" Patty leans out toward me. To her I have the answers to life somewhere inside my coat. I only keep questions in here.

Margaret ignores her sister, points a worn-tree-branch finger at me, and says, "Shame on you, whatever it is you're up to. Janice is a good woman and doesn't deserve to be put through anything by the likes of you. I'm calling."

I say, "Whoa, take it easy, Auntie Margaret. I'm telling the truth and I'm not here to hide things from Janice, just the opposite. I don't know how everything fits together yet, and I don't have all the puzzle pieces either. What I'm hoping is that you"—I turn to Janice—"can help me."

The sisters argue with each other. They have their considerable arms folded over their chests and they bump into each other like rams battling over territory. The swing seat complains and sways side to side, not in the direction the swing was intended to go. I yawn and hope nobody sees it.

Janice says, "Wait, wait. Stop!" Her aunts stop. "Are you really the son of Brendan's friend?"

"Yes. And what I'm working on, what Brendan wanted me

to figure out, is something from the past, the long past but not gone, and I think it involves both men in that picture, my father and the DA."

Janice says, "I already told you, I don't know anything about Brendan's past, never mind anything about your father and the DA."

I resist telling her that I know very little about my father's past and less about my own mother's present. I say, "That's okay. I think you'll still be able to help."

Margaret is shaking her head, silently *tsk-tsk*ing the proceedings. Patty has wide eyes and nods her head, yes. Janice is stoic, unreadable as a tabloid.

I say, "Janice, may I ask you some questions? Then I promise to tell you and show you what I know."

Janice nods. "Okay."

"How did you meet Brendan?" I start off with an easy question, get her used to talking about her and him, get her used to being honest and thinking about Brendan as past, maybe as something that can't hurt her, or can't hurt her much.

Janice cooperates. She gives a summary of their too-brief history. Her voice is low and calm, soothing, as if I'm the one who needs cheering up. Brendan was a truck driver and they met at a diner in New Hampshire. They sat next to each other at the counter. Janice worked at a local park, part of an environmental conservation and preservation team. They were married two months later, moved to Provincetown shortly thereafter, spent the last bunch of years bouncing around the Cape in accordance with Janice's varied environmental gigs. They loved the Cape and were going to stay forever, grow old, would you still need me, feed me, and the rest of the tune, happily ever after. . . .

Margaret is slapping me in the face, shouting. "What's wrong with you? Are you asleep? Wake up."

Patty hangs on her sister's arm, the nonslapping arm. "Stop it, Margaret, you'll hurt him!"

"I'm awake. I wasn't asleep. Jesus! Stop hitting me!" The old and familiar embarrassments swell, filling me with anger and hate for everyone, myself included. Makes me want to lash out, lie, share my poison with anyone around me. God help the person who finds my continued degradations and humiliations funny.

The twin aunts retreat to the kitchen, arm in arm, their cranky-hipped limps fitted together like the gears in a dying perpetual motion machine. Janice crouches at my feet. She says, "Are you okay? You just slumped in your chair. It looked like you passed out."

"I'm fine, I'm fine." I stand up, stumble a bit, but get my legs under me. I rub my face with my hands. If I could take my face off, I would.

Janice stands next to me, her hand on my elbow. It's a light touch, and comforting, but it's all I can do not to flinch and pull myself away. The twins come back. Margaret sits on the swing and has the cordless phone in her hand. Patty has a glass of water, which I assume is for me, until she takes a sip.

I swallow some air, willing the oxygen to do its goddamn job and keep me working right. "Sorry, I'm narcoleptic." I say it under my breath, the words cower and hide, and hope that only Janice hears my quick and unexpected confession.

Margaret says, "What?" Of course she heard me. She says it loud, like she's responding to a lie. This is not a lie.

I say, "I have narcolepsy." That's it. No explanation.

Patty appears at my left side like a spirit. "You poor dear. Drink this." There's lipstick on the glass. My job is so glamorous.

I say, "Please, everyone sit back down. I'm fine. It happens all the time and I know how to deal with it. I know how to live with it." I give back the community water. The women stare and investigate me. My status changing from potentially dangerous intruder to vulnerable afflicted person might just help my cause here.

I say, "Look. My narcolepsy is why I need to ask you questions, Janice. When Brendan came to my Southie office I fell asleep, like I did here, but not exactly like I did here because I probably looked awake to Brendan, did some sleep-talking and -walking like I do sometimes: automatic behavior, they call it." I stop talking and wave my hands in front of my own face, cleaning up the mess of words. "Anyway, I was out when he was in and all I've been able to piece together is that Brendan wanted me to find something, something that relates to my father and the DA." I pause and point at the picture again. It pays to have props. "I don't know what it is I'm supposed to find because I was asleep, and Brendan died before I could find out."

There. It's out. The truth as I know it and I feel fine. Everyone blinks at me a few times and I hear their eyelids opening and closing.

Margaret talks first. She says, "He's faking. Be careful, Janice."

Patty slaps her sister's hand.

Janice curls up her face and says, "Oh, be quiet, Margaret."

Margaret looks at me and shrugs, like we're commiserating, like I'm supposed to agree with her can-you-believe-these-knuckleheads-are-buying-what-you're-selling look. Can't say I'm all that fond of Aunt Margaret.

I say, "So, Janice, I assume you didn't know Brendan came to South Boston and hired me."

She says, "I knew he made a day trip to Boston, but I didn't know anything about you."

I nod. "I did talk with Brendan one other time. Is this a smokefree house? Do you mind if I smoke?" My timing has always been impeccable.

Janice shakes her head and is now exasperated with me. "Yes. I mean, no, you can't smoke in here. When did you talk to Brendan?"

I can't tell her it was the day before he died. It won't help anyone, especially me. I say, "A couple of days after his visit he called to check on my progress. Because I'm stubborn, I didn't come right out and admit to him that I slept through our face-to-face. I didn't ask him what I was supposed to find. I hoped during our phone conversation that those details of the case would just, you know, present themselves."

Margaret says, "I take it back. He's not faking. He's just a buffoon." She sets off another family brouhaha. Yeah, all this because of little old me. Janice clears the room of the battling aunts, banishing them to the kitchen.

When Janice returns to her seat on the swing, I say, "The important or odd part of our phone conversation was that Brendan seemed agitated, even paranoid. Does that mean anything to you?"

Janice turns on me quick and says, "No, that's not the important part." She leans closer to me and enunciates her words, sharpening them to a cutting point. "Brendan, my husband, killed himself, shot himself in the face with a gun. He was downstairs in our basement just a few days ago when he pulled the trigger. Your saying he was agitated and paranoid on the phone is not a surprise and certainly not the important part to me."

"I'm sorry. You're right. I'm sorry." I cannot say I'm sorry to her enough. I reach inside my coat and pull out the envelope. I'm careful to remove only one of the photos, the one with clothes. "While Brendan was there, the narcoleptic me managed to take some notes. Those are gone. Most of it was gibberish, but I'd written down South Shore Plaza. Do you know what that means? Brendan left me with this photograph, and I'm supposed to find something else, but obviously I haven't found it yet."

"South Shore Plaza means nothing to me. Brendan hated malls, wouldn't go in them if he could help it." Janice takes the picture, looks at it quick, and then looks away, like the photo might burn. "Who is she?"

"I don't know."

Janice looks at it again. "She looks a little like the *American Star* girl. The DA's daughter, right?"

I smile, and it doesn't feel right on my face. "It does look like her. But it's not her."

"No. I know. The photo is clearly older than she is."

I say, "Yes. Of course. Clearly. There was never any doubt."

"It does look a lot like her. Kind of spooky, in a way."

"Uncanny." I'm just going to agree with everything she says.

"Why did Brendan have this? Why did he give this to you?"

"I don't know, Janice. Like I said, he came to me to find something else. Not a person. An *it*."

She nods, even though I'm only answering her rhetorical questions, questions about her husband that will haunt her for the rest of her life because there might be no answers forthcoming. I don't know if she realizes that yet. Or maybe she does, and she's tolerating my presence with a staggering amount of dignity. Maybe she can share some dignity with me.

I say, "I'm sorry, but I have to ask this, Janice. Did Brendan act strange, do anything out of character, say anything odd in the days before he died?"

"You mean besides going to South Boston and hiring a private investigator?"

I don't say anything or do anything. I know that much, at least.

Janice loses herself again in the photo, the piece of her husband's past that has no place here, even though I'm trying to find it.

Finally, Janice says, "That girl on *American Star*. What's her name?"

"Jennifer Times."

"Right. Jennifer Times." Another pause, drinking in more of the photo; then she gives it back. "Brendan and I both watched the show together when this season started, but he stopped watching once they started picking the finalists. I feel like I remember him leaving the room when that local girl, Jennifer, was performing." Janice isn't looking at me but off into some corner of the porch, seeing those final days she shared with her husband. She's not talking to me now, either. She's talking to herself, trying to find her own answers.

"There was a night when Brendan came into the room with two glasses of wine, sat down next to me on the couch, but stood up and left as soon as he saw the show was on. He said something about how dumb it was, and that was strange because up until a week or two before, he was watching with me. We liked to make fun of the really bad singers.

"But I remember when he left the room it was Jennifer on the TV; she was singing. Brendan went into the kitchen, still talking to himself. He talked to himself quite a bit. He was a truck driver, and he said truck drivers talked to themselves a lot, even when they were talking to other people. I never told him, but I loved that about him and eavesdropped on him whenever I could. I'd feel guilty after, like I was reading a diary, but I still did it.

"He was in the kitchen, talking away." Janice pauses. "Sorry, but this is hard. I've been thinking about nothing but him for days now, and it's not getting any easier."

"Perfectly understandable."

Janice nods. Her eyes are wide and she's still not here. She's back at that night with Brendan, listening to him in the kitchen. Maybe this is what it was like for Brendan that day in the office, when he was talking to me and I wasn't there.

I say, "Did you hear what Brendan was saying in the kitchen?" I keep still, don't move in my seat, not even a wiggled pinky.

Janice says, "He was muttering and wasn't very loud. I didn't hear much. I got up and tiptoed to the doorway, like I usually did when I caught him talking to himself." She stops and smiles, but it falls apart, and I think she might start crying and never stop, but she doesn't. She goes on. "I didn't hear much, just snippets, nothing that made a whole lot of sense, so I walked into the kitchen. He was leaning on the kitchen island, talking and sipping his wine. When he saw me he smiled. I don't think he expected me to be there, but he smiled anyway. I walked over to him, gave him a kiss on the cheek, and thanked him for the wine. He said, 'Anytime,' squeezed my shoulder real quick, and I left him there, in the kitchen."

Janice sinks into the swing seat, slouching into the large green cushion. She's probably done, but I'm not moving. I won't move until I get what I need. I say, "When he was talking to himself, do you remember any phrases or words? Anything?"

Janice looks at me and covers her face with her hands. I know the feeling. She is done. She's going to tell me she doesn't remember anything else and that's it. She'll ask me, politely, to leave.

Then she sits upright again, her hands drop, and she says, "Yes. I think he said something about film, or more film."

My leg shakes, bobs up and down, tries to walk out of the room on its own. Is it more photos, then? An undeveloped roll, or more negatives, the rest of Tim's bedroom shoot? Maybe the rest of the pictorial includes more nudes, maybe the same girl, maybe a different girl, and I bet this missing portfolio includes some juicy eight-by-tens of Brendan and Billy Times, juicy enough to make the DA dangerously cranky. I say, "More film."

Janice nods. She wraps her arms around her chest, looks out the window, sits back in the swing seat, and sways. She says, "I have your card, Mark. I'll call you in a few days or a week. I need to know how this ends up."

I don't have to say anything, but I do. "Call me anytime. Thank you, Janice, you've been very helpful. And again, I'm so incredibly sorry about Brendan." I'm not going to tell her about the DA and his goons. I can't tell her it might be my fault that Brendan is dead. Not now, anyway. I need to finish this case first. There'll be time for the recriminations later.

Janice says, "Thanks. So am I."

It's past time to go. I get up and walk out of the porch, and I walk out fast, or as fast as I can handle. The twin aunts sit in the kitchen, huddled in two chairs they positioned near the breezeway entrance into the porch. They're whispering and they don't stop whispering as I walk by. Margaret has the phone in her hand, fingers hovering over buttons that spell 9–1–1. I'm sure they heard everything.

I say, "The pleasure was all mine. Don't get up, I can find the front door." I touch the brim of my hat for a faux tip, but the lid doesn't move, not for anyone.

Patty says, "Good luck." At least, I think it's Patty. I'm already out of the kitchen and through the dining room, where it's dark, so dark I can't really see, and I walk into the table shins first. Ow. The hutch and its china shakes. Nothing broken.

I right the ship, feel my way past the table, and find the front hallway and door. There are small curtained windows in the doorframe. My bull's charge through the dining room notwithstanding, I'm going to be as careful and cautious as I can the rest of the way. I know I'm close. I pull back the curtains for a little peekaboo.

The red car is outside. Can't say I'm surprised.

TWENTY-SIX

The red car idles in front of the gravel driveway. No, it's not idling, it's crawling, and it crawls by the house and down the road. They know I'm here. Maybe they planted some sort of homing device on me. I'm the endangered animal that needs to be tagged and tracked.

Or it's possible they don't know I'm here and they're just checking to see who's hanging at chez Sullivan. I didn't see the red car when I was in Brill's cab. Of course Brill could've spilled my beans for their twenty bucks. He strikes me as an equal opportunity kind of guy.

I take out my cell phone and dial. One ring and Brill answers. "Town Taxi, how can I help you?"

"Brill, it's me, Genevich. Can you pick me up on Rambler Road?"

He sighs. It doesn't sound nervous or guilty, just that he's pissed off to have to do his job. "Christ, where do you want to go now?"

The red car drives by again, in the opposite direction. It's moving faster, almost but not quite a normal, leisurely, obey-the-suburban-speed-limit pace. Then it's gone. I say with a mock British accent, "Home, James. Where else? Home."

Brill hangs up. I choose to believe that means he's coming to get me.

Voices from the kitchen: "Everything okay, Mark? Who are you talking to?"

I say, "I'm fine. Just calling a cab. He'll be here any minute. 'Bye and thanks." The weather is tolerable, it'd be hard to explain me standing inside, nose buried in the curtains by the front door, so I go outside, close the door gently behind me. Thinking better of sitting on the steps, in plain view of Rambler Road, I walk down the gravel driveway and conceal myself behind the blue SUV. Hopefully no one in the house is watching.

I go fishing for a cigarette and find one. It lights like it has been waiting for this moment all its life. I think about the red car and the goons. Are they planning another drive-by? Maybe they're getting the jump on my next destination. They'll be sitting in Ellen's kitchen when I get there, keeping the light on for me. They trashed my office and apartment, what's to say they won't do the same to the bungalow or to me? Nothing, far as I can tell.

Maybe I'm asking the wrong questions. I should be asking why haven't they ransacked the bungalow already? Would it look too fishy for break-ins and house-trashings to be following me around? Maybe they're not on such comfortable footing down here, away from the DA's stomping grounds. Didn't seem to bother them in Brendan's case, though. Maybe they're tired of looking for *it*, whether *it* is an undeveloped roll or a set of incriminating pictures, and they'll be happy just to deal with me after I do the grunt work for them.

Either or any way, doesn't matter to me anymore. What matters is that I have to find the goods before they find me again.

A car horn blasts two reports. That, or someone is trying to ride a goose sidesaddle. Brill's here. He beeps again. I step out from behind the SUV. He rolls down the passenger-side window and yells, "Come on, get in the goddamn car. We ain't got all day."

I say, "Ain't it the truth."

He says, "Did you get what you needed?"

"I was only offering my condolences and my flowers to the widow." I shouldn't be smug, but I am.

"Right. You didn't find shit."

I sit in Brill's backseat, and my ass picks up a strip of duct tape, which is just what my ass needs. I say, "The Genevich bungalow, Brill. You know where that is, right?"

He does. He drives down Rambler Road. According to my cell phone it's only 12:30. My cell phone doesn't tell lies. Ellen won't be home for another four hours, at least.

Brill pulls out onto the main drag. The library is just ahead. I try to turn around to see if anyone is tailing. I shift my weight in the seat and there's a loud and long ripping sound.

Brill says, "Goddamn it, you're tearing my seat apart!"

"Don't get your Depends in a bunch. It's your duct tape sticking to my ass like it's in love." I keep turning around, looking for the red car, and the duct tape keeps stripping off and clamping onto me.

He says, "Jesus Christ, stop moving around! What do you think you're doing back there anyway? It's going to take me the rest of the afternoon to fix that up right."

"Nothing. Just admiring the scenery." I stop moving, mostly because my legs are practically taped together. "Hey, did you see a red car today, earlier, when you were driving around?"

Brill's eyes get big. The wrinkles animate and release the hounds of his eyes. He says, "Yeah. It followed me to Rambler Road."

"No kidding." This isn't good. This—

Brill blows air through his lips, spitting laughter. Then it's out full. It's a belly laugh, a thigh-slapper. I'm not so amused. He says, "You are one sad sack, Genevich. Oooh, a red car, watch out for the red car! Ha! That's quite a gift for description you got there. You must solve all kinds of cases with those detailed detective powers of yours."

"All right, all right. Forget it."

"No, no, it's a good question. Except for holidays and a week off here and there, I've been driving around town ten hours a day, seven days a week for forty years, but I have never, ever, seen a red car on the road, not a one, until today. Man, I'm so glad you're on the case."

Brill laughs it up some more. I just might introduce my knuckles to the back of his head. He wheezes and chuckles until he drops me off at the bungalow. I don't tip. Let's see if he finds that funny.

He drives away. I'm here. I'm at the bungalow. And I know it's here. The rest of the film has to be here, if it's anywhere.

The sky has gone gray, the color of old newspapers. There's no red car in the driveway or anywhere on the block, but that doesn't mean the goons aren't inside. I have no weapon, no protection. I could grab something out of the shed, I suppose, but I don't know the finer points of Zen combat with pruning shears, and in the tale of the tape, trowels and shovels don't measure favorably when going against guns.

Play it straight, then. The front door is locked and intact. All the windows are closed. I peek inside a few, cupping my hands around my face. It's dark inside, but nothing seems out of place. I walk around to the backyard. It doesn't take me long. The house could fit inside my jacket. I hear the rain landing on my hat before I feel it.

I backdoor it into the kitchen. Everything is how we left it this morning: newspapers on the table, coffee mugs and toast crumbs on the counter. It's quiet, and I hope it stays that way. I won't turn on any lights, pretend I'm not here. It'll be easy.

Start at the beginning, the kitchen. I'll be thorough and check everything and everywhere: under the sink, between and behind pipes, the utensil and utility drawers. Maybe the film is hiding in plain view, just like Tim's photos on the walls, I don't know. There's a finite amount of space here in the old homestead; those family secrets can't stay hidden forever.

I look in the cabinets below the sink, past the pots and pans, the small pair of cabinets above the refrigerator that Ellen can't reach without a stool and neither can I. There's nothing but old phone books, a dusty bottle of whiskey, and books of matches, but I still push on the panels and wooden backings, seeing if anything will pop out or away, secret passages and hiding spots. I don't find any. The kitchen is clear.

The dining room and living room are next. Closets full of winter coats and dresses in plastic bags. No film. I move furniture and throw rugs, test for loose slats by rapping my foot on the floor. I go to my hands and knees and feel along the perimeters of the baseboards. Nothing and nothing. It's getting warm in here. My coat comes off, and the picture of Tim, Sullivan, and the DA goes back in its spot on the windowsill. It wasn't missed.

The guest room is next. There's only one closet and all it holds are two wooden tennis racquets, my old baseball glove—the one I pretend-signed with Carney Lansford's signature—four misshapen wire hangers, outdated board games that I open and rifle through, and empty luggage. The white suitcase and bag are as old as I am. I move the bed and bureau out, repeat my floor-and-baseboard checks, and find nothing.

It's all right. The nothing, that is. The first three rooms are only preludes, dry runs, practice searches for the real test. Ellen's room and the basement.

Ellen's room was their room. There are black-and-white photos on the walls, and they look to be half-and-half Tim pictures and antique finds. The Tim pictures are all of me, ranging in age from newborn to five years old. I'm in the pictures, but they're all someone else's memories, not mine. There's only one picture where Ellen shares the scene with me. It's a close-up and our faces are pressed together with Ellen in profile, hiding her smile behind one of my perfect chubby cheeks. My cheeks are still chubby.

No time for that. I do the bed and rug/floor check first, then the baseboard. I have a system, and I am systematically finding nothing. Then comes the nightstand, and I find her address book and flip through it. Nothing sinister, everything organized, all the numbers have a name. None of the names are Sullivan. Take that, Brill.

Next up, her antique wooden trunk that holds sweaters and sweatshirts, then her dresser, and yes, I'm going through her dresser, and I have to admit that I fear finding personal items that I don't want to find, but I can't and won't stop now. Underwear drawer, shirt drawer, pants and slacks, bras, and all clear.

Her closet is a big one, the biggest one in the house. It must be in the closet somewhere. I remove all the hanging clothes and place them on the bed. Then I pull out all the shoes from the floor and the shelves, along with hatboxes and shoeboxes, most of them empty, some of them trapping belts and scarves, tacky lapel pins and brooches, general shit Ellen never wears. No clown pants in here.

The back of the closet is paneled and some of the panels hang loose. I pull up a few but find only plaster. To the left, the closet goes deeper, until the ceiling tapers down, into the floor. There are stacks of cardboard boxes and I pull those out. One box holds tax and financial information, the other boxes are assorted memorabilia: high school yearbook, plaques, track-meet ribbons, unframed pictures, postcards. No rolls of film, no pictures.

I put everything back. It's 2:25. My back hurts and my legs are stiffening up, revolting against further bending against their will.

On the way to the basement, I do a quick run through the bathroom. I look inside the toilet tank, leaving no porcelain cover unturned. Then back to the kitchen, and it's grab a flashlight and pound the stairs down into the basement.

The basement, like the house, is small, seemingly smaller than the bungalow's footprint, though I don't know how that's possible. The furnace, washer, and dryer fill up an alcove. There's less clutter than I expected down here. There's a pair of rusty bed frames leaning against the foundation walls, a set of metal shelves that hold a mishmash of forgotten tokens of home ownership, and an old hutch with empty drawers. It looks like Ellen was down here recently, organizing or cleaning. I check the exposed ceiling beams and struts; the take-home prizes are spiderwebs and dead bugs, but no film.

A tip, an edge, of panic is starting to poke me in the back of the head, now that I haven't found it yet. The bungalow doesn't want to let go of its secrets.

Back to the alcove. Behind and above the washer and dryer is a crawl space with a dirt floor. I climb up and inside I have to duck-walk. Not wild about this. Dark, dirt floor, enclosed space: there's a large creepiness factor, and it's very easy to imagine there are more than metaphorical skeletons stuffed or buried here.

I find a Christmas-tree stand, boxes of ornaments and table-cloths, and one of my old kiddie Halloween costumes, a pirate. Christ. Everywhere I turn in the damn house is stuff that doesn't need to be saved, but it's there, like a collection of regrets, jettisoned and almost but not quite forgotten.

I use the flashlight to trace the length of the dirt floor into the corners and then, above me, on the beams and pipes. The film is not here. Is it buried? I could check, get a shovel and move some dirt around, like some penny-ante archaeologist or grave robber. Indiana Jones, I'm not. Goddamn, that would take too long. Time is my enemy and always will be.

Maybe the missing film isn't here. Maybe the DA and his goons already found it in my apartment or the office with their quaint search-and-seizure operation; it would explain why they haven't torn this place apart. But that doesn't work. Ellen's parents were still alive and living in the building when Tim died. He wouldn't have hidden film at their place. Even if he did hide it there, too much work and change has happened to the interior of the building in the intervening years. The years always intervene. It would've been found.

It could be anywhere. It could've been destroyed long ago, purposefully or accidentally. It could be nowhere. Or it's here but it's lost, like me. Being lost isn't the same as being nowhere. Being lost is worse because there's the false hope that you might be found.

I crawl out onto the washing machine ass first. I'm a large load, wash in warm water. Brush myself off and back upstairs to the kitchen. I sit heavily at the table with the newspapers. I want a cigarette but the pack is in my coat and my coat is way over in the other room. My legs are too heavy. My arms and hands are too heavy. If I could only get around without them, conserve energy, throw the extra weight overboard so I could stay afloat. Can't get myself out of the chair. You never get used to the total fatigue that rules your narcoleptic life, and it only gets more difficult to overcome. Practice doesn't make perfect.

TWENTY-SEVEN

The sun shines bright, just like the ones in cartoons. Cartoon suns sing and wink and have toothy smiles. Do we really need to make an impossibly massive ball of fire and radiation into our cute little friend?

Tim and I are in our backyard. Everything is green. It's the weekend again. Tools go back in the shed, but he keeps the hand trowel, the special one. We've all done this before.

Tim is still in the shed putting things away. I take a peek inside. Along with the sharp and toothy tools are bottles of cleaners and chemical fertilizers, their labels have cartoon figures on them, and they wink at me, ask me to come play. I remember their commercials, the smiley-faced chemical suds that scrub and sing their way down a drain and into our groundwater. Oh, happy days.

Tim closes the shed doors and locks them, even though he'll just have to unlock them again later. A loop of inefficiency. The doors are newly white, like my baby teeth. I can't go inside. He tells me I'm too young, but maybe I just don't know the secret password. There are so many secrets we can't keep track of them. We forget them and shed them like dead skin.

I stand next to the doors. The doors are too white. Brown paper bag. Pat on my head. Good boy. It's time to clean up the yard, again and again and again.

The sky is such a light shade of blue, it looks like water, and it shimmers. I don't much feel like singing for Tim today, but I will. He'd be devastated if I didn't.

I sing the old standard, "Take Me Out to the Ball Game." Tim switches the lyrics around and I put them back where they belong. It makes me tired. It's hot and the poop bag gets full. Tim never runs out of names for the dogs, the sources of the poop. We never see the dogs, so he might as well be naming the dog shit, but that wouldn't be a fun or appropriate game.

We dump the poop in its designated and delineated area, over the cyclone fence and into the woods behind the shed. It smells back here. As he dumps the bag, Tim says, "Shoo, fly, shoo."

We walk around to the front of the shed and Tim opens the doors. It's dark inside and my eyes need time to adjust. Tim says, "So, kid, whaddaya think?"

My hands ball up into tiny fists, no bigger than humming-birds' nests. The five-year-old me is pissed off and more than a little depressed that Tim was the photographer for those pictures, and for more pictures I can't find, some film that is a terrible secret and resulted in the death of his friend Brendan. Say it ain't so, Tim.

I say, "Where's the film? Who is she, Tim?"

Tim laughs, he loves to laugh, and he bends to one knee and chucks my chin with his fist, so fucking condescending. I should bite his knuckle or punch him in the groin, but I'm not strong enough.

Tim says, "I don't know and I don't know." He gets up and moves to lock the shed doors, but I make my own move. I jam my foot between the doors so they can't shut. I'm my own five-year-old goon, and my will is larger than the foot in the doors.

I say, "Who are you?"

Tim looks around, as if making sure the coast of our yard is clear, and says, "You don't know, and you never will."

He lifts me up when I'm not looking. I am all bluff and so very easy to remove from the doors. There's always next time. Tim puts me on his shoulders. I land roughly; my little body slams onto his stone figure. A sting runs up my spine and makes my extremities tingle. It hurts enough to bring tears.

I'm too high up, too close to that cartoon sun, which doesn't look or feel all that friendly anymore. My skin burns and my eyes hide in a squint that isn't getting the job done. The five-year-old has an epiphany. The cartoon sun is why everything sucks.

Tim walks with me on his shoulders. I'm still too high up. I wonder if he knows that I could fall and die from up here.

TWENTY-EIGHT

Full body twitch. A spasm sends my foot into the kitchen table leg. The table disapproves of being treated so shabbily and groans as it slides a few inches along the linoleum. My toes aren't crazy about the treatment either. Can't please anyone.

I'm in the kitchen and I'm awake. Two states of being that are not constant and should probably not be taken for granted. As a kid, I thought the expression was *taken for granite,* as in the rock. I still think that makes more sense.

All right. Get up. I go to the fridge and keep my head down because I do not want to look out the kitchen window, out in the backyard. I need to let the murk clear from my latest and greatest little sleep, to burn the murk away like morning fog before I'll allow a eureka moment. I don't want to jinx anything, not just yet. It's 3:36.

I make a ham and cheese on some whole-grain bread that looks like cardboard with poppy seeds. Tastes like it too. Everything sticks to the roof of my mouth. I eat one half of the sandwich and start the other half before I let myself look out into the backyard.

There it is, the answer as plain as my crooked face. Down at the bottom of the slanted yard: the shed. The missing film is hidden in the shed. It has to be.

I finish the sandwich and gulp some soda straight from the two-liter bottle. What Ellen doesn't know won't gross her out. Then I go into the living room for my jacket, my trusty exterior skin, and then to the great outdoors.

The sun is shining. I won't look at it because it might be the cartoon sun. I light a cigarette instead. Take that, cartoon sun. I ease down the backyard's pitch.

The shed has gone to seed. It's falling apart. Because of the uneven and pitched land, the shed, at each corner, sits on four stacks of cinder blocks of varying heights. The back end is up a couple of feet off the ground. The shed sags and tilts to the left. A mosquito fart could knock it to the ground. My ham-and-cheese sandwich rearranges itself in my stomach.

The roof is missing shingles, a diseased dragon losing its scales, tar paper and plywood exposed in spots. The walls need to be painted. The doors are yellowed, no longer newly white, just like my teeth. Looks like the doors took up smoking. The one window is covered with dust and spiderwebs. It's all still standing, though. Something to be said for that.

The shed was solely Tim's domain. Ellen is a stubborn city dweller with no interest in dirt or growing things, other than the cosmetic value live grass supposedly gives to her property. Ellen does not mow or rake or dig or plant. Even when I was a kid and we had no money, she hired landscapers to take care of the yard and they used their own equipment, not the stuff that has been locked in the shed for twenty-five years. After Tim died, the shed stayed locked. It was always just a part of the yard, a quirk of property that you overlooked, like some mound left by the long-ago glacial retreat.

The shed doors have a rusted padlock as their neglected sentinel. It has done the job and now it's time to retire. I wrap my hand around the padlock and it paints my hand with orange, dead metal. The lock itself is tight, but the latch mechanism that holds the doors closed hangs by loose and rusted screws. Two quick yanks and it all comes apart in my hand. The doors open and their hinges complain loudly. Crybabies.

Might as well be opening a sarcophagus, with all the dust and decay billowing into my face. One who dares disturb this tomb is cursed with a lungful of the stuff. I stagger back and cough a cough that I refuse to blame on my cigarettes.

I take a step inside. The floorboards are warped, forming wooden waves, but they feel solid enough to hold me. There's clutter. The years have gathered here. Time to empty the sucker. Like I said before, I'm not screwing around anymore.

I pull out rakes and a push mower, which seems to be in decent shape despite the long layoff. Ellen could probably sell it in her antiques store. Shovels, a charcoal grill, a wheelbarrow with a flat tire, extra cyclone fencing, bags of seed, fertilizer, beach toys, a toddler-sized sled, a metal gas can, an extra water hose, empty paint cans and brushes. Everything comes off the floor and into the yard. There's a lot of stuff, but it doesn't take long to carry it outside. The debris is spread over the grass; it looks like someone is reconstructing a Tim airplane after it crashed.

Shelves on the side walls hold coffee cans full of oily rags, old nails, washers, and screws. There's nothing taped underneath those shelves. The shed has no ceiling struts like the basement did, but I do check the frame, the beams above the door. Empty.

The rear of the shed has one long shelf with all but empty bottles of windshield washer fluid, antifreeze, and motor oil. Underneath the long plank of wood is a section of the rear wall that was reinforced with a big piece of plywood. There are nails and hooks in the plywood. The nails and hooks are empty, nothing hangs, but it looks like there's some space or a buffer between the plywood and the actual rear wall of the shed, certainly room enough for a little roll of film, says me.

How much space is there? I knock hard on the plywood, wanting to hear a hollow sound, and my fist punches through its rotten surface, out the rear wall of the shed, and into the sunlight. Whoops. I pull my bullying fist back inside unscathed. There's less space between the plywood and wall than I thought, and it's all wet and rotted back there, the wall as soft as a pancake from L Street Diner.

Ellen won't notice the fist hole in the wall, I don't think. When does she ever go behind the shed? I try to pry off more of the plywood, but another chunk of the back wall comes with it.

Dammit. I'll demolish the shed looking for the film, if I

have to. Can't say I have any ready-made excuses to explain such a home improvement project to Ellen, though.

Take a step back. The floorboards squeak and rattle. Something is loose somewhere. I back up some more, pressing my feet down hard, and in the rear left corner of the shed, where I was just standing and punching a second ago, the flooring rises up and off the frame a little bit and bites into the crumbling plywood above it. Maybe X marks the spot.

I go back out onto the lawn and fetch a hand trowel. It might be the poop-scooping shovel of yore, it might not. It ain't Excalibur. I use the thing like a crowbar and pry up that rear corner until I can grab it with my hands. The floorboard isn't rotted; the wood is tougher and fights back. I have a tight grip on the corner, and I pull and yank and lean all my weight into it. There's a clank and the hand trowel is gone, falling into the gap and beneath the floor, making a suitable time capsule.

The wood snaps and I fall on my ass. The shed shakes and groans, and for a second I think it's going to come down on my head, and maybe that wouldn't be a bad thing. Maybe another knock on my head will set me straight, fix me up as good as new.

The shed doesn't come down. The shaking and groaning stops and everything settles back. My fingers are red, raw, and screaming, but no splinters. I squeeze my hands in and out of fists and walk toward the hole in the floor. The sun goes behind a cloud and everything gets dark in the shed.

I go into snake mode, crawl on my belly, and hover my face

above the hole. I look down and see the ground and the hand shovel. Fuck it. Leave the shovel under the shed where it belongs. I don't need it to tear up more of the floorboards. My hands will do just fine.

Wait. There's a dark lump attached to one floor joint, a black barnacle, adjacent to the corner. I reach out a hand. I touch it: plastic. Two different kinds of plastic; parts feel like a bag and other parts feel more solid but still malleable. I jack my knees underneath my weight and the floorboard buckles and bows out toward the ground under the pressure, but I don't care. I need the leverage and both hands.

I lean over the dark lump; it's something wrapped in a garbage bag and duct-taped to the frame. My fingers get underneath, and it comes off with a quick yank. On cue, the sun comes out again. Maybe that cartoon sun is my friend after all.

Things get brighter and hotter in the shed. I move away from the hole and stand up. There's duct tape wound all around the plastic bag. I apply some even pressure and the inside of the package feels hard, maybe metal. Jesus Christ, my heart is beating, and—yeah, I'll say it—I am goddamn Indiana Jones, only I'm not afraid of snakes. If this thing were a football I'd spike it and do a little dance, make a little love. But I'm a professional. It's all about composure.

Through the plastic, I trace its perimeter. I'm Helen Keller, begging my fingers to give me the answers. It's shaped like a wheel, and it's too big to be a roll of film. It's a tin, or a canister, or a reel of film. A movie.

It gets darker inside the shed again, but the sunlight is still coming in through the punched-out hole in the back wall. My back is to the door and I feel their shadows brushing up against my legs. I've been able to feel their shadows on me since the first trip to Sullivan's house.

"Whaddaya say, Genevich?" says one goon.

"Jackpot!" says the other.

TWENTY-NINE

Looks like I was right about them choosing to wait me out, let me do all the heavy lifting. Seems to have worked out for them too. They get the gold stars, but I can't let them have the parting gift.

I turn around slowly, a shadow moving around a sundial. The two goons fill the doorway. They replace the open doors. They are mobile walls. The sun might as well be setting right behind them, or maybe one of them has the sun in his back pocket. I can't see their faces. They are shadows too.

One of them is holding a handgun, a handgun in silhouette, which doesn't make it look any prettier or any less dangerous. Its barrel is the proboscis of some giant bloodsucking insect. Its bite will do more than leave an itchy welt, and baking soda won't help.

I say, "If you're a couple of Jehovah's Witnesses, God isn't in the shed and I'm a druid."

"Looks like you're having a little yard sale. We thought we'd drop by, see what hunk of worthless junk I can get for two bucks," says Redhead. "Whaddaya say, Genevich? What can I get for my two bucks?" He's on the right. He's the one with the gun and it threatens to overload my overloaded systems. Things are getting fuzzy at the edges, sounds are getting tinny. Or it could be just the echoes and shadows in a small empty shed.

Even in silhouette, Redhead's freckles are visible, glowing future melanomas. Maybe if I keep him talking long enough he'll die of skin cancer. A man can hope.

Baldy joins in, he always does, the punch line to a joke that everyone sees coming. He says, "Two bucks? Nah, he'll ask for ten. He looks like a price gouger. Or maybe he's selling his stuff to raise money for charity, for other retards like him."

I'm not sure what to do with the plastic-wrapped package in my hands. They've seen it already. Hell, I'm holding it in front of my stomach, so I nonchalantly put it and my hands behind my back. Nothing up my sleeves.

I say, "What, you two pieces of shit can't read the KEEP OFF THE GRASS sign out there?"

They take a step inside the shed and have to duck under the doorframe to enter. The wood complains under their feet. I empathize with the wood. I did say I was a druid.

The goons take up all the space and air and light in the shed. Redhead says, "We're gonna cut the banter short, Genevich. You have two choices: we shoot you and take the movie or we just take the movie."

"And maybe we shoot you anyway," Baldy says.

I do register that they're confirming my find is in fact a movie, which is a plus, but I'm getting tingly again and the dark spots in my vision are growing bigger, ink leaking into a white shirt pocket. Come on, Genevich. Keep it together. I can't go out now, not now.

I shake my head and say, "That's no way to treat the gracious host. Bringing over a bottle of wine would've sufficed."

Redhead says, "We don't have manners. Sometimes I'm embarrassed for us. This isn't one of those times."

I say, "There's no way I'm giving you the flick. You two would just blab-blab-blab and ruin the ending for me." I don't think they appreciate how honest I'm being with them. I'm baring my soul here.

Baldy says, "Sorry, Genevich. We get the private screening."

They take another step forward; I go backward. We're doing a shed dance. I go back until the rear wall shelf hits me across the shoulders.

Redhead raises the gun to between-my-eyes level and says, "We do appreciate you clearing out a nice, clean, private space for your body. The way I see it, we shoot you, put all that crap back inside the shed, and no one will find you for days. Maybe even a week, depending on how bad the smell gets."

I say, "I didn't shower this morning and I sweat a lot."

Baldy says, "Give us the movie. Now."

That's right, I have the film, and until they get it, I have the upper hand. At least, that's what I have to fool myself into believing. I am a fool.

I can't move any farther backward, so I slide toward the

right, to the corner, to where I found my prize and to the hole I punched through the back wall. The rotted plywood and wall are right behind me.

I say, "All right, all right. No need for hostilities, gentlemen. I'll give it to you." I pretend to slip into the floorboard hole, flail my arms around like I'm getting electrocuted. Save me, somebody save me! The movement and action feels good and clears my head some. I might be hamming it up too much, hopefully not enough to get me shot, but I don't want them watching my sleight of hand with the package, so I scuff and bang my feet on the floor, the sounds are percussive and hard, and then, as I fall to my knees in a heap, I jam the film inside my jacket, right next to the manila envelope. The photos and film reunited and it feels so good.

Redhead traces my lack of progress with his gun. He says, "Knock off whatever it is you're doing, Genevich, and stand up."

I say, "Sorry. Tripped. Always been clumsy, you know?" I hold out my empty hands. "Shit, I dropped the movie. I'll get it." I turn around slowly. I'm that shadow on the sundial again.

Baldy says, "Get away from there, I'll get it," but it sounds tired, has no muscle or threat behind it because I'm trapped in the corner of the shed with nowhere to go, right? Redhead hesitates, doesn't say anything, doesn't do anything to stop me from turning around.

My legs coil under me. My knees have one good spring in them. I'm aimed at the fist-sized hole in the wall and ready to be fired. I'm a piston. I'm a catapult.

I jump and launch shoulder first toward the plywood and the rear wall underneath the shelf, but my knees don't have one good spring in them. My feet fall into the hole, lodge between the floor and the frame, and then I hit the plywood face first. The plywood is soft, but it's still strong enough to give me a good shot to the chops. There's enough momentum behind me and I bust through the shed and into the fading afternoon light. I'm a semisuccessful battering ram.

There's a gunshot and the bullet passes overhead; its sound is ugly and could never be confused with the buzz of a wasp or any living thing. The grass is more than a couple of feet below me. I tuck my chin into my chest, my hat falls off, and I dip a shoulder, hoping to land in some kind of roll. While dipping my shoulder, my body twists and turns, putting a tremendous amount of pressure on my feet and ankles; they're going to be yanked out of their respective sockets, but they come out of the corner. Upon release I snap forward and land awkwardly on my right shoulder, planting it into the ground. There's no roll, no tens from the judges. My bottom half comes up and over my head into a half-assed headstand, only I'm standing on my shoulder and neck. I slide on the grass in this position, then fall.

There are two loud snaps, one right after the other. Breaking wood. I'm on my stomach and I chance a look back at the shed, instead of getting up and fleeing for my life. Most of the rear wall is gone, punched through, and the hole is a mouth that's closing. The roof is falling, Chicken Little says so. Yet despite the sagging roof, the shed is growing bigger, a deflating balloon somehow taking in more air and taking up more of my view. Wait, it's moving, coming right at me. The cinder blocks are toppling, and so is the propped-up shed.

The goons. They're yelling and there's a burst of frantic footsteps but those end suddenly. The curtain drops on their show. I might meet a similarly sudden fate if I don't move. The shed falls and roars and aims for me. I roll left, out of the way, but I go back for my hat. I reach out and grab the brim right as that mass of rotted wood and rusty nails crash-lands on the hat and my fingers are flea lengths away from being crushed. More stale dust billows into my face. All four walls have collapsed, the doors broken and unhinged. Just like that, the shed that stood forever is no more.

I yank my hat out from beneath the rubble. It has nine lives. I stand up and put the hat on. It's still good.

Most of my body parts seem to be functioning, though my face is wet. My fingers report back from the bridge of my nose; they're red with blood. No biggie. Just a scratch, a ding, otherwise good to go.

I have the film. The goons don't and they're under a pile of suburban rubble. I step over the cyclone fence and remake myself into a woodland creature. I give one last look behind me.

The backyard of the Genevich family plot has the appearance of utter devastation and calamity, the debris of Tim's life destroyed and strewn everywhere, spread out for everyone to see, should they care to. Secrets no more. Tim's stuff, the stuff that defined Tim for the entirety of my life, is nothing but so much rusted and collapsed junk, those memories made material are asleep or dead, powerless and meaningless, but not harmless.

I walk away from the damage into the woods, thinking that Ellen won't be pleased when she finds the shed. Hopefully, I'll be around long enough to improvise a story.

THIRTY

I walk a mile, maybe two. Keep to the woods when I can, stay off the streets. When there aren't any woods, I cut through people's yards, stomp through bushes, trample on lawns, cross over driveways. I hide behind fences meant to keep riffraff like me out. I walk past their pools and swing sets. People are home, or coming home from work. They yell at me and threaten to call the police. But they don't, and I keep walking. Small children run away; the older ones point and laugh. I don't care. I wave them off, shooing away flies. I'm carrying the big secret. It gives me provenance to go where I need to go.

I'm hungry, thirsty, and tired. Not the same tired as usual, but more, with a little extra spice, a little kick. Buffalo tired, General Gao tired. I can't do much more walking. The aches and minor injuries from the rumble and tumble with the shed are building, combining into a larger pain. They aren't inert.

I have no immediate destination in mind other than away from the goons and my house, just to go somewhere they won't find me. That's it. No more walking. I find two homes that have an acre or more of woods between them. I go back into hiding, but get the street name and address numbers first.

I call Brill, tell him where to pick me up. He says he'll be there in ten minutes. That's a good Brill.

Being the only cab in town during the off-season, this is a risk. Assuming the goons have emerged from the woodpile, they'll do all they can to get back on my trail. They'll figure out he's the only way around town for me, if they don't know that already. I have to chance it. I need one more ride from him.

I sit on a tree stump. The street is twenty yards away, far enough away that I can see the road, but I'll only be seen if someone stops and searches for me. I won't be seen from a quick drive-by.

I take the film—what I presume to be the film—out of my coat. The wrap job is tight. After an initial struggle to get the unraveling started, the layers of tape and plastic come off easy and fast, the way I like it. It's a canister of film, maybe six inches in diameter. I open the canister and there's a reel of celluloid. I lift it out like a doctor extracting shrapnel, or like I'm playing operation, careful with that funny bone, can't touch the sides.

The film is tan and silky and beautiful, and probably horrible. It holds thousands of pictures, thousands of moments in time that fit together like the points in a line. It's getting dark in the woods and I try holding the film up to the vanishing light. There are shapes, but I can't make out much of anything.

I need equipment. Luckily, I know a film expert. She wears clown pants sometimes.

My cell rings. I dig it out of my pocket. I don't recognize the number, but it's the Boston area code.

"Hello."

"Hi, Mr. Genevich? It's me, Jennifer."

I look around the woods like she might pop out from behind a maple. I say, "What's wrong? Daddy doesn't know where I am?"

There's a beat or two of silence on the phone, long enough to make me think the call was dropped or she hung up. She says, "I'm sorry about what happened. I just thought my father was going to watch you, make sure you weren't dangerous or up to some crazy blackmail scam. That's all. I got your message and today I saw the break-in of your office and apartment in the paper. And I'm sorry, Mr. Genevich. Really, I didn't know he was going to do anything like that."

I'm in the middle of the woods, and I'm too tired to breathe. I want to sit down, but I'm already sitting down. Not sure what to believe or who to believe, not sure if I should believe in myself.

I say, "On the obscure chance you're telling it straight, thanks."

"Why would my father do that?"

"No *would* about it. Did. He did it."

"Why did he break into your apartment? Was he looking for those pictures?"

I say, "Your father was looking for a film to go along with those pictures I showed you. The pictures are meaningless; they can't hurt anyone. But the film. The film is dangerous. The film can do damage."

"Do you have it?"

"Oh, yeah. I have it. I'm getting copies made right now. Going to send them to the local stations as soon as I get off the phone with you." Dressing up the truth with some bluff can't hurt, especially if she's trying to play me on behalf of DA Daddy again.

"Oh, my God! Seriously, what's on it?"

"Bad stuff. It's no Sesame Street video."

"Is it that girl who looks like me?"

"What do you think, Jennifer?"

"How bad is it?"

"One man is already dead because of it."

There's a beat of silence. "What? Who's dead?" Her voice is a funeral, and I know she believes me, every word.

"Brendan Sullivan. Police report says he shot himself in his Osterville home. He was the one who hired me, sent me the pictures, and wanted me to find the film. I found the film. Sullivan was a childhood friend of my father and your father. We're all in this together. We should all hold hands and sing songs about buying the world a Coke."

More silence. Then: "Mr. Genevich, I want to see it. Will you meet me and show it to me?"

"Now that sounds like crazy talk. Even assuming that I don't think you're trying to set me up again, I don't know why I would show you the film."

"I know and I'm sorry. Just listen to me for a sec. After our dinner, I couldn't stop thinking about those photos, and then when I heard about your apartment, it got worse, and I have such a bad feeling about all this, you know? I just need to know what happened. I promise I'll help you in any way I can. I need to see this. I'll come to your office and watch it. I can come right now. It won't take me long to get there."

Jennifer talks fast, begging and pleading. She might be sincere, but probably not. With the goons having lost my trail, the timing of her call just plain sucks. That said, the DA can't go to her well too often. She'll know too much.

How about I keep the possibilities open? I say, "We'll see. Need to finish getting copies made. Maybe I can offer you a late-night showing. I'll call you later." I hang up.

The cell phone goes back in my pocket. I need to chew on this for a bit. For such a simple action, watching a film, there are suddenly too many forks and branches and off-ramps and roadblocks and . . .

Three loud beeps shake me off my tree stump. I land in a crouch. A white car crawls along my stretch of woods, stops, then beeps again. It's my man Brill.

I try to gather myself quickly, but it's like chasing a dropped bundle of papers in a windy parking lot. I come crashing through the woods. The film is back inside my coat pocket. There's a moment of panic when I expect the goons to be in the backseat waiting for me, but it's empty. I open the door and slide in. The seat's been retaped, just for me.

Brill says, "I'm not even gonna ask how you got out here."

"That's mighty fine of you."

"I won't ask what happened to your face, either. But I hope it hurt like hell because it's killing me."

"Just a scratch. The perils of hiking through the woods, my man."

"All right. Where to, Sasquatch?"

I say, "That's actually funny. Congrats."

Let's try a change of destinations. I can't rely on Brill anymore, too risky. I say, "Take me to the nearest and dearest car rental agency. One that's open."

THIRTY-ONE

I'm leaned back into the seat, relaxed. I feel magnanimous in my latest small victory. Let Brill have his cheap shots. Let the people have cake. At least I feel magnanimous until I wake up, not on a sleepy Osterville road but in the parking lot of a car rental agency.

Brill is turned around. The old bastard has been watching me. His skeleton arm is looped around the back of his seat, and he shows me his wooden teeth. I suppose it's a smile. I didn't need to see that. I'll have nightmares the next time I pass out.

I say, "What are you smiling at?"

He says, "Your little nap made me an extra ten bucks. If I had any kids, you'd be putting them through college one z at a time."

I say, "I wasn't asleep. Making sure the lot and inside was all clear. Sitting here thinking. You should try it."

"You must've been doing some hard thinking with all that twitching and snoring." He laughs and coughs. Can't imagine he has much lung left.

I don't have a comeback for him, so I change the thrust of

our departure conversation. "Nice tape job on the seats, Brill. You're first class all the way." I'm running low on cash. I have just enough to pay the grinning bag of bones.

Brill takes the bills. He says, "You here to rent a car?"

"No, I'm going to get my shoes shined and then maybe a foot massage. All that walking and my dogs are barking."

Brill turns back around, faces front, assumes the cabbie position. "You driving on my roads, any roads? That can't be legal."

I open my door. I don't have to explain anything to him, but I do. I say, "I have a driver's license and a credit card. I can drive a car. I'm sure the transaction will be quite easy. Wait for me here, we'll drag-race out of the lot. I'll let you be James Dean. You got the looks."

"No, thanks. I'm turning in early if you're going to be on the road." He revs the tiny four-cylinder engine. My cue to leave.

I get out. The lot is small and practically empty. The sun-bleached pavement is cracked and the same color as the overcast sky. Brill drives away. He's no fun.

Inside the rental agency, everything is bright yellow and shitty brown. There are cheery poster-sized ads hanging on the walls featuring madly grinning rental agents. Those madly grinning rental agents are at their desks but outside with a bright blue sky as their background. Apparently renting a car should be some sort of conversion experience for me. We'll see.

Before docking my weary ass at the service counter, I make a side trip to a small ATM tucked away between two mini palm trees. I need to replenish the cash supply. First I do a balance check: $35.16. Been spending too much and it's been weeks since I had a paying client. I'll take out twenty. While patiently waiting to add the exorbitant transaction fee to my ledger, I check my reflection in the handy-dandy mirror above the ATM. There's dried blood on the right side of my nose and cheek. The shed hit me with a pretty good shot but I won by TKO in the fifth.

No other customers in the joint, so I'm up next at the counter.

The agent says, "Can I help you?" He's a kid, skinnier than a junkie. Greasy hair parted all wrong, shadow of a mustache under his nose.

I say, "I need a car. Nothing fancy. But if you have something that has bumpers, real bumpers with rubber and reinforced, I don't know, metal. Not those cheap plastic panels they put on the front and back of most cars now. Real bumpers."

The kid stares at me. I know, I'm pretty. The dried blood adds character to a face already overburdened with character. He probably thinks I'm drunk with my slow, deep voice and my sudden bumper obsession. I suppose I should've cleaned myself up in the bathroom first. Can't do much about my voice, though. I am what I am.

He snaps out of his trance and types fast, too fast. There's no way he's hitting the keys in any sort of correct order. He says, "The only vehicles we have with what you described are a couple of small pickup trucks and three SUVs."

"Nah, I hate trucks and SUVs. Too big." I don't want to hurt anyone more than I already might. "I want something compact, easy to drive." I know enough not to add, *Won't cause a lot of collateral damage.*

"Okay. We have plenty of compacts." He types again at warp speed. It's actually kind of impressive. Good for him for finding his niche at such a young age.

I say, "A compact, but something safe. Air bags and all that stuff, and maybe with bumpers."

"I'm sorry, sir, but we don't have any compacts or sedans with the bumpers you described."

"Right, right, you already told me that. Sorry. Oh, and it should have one of those GPS thingies for directions."

"Our vehicles all come equipped with GPS."

Fantastic. I give him my license and credit card. All is well. We will complete our vehicular transaction and there will be joy.

I look outside the bay windows. No sign of the goons. There's a slowly creeping thought, bubbling its way up through the murk, the remnants of my cab nap. And here it is: I forgot to ask Brill where he dumped me. I was asleep and have no idea if we're still in Osterville or not. There's a nondescript strip mall across the street from the agency. It looks like every strip mall on the Cape. It has a pharmacy, bank, breakfast joint, gift shop, and water sports store. Maybe we're in Hyannis.

Wait. I find a life jacket. There's a stack of business cards on the counter; I paw at a couple and spy the address. Okay, still in Osterville, at its edge, but I know where I am now.

I say, "Oh, if you haven't picked me a car already, can I get one that has a lot of distracting stuff going on inside?"

He doesn't look up from his computer. He knows that won't help him. "You mean like a CD player?"

I say, "That's okay too, but I'm thinking more along the lines of a car that has a busy dashboard, tons of digital readings, lights, and blinking stuff."

"You want to be distracted?"

"When you say it like that, it sounds a little silly, but yeah, that'd be swell."

"I think we can accommodate you, Mr. Genevich."

"You're a pro's pro, kid."

I relax. I know I'm making a fool of myself, but the looming situation of me behind a steering wheel has me all hot and bothered. I know it's irresponsible and dangerous, reckless, and selfish. Me behind the wheel of a car is putting Mr. and Mrs. Q. Public and their extended families in danger. But I'm doing it anyway. I can't wait to drive again.

I'm done with Brill. Renting a car is the only way I'm going to get around without further endangering Ellen, and hopefully it'll be less likely the goons will pick up my scent again. They know my condition, they've been following me around; they won't be expecting me to rent a car.

I tell the kid I want the car for two days. He quotes me the price and terms. I cross my fingers and hope there's enough room on my credit card. Then he says, "Will you be buying renter's insurance for the vehicle?"

I laugh. Can't remember the last time I laughed like this. This could be a problem. For many narcoleptics, laughter is a trigger for the Godzilla symptoms, the ones that flatten Tokyo. But I know where I am and I know what I'm doing and I know where to go next. I feel damn good even if my contorted face reopens the cut along my nose.

I say, "Oh, yeah, kid. I'll take as much insurance as you'll give me. Then double the order."

THIRTY-TWO

My car is blue and looks like a space car. Meet George Jetson.

The kid has to show me how to start the thing, as it has no ignition key. Insert the black keyless lock/alarm box into a portal in the dash, push another dash button, and we're ready to go. Simple. The car is one of those gas-electric hybrids. At least I'll be helping out the environment as I'm crashing into shit. Hopefully I don't damage any wetlands or run over endangered owls or something similarly cute and near extinction.

Okay, I start the car up. My hands grip the wheel hard enough to remold the plastic, turn it into clay. White knuckles, dry mouth, the whole bit. I wonder what the air bag tastes like. Probably not marshmallow fluff.

I roll to the edge of the lot and onto the street, and I don't hit anything, don't pass out asleep, and the wheels don't fall off, so I relax a little bit. I join the flow of traffic, become part of the mass, the great unending migration, the river of vehicles, everyone anonymous but for a set of numbers and letters on their plates. My foot is a little heavy on the brake pedal; otherwise I'm doing fine. If millions of privileged stunted American lunkheads can operate heavy machinery, I can too. Driving is the easy part. It's staying awake that'll take some doing.

Yeah, I'm an accident waiting to happen, but I should be all right on a short jaunt into town. This first trip is only to downtown Osterville. It's the later excursion back to Southie that'll be my gauntlet.

I'm driving at the speed limit. I check all my mirrors, creating a little rotation of left sideview, rearview, right sideview, while sprinkling in the eyes-on-the-road bit. The OCD pattern might lull me to sleep so I change it up, go from right to left. I forgot how much you have to look at while driving, the proverbial everywhere-at-once. It's making me tired.

Of course, the roads are congested all of a sudden and out of nowhere. Did I run over a hive or something? Cars swarming and stopping and going and stopping. The town has been deader than the dinosaurs since I've been here, and all of a sudden it's downtown LA.

No signs of the red car, or at least one particular red car and its goons. I should've asked for a car with tinted windows so nobody could see me. I wasn't thinking. My windshield is a big bubble and I'm on display, behind glass; don't break in case of emergency.

Traffic stretches the ride out to fifteen minutes before I penetrate the downtown area. There's Ellen's photography studio/antiques store. The antiques side is dark. During the off-season, she only opens on Fridays and weekends. There are lights on in her studio, though, so she's still here. Not sure if that's a good thing or bad thing. I take a left onto a one-lane strip of pavement that runs between Ellen's building and the clothing boutique next door, and I tuck me and my rental behind the building. There's no public parking back here, only Ellen's car, a Dumpster, and the back doors.

I get out and try the antiques shop first. There are two large wooden doors that when open serve as a mini-bay for larger deliveries. The doors are loose and bang around in the frame as I yank on them, but they're locked. Damn. It's where I need to go and I don't have any keys.

Door number 2, then, the one I wanted to avoid. Up three wooden stairs to a small landing and a single door, a composite and newer than the antique doors, which is how nature intended. That's locked too. I'm not walking around out front on the off-chance the goons do a drive-by. I ring the bell. It doesn't ring. It buzzes like I just gave the wrong answer to the hundred-dollar question.

Footsteps approach the door and I panic. Ellen can't know that I drove here. I'm parked behind the Dumpster, my shiny space car in plain view. Crap. I try to fill the doorway with my bulk, but Ellen will be half a step above me, elevated. The door opens.

Ellen's wearing her clown pants again. She says, "Hey. What are you doing back here?"

I yawn and stretch my arms over my head, trying to block her view. For once, me being tired is schtick. I say, "I don't know. There was a lot of traffic out front and Brill came back here to drop me off. He's kind of a surly guy."

"Stop it. He's a sweetheart." Ellen is whispering and throwing looks over her shoulder. "I've got a client and I'm in the middle of a shoot. Go around front."

I say, "Come on, I'm here, my knees have rusted up, and I'm dead tired. Let me in. Your client won't even notice me limp through." I lay it on thick but leave out the pretty please.

She says, "Yeah, right," but steps aside, holds the door open, and adds, "Just be quick."

"Like a bunny," I say. I shimmy inside the door, crowding her space purposefully so she has a harder time seeing over me and into the lot. I compress and crumple her clown pants. It's not easy being a clown.

She says, "What the hell is that car doing back here?"

My hands go into my pockets. Instead of balls of lint and thread, maybe I'll find a plausible excuse. I say, "Oh, some guy asked if he could park there real quick. Said he was just returning something next door. I told him it was fine." Lame story, but should be good enough for now.

Ellen lets out an exasperated sigh. "If he's not out in five minutes, I'm calling a tow truck. I can't have people parking back here." She's all talk. She'll forget about the car as soon as the door is shut. I bet.

Ellen leads me through a small back hallway and into the studio. The background overlay is a desert and tumbleweeds, huge ones, bigger than my car. A little kid is dressed up as a cowboy with hat, vest, chaps, six-shooters, spurs, the whole bit. He must've just heard the saddest campfire song ever because he's bawling his eyes out while rocking on a plastic horse.

Those UFO-sized photographer spot lamps are everywhere, warming the kid up like he's a fast-food burger that's been sitting out since the joint opened. I don't blame him for being a little cranky.

His mom yaks on her cell phone, sniping at someone, wears sunglasses and lip gloss shinier than mica, and has a purse bigger than Ellen's mural tumbleweed. It ain't the OK Corral in here.

I say, "Sorry to interrupt. As you were."

The little kid jumps at the sound of my voice, cries harder, and rocks the wooden pony faster, like he's trying to make a break for it.

I say, "Remember the Alamo, kid."

Ellen apologizes, puts on a happy face like it's part of her professional garb, something that hangs on a coatrack after work is over. She ducks behind her camera. "Come on, Danny boy, you can smile for me, right? Look at my pants!"

Yikes. I'm out of the studio, door closed behind me, and into her nondescript reception area. Ellen has a desk with a phone, computer, printer, and a buzzer. Next to that is a door to the antiques store. That's locked too. The doorknob turns but there's a dead bolt about chest high. I need me some keys. Don't want to have to see the clown pants and cowboy-tantrum show again. I go behind her desk and let my fingers do the walking through her drawers. I find a ring of ten or so keys.

Guess and check, and eventually the right key. I don't turn on the lights, as the store's bay window is large and I could easily be seen from outside. The afternoon is dying, but there's enough light in here that I can see where I'm going.

The antiques store is packed tight with weekend treasures: wooden barrels filled with barely recognizable tools that might've come from the dawn of the Bronze Age, or at least the 1940s; home and lawn furniture; kitschy lamps, one shaped like a hula girl with the shade as the grass skirt; fishing gear; a shelf full of dusty hardcover books; tin advertising placards. Piles of useless junk everywhere. If it's old, it's in here somewhere. I never understood the appeal of antiques. Some things are meant to be thrown away and forgotten.

The photography and film stuff has its own corner in the rear of the store. There's a display counter with three projectors under glass. Short stacks of film reels separate the projectors. Nice presentation. No price tags, but the specs and names of the projectors are written on pieces of masking tape that are stuck to the counters. The curling and peeling tape is in much worse condition than the projectors, which look to be mint.

All right. I assume the film is 8 millimeter, but I'm not exactly sure what projector I need to play it, and even if I had the right projector I don't know how to use it. I need Ellen's help. Again.

Out of the dusty store and back into the reception area, I stick my head inside the studio. Glamour Mom is still on the phone, talking directly to a Prada handbag maybe. The kid continues to wail. Ellen dances some crazed jig that pendulums back and forth behind her tripod. She makes odd noises with her mouth. A professional at work.

I say, "Hey, Bozo. I need your expertise for a second."

Under normal circumstances (maybe these are her normal circumstances, I don't know), I'd assume she'd be pissed at me for interrupting. She mumbles something under her breath that I don't quite hear, but it might be *Thank Christ*.

Ellen has to say, "Excuse me," three times before the woman puts down her phone. "Maybe we should try something else. I don't think Danny likes being a cowboy. Why don't we change him, let him pick something else out of that bin over there, and I'll be right back?"

The brat has worked her over pretty good, softened her up, and hopefully made her head mushy enough so she can't add one and one together. I need to take advantage and throw stuff at her quick.

Ellen has only one foot in the reception area and I'm sticking the film canister in her face. I say, "I just need a little help. This is eight-millimeter film, right? Or super eight? Or something else?"

Ellen blinks a few times, clearly stunned after trying to wrangle Danny the Kid into an image. She says, "Let me see."

I open the can and let a six-inch tail grow from the spool. She reaches for it. I say, "Don't get your grubby fingerprints on it."

"I need to see the damn thing if I'm going to tell you what it is." I give it to her, ready to snatch it back out of her hands should she hold it up to the light and see something bad. "This isn't super eight, it's too dark. Eight millimeter." She gives it back, yawns, and stretches. "My back is killing me. Where'd you get that?"

I don't answer. I say, "I need a projector. I need to watch this. Got anything I can borrow?"

"Yeah, I have projectors. Silent or sound?"

"I don't know. Do you have one that plays both?"

I take her by the arm and lead her into the store. She doesn't turn on the lights. What a good clown.

Small key goes into small lock, and the glass slides open to the left. "This one will play your movie, sound or no sound. It's easy to use too."

I read the tape: Eumig Mark-S Zoom 8mm magnetic sound projector.

She picks it up, shuts the glass case, and rests it on the counter. It's a mini-robot out of a 1950s sci-fi flick, only the earth isn't standing still.

She says, "Let me finish up the shoot and I can set up the projector in here. I've got a screen in the closet."

"No, I can't watch it here. This film, it's for a client. Just need to make sure what's in the can is the real deal, that it's what I think it is. No one else but me can see it."

"Why? Where did you get it?"

"Sorry. Secrets of state. I can't tell you."

"Wait. What client? How have you had any contact with a client since we've been down here?"

I think about the backyard and demolished shed. She'll know where I found it.

I hold out my cell phone, wave it around like it's Wonka's golden ticket. "I've been on the phone with my clients all day.

I'm not gonna just sit on my ass the whole time I'm down here. That wouldn't be very professional, would it? Don't worry. It's no big deal. I watch the flick for simple verification, then stick it in a FedEx box, case closed. You go. Go finish up with that little cherub in there. I'm all set."

Ellen folds her arms across her chest. She's not having any of it. She digs in, entrenches, a tick in a mutt's ear. She says, "I think you're lying to me."

"Frankly, I'm nonplussed. Would I lie to you, Clowny?"

"Yes. You do, all the time."

"True. But this time everything is kosher." I spread the word *everything* out like it's smooth peanut butter.

Ellen sighs and throws up her hands. "I don't know what to do with you, and I don't have time to argue. I'll set up the projector, then go back into the studio, and you can watch it in here by yourself."

Okay, I'm by one hurdle; now on to the next. I talk as fast as I can, which isn't very. "No good. I need someplace private. Not rush-hour downtown Osterville in an antiques store with a huge bay friggin' window. Let me borrow it. I promise to return it in one piece. I'll set it up and watch it at the house before you come home."

"You're a giant pain in my butt, you know that, right?"

I say, "I'll have a bowl of popcorn ready for you when you get back. Extra butter."

"Fine. Let me see if the bulbs still work." Ellen plugs it in, turns it on. A beam of light shines out of the projection bulb and onto a bearskin rug and its matted fur. I resist the urge for a shadow puppet show. She turns off the projection bulb and two small lights come on within the body of the projector.

I say, "What are those lights?"

"You could thread the film in the dark, if you needed to."

"Good to know."

"This projector will automatically thread through the film gate, which is nice. If you think it's a sound film, you'll have to thread it manually through the sound head and then to the take-up reel. It's easy, though." Ellen points out the heads, loops, and hot spots. I should be taking notes, drawing diagrams.

She says, "The instruction manual is taped underneath the projector if you want to mess around with it. If you can figure out how to do it yourself, great, or just wait until I get home. I won't be long. This kid is my last shoot of the day." She shuts off the projector and unplugs it.

I say, "Thanks. I think I can handle it from here."

Ellen walks to the other side of the counter, then ducks down and disappears. Momentarily inspired, I take one of the display case's stacked film reels and tuck it inside my coat. The reel is black, not gray, but about the same size as the one I found. I'm a collector now.

Ellen emerges with a carrying case. "This was Tim's projector. If you break it, you're a dead man." The little robot disappears into the case. I hope it won't be lonely, separated from its friends.

Tim's projector for Tim's film that was in Tim's shed. I've

opened one of those sets of nested Russian dolls, and I don't know when the dolls will stop coming out or how to stop them. I grab the case by the handle and let the projector hang by my hip. It's heavy. It's all heavy.

"How come you don't sell these projectors, or the cameras on the wall?"

"What? We don't have time for this."

"You're right, we don't, but I want to know. Maybe the answer is important. Give me your gut-shot answer. Quick. Don't think about it. Don't think about what I'd want to hear or don't want to hear. Just tell me."

She says, "Because no one else should be using Tim's stuff."

I want to take the question back because she can't answer it. It wasn't fair to try and distill something as complex as her twenty-five-plus years of being a widow into a reaction. She gave it an honest try. Don't know what I was expecting, maybe something that would make Tim seem like a real person, not a collection of secrets, clues, and consequences. Something that helps me to get through tonight.

I say, "Fair enough. There will be no breaking of the projector. I'm a gentle soul."

Ellen puts her hands in her hair. "You've got me all frazzled. I need to go back. There's a stand-alone screen in that closet over there. Take it with you."

I scoot down to the end of the display cabinet, boxing her in while I root through the closet for the screen. I hold up a long heavy cardboard box. "Is it in the box?"

"Yes! Now get out of the way. Shoo!"

I hustle after Ellen, my arms full of film equipment. Let's all go to the lobby. I follow her into the reception area, to the studio. Ellen stops at the door.

"Where are you going?"

I say, "I'm going out the way I came in. Brill is going to meet me out back. He went to get a coffee and a pack of smokes and a *Playboy*. I'm telling you, he's a sick old man."

Ellen ignores me and walks into the studio. "Okay, so sorry for the interruption. He's leaving, finally."

It's true.

Ellen breaks into a fake-cheery voice. She's a pro at it, which makes me wonder how many years she used that voice on the kid me: everything is great and happy and there's nothing wrong here, nothing can hurt you.

She says, "How's Danny doing? Is he ready? You're going to look so cool in the pictures, Danny. Picture time!"

The movie-show equipment is cumbersome. I flip the screen up onto my left shoulder, lugging it like a log. Balancing and carrying it is not easy.

Glamour Mom couldn't care less about the goings-on and continues to talk on the phone. Danny is still crying, and is now dressed like a duck; yellow feathers and orange bill split wide open over his face, the suit swallows him. His wings flap around as Ellen changes the desert scene to a sunset lake.

I'm no duck. I am the guy waddling out, away from the sunset lake and into a back alley.

THIRTY-THREE

The sun is setting but there's no lake back here. I buckle the projector into the passenger seat. It could be a bumpy ride and I don't want it rolling around the trunk or backseat. It needs to survive the trip.

Before I climb behind the wheel, I take out the cell phone. No messages. I consider calling Brill, but I won't. There's no way he'd give me a ride to Southie, even if I did have enough cash, which I don't. I turn off the cell phone. I'm sure Ellen will be calling me as soon as she gets home.

Yeah, Southie. I've made a decision. Don't know if I'm going to call Jennifer, but I'm going back to Southie and my apartment. This is the only way to finish the case. My case. I don't think I have the cash or credit card balance left to hole up in a local motel, or any motel on the way to Southie, and watch the film. Besides, this isn't about hiding anymore. That skulking-around shit I went through today is not for me. It makes me irritable and fatigued. This is about doing it my way. I'm going to go back to my office and my apartment, where I will watch this film and solve this case. It's going to end there, one way or the other, because I say so.

Okay, the drive. The downtown traffic has decreased considerably. The townies are all home, eating dinner, watching the local news. I wonder what Janice Sullivan is doing tonight. I don't remember if Brendan's wake was today or not. I wonder how long her twin aunts are staying at the house. I think about Janice's first day alone, and then the next one, and the next one. Will I be able to tell her, when all this is over, about the death of her husband?

Stop. I can't lose myself in runaway trains of thought. Those are nonstop bullets to Sleep Town.

Motoring through the outskirts of Osterville and I need to make a pit stop before the big ride. I pull into a convenience store. Mine is the only car in the lot. If this was Southie, the townie kids would be hanging out here, driving around and buzzing the lot because there's no other place to go. They'd spike their slurpies and drink hidden beers. But this isn't Southie. I'm not there yet, not even close.

Inside, a quick supply run: supersized black coffee, a box of powdered donuts, and a pack of smokes. Dinner of champions. Let's hope it brings on a spell of insomnia.

Back behind the wheel with my supplies, I check the seat belt rig on my copilot. I apologize for not getting it a Danish. I'm so inconsiderate.

I turn on the space car. The dashboard is a touch-screen computer with settings for the radio, CD player, climate control, fuel efficiency ratings for the trip, and a screen that displays an animated diagram of the hybrid engine and when the power shifts from gas to electric. Have to hand it to the rental agent, I wanted distracting and the kid gave it to me.

Next is the GPS. I plug in the convenience store's address, then the destination, my apartment. I choose AVOID HIGHWAYS instead of FASTEST TRIP. Driving on the highway, especially the expressway when I get closer to Boston, would be too dangerous for everyone. I know the drive, normally ninety minutes, will take twice, maybe even three times as long by sticking to back roads, but there's always congestion on the highways and the likelihood of me killing myself and someone else with my car at highway speeds is too great. I'll take it slow and steady and win the race on the back roads.

The GPS estimates driving time to be three hours and twenty-two minutes. I pat the projector, say, "Road trip," and pull out of the lot. The GPS has a female voice. She tells me to turn left.

"You're the boss."

I drive. Osterville becomes Centerville becomes Barnstable becomes Sandwich. My coffee is hot enough to burn enamel, the way I like it. The combination of excitement, fear, and caffeine has me wired. I feel awake. I know it's the calm before the storm. I still could go out at any minute, but I feel good. That's until I remember there's only two ways off the Cape. Both include a spot of highway driving and a huge bridge.

It's past dusk and there's no turning back. The sun is gone-daddy-gone and might never come up again if I'm not careful, as if careful ever has anything to do with narcolepsy. I'm in

Sandwich when the GPS tells me to get on Route 6. She's too calm. She doesn't realize what she's telling me to do.

The on-ramp to the highway winds around itself and spits me onto a too-small runway to merge into the two-lane traffic. I jump on with both feet and all four tires, eyes forward, afraid to check my mirror. A hulking SUV comes right up my behind and beeps. The horn is loud enough to be an air raid siren. I jerk and swerve right but keep space car on the road. Goddamn highway, got to get off sooner than soon.

The Sagamore Bridge is ahead, a behemoth, seventy-plus years old. That can't be safe for anyone. It spans the Cape Cod Canal and is at least 150 feet above the water. Its slope is too steep, the two northbound lanes too narrow. No cement dividers, just double yellow lines keep northbound and southbound separated. They need more than lines. North and south don't like each other and don't play well together. Doesn't anyone know their history anymore?

There are too many cars and trucks squeezing over the towering Cape entrance and exit. I stay in the right lane. I'm so scared I'm literally shaking. White powder from a donut I stuff in my mouth sprinkles all over my pants. I probably shouldn't be eating now, but I'm trying for some sort of harmless everyday action while driving, just like the other slob motorists on the death bridge.

The steel girders whisper at my car doors. I'm on an old rickety roller coaster. The car is ticking its way up the big hill, still going up, and I'm anticipating the drop. My hands are empty of donut and back on the wheel, still shaking. This is a mistake.

I can't manage my narcolepsy and I can't manage who or what I'll hit with the space car when I go to sleep. No if. When. I don't know when an attack will happen. There's no pattern. There's no reason.

I try to drink the coffee but my tremors are too violent and I get my lips and chin scalded for the trouble. The swell of traffic moves at a steady 45 miles per hour. There are other vehicles on the front, back, and left of me. I can't slow down and can't switch lanes. I won't look right and down, to the water. I'm not afraid of the bridge or the fall. I'm afraid of me, of that curtain that'll just go down over my eyes.

I crest the top of the bridge. A blast of wind voices its displeasure and pushes me left a few inches. I correct course, but it's not a smooth correction. The car jerks. The wind keeps blowing, whistling around the car's frame. My hands want to cry on the steering wheel. They're doing their best. They need a drink and a cigarette.

After the crest is down. The down is as steep as the up, and almost worse. The speed of the surrounding traffic increases. We have this incredible group forward momentum and nothing at the bottom of the hill to slow us down. I tap my brakes for no reason. I chance a look in the rearview mirror and the bulk of the bridge is behind me. Thank Christ. I'm over the canal and off the Cape. I breathe for the first time since Sandwich. The breath is too clean. Need a smoke, but that will have to wait until I get off the highway.

I'm finally off the bridge. Ms. GPS says she wants world peace and Route 6 is now Route 3 north, and I need to take the first exit to get with the back-roads plan again. Easy for her to say. I still have some highway to traverse.

I'm putting along Route 3 in the right lane, going fifty while everyone else passes me. The flat two lanes of highway stretch out into darkness, and the red taillights of the passing cars fade out of sight. I think about staying on the highway, taking it slow, pulling over when I get real tired and getting to Southie quicker, but I can't chance it. I crash here, I'm a dead man, and I'll probably take someone with me.

I'm already yawning by the time the first Plymouth exit shows up on my radar screen. Maybe I'll show my movie on Plymouth Rock. I take the exit and pull over in a gully soon after the off-ramp. Need to reset my bearings, take a breather. My hands and fingers are sore from vise-gripping the wheel.

I light a cigarette and turn on my cell phone. It rings and vibrates as soon as it powers up. It's Ellen. I let it ring out, then I call her back. My timing is good. She's still leaving a message for me so my call is directly shuffled off to her voice mail.

Talk after the beep. "I'm okay, Ellen. No worries. Just so you know, the DA is crooked, can't be trusted. You stay put and call the police if you see a couple of mountain-sized goons on your doorstep, or if any red cars pull into the driveway. Or if that doesn't make you feel safe, go to a motel. I'm being serious. I'd offer to treat but I'm just about out of cash. I've almost solved my case. I'll call you back later, when it's over."

It is possible the goons are in the house, have Ellen tied to a chair, gun to her head, the whole mustache-twisting bit, and are making her call me under the threat of pain. Possible but not likely. Sure, it's getting late and the DA and his squad are desperate to get the film, but they also have to be careful about how many people know what they're doing. They start harassing too many folks, the cleanup gets too big and messy. Then again, maybe I shouldn't underestimate their desperation.

I can't turn back now. If the goons want me, they can call from their own phone.

The cell rings. It's Ellen and I don't answer it. She must've heard my message. I'll make it up to her later, if there is a later. I turn on the car, and it's back on the road again for me.

Plymouth is its own state. The biggest city in Massachusetts by square mileage, and I'm feeling it. Drive, drive, drive. Lefts and rights. Quiet back roads that range from the heart of suburbia to the heart of darkness, country roads with no streetlamps and houses that don't have any neighbors.

It's a weeknight and it's cold, so no one is out walking or riding their bikes. Mostly, it's just me and the road. When another car approaches in the opposite lane, I tense up, a microwave panic; it's instant and the same feeling I had on the highway. I think about what would happen if I suddenly veered into that lane, into those headlights, and I'm the Tin Man with no heart and everything starts to rust. Then the car passes me and I relax a little, but the whole process is draining.

I pull over and eat a few donuts. I pull over and take a leak, stretch my legs. I pull over and light another fire in my mouth. I pull over and try to take a quick nap, but as soon as I park the car, shut everything off, I'm awake again. The almost-asleep feeling is gone. I close my eyes, it's lost, and for once I can't find it.

Drive, drive, drive. The GPS says I'm in Kingston, but I don't remember leaving Plymouth. That's not good. My stomach fills with acid, but that's what I get for medicating with black coffee and powdered donuts.

I think about calling someone, just to shoot the shit. Talking can help keep me awake, but there's no one to call. I try to focus on the GPS, its voice, maps, and beeps. I learn the digital pattern, how soon before a turn she'll tell me to turn. This isn't good either. The whole trip is becoming a routine. I've been in the car long enough that driving is once again automatic behavior.

I sing. I play with the touch screen, changing the background colors. Kingston becomes Pembroke. Pembroke becomes Hanover.

More than ninety minutes have passed since the start. I'd be in Southie by now if I could've driven on the highway. That kind of thinking isn't helping. Stay on the sunny side of the street, Genevich.

The road. The road is in Hanover, for now. I flick the projector's latches up and down. The projector doesn't complain. The road. How many roads are there in Massachusetts? Truth is, you can get they-uh from hee-uh. You can even find roads to the past. Everything and everyone is connected. It's more than a little depressing. I flick the latches harder; apparently I'm sadistic when it comes to inanimate objects. The road. Flick.

Then everything is noise. The engine revs and the space car fills a ditch. My teeth knock and jam into each other with the jolt. The car careens left into bushes and woods. Budding branches scratch the windshield and side panels. I cut the wheel hard right and stomp on the brake pedal. The car slows some, but the back end skids out, and it wants to roll. I know the feeling. The car goes up and I'm pitched toward the passenger seat and the projector. The space car is going to go over and just ahead is the trunk of a huge tree.

Then the car stops. Everything is quiet. The GPS beeps, tells me to turn right.

I climb out. The car is beached on a swale, a foot away from the big tree. It's pitch dark and I can't see all that much, but the driver's-side door feels dented and scratched. I crossed over the right lane and into some woods. There's a house maybe two hundred yards ahead. I walk around to the passenger side and check the projector, and it seems to be in one piece.

"Now that we've got that out of the way."

I climb back in the car and roll off the hill; the frame and wheel wells groan but I make it back to the road and go a half mile before I pull over again. The space car's wounds seem superficial. Tires still inflated. No cracked glass, and I have no cracked bones.

The GPS and distracting dashboard aren't enough to keep me conscious. I need another stay-awake strategy. I dig a notepad and pencil out of my coat and put it in the passenger seat. It's worth a shot.

Hanover becomes Norwell. I'm keeping a running tally of yellow street signs. Whenever I pass one, I make a slash on the notepad, a little task to keep me focused and awake. Norwell becomes Hingham. I'm driving with more confidence. I know it's a false confidence, the belief that the disaster has already happened, lightning struck once, and it won't happen again. I know that isn't true but after a night spent in a car, by myself, it's easy to cling to my own lies.

I keep up with the tally marks. I play with the dashboard some more. I still get sleepy. I push on. Hingham becomes Weymouth. I pull over twice and try to sleep. Again, no dice. I walk around, take deep breaths, alternating filling up my lungs with hot smoke and with the cold March air. I pee on someone's rosebushes.

It's almost midnight, but as I creep closer to the city there are more lights, a neon and halogen path. Things are getting brighter. Weymouth becomes Quincy. Despite the late hour, there are more cars around. I let them box me in and go where the currents take me. Quincy becomes the outskirts of Dorchester. I pass the JFK library and UMass Boston and BC High School. Dorchester becomes Southie.

I've made it. Bumped and bruised, scratched, damaged, more than a little weary, but I'm here.

THIRTY-FOUR

I drive by my building three times, approaching it from differ-ent angles and streets. I'm circling, only I'm not the buzzard. I watch the local traffic and eyeball the parked cars. No sign of the goon car. My office and apartment windows are darkened. No one left the light on for me.

Time to end the magical mystery tour. I park on West Broadway, a block away from my building, across from an empty bank parking lot. I wait and watch the corner, my cor-ner. There's nothing happening around my apartment. Cabs trolling the streets, homeless sinking inside their upturned collars and sitting on benches, and pub crawlers are the only ones out.

I take out my cell and flip it around in my hands, giving the fingers something to hold besides the steering wheel. I'm not going to call Jennifer right now. Maybe later. Maybe after I watch the film. Maybe not at all. I don't care all that much about what happens after the film. I just need to see it before everything falls apart and on top of me.

Phone goes back inside the jacket and the manila envelope

comes out. I check that the photos are still inside, that they haven't run and hid anywhere. The photos are still there, so are the young woman and those three letters. LIT, Tim's signature. I tuck the envelope under the driver's seat, a pirate hiding his booty. I don't know if I'll be able to reclaim the pictures later, but I want to keep the film and the photos separate, just in case.

I get out of the car and remove a small branch that was pinned under a wiper blade. That's better. Here, under the streetlights, the damage to the space car looks severe and permanent, more a bite from a pit bull than a bee sting. Bumpers wouldn't have helped, either.

I unload the screen and projector, the precious cargo. My muscles are stiff and the joints ache from the drive. They don't want to move and they liked it in the car. Sorry, fellas. There's work to do.

Screen lying across my shoulders and the projector dangling from my left hand, I hike up the street. I'm some limping and bent documentary director about to see my life's work for the first time. I have no idea what kind of story, what kind of truth I've discovered, documented, even created. I'm afraid of that truth and wish I could hide from it, but I can't. Won't. Yeah, I'm a kind of hero, but the worst kind; the one acting heroic only by accident and because of circumstance.

There's a cold breeze coming off the bay. It's insistent and gets trapped and passed between the rows of buildings, bouncing around like a ricocheting bullet, hitting me with multiple shots. No tumbleweeds, but wisps of paper wrappers and crushed cans roll on the sidewalks. West Broadway isn't deserted, but it might as well be. There's a distinct last-person-on-earth vibe going on. I'm alone and have been for a long time.

I make it to my front door and put my burdens down on the welcome mat. The door is locked, both knob and dead bolt. I feel so protected. My keys fit into their assigned slots and Open Sesame. I should have a flashlight. I should have a lot of things. I lump the equipment inside and I turn on the hall and office lights for a quick peek.

The office and hallway have been cleared and cleaned out, the carcass picked over and stripped. Only the file cabinet and the desk remain in the office. The desk is missing a leg and leans crookedly toward a corner of the room. It's almost like I was never there. I'm a ghost in a ghost office. I don't bother to check if any of my files survived the purge. I don't want to advertise my triumphant return, the not-so-prodigal son, so I shut the lights off. The darkness comes back, slides right in, settles over everything, a favorite blanket.

The ascent up the stairs to the second-floor landing isn't quite blind, since leftover streetlight spills through the landing window. I huff and puff up the stairs, then put down the equipment next to my door. It's shut. Ellen's peeps have already fixed it. I take out my lighter and the half-inch flame is enough to guide my entry into the apartment. Unlike the office, my apartment has yet to be cleaned or even touched. The shambles and wreckage of my personal life are right where I left them, which is nice. Seems an appropriate scene as any for this little movie.

I scavenge some scraps of paper, find an ashtray, and light a small fire. The fire burns long enough for me to find two small candles in the kitchen. I light those. Don't know if their orange glow can be seen from the street, so I get a couple of wool blankets out of my bedroom and hang them over the windows, tucking and tying their corners into the curtain framing. A makeshift darkroom.

I set the screen up in front of my bedroom door, which is opposite the blanket-covered windows. Next up, quietly as I can, because anyone could be listening, I clear out some space and bring in the kitchen table. Two legs are broken. I experiment with varied hunks of the living room flotsam and jetsam and manage to jury-rig a flat stable surface for the projector. It'll hold the weight even if I can't.

I take the projector out of its case, careful, reverential, a jeweler plucking a diamond from the setting of an antique ring. The projector goes on the table. Its dual arms are stubby and upright. I plug it in, turn it on. Out spits a ray of blinding light, a spotlight that enlarges to a rectangle that's half on and half off the screen. I shut off the projection bulb and small pilot lights glow around the feeds. I read the manual. It has directions in English and French. It seems like straightforward stuff, but then I think I should try the other film I nabbed from Ellen's store first, just a little film-threading practice. Never mind. I don't have the time. I make adjustments to the height of the projector. I place the film on the front reel and thread it through the sound head like Ellen showed me. It's working.

I fear I might do something to tear or snap the tape, this collection of lost memories is so fragile its impossible thinness passes between my fingers, but the film feeds smooth and the take-up reel gathers frames. A quick adjustment to the lens and everything is in focus. I stand next to the projector and the table with its two legs. The projector is doing its projecting. I'm standing and watching. The film is playing.

THIRTY-FIVE

White empty frames are accompanied by a loud hiss, a loud nothingness. Then the white explodes into sound and color. The projector's speaker crackles with off-camera laughter, laughter that momentarily precedes any clear images. It's the laughter of boys, full of bravado and mischief and oh-shit-what-have-we-got-ourselves-into? The bedroom is drab with its green bedspread and off-white paint-chipped walls; nightstand and bookcase are splintering and warped. A neglected, dying bedroom in a Southie project. The scene is fixed; the camera is on a tripod.

She sits on the bed wearing her white T-shirt and short denim skirt, but also wearing big purple bruises and rusty scrapes. In color, she looks even more like Jennifer, but an anorexic version. Her arms are thinner than the film running past the projector's lens, skin washed with bleach. Her eyes are half open, or half closed. I want her to have a name because she doesn't have one yet. She sways on her knees and pitches in her own two cents of laughter. It's slurred and messy, a spilled drink, a broken cigarette. She's not Jennifer.

Off camera, the boys speak. Their voices are boxed in, tinny, trapped in the projector's speaker.

"Let me take a couple of quick shots."

"What the fuck for?"

"So he can beat off to 'em later."

"Fuck off. For cover shots, or promos. It'll help sell the movie, find buyers. What, am I the only one here with any business sense?"

"You ain't got no fuckin' sense."

"And you ain't got no fuckin' dick."

More of that boy laughter, plus the clinking of bottles, then Tim appears on-screen, backside first. He turns around, sticks his mug into the camera and travels through decades. He fills the frame, fills the screen in my apartment. He's a kid. Fifteen tops. Dark hair, pinched eyes, a crooked smile.

Ellen was right. He does look like me, like I used to look. No, that isn't it. He looks like how I imagined my own appearance, my old appearance in all the daydreams I've had of the pre-accident me. He is the idealized Mark Genevich, the one lost forever, if he ever existed in the first place. He's young, whole, not broken. He's not the monster me on that screen. He's there just for a second, but he's there. I could spend the next month wearing this scene out, rewinding and watching and rewinding, staring into that broken mirror.

Then Tim winks and says, "Sorry. I'll be quick, just like the boys will."

Off camera: a round of *fuck you*s and *you pussy*s mixes in with laughter. Tim turns away from the camera and snaps a picture. He says, "One more. How 'bout a money shot. Take the shirt and skirt off." The chorus shouts their approval this time. The camera only sees Tim's back. He completely obscures her. She mumbles something and then the sound of clothes being removed, cloth rubbing against itself and against skin. T-shirt flutters off the bed, a flag falling to the ground. Tim snaps a second picture, then hides behind the movie camera.

No one says anything and the camera just stares. She's shirtless and skirtless. She opens her eyes, or at least tries to, and says, "Someone gimme a drink."

Off camera. "When are we gonna start this shit?"

Tim says, "Whenever you're ready. Start now. I'll edit out your fuckups later."

Two bare-chested teens enter the scene, both wearing jeans. Their skin is painfully white and spotted with freckles and pimples. These guys are only a couple of years removed from Ellen's keepsake picture on the stairs, boys in men's bodies. Sullivan is on the right and Times on the left; both have wide eyes and cocksure sneers. Unlike in the stair picture from Ellen's house, Sullivan is now the bigger of the two, thick arms and broad shoulders. He's the muscle, the heavy lifter, the mover, the shaker. Times has a wiry build, looks leaner, quicker, and meaner. Here's your leader. He's holding a bottle of clear liquid, takes a swig.

Times kneels on the bed beside the woman and says, "You ready for a good time?" No one responds to or laughs at the porn cliché, which probably isn't a cliché to them yet. It's painfully earnest in this flick.

The new silence in the room is another character. Times looks around to his boys, and it's a moment when the whole thing could get called off, shut down. Sullivan and Tim would be all right with a last-second cancellation of this pilot. I can't know this but I do. The moment passes, like all moments must pass, and it makes everything worse, implicates them further, because they had a chance to stop and they didn't.

Times says, "Here." He gives her the bottle and she drinks deep, so deep I'm not sure she'll be able to come back up for a breath. But she does, and hands back the bottle and melts out of her sitting position and onto her back. Sullivan grabs a handful of her left breast and frantically works at the button and fly of his pants with his free hand.

Her right hand and arm float up in front her face slowly, like an old cobra going through the motions for some two-bit snake charmer, and her hand eventually lands on Times's thigh. She's like them, only a kid. And she's a junkie. I wonder if those three amigos could see that and were banking on it, or if they were too busy with their collective tough-guy routine to see anything.

Times says, "Lights, camera, action."

The sex is fast, rough, and clumsy. With its grim and bleak bedroom setting, drunk, high, and uninterested female star, and two boys who are awkward but feral and relentless, it's a scene that is both pathetic and frightening at the same time.

The vibe has flipped 180 degrees, from should-we-do-this to where the potential for violence is an ogre in the room. Like someone watching a scary movie through his fingers, I cringe because I know the violence is coming.

The camera stays in one spot and only pans and scans. There's never a good clear shot of the woman's face. We see her collection of body parts in assorted states of motion but never her face. She's not supposed to matter, and even if nothing else were to happen, this is enough to make me hate the boy behind the camera and the man he became. Tim says nothing throughout the carnal gymnastics. He's the silent but complicit eye.

Sullivan finishes first and stumbles out of the scene. He gives Tim—not the camera—a look, one that might haunt me for the rest of my little sleeps and short days. When that kid's middle-aged version killed himself in the basement of his Cape house, I imagine he had the same look on his face when he pulled the trigger. A look one might have when the truth, the hidden and ugly truth of the world, that we're all complicit, has been revealed.

Times is still going at her. He's on top and he speeds up his thrusts for the big finish. Then there's a horrible choking cough. It's wet and desperate and loud, practically tears through the projector's speaker, and makes Brill's lung-ejecting hacks sound like a prim and proper clearing of the throat.

"Jesus, fuck!" Times jumps off the bed like it's electrified.

It's her. She's choking. I still can't see enough of her face; she's lying down and the camera isn't up high enough. She coughs but isn't breathing in. Out with the bad but no in with the good. Yellow vomit leaks out of her nose and mouth and into her hair. Her hands try to cover her face but fall back onto the bed. She shakes all over, the convulsions increasing in speed and violence. I think maybe I accidentally sped up the film but I didn't; it's all her. Maybe the bed is electrified.

From behind the camera, and it sounds like he's behind me, talking over my shoulder, Tim says, "What's fuckin' happening?" He doesn't lose the shot, though, that son of a bitch. The camera stays focused on her.

"Oh, fuck, her fucking eyes, they're all white. Fuck! Fuck!"

Sullivan says, "She's freaking out. What do we do?"

The camera gets knocked to the floor, but it still runs, records its images. A skewed, tilted shot of under the bed fills the screen. There's nothing there but dust and cobwebs and darkness.

The bed shakes and the springs complain. The choking noises are gone. The boys are all shouting at the same time. I can only make out snippets, swears, phrases. It's a mess. I lean closer to the screen, trying to hide under that bed, trying to hear what they're saying. Their voices are one voice, high-pitched and scared.

Then the three voices become only two. One is screaming. I think it's Times. He's says, "Shut the fucking camera off!" He shouts it repeatedly, his increased mania exploding in the room.

And I hear Tim—I think it's Tim. He's whispering and getting closer to the camera. He's going to shut it off, taking orders like a good little boy. He's repeating himself too, has his own mantra. Tim is saying, "Is she dead? Is she dead?"

The screen goes white. The End. *Fin.*

The take-up reel rattles with a loose piece of film slapping against the projector. My hands are sweating and I'm breathing heavy. I shut off the projector, the screen goes black, the take-up reel slows, and I stop it with my hand. The used engine gives a whiff of ozone and waves of dying heat. Everything should be quiet, but it isn't.

"Who is she?" A voice from my left, from the front door.

I say, "Don't you mean, who was she?"

THIRTY-SIX

Jennifer Times stands in the front doorway. She looks like she did at the mall autograph session. Sweatpants, jean jacket over a Red Sox T, hair tied up into a tight ponytail. It might be the weak candlelight, shadows dampening her cheekbones and eyes, but she looks a generation older than when we were at the restaurant. We're both older now.

I say, "I don't remember calling and inviting you over. I would've cleaned up a bit first. Maybe even baked a cake."

She walks in, shuts the door behind her. Someone raised her right. She says, "Who was she? Do you know?"

I say, "No idea. No clue, as it was. How much did you see?"

"Enough."

I nod. It was enough.

She says, "What are you going to do now?"

"Me? I'm done. I'm taking myself out of the game, making my own call to the bullpen. I'm wrapping this all up in a pretty red bow and dumping into the state police's lap. Or the FBI. No local cops, no one who knows your dad, no offense. I was hired to find it. I found it."

Jennifer carefully steps over the rubble and crouches next to me, next to the projector. She stares at it like she might lay hands on it, wanting to heal or be healed, I don't know. "What do you think happened to her after?"

I say, "How did you get in here?"

"I checked the welcome mat and there were keys duct-taped underneath."

Keys? I never left any keys. I don't even have spares. Ellen wouldn't do that either. Yeah, she's the de facto mayor of Southie, friends with everyone, but she's also a pragmatist. She knows better than to leave keys under a welcome mat on one of the busiest corners of South Boston. All of which means Jennifer is lying and also means I'm screwed, as I'm sure other unexpected guests are likely to arrive shortly.

Jennifer holds up a ring of two keys on a Lithuanian-flag key chain.

Shit. Those are Ellen's keys. I say, "How did you know I was here?"

"Why are you interrogating me?"

"I'm only asking simple questions, and here you go trying to rush everything to the interrogation level."

She says, "I was parked outside of your apartment and saw you. I waited a few minutes and let myself in, then I sat outside your door listening. I came in when I heard them yelling."

I fold up and break down the projector as she talks. I don't rewind the film but, instead, slip the take-up reel into my coat pocket, next to the other film. I wrap up the cord and slide the projector into its case, latch the latches twice for luck. I say, "Why are you here?" and walk past her to the screen.

"I needed to see if you were telling me the truth on the phone. I had to know."

The screen recoils quickly and slides into its box nice and easy. I say, "And now that you know, what are you going to do?"

Jennifer walks past the table and sits on the couch. "How about answering my question?"

"What question was that? I tend to lose track of things, you know?"

"What do you think happened after? After the movie? What did they do?"

My turn to play the strong silent type. I lean on the screen, thinking about giving an answer, my theory on everything, life, death, the ever-expanding doomed universe. Then there's a short bang downstairs. Not loud enough to wake up neighbors, a newspaper hitting the door.

Jennifer whispers, "What was that?"

"It ain't no newspaper," I say. "Expecting company, Jennifer? It's awful rude to invite your friends over without asking me."

"I didn't tell anyone where I was going or what I was doing." She gets up off the couch, calm as a kiddie pool, and tiptoes into my bedroom. She gestures and I lean in close to hear. She whispers, "See if you can find out who that woman was and what they did with her after. You know, do your job. And if things get hairy, I'll come out and save you." Jennifer shuts the door.

No way. I'm going to pull her out of the room and use her as a human shield should the need arise. I turn the knob but it's locked. Didn't know it had a lock.

If things get hairy. I'm already hairy and so are the things. Yeah, another goddamn setup, but a bizarre one that makes no sense. Doesn't matter. Prioritize. I need to hide the equipment, or at least bury it in junk so it doesn't look like I'd just watched the film for the first time. I lay the screen behind the couch, unzip a cushion and stuff the film inside, then go to work with the projector and case, putting it under the kitchen table, incorporating it into one of the makeshift legs. I move the candles to the center of the table.

Maybe my priorities are all out of whack. I give thought to the back exit and the fire escape off the kitchen, but the front door to my apartment is currently under assault. I'm not much of a runner or climber, and I'd need one hell of a head start. I could call the police, but they'd be the DA's police, and even if they weren't, they wouldn't get here in time. No sense in prolonging this. I walk over to the front windows and pull down the blankets. I lean against the wall between the windows, light a cigarette, shine the tops of my Doc Martens on the backs of my calves, adjust my hat, pretend I have style.

The door flies open and crashes into the wall. The knob sinks into the plaster. The insurance bill just got a little bigger. As inevitable as the tides, the two goons are in my doorway.

I say, "That ain't the secret knock, so I'm going to have to ask you gentlemen to leave."

Redhead says, "Candles. How romantic."

Yeah, even with the added ambience of streetlamps and assorted background neon, the light quality isn't great, but it's enough to see a hell of a shiner under his right eye, scratches on his face, and the gun in his hand. He holds it like he's King Kong clutching a Fay Wray imposter and can't wait to squeeze.

Can't focus on the gun. It gets my panic juices flowing. This time with the goons, it feels different already, like how the air smells different before a thunderstorm, before all the action. My legs get a jump on the jellification process.

Baldy says, "Romancing yourself there, retard? You're fuckin' ugly enough that your right hand would reject you."

I blow some smoke, don't say anything, and try to give them smug, give them confidence. My bluff will work only if I get the attitude right. And even then, it still might not work.

Redhead is a totem to violence. He wears threat like cologne. He says, "I wouldn't be standing there fucking smiling like you know something. Smiling like you aren't never gonna feel pain again, Genevich."

I say, "Can't help myself, boys. I'm a happy guy. Don't mean to rub your noses in it."

Baldy says, "We're gonna rub your nose all over our fists and the fuckin' walls." He cracks his knuckles, grinding bone against bone.

They walk toward me, necks retracted into their shoulders, and I can just about hear their muscles bulging against their dress shirts and suit coats. Dust and sparks fall out of their mouths. Oh, and the gun is still pointed at me.

Can't say I've thought my Hail Mary bluff all the way

through, but I'm going with it. I open my jacket and pull out the dummy film, the black one, the one from Ellen's store. Only what I'm holding isn't the dummy film. Apparently I put that one inside the couch cushion. What I'm waving around in front of the goons is the take-up reel, half full with Tim's film.

Oh, boy. Need to regroup, and fast. I say, "Have you boys seen this yet? Some of the performances are uneven, but two thumbs way up. You know, you two fellas remind me of the shit-talking boys that star in the movie. Same intensity and all that. I'm sure the reviews will be just as good when it gets a wide release. Twelve thousand theaters, red-carpet premiere somewhere, Golden Globes, then the Oscars, the works."

The goons stop their advance, share a look. My cigarette is almost dead. I know the feeling well.

Redhead laughs, a car's engine dying. He says, "You trying to tell us you made a copy?"

Baldy's head is black with stubble. I guess, with all the *mishegas*, he hasn't had time for a shave. He should lighten his schedule. He says, "You haven't had time to make any copies."

"Says you. I had it digitized. Didn't take long, boys. Didn't even cost that much. Oh, I tipped well for the rush and all. But it got done, and done quick. Even made a few hard copies for the hell of it. You know, for the retro-vibe. The kids love all the old stuff."

Baldy breaks from formation and takes a jab step toward me. I think he's grown bigger since he first walked into the room. His nostrils flare out, the openings as wide as exhaust pipes. I'm in big trouble. He says, "You're fuckin' lying."

I don't know if that's just a standard reply, maybe Baldy's default setting. The goons creep closer. My heart does laps around my chest cavity and its pace is too fast, it'll never make it to the end of the race. Appearing calm is going to be as easy as looking pretty.

I say, "Nope. This one here is one of the copies. You don't think I'd wave the original around, do you? I figure I can make a quick buck or two by putting that puppy on eBay."

It's their turn to talk, to give me a break, a chance to catch my breath, but my breath won't be caught. It's going too fast and hard, a dog with a broken leash sprinting after a squirrel. Black spots in my vision now. They're not buying any of this, and I'm in a barrel full of shit. I move back, away from the window. My legs have gone cold spaghetti on me and I almost go down, stumbling on my twisted and bent CD tower. Muscles tingle and my skin suddenly gets very heavy.

I say, "If my video guy doesn't see me on his doorstep tomorrow morning, alone and in one piece, he uploads the video onto YouTube and drops a couple of DVDs into FedEx boxes, and the boxes have addresses, important addresses, on them, just in case you were wondering."

The goons laugh, split up, and circle me, one goon on each side. I'll be the meat in the goon sandwich. Looks like I should've gone with a frantic fire-escape escape. There isn't always a next time.

Redhead scratches his nose with the gun barrel and says, "You're bullshitting the wrong guys, Genevich. We don't believe you, and we don't really care. We're getting paid to find the film, take that film, copy or not, and then knock the snot out of you."

Things are getting more than hairy. Things are going black and fuzzy and not just at the edges. I say, "Don't make me drop another shed on your asses."

Baldy lunges, his coat billowing behind him like giant bat wings. The wings beat once, twice, he hangs in the air, and I feel the wind, it's hot and humid, an exhaled breath on glass that lifts the hat off my head. Then he takes a swing, but he doesn't land the blow because I'm already falling, already going down.

THIRTY-SEVEN

I open my eyes and everything is wrong. Cataplexy. My waking coma. The wires are all crossed, the circuit breakers flipped. I can't move and won't be able to for a while.

DA Times sits in front of me. He's wearing black gloves and holds a gun. Maybe I should get me one of those; seems like everyone else is buying. I'm always the last one in the latest trends. I'm the rotten egg.

"Mark? You there?"

I try to say, "Yeah," but it's only loosened air, don't know if he hears it so I blink a few times. Yeah, I'm here, and here is wrong. Here is my couch. The projector is on the kitchen table, the take-up reel and the film hang off the rear arm. The candles are two fingers from burning out, white melted wax pools around the holders. The screen is set up in front of my bedroom door. The blankets are over the windows.

The DA is dressed all in black: tight turtleneck and pants. He says, "I never realized how awful narcolepsy was, Mark. Are you currently experiencing cataplexy?" He shakes his head, his faux pity the answer to his own question. "These symptoms of yours are just dreadful. I feel for you, I really do. I don't know how you make it through the day."

"Positive thinking," I say. "I'm fine. I could get up and pin your nose to the back of your head if I wanted to, but it'd be rude." The murk is still in my head and wants me to go back under, back down. It'd be so easy just to close my eyes.

He frowns and talks real quiet. He's a dad talking to a screwup kid, the one he still loves despite everything. "From what Ellen tells me, you've had a real tough go of it."

"Ellen likes to worry." Luckily, I'm in no condition to present a state of shock or agitation at the mention of Ellen's name.

"I'd say she has reason to. Look at the couch you're sitting on, Mark. It's absolutely riddled with cigarette holes. Ellen mentioned the couch to me, but I thought she was exaggerating. It's a minor miracle you haven't burned this place to the ground. Yet."

I say, "Those aren't cigarette burns. I have a moth problem." My voice is weak, watery. It usually takes me twenty minutes to fully recover from cataplexy. I need to keep the chatter going. Despite his daddy-knows-best schtick, the gun and black gloves broadcast loud and clear what his real plan is for the evening.

The DA gets up and fishes around in my pockets. I could breathe on him real heavy, but that's about the only resistance I can offer. The DA takes my lighter out. No fair, I didn't say he could have it. Then he finds my pack of smokes, pulls one out, sticks it in my mouth, and lights it. It tastes good even though I know it's going to kill me.

Time to talk. Just talk. Talking as currency to buy me time. I hate time. I say, "Don't know why you and the goons bothered setting the equipment back up. But who am I to critique your work?" The cigarette falls out of my mouth, rolls down my chest and onto the floor between my feet. I hope it's on the hardwood floor, not on rug or debris.

The DA pulls out another cigarette and fills my mouth with it. He says, "Goons?"

I concentrate on the balancing act of talking and keeping the butt in my mouth. I'll smoke this one down to the filter if I have to. "Yeah, your boys, your goons. Redhead and Baldy. I'd like to make an official complaint to their supervisor when all this is over."

The DA leans in and hovers the gun's snub nose between my eyes. It's close enough that I smell the gun oil. The DA waving that thing in my face isn't going to speed up my recovery any.

He says, "Are these the same imaginary goons you warned Ellen about in a voice mail? You said something about a red car and a crooked DA too."

An upper cut to my glass chin. He really did talk to Ellen. I say, "If you did anything to Ellen, I'll—"

"She called me, Mark. Tonight. She was distraught, didn't know where you were. She said you had destroyed the shed today, emptied your bank account, and maxed out your credit cards in the last week. She told me how strangely you'd been behaving and said your symptoms seemed to have been worsening.

"We had a nice long chat. Ellen is a wonderful and brave

person. She told me everything about you and your narcolepsy, Mark. She told me that stress triggers the worst of your symptoms." He moves the gun all around my face, tracing the damaged features but not touching me. "I told her I'd check up on you. And here I am." He switches hands with the gun.

I can't think about Ellen and her motivations for calling the DA despite my pointed instructions to the contrary. It would ruin what little resolve I have left.

I say, "Gee, thanks. You're like a warm blanket and cup of hot chocolate, even if you are lying about the goons through your capped and whitened teeth." Despite my apartment being made to appear that I didn't break down all the film equipment before everyone showed up, I know he's lying.

He leans in and says, "For what it's worth, and that's not much because it has no bearing on what will happen here tonight, I'm telling the truth. No goons. You hallucinated or dreamed them up. This is all about me and you." His voice goes completely cold, can be measured only in the Kelvin scale.

I say, "And a woman. You know, the one who looks like your daughter? Except dead."

The DA doesn't say anything but leans back into his chair.

Need to keep the chatter going. I say, "What about your old pal Brendan? He's dead too."

The DA pushes the gun into my face again and says, "Are you stressed, Mark?" He looks down toward the floor, to something between my feet. "That cigarette has already caught on something. Can you smell the smoke? You need to be more careful and take care of yourself. No one else will."

He's bluffing about a fire, I hope. The paranoid part of me feels the temperature rising around my ankles, a fledgling fire starting right under my feet, a hotfoot joke that isn't so funny. I try to move the feet—and nothing. Might as well be trying to move the kitchen table with my mind.

I wiggle my fingers a little bit but can't make a fist, wouldn't even be able to hitchhike. But they'll be back soon. My legs are another matter. Those won't be able to hold me up for at least fifteen minutes, maybe longer. My second cigarette is burning away like lost time.

I say, "Jennifer is here."

"Mark, I really am sorry about all of this. I know you don't want to hear it, but at least your suffering will be over. You won't be a burden to Ellen or yourself anymore. It's really going to be for the best."

Now I'm getting mad. The fucker is talking to me like I'm some drooling vegetable and should pull my own plug.

I say, "Jennifer is hiding in my bedroom. Go take a look. I apologize if my bed isn't made. I've been a little busy." My cigarette jumps up and down, performing carcinogenic calisthenics as my volume rises. This is desperation time. I need him to go into that bedroom.

He says, "Mark, enough, really."

"Listen to me! If she isn't in there, you win, and I'll close my eyes and you can burn me up and stub me out like the rest of my cigarettes. But go fucking look, right now!" My voice breaks on the last line.

The DA stands up, puts his gun down on the projector table

and his hands in his pockets. Then he leans forward, sticking his face in mine, our noses a fly hair away from touching. His eyes line up with mine and I don't see anything there that I recognize or understand. Anyone who tells you they can read someone's eyes is lying.

I blow smoke in his face and say, "Be careful, that second-hand smoke is a killer."

He hits me in the arms, chest, stomach, and the groin, looking for reactions, movement. I'm the dead snake and he's poking me with a stick.

I feel it all, but I don't move. I say, "Stop it, I'm ticklish."

He backs off, picks up the gun. "All right, Mark, but only because you're Tim's kid. I shouldn't be an enabler, but I'll go look in your bedroom, and then we'll be done."

"Say hi to Jennifer for me."

The DA backs away from the couch, moves the screen out from the front of my bedroom door. Still watching me, he turns the knob and pushes the door open. Yeah, I know now that Jennifer and the goons were a hallucination, but part of me is still surprised that the door is unlocked. Times ducks inside my bedroom.

My right hand is heavier than a mountain and moves like a continent, but it moves, aiming inside my jacket pocket. I don't need more smokes, but I do need my cell phone. I'm moving too slow. I have only moments, moments that can't be defined or measured in seconds, not by me anyway. My fingers are clumsy and thick, but they find the hunk of plastic, hold on, and pull it out. I can't hold the phone up in front of my face, so

I flip it open and rest my hand, arm, and phone on my stomach. The LCD screen glows brightly in the dark room.

The DA says, "Drop the phone, Mark." Gun held out like he means it, but he won't shoot me unless he absolutely has to. I'm banking that it would be too messy to cover up. Here's hoping there isn't a run on the bank.

I say, "No need to get your tassels in a twirl, DA, I just wanted to show you I had a little phone chat of my own, earlier."

Goddamn it, the buttons are so small and my thumb isn't ready for the minute motor coordination test. I hit the wrong buttons. The DA lunges across the room. My thumb cooperates, I select incoming calls from the main menu, scroll down, and there it is. The magic number. Phew. It's actually there.

The DA grabs the cell phone, but he's too late.

I'm breathing heavy. Ash floats onto my chest. Cigarette two is getting low. I say, "Take a gander at the screen. That's a list of incoming calls, not outgoing. See that menu heading, DA? Tell me, what does it say?"

He complies without looking up. Good DA. "Incoming calls."

I say, "Oh, I lied about Jennifer being here. Sorry about that. If I had told you to check the incoming calls of my cell phone, you either wouldn't have or would've lied about what you saw. That, and it was nice to have a few seconds of me time."

The DA doesn't say anything, just stares at the phone and then up at me.

I say, "I think you recognize Jennifer's number, unless that's some secret line you don't know about. Nah, you know that number. I can tell. Note the time too. She called me this afternoon. Hours and hours ago. And now I'm wondering: have you talked to her since she called me? I'm guessing not. I'm guessing that if she was home, she avoided you like herpes."

He says, "Why would she call you?"

I say, "I'm also guessing she didn't really tell you about our date at Amrheins either. Did she tell you I showed her the pictures? No? Fancy that. Tell me, are you stressed now, Billy?"

He yells, "What did you tell her?"

Cigarette number two is a bullet between my teeth, and I'm chomping the hell out of it. I say, "I told her everything. I told her that once upon a time there were three musketeers, you, my father, and Brendan Sullivan, the lords of Southie—or lords of their project at least—and they decided to try their hand at an amateur porno. Tim was the director, Brendan an actor, and everyone's local hero, Billy, was costar and producer. They found and bribed some young barely-there junkie, and a star was born. Only she OD'd, or was just so drunk she choked on her own vomit, and died on camera as you guys just sat and watched with your thumbs up your asses.

"Some bad luck there, I guess, but you three of Southie's finest never reported the death. No. You see, Billy Times used to go around bragging about mob and Whitey Bulger contacts to whoever would listen. Yeah, you had a big mouth and it was always running, but maybe it wasn't all talk, maybe you weren't just full of shit. So the junkie died in your bedroom, you called in a favor, and the body magically disappeared. But what you weren't expecting was that two of your musketeers, your pals,

Tim especially, didn't trust you. Not one goddamn bit. He didn't destroy the pictures or the film. He split them up with Brendan, a two-man tontine of your former musketeers. That's gotta hurt a little, eh, DA?"

While I'm talking, the DA drops my cell phone and it disappears into the rubble. He jams the gun in his waistband, by his left hip, and slumps over to the projector. He plucks the take-up reel and film from the rear arm.

I say, "Fast-forward to last week. Brendan saw Jennifer performing on *American Star*, and she looked so much like the junkie, like the dead girl, and your name was being bandied about on fluff news pieces all over the state, Brendan had a belated attack of conscience. He brought me the photos and hired me to find the film. Of course I was, shall we say, indisposed when he was in my office and I thought it was Jennifer who gave me the pics. This is where you come in again. Yeah, this Monday morning quarterback knows taking the pictures to you was a full ten on the Richter scale of mistakes, which resulted in my apartment and office being torn apart and your goons putting the lean on me and making sure Brendan Sullivan was out of the picture, so to speak, or dead if you prefer I speak plainly. But I found the film.

"Oh—and this last bit is pure conjecture, but Jennifer thought it sounded plausible—the narcoleptic me had taken some notes when Brendan was here. The only piece of automatic writing that wasn't gibberish was *South Shore Plaza*, and that notepad was stolen from my office. Haven't had a chance to check dates yet, but I'll bet more than two bits there was some heavy construction going on at that mall back in your day, and Dead Girl has herself a cement plot, maybe parking-garage Level Three?

"That's what I told Jennifer. All of it. She found it to be riveting stuff. Begged me to show her the film and told me she'd help me if I needed it. So, Billy boy, what do you think? How'd I do? Did I get it right?"

He says, "Not perfect. But you're more right than wrong."

He doesn't accuse me of bluffing, doesn't deny the goons, either. I nailed it. Perfect dismount. I broke him down. I'm the one with all the hand. In the midst of the mental back pat, cigarette number two falls out of my mouth and onto my chest. My arms are tree trunks, but I slowly manage to brush the glowing stub off onto the couch—but still too close to me. Wasn't thinking right. Should've flicked it across the room with my fingers.

I still smell smoke, and now I see it. It's coming up from the floor, from between my legs. Unless my floor has taken up smoking, there's a fire down below. I try to move my legs; still no go. I don't have much time.

The DA has gone all quiet. He's the secret that everyone knows. He passes the film from hand to hand. He says, "Jennifer wouldn't believe you."

I try to move, but all I manage is some feeble twisting of my torso and some hip movement. It's not the Twist and I'm no Chubby Checker. The dummy film inside the couch cushion digs into my ass as I move. It's not helping. I say, "Why wouldn't she believe me? Especially after I wind up quote *accidentally dead* unquote."

The DA looks at me, his wheels turning, but they aren't taking him anywhere. He says, "She'll believe me over you. Time will pass, and she'll believe me." He says it, but I don't think he buys it, not even at discount. He stands in the dark of my ruined apartment.

Need to keep those wheels a-spinnin'. I say, "Who was Dead Girl? Tell me."

He says, "I don't know, Mark. I really don't."

The couch on my too-close left is smoking now. Maybe it's my imagination but the apartment is getting brighter. The heat down by my feet is no longer a phantom heat. It's real.

I say, "Come on. It's over, Times. Just cross the Ts for me."

The DA pulls his gun out. I might've pushed him too far into desperation mode. "I can't tell you what I don't know. We found her in Dorchester. Tim had seen her wandering the streets for days, bumming smokes and offering five-dollar blowjobs. We didn't even know her name, and after—after, no one missed her. No one asked about her."

I say, "That's not good enough—" and then a searing pain wraps around my left ankle, worse then anything I've ever felt, worse than anything I've ever imagined. I scream and it's enough of a jolt to bend me in half, send my arms down to the emergency scene. My left pant leg is engulfed in flame; so is most of the floor beneath my feet. I beat frantically at my pant leg, each swipe of my paw like mashing a nest full of yellow jackets into my ankle. I quickly and without thinking or planning try to stand, and manage a somewhat upright position but fall immediately to the left, crash-landing on shards of broken coffee table. That hurts too. The high-intense pain of my actively burning flesh is gone, replaced by a slow, throbbing, and building ache. I belly-crawl away from the flames, but things are getting hotter and brighter in the apartment.

I look up. Times is still there, looking down, watching me, gun in one hand, film in the other. I say, "Burning me up isn't gonna solve anything. You'll still have questions to answer." The flames are speaking now, the greedy crackle of its expanding mouth.

He says, "I'm sorry it has to be this way. I'm not a good guy." He bends down, knocks my hat off, grabs a handful of my hair, and yanks my head up. Can't say I'm thrilled with this by-the-scruff treatment. He says, "Your father wasn't a good guy either, Mark. But I liked him anyway."

The pain in my leg starts to subside and this isn't a good sign, because it likely means I'm going out again, and this time the sleep won't be a little one. I yell, and scream, and bang my forehead on the floor, anything to keep myself awake.

The fire races up the blankets over the windows, throwing an orange spotlight on the room and waves of powerful heat. The DA stands up, coughs, and takes a step toward the front door.

I reach out with my right hand and clamp down on his ankle. I'm a leech, a barnacle, and I'm not letting go. I yell, "Go ahead, shoot me!" He won't. If he's careful, he won't even step on my hand to break it, or mark me up with bruises. He can't chance ruining his quaint narcoleptic-burned-himself-up-smoking setup.

The DA halfheartedly tries to pull his leg out of my hand,

and it gives me time and an opening to pull my torso close and wrap myself around his leg. Now I'm an anchor, a tree root, and he isn't going anywhere.

Apparently my apartment isn't very flame retardant, because a full-on blaze is roaring now. I curl up into a tighter ball, trying to keep my assorted parts out of the fire. The DA is yelling, getting more violent and desperate.

I turn my head and pin my face to his leg, trying to protect it. I close my eyes, waiting for a bullet that doesn't come. Instead, he kicks me in the back of the head and kicks me in the ribs, but I'm not letting go. No way.

The DA drags me and his leg behind him, toward the front door. He gives me a few more kicks, then pulls us out into the hallway. My legs are weak, but they have something in them, they have to.

He sticks the gun barrel in my ear, jams it inside, trying to poke at my brain. The pain is like that pressure-point pain where your whole body involuntary gives up. He yells, "Fucking let go! Right now!"

I twist and load my legs under my weight, like I did in preparation for my ill-fated shed leap. Then I lift his leg off the ground and I'm in a crouch. The gun hand goes away with the sudden shift and he stands and waves his arms like a kid on a balance beam. I throw his leg left, which spins the DA around, away from me and facing the stairs.

I jump up, my burned leg erupting into new pain, but I get into a standing position right behind the DA. I grab handfuls of his turtleneck first, fixing to twist his gun arm and pin it behind his back, disarm him, and be the hero, but my legs go out like they were never there. My momentum takes me forward into the DA's back and my legs tangle and twine in his, knocking out his knees. He can't hold us and we pitch down the wooden stairs.

The DA lands almost halfway down the flight, face first, with me on his back, clinging, hands still full of turtleneck, and I'm driving, forcing all my weight down, not that I have a choice. We land hard. There's a crack and I bounce up and manage to stay on his back, riding him like a sled, until we hit the first-floor landing. I involuntarily roll off him, crashing back first into the outside door. The glass window rattles hard in the frame but holds together.

The DA comes to a stop at my feet, sprawled and boneless, his head bent back, too far back, a broken doll. The gun is still in one gloved hand. The take-up reel of film sits on the bottom step, between the DA's feet.

I think about sitting here and just closing my eyes, letting that orange warmth above rock me to sleep. I think about crawling into my office, maybe that bottle of whiskey is still in the bottom drawer of my file cabinet. Those scenarios have a nice captain-going-down-with-the-ship appeal to them, but that's not me.

I grab the film, open the front door, and crawl out onto the sidewalk, the gritty and cold sidewalk, and the door shuts behind me. Everything goes quiet, but below the quiet, if my ears dig hard enough, is the not-so-subtle rumble of flames doing their thing inside the building.

I crawl the first fifty feet down the street, then struggle onto unsteady feet. I use the facades of apartment buildings and pizza joints and convenience stores to rappel down West Broadway and to my rental car.

Inside. I start the car. The dash lights up and I have plenty of gas, enough for another road trip. Beneath my seat, the manila envelope is still there, the pictures still inside, the girl still dead and anonymous. The film goes inside the envelope. It fits.

The sound of flames has disappeared but there are sirens now. One fire truck roars up Broadway past me. I watch it go by; its sound and fury stops at the corner, my corner. Maybe they're in time to save the building and some of my stuff, like the projector. I know better. They won't be able to save anything or anyone.

It's the wee hours of someone's morning. I'm all out of cigarettes, but my leg feels like a used one. Hands on the wheel at two and ten. I check my mirrors. No one is double-parked. My U-turn is legal and easy, and I drive away.

THIRTY-EIGHT

I'm back at the bungalow. Ellen isn't home and she didn't leave the lights on for me. I'm used to it. I limp inside the back door and into the kitchen. First I grab that dusty bottle of whiskey from the cabinets above the refrigerator, take a couple of pulls, and then head to the bathroom to check out my leg. Priorities, man, priorities.

I took the back roads to the Cape, made a pit stop or two, pulled over and napped a couple of times. The sun was coming up as I white-knuckled it over the Sagamore Bridge again, but I made it here. And I made it here without another car accident, although I think I ran over a squirrel when I found myself two-wheeling it up a sidewalk. Sorry, fella.

Bathroom. I roll my pants up and the burned parts stick to my leg. I clean it up best as I can in the tub, but the water hurts. The whiskey doesn't help as much as it should. The skin on my ankle and about halfway up my calf is burned pretty good. I have no idea of the degree scale, but the skin is red and has oozing blisters. I squeeze some Vaseline onto gauze pads and wrap things up tight, but not too tight. It's a bad wrap job, gauze coming undone and sticking out, Christmas presents wrapped in old tissue paper. But it'll have to do.

Me and the bottle of whiskey, we hobble into the living room and I sit on the couch like a dropped piano. I take out the manila envelope and one of the pictures, the picture of Dead Girl wearing the white T-shirt and skirt. The photo is black-and-white but I'll remember her in color, like in the film. She seems a little more alive in this picture, as if the second picture, taken moments later, wears that spent time instead of clothes. The girl in the second photo is that much closer to death, and you can see it.

The living room is getting brighter and my eyes are getting heavier, but I can't go to sleep just yet. I walk to the front windowsill and grab the picture of the old fisherman holding whatever it is next to his head, and I still think it looks like a gun. I also take the picture of the three muske-teers: Tim, Billy, and Brendan, those clean-looking carefree preteens sitting on the stairs. I escort the pictures back to the couch and put them on the coffee table, whiskey bottle between them.

I pick up the old fisherman, flip it around to the back, undo the golden clasp, and remove the photo from the frame. I put the picture facedown on the table. Don't mean any disrespect to the guy.

I stick the first picture of the girl into the frame. Don't need to trim the edges or margins. It's a perfect fit. I spit-polish the glass. Looks good as new. I put her down next to the boys. LIT in the lower left of both pictures.

The boys. Those goddamn buzz cuts and soda-pop smiles. That picture might as well be of anyone. I don't know them, any of them, never did, never will, and don't really want to, but I know their lies.

I think about taking down all the photos off the walls, making a pile, mixing these two in, then reshuffling the deck and hanging everything back up. Maybe I could forget that way and no one would ever find them again.

I think about Jennifer, Ellen, Janice, and me and of how, because of them, our lives will always be about lies and lost time, just like my little sleeps. I think about the dead girl, the stubborn memory that everyone has forgotten. Maybe tomorrow someone will remember.

I gather up my cargo and walk into the hallway. Framed black-and-white pictures hang on the walls on both sides of my bedroom doorway. Faux-lantern lamps hang on either side of the doorway, and beneath the lamps are two pictures. I take those two frames down and stack them on the floor.

I double-check that the manila envelope with the other photo and the film is still inside my jacket. It is. I'm holding on to that sucker like a mama bird with a wing around her egg.

The other photos, those I hang on the wall. The girl and the boys fit the nails and fill those glowing empty spots on the walls, one picture on each side of my door for all the world to see.

I open the bedroom door. Unlike the hallway, it's dark

inside. I won't open the curtains or pull the shade. I won't turn on the light. I know where I am and I know where I'm going.

Tomorrow, if there is one, will be for remembering. Now? I'm going to sleep, even if it's just a little one.

THIRTY-NINE

The sun shines bright and hot, too hot. It's a remorseless desert sun, a sun completely indifferent to the effect of its heat and radiation. It's the real sun, not a cartoon. Can't even be bothered to say *fuck you*.

It's the weekend. Tim and I are in our backyard. I'm five years old. Not everything is green. Debris and old equipment cover the yard. Someone's life has exploded. The shed has been destroyed and is nothing but a pile of sharp and splintered pieces. All the king's men can't put it back together again. The shed is dead.

Tim and I stand in front of the fallen shed, hand in hand. His big hand sweats around my little one and I want to let go. I really want to let go, but I can't.

He pats me on the head, hands me the brown paper bag, and says, "Come on. Let's clean up all this shit."

I follow Tim around the yard. He picks up his old lawn mower along with the sharp and toothy tools that used to wink and gleam at me from inside the shed. They go inside my little brown paper bag. Next into the bag are the bottles of cleaners and bags of fertilizer. There's no game today and Tim doesn't name dogs after the stuff we pick up.

He says, "You can still sing your song, buddy."

I don't. And I won't.

Some of the stuff we find lying on the grass is charred and smoking. He picks up a projector, a screen, and a film can, all empty secrets, and they go into the bag. There are other bits and pieces burned beyond recognition, and I get the sense that this is a good thing. Everything goes into the bag. The bag is getting heavy.

We still have much more to pick up, haven't made a dent with our cleanup effort, but Tim leads me behind the fallen shed, takes the brown bag, and tips it upside down behind the fence. Nothing comes out. Tim says, "Goodbye," as he shakes out the empty bag.

We walk around to where the front of the shed used to be. He kicks at the fallen cinder blocks, gray as tombstones, and paces in the rectangular dirt spot left by the shed. I stay where the shed's front doors used to be, like a good boy.

Tim stops walking and stands in the middle of the dirt spot. He says, "So, kid, whaddaya think?"

The five-year-old me is tired, tired of the cleanup and the questions, tired of everything. I say, "I think you're a coward." It has no ring of authenticity to it, not one bit, because I think I'm a coward too. Like father, like son.

Tim doesn't offer me any apologies, recriminations, or excuses. He doesn't tell me what I know already, that I have to clean up the mess by myself. He doesn't even say goodbye. He turns, walks over the pile of wood and glass and tar, and disappears into the woods behind our house.

FORTY

The real sun shines bright and hot. It has some bite to it. Spring has become summer. I guess there was a tomorrow after all. Fancy that.

Ellen and I are in the bungalow's backyard. It's my first time in Osterville since I was allowed back into my apartment and office just over a week ago.

Ellen cooks chicken and hot dogs on the small charcoal grill, the grill from the old shed. I think it's the only piece of the lost treasure she kept. The shed is long gone and she hasn't put up a new one. Landscapers spread topsoil and planted grass over the site. Grass grows, but the footprint of the shed is still visible. It's the backyard's scar.

Ellen wears black gym shorts that go past her knees and a green sleeveless T-shirt that's too small. She has a cigarette in one hand, spatula in the other.

She says, "The hot dogs will be ready first." It might be the longest sentence offered to me since arriving at the bungalow.

"Great. I'm starving." A cigarette rolls over my teeth. I'm sitting on a chaise longue, protected by the shade of the house while I wrestle with a newspaper. There are cigarette ashes in my coffee cup. I don't mind.

Almost four full months have passed since the night of the fire in my apartment. Newspaper articles and TV exposés about the DA and the repercussions of my case are still almost a daily occurrence. Today's page 2 of the *Boston Globe* details the complexities associated with the planned exhumation of the body from the foundation of the South Shore Plaza's parking garage.

We know her name now too. Kelly Bishop. An octogenarian aunt, her only living relative, recognized Kelly in the photos, but very little is known or has been reported about Kelly's life. Other than the photos and film, the evidence of their shared time, no further link between Kelly and the boys from Southie has been unearthed.

I don't think the DA was lying to me when he said they didn't know who she was. She was already an anonymous victim, which is why the press drops her story and sticks with the headliners, the DA and his daughter. Kelly's story is too sad and all too real. No glamour or intrigue in the death of the unwanted and anonymous. I remember her name, though, and I'll make it a point not to forget.

I flip through the paper. There's a bit about Jennifer Times in the entertainment section.

I say, "Looks like somebody is cashing in, and it isn't me."

Ellen gives me a hot dog and bun, no ketchup or mustard. She says, "Who are you talking about?"

I say, "Jennifer Times is forging an alternate path back to celebrity land. She's due to be interviewed on national TV again.

Tonight and prime time. She has plans to announce that a book and a CD are in the works."

Ellen shrugs, finishes her cigarette, and grinds it under her heel. Her heel means business. It's the exclamation point on the months of stilted conversations and awkward silences. I probably shouldn't be mentioning Times around her. She clearly doesn't want to talk about that.

Then Ellen hits me with a knockout punch. She says, "I saw Tim with her."

I drop the hot dog and ash-filled coffee cup to the grass. I say, "Who?" but I know the answer.

Ellen says, "Kelly Bishop."

I struggle out of the chaise longue. I need to stand and pace or run away. I need to do something with the adrenaline dump into my system. I'm still in the shade but everything is hot again. I repeat what Ellen said, just to get the facts straight like a good detective should. "You saw Kelly with Tim."

Ellen opens the grill's lid, and gray smoke escapes and makes a run for it. She crosses her arms, knotting them into a life jacket. Then she takes off her glasses and hides her eyes. I might not be able to find them.

She says, "It was early evening, and it was already dark. I was leaving Harbor Point to meet my friends on Carson Beach. I'd stolen a quarter bottle of gin from the top of our refrigerator. I got busted later, when I came home drunk.

"I was fourteen. I remember running down the front steps, hiding the bottle in my fat winter coat even though it was summer. I was so proud of myself and thought I was so smart. Well, there was Tim and the girl, arm in arm, walking through the parking lot. He was holding her up, really. She was obviously drunk or high and couldn't walk. I had no idea who she was. She was so skinny and pale.

"Tim said, 'Hey, Ellen.' Then he smiled. It wasn't a good smile. It was a smile I used to get from the boys who snapped my bra strap or grabbed my ass when I wasn't looking. I didn't say anything back to him. That Kelly looked at me but she couldn't focus. She giggled and rested her head on Tim's shoulder. Then they just stumbled away, into the building.

"I invited you down today to tell you this, Mark." Ellen closes the lid on the grill and the smoke goes back into hiding.

I don't know what to think, but I'm angry. I probably shouldn't be. "Why didn't you tell anybody else?"

"I told the police. I told them as soon as I saw the pictures of her. I just didn't tell you."

My anger evaporates instantly and leaves only sadness. Sadness for us and for everything. The truth is sadness. I walk over toward Ellen and the grill and say, "Why didn't you tell me?"

Ellen isn't hiding her eyes anymore. I get the double barrel. "You kept that case a secret from me. You kept everything he did from me."

"I told you everything I knew once I'd solved the case."

"Only because you had to, Mark. Would you have told me anything if you managed to solve your case without destroying the shed and setting my building on fire?"

I take off my hat and scratch my head. "Yeah, Ellen. Of course I would've told you."

Ellen turns away and opens the grill again. The chicken hisses and steams. It's done. She plucks the meat off the grill with tongs, then dumps on the barbecue sauce. She says, "I know, Mark. I'm sorry. I'm not being fair. But I'm still so angry. I wish you'd told me about what was going on earlier."

"I didn't want to say anything until I knew exactly what had happened. There was no guarantee I was going to figure it all out. Giving you the bits and pieces and then living with the doubt would've been worse."

Ellen breathes in sharp, ready to go on offense again, but then she exhales slowly and shakes her head. She says, "I've tried telling myself that it wasn't Kelly I saw with Tim that night. Maybe I'm just putting that face from those pictures onto someone else's body. It's possible, right?" She pauses and fiddles with the burner knobs. "I do know that just a few days after I saw him with that girl, Tim stopped hanging around with Times and Sullivan and started chasing after me. He was a different kid. He wasn't obnoxious and loud and cocky like the rest of them. He got real quiet, listened way more than he talked. At the time, I thought it was because of some puppy-love crush he had on me. Jesus Christ, I thought he was acting like that because of me. Ridiculous, right?"

Ellen talks just above a whisper but waves the spatula over her head and scrapes the blue sky. "Now, I don't know what to think. Did he only start pursuing me and dating me because of what happened, because of what he did? Was he using me to hide his guilt, to try and somehow make up for that night, to try and become some person that he wasn't? What do you think, Mark? I want to know. I have to know. Can you answer any of those questions for me, Mr. Private Detective?"

I could tell her that maybe it was her and that she somehow saved Tim, redeemed him. But she knows the truth; I can't answer any of those questions. No one can. I don't even try.

I say, "I'm sorry, Ellen," and I give her a hug. She accepts it grudgingly. It's the best I can do.

Ellen releases me quick. "Let's eat before the flies and yellow jackets find us."

So we sit outside, next to each other on adjacent chaise longues, and eat our barbecued chicken and hot dogs. We don't talk because we don't know what to say anymore. When we finish eating we each smoke a cigarette. The filters are pinched tight between our fingers. We're afraid to let go.

Eventually, I get up and say, "Thanks for dinner, Ellen. It was great. I'm getting tired. Should probably move around a bit or I'm gonna go out." I get up and gather the dirty dishes and makeshift ashtrays.

Ellen says, "Thank you, Mark." She doesn't look up at me. She starts in on another cigarette and stares out to where the shed used to be, to where the grass isn't growing fast enough.

I say, "You're welcome."

I walk through the back door, dump the dishes in the sink, then mosey down the hallway and into the living room. I dock myself on the couch as the murk and fatigue come rolling in.

My eyelids are as heavy and thick as Dostoyevsky novels and my world is getting dim again, but I see all the black-and-white pictures are still on the walls. Ellen hasn't taken any of them down. Not a one. Maybe it means that, despite everything, Ellen is determined not to forget, determined to keep her collected memories exactly where they were before, determined to fight against her very own version of the little sleep.

I don't think she'll succeed, but I admire the effort.

ACKNOWLEDGMENTS

There are so many people who need proper thanks that I won't be able to thank them all, but I'll give it a try. If I've forgotten anyone, it wasn't intentional and mea culpa.

Gargantuan thanks to Lisa, Cole, Emma, Rascal, Kathleen M., Paul N. T., Erin, Dan, Jennifer, the Carroll and Genevich clan, and to the rest of my family and friends for their love and support and for putting up with my panics, mood swings, and egotistical ramblings. Special acknowledgment to Michael, Rob, and Mary (along with the tireless and wonderful Lisa and Dad) for acting enthusiastically as my first readers way back when I wrote just awful, terrible stuff.

Giant, sloppy, and unending thanks and admiration to Poppy Z. "I love Steve Nash, really" Brite, Steve "Big Brother" Eller, and Stewart "Don't hate me because I root for the Raiders" O'Nan. They have been and continue to be invaluable mentors, supporters, and friends. I will never be able to thank them enough.

Big, aw-shucks, punch-you-in-the-shoulder thanks to the following who have shared their talent and helped me along the way: assorted Arrows, Laird "Imago" Barron, Mairi "seismic" Beacon, Hannah Wolf "da Bulls" Bowen, Michael "The Kid" Cisco, Brett "They call me F" Cox, JoAnn "He's not related to me" Cox, Ellen "Owned by cats" Datlow, dgk "kelly" goldberg (you are missed), Jack "I know Chandler better than you" Haringa, John "Don't call me Paul" Harvey, and the rest of the Providence critique crew, Brian "bah" Hopkins, Nick "I hate TV" Kaufmann, Mike "Blame Canada" Kelly, Dan "Samurai" Keohane, Greg "Hardest working man in horrah" Lamberson, John "Purple flower" Langan, Sarah "He's not related to me" Langan, Seth "I'm taller than you" Lindberg, Simon "IO" Logan, Louis "A guy called me Louie . . . once" Maistros and his family, Nick "nihilistic kid" Mamatas, Dallas "They call me . . ." Mayr, Sandra "I can whup Chuck Norris" McDonald, Kris "Mudd" Meyer, Kurt "Fig" Newton, Brett "el Presidente" Savory, Kathy "I played Mafia before you" Sedia, Jeffrey and Scott "But not Kristen" Thomas, M. "Not related to them" Thomas, and Sean "Cower as I crush you" Wallace.

Special thanks to my agent, Stephen "They're coming to get you" Barbara, who understands my work and tolerates my occasional tantrums and delusions.

More special thanks to the entire Henry Holt team, and especially to Sarah "The Dark" Knight for her thousand-watt enthusiasm and for believing in *The Little Sleep* and in Mark Genevich.

Thanks to (give yourself a nickname) for reading *The Little Sleep*. Now, go tell your friends and neighbors or blog about it. Blogging would be good.

Cheers!